# 必考！
# 文法速解

**www.learnerhall.org**

Google 熱蒐文法網站

大學堂英文　編著

創學堂文教事業股份有限公司

　　別怕！這本書不是你以為的那種文法百科大全。別擔心！書裏面既沒有密密麻麻的細則，也沒有艱澀的術語、繁瑣的講解。我們分享的是我們的私房撇步。幾條百用不厭的大規則，加上簡單的例句，你就可以輕鬆掌握語法概念。但是我們知道這樣還不夠。只有在「理解」語法的功能和使用理由後，才能擺脫死記硬背、學過即忘的夢魘迴圈，也才能將語法內化、活化，促成口語或寫作溝通的可能。所以，每個短小精悍的單元裏，我們要教會你 what (the rule is)，也會清楚說明 why (the rule is used)。

　　我們認為能否學好英文取決於三個條件：方法、教材、毅力，缺一不可。這本書幫你備齊了前兩項。相較於坊間的文法書，每個單元動輒二、三十頁，我們不出三頁就能道破個中訣竅。也因而能將大部份篇幅留給可以偵測出你是否已融會貫通的魔鬼練習題。藉由大量答題，及時驗證、強化所學，或找出自己犯錯的癥結，始終是最有效的學習法。同時，從做中學，也能練就你對考點的敏銳度，讓你一眼識破老師的命題梗。題目下方，清楚易懂的解題邏輯，讓這本書成為

自修的最佳選擇。當你學得通，答得對，看得到成果，自然就有動力持續深度學習。

　　選材時，我們歷經兩階段才敲定書裏要收錄的主題。首先由經驗豐富的教學團隊羅列出最易卡關的文法清單。接著，統計自 2012 年大學堂英文網站開站以來，最多網友們瀏覽、求助的文法類型。兩相比對後，精選出關係代名詞、分詞構句等十個單元，我們很有信心可符合你學習的需求。十個單元，各自獨立。你可以挑選自己覺得最棘手的單元先讀，立馬解決困擾已久的文法問題。書後收錄五回合，共 250 道題目，讓你再次檢驗自己是否已徹底吸收全書精華。解析處，明確標示考點，方便你回頭複習相關文法概念。通過道道題目「千錘百鍊」的你，將發現自己已練就出答題快、準的好功夫。

　　我們希望這本書可扭轉文法學習給人的繁瑣印象。若你有任何建議或疑問，歡迎到大學堂英文網站上留言。大學堂英文的網址：http://www.learnerhall.org/

# 目錄 Contents

## Unit 1　關係代名詞、關係副詞、複合關係代名詞
## 1–1 關係代名詞

■ 關係代名詞的功能

關係代名詞本身並無意思，但具備兩大功能：

1. 可當「連接詞」，連接兩個句子。
2. 可當「代名詞」，代替之前已說過的「名詞」。

由此可見，善用「關係代名詞」除可去除贅字、連接兩個句子，也讓句意更形緊密。請見下方例句：

例 富有的羅馬人喜歡舉辦主打異國風味菜餚，如：烤孔雀等的奢華餐宴。

> 句 1　Rich Romans loved to serve fancy **banquets**.
> 句 2　**The banquets** featured lots of exotic dishes such as roasted peacock.

使用關係代名詞連接
Rich Romans loved to serve fancy banquets **which / that** featured lots of exotic dishes such as roasted peacock.

> 解 由上可知，關係代名詞除取代了句 1 與句 2 重複的名詞 banquets 外，同時也將兩句併成一句。關係代名詞 which / that 所帶出的關係子句 which / that...peacock 放在名詞 banquets 後，為「形容詞子句」，意指「... 的」餐宴。

■ 如何找出關係代名詞、造關係子句及合併句子

造關係子句的三大步驟：

> 步驟 1　先找出兩個句子裡「相同的名詞」，即「先行詞」。
> 步驟 2　參考下方關係代名詞表格，找出合適的關係代名詞。

| 先行詞 | 主詞 | 受詞 | 所有格 |
|--------|------|------|--------|
| 人 | who | whom | whose |
| 事物 | which | which | whose |
| 人、事物 | that | that | 無 |

先行詞在主要句裡的屬性可分成「人」和「事物」兩類，在次要句中則依所處位置分成「主格」、「受格」和「所有格」；循屬性和位置兩條件，交叉比對，即可找出合適的關係代名詞。

步驟3 以「先行詞＋關係代名詞＋關係子句」的順序將兩句合併。

兩句合併時，主要句不動，將次要句與主要句重複的名詞改成關係代名詞。次要句裡剩下的部分即為關係子句。接著再以主要句的先行詞先跑，跑在關係代名詞前，關係代名詞再帶出次要句剩下的部份，即關係子句，的概念將兩句合併。請見下方例句：

例 請用關係代名詞將下方兩句併成一句。

句1 **The tiger** has been shot to death.
句2 **The tiger** attacked three visitors this morning.

步驟1 先找出兩個句子中相同的名詞 the tiger，句1的 the tiger 即為「先行詞」。

步驟2 句1不動，句2裡「物」性質的 the tiger，放句首當「主詞」可換成「物／主詞性質」的關係代名詞 which 或 that。句2，the tiger 換成 which / that 後，剩下的部份 attacked … morning 就是所謂的關係子句。

步驟3 以「先行詞＋關係代名詞＋關係子句」的順序將句2併入句1，即得：
今天早上攻擊三名遊客的那隻老虎已被射殺。
The tiger which / that attacked three visitors this morning has
　先行詞　　　關代　　　　　　關係子句
been shot to death.

■ 關係代名詞的六大使用規則

1. 「受詞」性質的關係代名詞可省略，但若受詞性質的關係代名詞前有「介係詞」，或「逗號」時，則不可省略關係代名詞。

例 他出生在一個極重視教育的家庭。

句 1 He was born in **a family**.
句 2 Education is highly valued in **the family**.

使用關係代名詞連接
He was born in a family **which / that** education is highly valued in.
He was born in a family education is highly valued in.
He was born in a family **in which** education is highly valued.
He was born in a family **where** education is highly valued.

> 解 先行詞 the family 屬物，又在句 2 的位置屬受詞，故連接兩句時，需用「物 / 受詞性質」的關係代名詞，that 或 which 皆可，見 a。又受詞性質的關係代名詞可省略，故 b 也對。但若將句尾的介係詞 in 搬到關係代名詞前，則受詞性質的關係代名詞不可省略。in that 為錯誤寫法，因關係代名詞 that 前不可放介係詞，故只能用 in which，見 c。再者「介係詞 + which」可換成代替地點的「關係副詞」where，見 d。四種寫法中，以 c 和 d 為佳。
>
> 註 關係子句從關係副詞開始，往後推，到第二個動詞前結束。若沒有第二個動詞，則到句點為止。關係子句 where education … valued，放在名詞 family 後方，為形容詞子句，意指「… 的」。請見下方句構分析：
>
> He was born in a family where education is highly valued.
> 主詞　動詞　　　　　　　　　　　　　　形容詞子句

2. 關係代名詞 that 前，不可有逗號，也不可放介係詞。

例 John 暗戀的那個女孩剛剛走過他身邊。

句 1 **The girl** walked past him.
句 2 John has a crush on **the girl**.

使用關係代名詞連接

The girl **whom / that** John has a crush on just walked past him.
The girl John has a crush on just walked past him.
The girl **on whom** John has a crush just walked past him.

> 解 先行詞 the girl 屬人，又在句 2 的位置屬受詞，故連接兩句時，需用「人 / 受詞性質」的關係代名詞，whom 和 that 皆可，見 a。又受詞性質的關係代名詞可省略，故 b 也對。若將句尾的介係詞 on 搬到關係代名詞前，則受詞性質的關係代名詞不可省略。on that 為錯誤寫法，因關係代名詞 that 前不可放介係詞，故只能用 on whom，見 c。三種寫法中，以 c 為佳。

> 註 關係子句從關係代名詞開始，往後推，到第二個動詞前結束。若沒有第二個動詞，則到句點為止。關係子句 on whom … crush，放在名詞 the girl 後方，為形容詞子句，意指「… 的」。請見下方句構分析：

> The girl | on whom John has a crush | just walked past him.
> 主詞 | 形容詞子句 | 動詞

3. 關係代名詞 that 不具所有格性質。所有格性質的關係代名詞為 whose。

> 例 姓氏結尾為 stein 的人，可能他的祖先來自德國。

句 1 **A person** may have forefathers from Germany.
句 2 **A person**'s surname ends with stein.

使用關係代名詞連接

A person **whose** surname ends with stein may have forefathers from Germany.

> 解 先行詞 a person 屬人，又在句 2 的位置屬所有格，故連接兩句時需用「人 / 所有格性質」的關係代名詞 whose。切記別誤寫成 that，因關係代名詞 that 不能當所有格。

> 註 關係子句從關係代名詞開始，往後推，到第二個動詞前結束。若沒有第二個動詞，則到句點為止。關係子句 whose … stein，放在名詞 a person 後方，為形容詞子句，意指「… 的」。請見下方句構分析：

> A person | whose surname ends with stein | may have forefathers
> 　　主詞　　　　　　　形容詞子句　　　　　　　　動詞
> from Germany.

4. 先行詞包括人和物時，只能用關係代名詞 that。

　例 受困在著火的房子裡的小孩與狗已被救出。

　　句 1 **The kid and the dog** have been rescued.
　　句 2 **The kid and the dog** were trapped in the burning building.

　　使用關係代名詞連接
　　The kid and the dog **that** were trapped in the burning building have been rescued.

> 解 先行詞 the kid and the dog，有人也有物，故連接兩句時只能用既可代替人，也可代替物的關係代名詞 that。若用關係代名詞 which 只代替了「物」the dog，而用關係代名詞 who 只能代替「人」the kid，兩者均非正解。
>
> 註 關係子句從關係代名詞開始，往後推，到第二個動詞前結束。若沒有第二個動詞，則到句點為止。關係子句 that ... building，放在名詞 the kid and the dog 後方，為形容詞子句，意指「... 的」。請見下方句構分析：
>
> The kid and the dog | that were trapped in the burning building
> 　　主詞　　　　　　　　　　　　形容詞子句
> have been rescued.
> 　　動詞

5. 若遇上 who 或 which 開頭的疑問句，句中的關係代名詞得用 that，才可避免和疑問詞 who 或 which 混淆。

　例 坐在 Tim 隔壁的那個女人是誰？

　　句 1 Who is **the woman**?
　　句 2 **The woman** sits next to Tim.

使用關係代名詞連接

Who is the woman **that** sits next to Tim?

> 解 先行詞 the woman 屬人，又在句 2 的位置屬主詞，連接兩句時，本需用「人 / 主詞性質」的關係代名詞 who，但因為句首有疑問詞 who，為避免混淆，故改用關係代名詞 that。
>
> 註 關係子句從關係代名詞開始，往後推，到第二個動詞前結束。若沒有第二個動詞，則到句點為止。關係子句 that … Tim，放在名詞 the woman 後方，為形容詞子句，意指「…的」。請見下方句構分析：
>
> Who　is　the woman　that sits next to Tim?
> 疑問詞 動詞　　　　　　形容詞子句

6. 補充說明「虛主詞」it，除了可用「不定詞」(to 動詞原形) 外，也可用「that 關係子句」。

> 例 據說 Jennifer 將成為知名化妝品公司的品牌大使。

It is said **that** Jennifer will become the brand ambassador for a renowned cosmetics company.

> 解 關係子句從關係代名詞開始，往後推，到第二個動詞前結束。若沒有第二個動詞，則到句點為止。關係子句 that … company，補充說明主詞 it 究竟為何，屬名詞子句。請見下方句構分析：
>
> It　is said　that Jennifer will become … cosmetics company.
> 主詞 動詞　　　　補充說明 it 的名詞子句

## 小試身手：請選出正確解答

**01.** The naughty boy stood on the brink of a steep cliff and slowly leaned forward, _____ scared his mom out of her mind.

(A) which      (B) who      (C) that      (D) what

> **解** 頑皮的男孩站在陡峭的懸崖邊，慢慢地將身子往前傾，這舉動讓他媽媽嚇壞了。
>
> stood / leaned / scared 三個動詞，代表三個句子，需兩個連接詞（或關代），故除連接詞 and 外，劃線部分應為具連接句子功能的關係代名詞。讓媽媽嚇壞了的是 "The naughty boy stood on the brink of a steep cliff and slowly leaned forward" 這件事，故 scared 這句的先行詞為一整個句子，性質屬「事」，又 scared … 這句缺「主詞」，連接兩句需用「事 / 主詞性質」的關係代名詞 which。先行詞為「1」件事，關係代名詞前方需打逗號。綜合以上，**A** 選項為正解。關係代名詞 which 帶出來的關係子句 which … mind 為補充說明用的「名詞子句」。英文的逗號等同於中文的括號，括號裏的內容，多為補述用的名詞子句。

**02.** We all make assumptions about people based on what they wear. For example, women _____ work-wear is "provocative" are considered to be less competent.

(A) who      (B) which      (C) whose      (D) that

> **解** 我們都會依據人們的衣著作出臆測。比如說，上班穿著較性感的女性，常被視為較不具有專業能力。
>
> is / are considered 兩個動詞，代表兩個句子，故劃線部分應為具連接句子功能的關係代名詞。將先行詞 women 放回後方 work-wear is provocative 這句子排排看，得出：women's work-wear is provocative，由此可知需用「人 / 所有格性質」的關係代名詞 whose，**C** 選項為正解。關係子句從關係代名詞開始，往後推，到第二個動詞 are considered 前結束。關係代名詞 whose 帶出來的關係子句 whose … provocative 放在名詞 women 後，為「形容詞子句」。

**03.** The sudden burst of flames sends terrified people, most of _____ are in their teens and 20s, running for their lives.

(A) that      (B) which      (C) whom      (D) who

Unit 1
關係
代名詞

Unit 2
被動
語態

Unit 3
分詞
形容詞

Unit 4
分詞
構句

Unit 5
假設
語法

Unit 6
倒裝
句

Unit 7
間接
問句

Unit 8
特殊
動詞

Unit 9
主動詞
一致

Unit 10
對稱
結構

特別收錄
Unit 11
五回
試題

解 突然爆出的火球，讓驚恐的人們（大多為青少年或 20 多歲的年輕人）趕緊逃命。

sends / are 兩個動詞，代表兩個句子，故劃線部分應為具連接句子功能的關係代名詞。將先行詞 people 放回後方 most of...their lives 這句子排排看，得出：most of the people are in their teens and 20s，由此可知需用「人／受詞性質」的關係代名詞 whom，**C** 選項為正解。關係子句從關係代名詞開始，往後推，到斷句用的逗點為止。關係代名詞 most of whom 帶出來的關係子句 most of whom … and 20s 為補充說明 people 狀態的「名詞子句」。逗號等同於中文的括號，括號裏的內容，為補述用的名詞子句。

04. McDonald's _____ the term "McJob" originally came, is "not loving" the entry in Oxford English Dictionary at all and demands that it be axed entirely.

(A) which　　　　(B) that　　　　(C) , from which　　(D) , whose

解 麥當勞（即 McJob 一詞的起源處）對牛津英文字典收錄 McJob 感到反感，要求撤除這詞條。

came / is 兩個動詞，代表兩個句子，故劃線部分應為具連接句子功能的關係代名詞。將先行詞 McDonald's 放回後方 the term … came 這句子排排看，得出：the term "McJob" came from McDonald's，由此可知需用「物／受詞性質」的關係代名詞 which。但是關係代名詞只能代替名詞 McDonald's，無法代替介係詞 from，故答案應為 from which，或代替地點的關係副詞 where，**C** 選項為正解。關係子句從關係代名詞開始，往後推，到第二個動詞 is 前結束。關係代名詞 from which 帶出來的關係子句 from which … came 為補充說明 McDonald's 的「名詞子句」。先行詞 McDonald's 為「1」家公司，關係代名詞 from which 前方需打逗號。逗號等同於中文的括號，括號裏的內容，為補述用的名詞子句。

05. Cryptozoology is literally "the study of hidden animals" and involves the search for animals _____ existence has not been verified such as the Yeti or Bigfoot.

(A) that　　　　(B) those of which　　(C) whose　　　　(D) , which

解 「傳說動物學」是一門研究潛藏動物的學問，包括搜尋那些仍未被證實是否存在的動物，如：雪人或大腳怪。

is / involves / has not been verified 三個動詞，代表三個句子，需兩個

連接詞（或關代）。故除了連接詞 and 外，劃線部分應為具連接句子功能的關係代名詞。將先行詞 animals 放回後方 existence has not been verified … Bigfoot 這句子排排看，得出：the animals' existence has not been…Bigfoot，由此可知需用「物／所有格性質」的關係代名詞 whose，**C** 選項為正解。關係子句從關係代名詞開始，往後推，找不到第二個動詞，所以到句點為止。關係代名詞 whose 所帶出來的關係子句 whose … Bigfoot 放在名詞 animals 後，為「形容詞子句」。

**06.** It was said _____ the US paid Russia over 63 million dollars per seat to fly its astronauts to and from the space station.

(A) that　　　　　(B) what　　　　　(C) which　　　　　(D) why

解 據說，為了運送太空人往來太空站，每個座位，美國付給蘇聯超過美金 6300 萬元。

補充說明虛主詞 it 可用「不定詞」（to 動詞原形），或「that 子句」，故 **A** 選項為正解。關係子句從關係代名詞開始，往後推，paid 和 fly 間，已用不定詞（to fly）處理過，應視為一組動詞。找不到第二個動詞，所以關係子句到句點為止。關係代名詞 that 帶出來的關係子句 that … station 為補充說明虛主詞 it 的「名詞子句」。

**07.** The ideal world is one _____ all countries cooperate with one another.

(A) , which　　　　(B) that　　　　(C) in which　　　　(D) whose

解 理想的世界是一個所有國家都互助互惠的世界。

is / cooperate 兩個動詞，代表兩個句子，故劃線部分應為具連接句子功能的關係代名詞。將先行詞 one（即：one world）放回後方 all countries cooperate… another 這句子排排看，得出：all countries cooperate … in one world，由此可知需用「物／受詞性質」的關係代名詞 which。但因為關係代名詞只能代替名詞 one world，無法代替介係詞 in，故答案應為 in which，或代替地點的關係副詞 where，**C** 選項為正解。關係子句從關係代名詞開始，往後推，找不到第二個動詞，所以到句點為止。關係代名詞 in which 帶出來的關係子句 in which … another 放在名詞 one 的後方，為「形容詞子句」。

**08.** Amy is such a courageous girl _____ she stands up against the odds without flinching.

(A) which　　　　(B) that　　　　(C) who　　　　(D) whose

解 Amy 是個如此有勇氣的女孩，以致於她毫不退縮地起身對抗困境。

本題考點為「如此 ... 以致於 ...」句型：such + 名詞 + that 子句，故 **B** 選項為正解。關係子句從關係代名詞開始，往後推，找不到第二個動詞，所以到句點為止。

**09.** Cigarette smoke is a mixture of over 4000 chemical substances, many of _____ are harmful to your health.

(A) that　　　　(B) what　　　　(C) them　　　　(D) which

解 香菸的煙霧內含 4000 多種化學物質，其中許多都對你的健康有害。

is / are 兩個動詞，代表兩個句子，故劃線部分應為具連接句子功能的關係代名詞。將先行詞 substances 放回後方 many of...your health 這句子排排看，得出：many of the substances are harmful to your health，由此可知需用「物 / 受詞性質」的關係代名詞 which，**D** 選項為正解。關係子句從關係代名詞開始，往後推，找不到第二個動詞，所以到句點為止。關係代名詞 which 帶出來的關係子句 many of which...health 為補充說明 substances 性質的「名詞子句」。逗號等同於中文的括號，括號裏的內容，為補述用的名詞子句。若選 C，得另外補上連接詞 and 才能連接兩個句子，即：Cigarette smoke is a mixture of over 4000 chemical substances, and many of them are harmful to your health.。也可省略掉 are，只剩一個動詞，就不需要關係代名詞，也不需連接詞，即：Cigarette smoke is a mixture of over 4000 chemical substances, many of them harmful to your health.

**10.** I know that fried foods are harmful for my health _____ I shouldn't eat them; however, I cannot resist my cravings and always feel drawn towards them.

(A) and that　　(B) which　　　(C) when　　　(D) what

解 我知道油炸食物對我的健康有害，也知道我不該吃油炸食物，但是我就是抗拒不了我對油炸食物的渴望，且總是覺得被它們吸引。

動詞 know 後方有兩個受詞，都以關係代名詞 that 帶出來的關係子句對稱呈現，且用連接詞 and 連接兩個受詞，故 **A** 選項為正解。請見下方句構分析：

I know that fried foods are harmful for my health _____ I shouldn't eat them.
　　　　that 關係子句 1　　　　　連接詞　　that 關係子句 2

關係代名詞 that 帶出來的關係子句 1 為「名詞子句」，放在 know 後方當受詞。

# Unit 1

關係代名詞、關係副詞、複合關係代名詞
## 1-2 關係副詞

關係副詞 = 介係詞 + 關係代名詞 which。常用的關係副詞有三個：代表地點的 where、代表時間的 when，及說明理由的 why。

| 關係副詞 | 地點 | 時間 | 理由 |
|---|---|---|---|
| 介係詞 + which | where | when | why |

例 她出生在一個極重視教育的家庭 。

句1 She was born in **a family**.
句2 Education is highly valued in **the family**.

使用關係代名詞連接
She was born in a family **which** education is highly valued **in**.

將介係詞搬到關係代名詞前
She was born in a family **in which** education is highly valued.

使用關係副詞連接
She was born in a family **where** education is highly valued.

> 解 先行詞 a family 屬物，又在句 2 的位置屬受詞，故連接兩句時可用「物 / 受詞性質」的關係代名詞 which。因關係代名詞只能代替名詞，無法代替介係詞，故介係詞 in 仍須寫出來。接著將介係詞 in 搬到關係代名詞 which 前，in 和 which 合併就成了代替地點 family 的關係副詞 where。

例 曾經有段時間，這名大亨只不過是個月領 22K 的工廠員工。

句1 There was **a time**.
句2 The tycoon was just a factory worker earning 22K a month at **that time**.

使用關係代名詞連接
There was a time **which** the tycoon was just a factory worker earning 22K a month **at**.

將介係詞搬到關係代名詞前
There was a time **at which** the tycoon was just a factory worker earning 22K a month.

使用關係副詞連接
There was a time **when** the tycoon was just a factory worker earning 22K a month.

> 解 先行詞 a time 屬物，又在句 2 的位置屬受詞，故連接兩句時可用「物 / 受詞性質」的關係代名詞 which。因關係代名詞只能代替名詞，無法代替介係詞，故介係詞 at 仍須寫出來。接著將介係詞 at 搬到關係代名詞 which 前，at 和 which 合併就成了代替時間 a time 的關係副詞 when。

例 她之所以辭職有許多原因。

句 1 There are **many reasons**.
句 2 She quits her job for **many reasons**.

使用關係代名詞連接
There are many reasons **which** she quits her job **for**.

將介係詞搬到關係代名詞前
There are many reasons **for which** she quits her job.

使用關係副詞連接
There are many reasons **why** she quits her job.

> 解 先行詞 many reasons 屬物，又在句 2 的位置屬受詞，故連接兩句時可用「物 / 受詞性質」的關係代名詞 which。因關係代名詞只能代替名詞，無法代替介係詞，故介係詞 for 仍須寫出來。接著將介係詞 for 搬到關係代名詞 which 前，for 和 which 合併就成了代替理由 reasons 的關係副詞 why。

# Unit 1

關係代名詞、關係副詞、複合關係代名詞
## 1–3 複合關係代名詞 what

■ 複合關係代名詞 what

代替「物」的複合關係代名詞 what = 先行詞 + 關係代名詞。當發現關係代名詞前沒有「先行詞」，即沒有「名詞」時，就可使用複合關係代名詞。

常用的複合關係代名詞有：what（代替物）、whatever（代替物）、whoever（代替人）、whomever（代替人）、whosever（代替人的）和 whichever（代替哪一個東西）。~ ever 的語氣比沒有 ever 字尾的複合關係代名詞來得強。請見下方例句：

例 金錢常引誘我們做不該做的事。

句 1 Money often tempts us to do **the things**.
句 2 We shouldn't do **the things**.

使用關係代名詞連接
Money often tempts us to do **the things which** we shouldn't do.

使用複合關係代名詞連接
Money often tempts us to do **what** we shouldn't do.

> 解 先行詞 the things 屬物，又在句 2 的位置屬受詞，故連接兩句時可用「物／受詞性質」的關係代名詞 which。接著把先行詞 the things 和 which 合併，就成了代替「物」的複合關係代名詞 what。關係子句從複合關係代名詞開始，往後推，找不到第二個動詞，所以到句點為止。從例句可看出，複合關係代名詞 what 前「沒有先行詞」，且帶出來的關係子句 what … do 放在動詞 do 後，為受詞，即「名詞子句」。

■ 關係代名詞 that 和複合關係代名詞 what 的使用時機

關係代名詞 that 和複合關係代名詞 what 都可用於「沒有先行詞」時。若關係子

句「意思完整」時，需用關係代名詞 that 當連接詞。相反地，若關係子句「意思不完整」時，則用關係代名詞 what 當連接詞。請見下方例句：

例 Tracy 上個月和她老公離婚了，這件事是千真萬確的。

That Tracy divorced her husband last month is true.
關係代名詞　　　　　　關係子句

> 解 關係子句從關係代名詞開始，往後推，到第二個動詞 is 前結束。關係代名詞 that 帶出一個「意思完整的」關係子句 (Tracy 上個月和她老公離婚了)。1 句關係子句 that Tracy … month 放句首當主詞。單數主詞，搭配單數動詞 is。請見下方句構分析：
>
> That Tracy divorced her husband last month is true.
> 　　　　　　主詞　　　　　　　　　　動詞

例 他說的關於 Tracy 的事都是真的。

What　he said about Tracy　is true.
複合關係代名詞　關係子句

> 解 關係子句從複合關係代名詞開始，往後推，到第二個動詞 is 前結束。複合關係代名詞 what 帶出一個「意思不完整的」關係子句 (他說了什麼關於 Tracy 的事呢？)。1 句關係子句 what he said about Tracy 放句首當主詞。單數主詞，搭配單數動詞 is。請見下方句構分析：
>
> What he said about Tracy is true.
> 　　　　主詞　　　　　動詞

## 小試身手：請選出正確解答

**01.** **A Dutch bank has unveiled plans for a new telephone banking system _____ a customer's identity will be confirmed by their voice.**

(A) whose　　　(B) when　　　(C) that　　　(D) where

> **解** 有家丹麥的銀行已推出可透過聲音確認客戶身分的新電話銀行服務系統。
>
> has unveiled / will be confirmed 兩個動詞，代表兩個句子，故劃線部分應為具連接句子功能的關係代名詞。將先行詞 system 放回後方 a customer's…their voice 這句子排排看，得出：a customer's identity will be confirmed by their voice in the system，由此可知需用「物／受性質」的關係代名詞 which。但因關係代名詞只能代替名詞 the system，無法代替介係詞 in，故答案應為 in which，或代替地點的關係副詞 where，**D** 選項為正解。關係子句從關係副詞開始，往後推，找不到第二個動詞，所以到句點為止。關係副詞 where 帶出來的關係子句 where … voice 放在名詞 system 後，為「形容詞子句」。

**02.** **The most stressful day of the week is Monday _____ people return to work after a relaxing weekend.**

(A) that　　　(B) , when　　　(C) , which　　　(D) why

> **解** 一星期裏，壓力最大的一天，就是星期一（大家度過輕鬆的週末後，再返回工作崗位的日子）。
>
> is / return 兩個動詞，代表兩個句子，故劃線部分應為具連接句子功能的關係代名詞。將先行詞 Monday 放回後方 people return…weekend 這句子排排看，得出：people return to work after a relaxing weekend on Monday，由此可知需用「物／受詞性質」的關係代名詞 which，但因關係代名詞只能代替名詞 Monday，無法代替介係詞 on，故答案應為 on which，或代替時間的關係副詞 when，**B** 選項為正解。關係子句從關係副詞開始，往後推，return to work，已用不定詞處理過，視為一組動詞。找不到第二個動詞，所以到句點為止。關係副詞 when 帶出來的關係子句 when … weekend，為補充說明星期一是什麼日子的「名詞子句」。又因為先行詞 Monday 為「1」天，故關係副詞 when 前方需打逗號。逗號等同於中文的括號，括號裏的內容，為補述的名詞子句。

**03.** An area code is a section of a telephone number generally representing the geographical area _____ the phone receiving the call is based in.

(A) where      (B) what      (C) when      (D) which

> 解 區域碼是電話號碼中的一段，通常代表受話者身處的地理區域。
>
> is / is based 兩個動詞，代表兩個句子，故劃線部分應為具連接句子功能的關係代名詞。將先行詞 area 放回後方 the phone … in 這句子排排看，得出：the phone receiving the call is based in the area，由此可知需用「物／受詞性質」的關係代名詞 which，但因關係代名詞只能代替名詞 area，無法代替介係詞 in，故答案應為 which … in，**D** 選項為正解。關係子句從關係代名詞開始，往後推，找不到第二個動詞，所以到句點為止。關係代名詞 which 帶出來的關係子 which … based in 放在名詞 area 後，為「形容詞子句」。若將句尾的介係詞 in 搬到關係代名詞 which 前，in 和 which 可合併成代替地點的關係副詞 where。

**04.** By understanding better the reason _____ flu spreads in winter but naturally fades in summer, we can find simple measures to stop its transmission.

(A) why      (B) when      (C) what      (D) which

> 解 藉著多了解感冒為何在冬天容易擴散，卻在夏天自然而然地消退的理由，我們就能找出阻止它傳播的簡易方法。
>
> spreads / fades / can find 三個動詞，代表三個句子，需要兩個連接詞 (或關代)。所以除連接詞 but 外，劃線部分應為具連接句子功能的關係代名詞。將先行詞 the reason 放回後方 flu spreads … summer 這句子排排看，得出：flu spreads in winter but naturally fades in summer for the reason，由此可知需用「物／受詞性質」的關係代名詞 which，但因關係代名詞只能代替名詞 the reason，無法代替介係詞 for，故答案應為 for which，或代替理由的關係副詞 why，**A** 選項為正解。關係子句從關係副詞開始，往後推，spreads … but … fades，已用連接詞處理過，視為一組動詞。找不到第二個動詞，所以到斷句用的逗號 summer, 為止。關係副詞 why 帶出來的關係子句 why … in summer 放在名詞 reason 後，為「形容詞子句」。

**05.** Jobipedia is a website _____ unemployed young people can ask questions about recruiting and get advice from human resources managers at 30 major companies.

(A) that      (B) where      (C) whose      (D) when

解 Jobipedia 是個無業的年輕人可向 30 家大公司的人資經理請益關於招募的問題，並聽取他們建議的網站。

is / can ask 兩個動詞，代表兩個句子，故劃線部分應為具連接句子功能的關係代名詞。將先行詞 the website 放回後方 unemployed young … companies 這句子排排看，得出：unemployed young people can ask questions ... and get advice from ... companies on the website，由此可知需用「物 / 受詞性質」的關係代名詞 which，但因為關係代名詞只能代替名詞 website，無法代替介係詞 on，故答案應為 on which，或代替地點的關係副詞 where，B 選項為正解。關係子句從關係副詞開始，往後推，ask … and get …，已用連接詞處理過，視為一組動詞。找不到第二個動詞，所以到句點為止。關係副詞 where 帶出來的關係子句 where … companies 放在名詞 website 後，為「形容詞子句」。

06. **Jimmy fell into the habit of saying _____ came to his mind, wild nonsense included, as a way of getting attention.**

(A) whose      (B) when      (C) what      (D) that

解 Jimmy 養成了想到什麼就說什麼的習慣，包括一些胡言亂語，並藉此引人關注。

fell / came 兩個動詞，代表兩個句子，故劃線部分應為具連接句子功能的關係代名詞。又關係代名詞前只有偏重動詞意思的動名詞 saying，並無先行詞，故答案不是 that 就是 what。關係子句從複合關係代名詞開始，往後推，找不到第二個動詞，所以到斷句用的逗點 mind，為止。又關係子句 came to his mind「意思不完整」，他想到了什麼呢？綜合以上，C 選項為正解。複合關係代名詞 what = the things which。複合關係代名詞 what 帶出來的關係子句 what … mind 放在動詞 say 後方當受詞，為「名詞子句」。

07. **Taiwan has been upgrading facilities on the island, _____ about 180 people live, most of them coastguard personnel.**

(A) what      (B) which      (C) when      (D) where

解 台灣一直提升這個島上的設施。這島上住了約 180 人，大多數都是海巡人員。

has been upgrading / live 兩個動詞，代表兩個句子，故劃線部分應為具連接句子功能的關係代名詞。將先行詞 the island 放回後方 about 180 people live 這句子排排看，得出：about 180 people live on the island，由此可知需用「物 / 受詞性質」的關係代名詞 which，但因為關係代名詞

只能代替名詞 island，無法代替介係詞 on，故答案應為 on which，或代替地點的關係副詞 where，**D** 選項為正解。關係子句從關係副詞開始，往後推，找不到第二個動詞，所以到斷句用的逗點 live, 為止。關係副詞 where 帶出來的關係子句 where ... live，為補充說明島上狀況的「名詞子句」。因為先行詞 the island 為「1」個島，故關係副詞 where 前方需打逗號。逗號等同於中文的括號，括號裏的內容，為補述用的名詞子句。

**08.** The scientists are keen to emphasize _____ measures like vaccines and good personal hygiene are still the best ways to protect yourself from a terrible cold.

(A) that          (B) where          (C) which          (D) what

解 科學家積極強調，如：疫苗和好的個人衛生等，仍然是避免重感冒的最佳方式。

are / are 兩動詞，代表兩個句子，故劃線部分應為具連接句子功能的關係代名詞。又關係代名詞前只有動詞 emphasize，無先行詞，故答案不是 that 就是 what。關係子句從關係代名詞開始，往後推，are ... to protect，已用不定詞處理過，視為一組動詞。找不到第二個動詞，所以到句點為止。關係子句 measures like vaccines ... are the best ways to protect ... yourself「意思完整」，**A** 選項為正解。關係代名詞 that 帶出來的關係子句 that measures ... from a terrible cold 放在動詞 emphasize 後方當受詞，為「名詞子句」。

**09.** With social media and a 24/7 news cycle, how do we, as news consumers, make sense of _____ we hear and read?

(A) that          (B) what          (C) which          (D) when

解 有了社群媒體，和 24 小時天天不間斷的新聞週期，身為新聞消耗者的我們，該如何解讀我們所聽所讀的事呢？

make / hear 兩個動詞，代表兩個句子，故劃線部分應為具連接句子功能的關係代名詞。又關係代名詞前只有介係詞 of，且關係代名詞若代替前方名詞 news consumers 語意也不合，因為我們不會 hear and read news consumers，可見無先行詞，故答案不是 that 就是 what。關係子句從關係代名詞開始，往後推，hear and read，已用連接詞處理過，視為一組動詞。找不到第二個動詞，所以到句點為止。關係子句 we hear and read「意思不完整」，我們到底聽到和看到什麼呢？綜合以上，**B** 選項為正解。複合關係代名詞 what = the things which。複合關係代名詞 what 帶出來的關係子句 what we ... read 放在動詞 make sense of 後方

當受詞，為「名詞子句」。

10. **A witness at the scene indicated that the attack was more organized than the police described and _____ deadly weapons were used.**

    (A) which       (B) why       (C) whose       (D) that

    > 解 現場目擊證人指出，這宗攻擊案比警方描述得更有組織，且歹徒使用了致命的武器。
    >
    > 動詞 indicated 後方有兩個受詞，都以 that 關係子句對稱呈現。再用連接詞 and 連接兩個受詞，**D** 選項為正解。請見下方句構分析：
    >
    > …indicated that the attack…described and _____ deadly weapons were used.
    >                  that 關係子句 1       連接詞          that 關係子句 2
    > 關係代名詞 that 帶出來的關係子句 that … described 和 that deadly … used 放在 indicated 後方當受詞，為「名詞子句」。

# Unit 1

關係代名詞、關係副詞、複合關係代名詞
## 1-4 最後小叮嚀

■ 框出關係子句，並熟悉它的兩大用途

關係子句從關係代名詞開始，往後推，到第二個動詞前結束。若找不到第二個動詞，則到句點或斷句用的逗點為止。且按用途，關係子句可分成兩種：「形容詞子句」和「名詞子句」。

1. 形容詞子句：關係子句放在名詞後，當形容詞使用。形容詞子句前後不會有逗點。

例 Teachers whose students performed well on the exam received bonuses.
　　　　　　形容詞子句

解 學生考試表現好的老師，領到了獎金。

關係子句從關係代名詞 whose 開始，經過第一個動詞 performed，到第二個動詞 received 前結束。關係代名詞 whose 帶出關係子句 whose … exam，放在名詞後當形容詞使用，意指「… 的」老師。

2. 名詞子句：名詞子句可放句首當主詞，或放動詞 / 介係詞後當受詞，或夾在逗點間當補述用。

例 What a spacecraft needs is a reliable energy storage system.
　　名詞子句當主詞　　動詞

解 太空船需要的是一個可靠的能源儲存系統。

關係子句從複合關係代名詞 what 開始，經過第一個動詞 needs，到第二個動詞 is 前結束。複合關係代名詞 what 帶出關係子句 what … needs，放在句首當主詞，屬名詞子句。主詞為「1 句」關係子句，單數主詞，搭配單數動詞 is。

20

例 Evidence shows that swearing has the effect of preventing physical violence.

名詞子句當受詞

解 證據顯示，罵髒話有預防肢體暴力的效果。

關係子句從關係代名詞 that 開始，往後推，經過第一個動詞 has，卻找不到第二個動詞，所以到句點為止。關係代名詞 that 帶出關係子句 that ... violence，放在動詞 shows 後方當受詞，為名詞子句。

例 The castle, which is located on the cliff, provides superb views of the city.

補述用的名詞子句

解 這城堡，位於懸崖上，提供絕佳的都市景色。

關係子句從關係代名詞 which 開始，往後推，到第二個動詞 provides 前，同時也是斷句用的逗點 cliff, 為止。關係代名詞 which 帶出來的關係子句 which ... cliff，夾在兩個逗點間，為補充說明城堡狀況的「名詞子句」。逗號等同於中文的括號。

■ 限定和非限定關係子句，一個逗號差很大。

大家在學限定和非限定關係子句時，老師總會說：關係代名詞前有逗號時為「非限定」用法，而沒有逗號時為「限定」用法。但是我建議大家以「形容詞子句」和「名詞子句」來區分是否需在關係代名詞前打逗號。一般而言，若關係子句當「形容詞」使用時，關係代名詞前不需打逗號，但若關係子句當「補充說明」用的名詞子句時，關係代名詞前就得打逗點。

例 請看下方 a 和 b 例句：

a. Andy has a girlfriend **who lives in Taipei**.

解 關係代名詞前不打逗號，則關係子句當「形容詞」使用，意指「...的」。句子翻譯：Andy 有個「住在台北的」女朋友。那別的地方呢？或許暗示 Jeff 是個花心大少，女友眾多，而其中一個住在台北。

b. Andy has a girlfriend, **who lives in Taipei**.

> 解 關係代名詞前打了逗點，則關係子句有「補充說明」的功能。逗號等同於中文的括號，括號裏的內容，多為補述用。句子翻譯：Andy 有女朋友了（她住在台北）。可見 Jeff 只有一個女友，而且他的女友就住在台北。

從上方例子，我們也可將關係代名詞前方打不打逗號的原則更進一步簡化成：若先行詞的數量只有「1 個」時，就需打逗號，很多個時，則不須打逗號。

例 This summer, the dengue fever hits tourism in Tainan, **which** enjoys a reputation as Taiwan's best food destination.

> 解 先行詞 Tainan 只有一個，故關係代名詞 which 前需打逗號。逗號等同於中文的括號，括號裏的內容，多為補述用。句子翻譯：今年夏天，登革熱重創台南觀光（台南享有台灣美食之都的美名）。

## 小試身手：請選出正確解答

**01.** It's early September _____ the days are bright and warm but nights are already creeping below 0°C.

(A) that      (B) why      (C) , when      (D) , whose

> **解** 現在是九月初。九月初白天明亮溫暖，但是夜裡氣溫卻已經悄悄落到攝氏零度以下。
>
> is / are / are 三個動詞，代表三個句子，需兩個連接詞 (或關代)。除了連接詞 but 外，劃線部分應為具連接句子功能的關係代名詞。將先行詞 September 放回後方 the days are ... below 0°C 這句子排排看，得出：the days are bright and warm but nights are already creeping below 0°C in September，由此可知需用「物 / 受詞性質」的關係代名詞 which，但因為關係代名詞只能代替名詞 September，無法代替介係詞 in，故答案應為 in which，或代替時間的關係副詞 when，**C** 選項為正解。關係子句從關係副詞 when 開始，往後推，... days are ... but nights are ...，已用連接詞處理過，視為一組動詞。找不到第二個動詞，所以到句點為止。關係副詞 when 帶出來的關係子句 when ... below 0°C 為補充說明九月日夜氣候的「名詞子句」。又先行詞 September 為「1 個」月份，故關係副詞 when 前方需打逗號。

**02.** According to Alan Arnette, a mountaineer based in Colorado _____ blog is a trusted source of Everest information, from 1924 to August 2015, 283 people have died on the mountain.

(A) whose      (B) that      (C) what      (D) where

> **解** 據 Alan Arnette (一名以科羅拉多州為基地的登山者，他的部落格是獲取珠穆朗瑪峰可靠訊息的來源) 所言，從 1924 年到 2015 年八月，共有 283 人命喪喜馬拉雅山。
>
> is / have 兩個動詞，代表兩個句子，故劃線部分應為具連接句子功能的關係代名詞。登山者 (mountaineer) 才會經營部落格 (blog)，將先行詞 mountaineer 放回後方句 blog is ... information 這句子排排看，得出：the mountaineer's blog is a trusted source of Everest information，由此可知需用「人 / 所有格性質」的關係代名詞 whose，**A** 選項為正解。關係子句從關係代名詞開始，往後推，找不到第二個動詞，所以到斷句用的逗點 information, 為止。關係代名詞 whose 帶出來的關係子句 whose blog ... information 放在名詞 a mountaineer ... 後，為「形容詞子句」。

Unit 1
關係
代名詞

Unit 2
被動
語態

Unit 3
分詞
形容詞

Unit 4
分詞
構句

Unit 5
假設
語法

Unit 6
倒裝
句

Unit 7
間接
問句

Unit 8
特殊
動詞

Unit 9
主動詞
一致

Unit 10
對稱
結構

特別收錄
Unit 11
五回
試題

**03.** **There is an underlying dissatisfaction which makes some people resort to cosmetic surgery _____ the surgery may not solve.**

(A) that      (B) and which      (C) by what      (D) when

> 解 潛在的不滿或許讓人們退而求助整形手術,又或連整形手術也無法解決這種不滿。
>
> 名詞 dissatisfaction 後方有兩個形容詞子句,都以 which 關係子句對稱呈現。再用連接詞 and 連接兩個形容詞,**B** 選項為正解。請見下方句構分析:
>
> There　is … dissatisfaction which … surgery　and which … solve.
> 　主詞　動詞　　　　　　　　　　　形容詞子句 1　　　　形容詞子句 2

**04.** **This fantasy writer was known to form good relationships with a large group of vampires _____ he had interviews regularly.**

(A) with whom      (B) who      (C) of which      (D) what

> 解 這個奇幻作家以和他常訪問的一大群吸血鬼關係良好而為人津津樂道。
>
> was / had 兩個動詞,代表兩個句子,故劃線部分應為具連接句子功能的關係代名詞。將先行詞 vampires 放回後方句 he had … regularly 排排看,得出:he had interviews with the vampires regularly,由此可知需用「人 / 受詞性質」的關係代名詞 whom,但因關係代名詞只能代替名詞 vampires,無法代替介係詞 with,故答案應為 with whom,**A** 選項為正解。關係子句從關係代名詞開始,往後推,找不到第二個動詞,所以到句點為止。關係代名詞 with whom 帶出來的關係子句 with whom … regularly 放在名詞 vampires 後方,為「形容詞子句」。

**05.** **When carbon monoxide and nitrogen dioxide find their way high into the atmosphere, they often get transformed through chemical reactions into _____ scientists refer to as secondary pollutants.**

(A) which      (B) why      (C) whose      (D) what

> 解 當一氧化碳和二氧化氮高升到空中時,它們常透過化學反應,轉化成科學家所說的次級污染物。
>
> find / get / refer 三個動詞,代表三個句子,需兩個連接詞 (或關代),除連接詞 when 外,劃線部分應為具連接句子功能的關係代名詞。關係代名詞前只有介係詞 into,並無先行詞,故答案不是 that 就是 what。關

係子句從關係代名詞開始，往後推，找不到第二個動詞，所以到句點為止。關係子句 scientists refer to as secondary pollutants「意思不完整」，究竟科學家將什麼稱為次級污染物呢？綜合以上，**D** 選項為正解。複合關係代名詞 what 帶出來的關係子句 what … pollutants 放在介係詞 into 後方，當受詞，為「名詞子句」。片語「把 A 看作 B」refer to A as B。

**06.** Due to the unique environment _____ they operate, spacecraft power systems must also be able to function smoothly in zero gravity and in a vacuum, as well as endure immense amounts of radiation.

(A) when　　　　(B) by whom　　　　(C) what　　　　(D) where

解 由於太空梭電力系統運作的環境特殊，它們必須能夠在無重力和真空環境中流暢運轉，也必須能夠忍受極大量的輻射。

operate / must also be 兩個動詞，代表兩個句子，故劃線部分應為具連接句子功能的關係代名詞。將先行詞 environment 放回後方句 they（指 spacecraft power systems）operate 排排看，得出：they operate in the environment，由此可知需用「物 / 受詞性質」的關係代名詞 which，但因關係代名詞只能代替名詞 environment，無法代替介係詞 in，故答案應為 in which，或代替地點的關係副詞 where，**D** 選項為正解。關係子句從關係副詞開始，往後推，找不到第二個動詞，所以到斷句用的逗點 operate, 為止。關係副詞 where 帶出來的關係子句 where they operate 放在名詞 environment 後方，為「形容詞子句」。

**07.** The general sales tax has been a major source of income for state governments, _____ derive more than half of their budgets from it.

(A) much of which　　　　　　(B) none of whom
(C) many of them　　　　　　(D) most of which

解 一般消費稅已成為州政府主要的收入來源。大多數州政府從中取得一半以上的預算。

has been / derive 兩個動詞，代表兩個句子，故劃線部分應為具連接句子功能的關係代名詞。將先行詞 state governments 放回後方句 derive more than … it 句子排排看，得出：state governments derive more than half of their budgets from it（即 the general sales tax），由此可知需用「物 / 主詞性質」的關係代名詞 which，且數量詞應為複數，才能搭配複數動詞 derive，**D** 選項為正解。關係子句從關係代名詞開始，往後推，找不到第二個動詞，所以到句點為止。關係代名詞 most of which 帶出來的關係子句 most of which derive … it 放在 state government 後

Unit 1
關係
代名詞

Unit 2
被動
語態

Unit 3
分詞
形容詞

Unit 4
分詞
構句

Unit 5
假設
語法

Unit 6
倒裝
句

Unit 7
間接
問句

Unit 8
特殊
動詞

Unit 9
主動詞
一致

Unit 10
對稱
結構

特別收錄
Unit 11
五回
試題

方，補充說明州政府的財源來源，為「名詞子句」，故關係代名詞 most of which 前要打逗號。

**08.** Although tea and coffee contain many different substances, the one _____ most research focuses is caffeine.

(A) about what　　(B) that　　　　(C) on which　　(D) whose

解 雖然茶和咖啡內含許多不同物質，但大多數研究偏重的物質就是咖啡因。

contain / focuses / is 三個動詞，代表三個句子，需要兩個連接詞（或關代），除連接詞 although 外，劃線部分應為具連接句子功能的關係代名詞。將先行詞 the one（即 the substance）放回後方句 most research focuses 排排看，得出：most research focuses on the substance，由此可知需用「物／受詞性質」的關係代名詞 which，但因為關係代名詞只能代替名詞 substance，無法代替介係詞 on，故答案應為 on which，**C** 選項為正解。關係子句從關係代名詞開始，往後推，到第二個動詞 is 前結束。關係代名詞 on which 帶出來的關係子句 on which most research focuses 放在名詞 the one 後方，為「形容詞子句」。

**09.** There was about a 10 to 15% difference in earnings between the most and the least attractive people in the group _____ added up to about $230,000 over a lifetime.

(A) who　　　　(B) , where　　(C) what　　　(D) , which

解 團體中，外貌出眾和最不起眼的人，收入差距約為百分之 10 到 15，甚至一輩子累積下來的收入差距還可高達約美金 23 萬元。

was / added 兩個動詞，代表兩個句子，故劃線部分應為具連接句子功能的關係代名詞。錢加起來（added up）才會變成 $230,000，故先行詞應為 difference in earnings，放回後方句 added up ... lifetime 排排看，得出：the difference in earnings added up to about $230,000 over a lifetime，由此可知需用「物／主詞性質」的關係代名詞 which。關係子句從關係代名詞開始，往後推，找不到第二個動詞，所以到句點為止。關係代名詞 which 帶出來的關係子句 which added ... lifetime 放在名詞 difference in earnings 後方，補充說明收入的差距有多大，為補述用的「名詞子句」，故關係代名詞 which 前要打逗號，**D** 選項為正解。

10. The most popular course, "Hostessing," costs 100,000 yuan for 12 days _____ the client learns skills from engaging in small talk to pairing wines with a meal.

(A) , when　　　(B) of which　　　(C) , what　　　(D) where

> 解 最熱門的課程－如何做東道主－為期 12 天，費用為人民幣 10 萬元。在這12天裏，客戶將學習許多技巧，從熱絡交談到挑選搭配餐點的酒等。
>
> costs / learns 兩個動詞，代表兩個句子，故劃線部分應為具連接句子功能的關係代名詞。將先行詞 12 days 放回後方句 the clients … a meal 排排看，得出：the clients learns skills from engaging in small talk to pairing wines with a meal during the 12 days，由此可知需用「物 / 受詞性質」的關係代名詞 which。但因關係代名詞只能代替名詞 12 days，無法代替介係詞 during，故答案應為 during which，或代替時間的關係副詞 when，A 選項為正解。關係子句從關係副詞開始，往後推，找不到第二個動詞，所以到句點為止。關係副詞 when 帶出來的關係子句 when the clients … meal 放在名詞 12 days 後方，補充說明為期 12 天的課程內容為何，為補述用的「名詞子句」，故關係副詞 when 前方要打逗號。

11. Some of _____ seem unusual or even weird to foreigners, such as chicken feet, stingy tofu or pig's blood cake, are mind-blowing delicacies for the locals.

(A) those　　　(B) what　　　(C) whom　　　(D) which

> 解 有些被外國人視為不尋常，甚至怪異的食物，如：雞腳、臭豆腐或豬血糕等，對當地人而言卻是好吃度爆表的美食。
>
> seem / are 兩個動詞，代表兩個句子，故劃線部分應為具連接句子功能的關係代名詞。又關係代名詞前只有介係詞 of，並無先行詞，故答案不是 that 就是 what。關係子句從關係代名詞開始，往後推，到斷句用的逗號 foreigners, 前結束。關係子句 seem unusual or even weird to foreigners「意思不完整」，究竟外國人把什麼視為不尋常或甚至怪異呢？綜合以上，B 選項為正解。複合關係代名詞 what = the foods which。複合關係代名詞 what 帶出來的關係子句 what … foreigners 放在介係詞 of 後方，當受詞，為「名詞子句」。

12. After completing senior high school, Andy tried out for the police academy _____ sprawling campus was located in the suburbs of Paris.

(A) that　　　(B) when　　　(C) where　　　(D) whose

> 解 高中畢業後，Andy 試著申請位於巴黎郊區，且校園不斷向外擴張的警察學校。
>
> tried out / was located 兩個動詞，代表兩個句子，故劃線部分應為具連接句子功能的關係代名詞。將先行詞 police academy 放回後方句 sprawling campus... Paris 排排看，得出：the police academy's sprawling campus was located in the suburbs of Paris，由此可知需用「物／所有格性質」的關係代名詞 whose，**D** 選項為正解。關係子句從關係代名詞開始，往後推，找不到第二個動詞，所以到句點為止。關係代名詞 whose 帶出來的關係子句 whose ... Paris 放在名詞 the police academy 後方，為「形容詞子句」。

13. A common rule of thumb to remember about Aussie lingo is _____ words are often shortened at the end and take the –ie suffix. For example, Brisbane is often called "Brizzie" and breakfast becomes "brekkie."

(A) what      (B) which      (C) that      (D) why

> 解 記得，澳洲式英文的通則之一就是單字常被縮短且以 ie 收尾，例如：Brisbane 常被說成 Brizzie，而 breakfast 則變成了 brekkie。
>
> is / are shortened 兩個動詞，代表兩個句子，故劃線部分應為具連接句子功能的關係代名詞。又關係代名詞前只有動詞 is，沒有先行詞，故答案不是 that 就是 what。關係子句從關係代名詞開始，往後推，are shortened ... and take ...，已用連接詞處理過，視為一組動詞。找不到第二個動詞，所以到句點為止。關係子句 words are ... suffix「意思完整」，**C** 選項為正解。

14. In 2013, the British Association of Aesthetic Plastic Surgeons carried out 50,000 procedures _____ the most common was breast augmentation.

(A) , of which      (B) , by whom      (C) that      (D) where

> 解 2013 年，英國醫美外科醫師協會開了五萬台刀，當中最常見的項目就是隆乳手術。
>
> carried out / was 兩個動詞，代表兩個句子，故劃線部分應為具連接句子功能的關係代名詞。將先行詞 50,000 procedures 放回後方句 the most common was ... augmentation 排排看，得出：of the 50,000 procedures, the most common was breast augmentation，由此可知需用「物／受詞性質」的關係代名詞 which。但因為關係代名詞只能代替名詞 procedures，無法代替介係詞 of，故答案應為 of which，**A** 選項為正解。關係子句從關

係詞代名詞開始，往後推，找不到第二個動詞，所以到句點為止。關係代名詞 of which 帶出來的關係子句 of which the most ... augmentation 放在名詞 procedures 後方，補充說明 procedures 的內容為何，為補述用的「名詞子句」，故關係代名詞 of which 前方要打逗號。

15. The eye implant, a 3mm square array of about 1,500 light sensors, _____ sends pulsed electrical signals to nerve cells, is connected to a tiny computer that sits underneath the skin behind the ear.

(A) what      (B) which      (C) through which    (D) who

解 這眼內植入物（即三平方毫釐大小的矩陣，內含約 1500 個可傳送震動的電波訊號到神經細胞的光感應器）將連接到一個位於耳後皮下的迷你電腦。

sends / is connected 兩個動詞，代表兩個句子，故劃線部分應為具連接句子功能的關係代名詞。從單數 sends 可知先行詞不是 sensors，而是單數的 a 3mm square array。將先行詞 a 3mm square array 放回後方句 sends ... cells 排排看，得出：a 3mm square array sends pulsed electrical signals to nerve cells，由此可知需用「物／主詞性質」的關係代名詞 which，B 選項為正解。關係子句從關係代名詞開始，往後推，到第二個動詞 is connected 前結束。關係代名詞 which 帶出來的關係子句 which sends ... cells 放在名詞 a 3mm square array 後方，補充說明感光矩陣的功能，為補述用的「名詞子句」。逗號夾住的 a 3mm square array ... light sensors，則為同位格，補充說明眼內植入物的外觀。

16. Just as the astronaut has been trained to use medical equipment and act like a space paramedic, similar training can be given to people in areas _____ there are shortages of doctors and healthcare workers.

(A) where      (B) so that      (C) when      (D) which

解 正如太空人接受使用醫療器材方面的訓練後，繼而表現得像太空醫護人員一般，醫生或健康照護人員短缺地區的人們，也可接受類似的訓練。

has been trained to use / act / can be given / are 四個動詞，代表四個句子，需有三個連接詞（或關代），除連接詞 as 和 and 外，劃線部分應為具連接句子功能的關係代名詞。將先行詞 areas 放回後方句 there are ... workers 排排看，得出：there are shortages of doctors and healthcare workers in the areas，由此可知需用「物／受詞性質」的關係代名詞 which。因關係代名詞只能代替名詞 areas，無法代替介係詞 in，故答案應為 in which，或代替地點的關係副詞 where，A 選項為正解。關係

Unit 1
關係
代名詞

Unit 2
被動
語態

Unit 3
分詞
形容詞

Unit 4
分詞
構句

Unit 5
假設
語法

Unit 6
倒裝
句

Unit 7
間接
問句

Unit 8
特殊
動詞

Unit 9
主動詞
一致

Unit 10
對稱
結構

特別收錄
Unit 11
五回
試題

> 子句從關係副詞開始，往後推，找不到第二個動詞，所以到句點為止。
> 關係副詞 where 帶出來的關係子句 where there … workers 放在名詞
> areas 後方，為「形容詞子句」。

**17.** _____ e-books have surged in popularity in recent years is not news, but where they are headed and what effect this will have on the printed world is unknown.

(A) When      (B) What      (C) That      (D) Why

> 解 近幾年來，電子書備受歡迎已非新聞，但它們未來的趨勢和這趨勢對印刷界產生的影響仍屬未知。
>
> have surged / is 兩個動詞，代表兩個句子，故劃線部分應為具連接句子功能的關係代名詞。又關係代名詞前無先行詞，答案不是 that 就是 what。關係子句從關係詞代名詞開始，往後推，到第二個動詞 is 前結束。關係子句 e-books … recent years「意思完整」，C 選項為正解。關係代名詞 that 帶出來的關係子句 that ebooks … recent years 放在句首當主詞，屬「名詞子句」。「1 句」關係子句當主詞，單數主詞，搭配單數動詞 is。

**18.** Decline in belief seems to be occurring across the board, including in places _____ are still strongly religious such as Brazil.

(A) that      (B) where      (C) at which      (D) what

> 解 信教人數的下滑似乎是全面性的，包含如：巴西等信仰極度虔誠的地區，也是如此。
>
> seems to be / are 兩個動詞，代表兩個句子，故劃線部分應為具連接句子功能的關係代名詞。將先行詞 places 放回後方句 are…Brazil 排排看，得出：the places are still strongly religious such as Brazil，由此可知需用「物 / 主詞性質」的關係代名詞 which / that，A 選項為正解。關係子句從關係詞代名開始，往後推，找不到第二個動詞，所以到句點為止。關係代名詞 that 帶出來的關係子句 that are … Brazil 放在名詞 places 後方，為「形容詞子句」。

**19.** Dubbed "Cubs of the Caliphate," these children in the training camps, _____ are as young as five years old, are drilled every day, eventually graduating to the front lines of battles.

(A) most of who          (B) several of which
(C) some of whom       (D) all of them

解 這些訓練營中的小孩被暱稱為「哈理發國幼獅」，有些甚至年僅五歲。他們每天接受訓練，最終結業後被送往戰爭前線。

are / are drilled 兩個動詞，代表兩個句子，故劃線部分應為具連接句子功能的關係代名詞。young 用來形容 children，故先行詞為 children，而非 camps。將先行詞 these children in the training camps 放回後方句 are … old 排排看，得出：數量詞 of the children in the training camps are as young as five years old，由此可知需用「人 / 受詞性質」的關係代名詞 whom，且數量詞需為複數才能搭配複數動詞 are。綜合以上，C 選項為正解。關係子句從關係詞代名詞開始，往後推，到第二個動詞 are drilled 前 / 或斷句用的逗號 old, 結束。關係代名詞 whom 帶出來的關係子句 some of whom are … old 補充說明訓練營裏小孩的狀況，為補述用的「名詞子句」，故 some of whom 前需打逗號。

20. In my opinion, _____ others label or might call failure is just God's way of pointing you in a new direction.

    (A) that        (B) which        (C) what        (D) when

解 在我看來，被其他人貼上「失敗」標籤，或稱為失敗的事，只不過是老天爺指引你新方向的方法。

label / might call / is 三個動詞，代表三個句子，需要兩個連接詞（或關代）。除連接詞 or 外，劃線部分應為具連接句子功能的關係代名詞。關係代名詞前，沒有先行詞，故答案不是 that 就是 what。關係子句從複合關係詞代名詞開始，往後推，label or might call，已用連接詞處理過，視為一組動詞，所以到第二個動詞 is 前結束。關係子句 others label or might call failure「意思不完整」，其他人可能將什麼稱為失敗呢？綜合以上，C 選項為正解。複合關係代名詞 what 帶出來的關係子句 what others … failure 放在句首當主詞，屬「名詞子句」。「1 句」關係子句當主詞，單數主詞，搭配單數動詞 is。「就我看來」in my opinion，為放句首的「副詞」。

# Unit 2　被動語態

■ 使用被動式的時機

被動式常用於以下四個狀況：

1. 當主詞無法執行動作時，需用「被動式」。
2. 當執行動作的主詞不明確時，需用「被動式」，且「by + 受詞」部分也可省略，如 "by people"或"by us"等，都可略去不寫。
3. 當全句重點在於受詞而非主詞時，可用「被動式」。
4. 科普類文章或發表研究結果時，為表示「客觀」，也常用「被動式」。

■ 主動語態和被動語態互換的三步驟

步驟1 主動句的主詞變成被動句的受詞，且放在介係詞 by（被）的後面。
步驟2 主動句的受詞變成被動句的主詞。
步驟3 主動句的動詞改成被動式的動詞，基本架構為「be + p.p.」。

請見下方圖示：

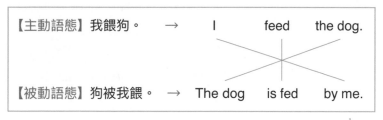

由上圖可知，被動語態的記號為介係詞「by（被）」和動詞「be + p.p.」。

■ 被動式的時態

被動式動詞的基本架構為「be + p.p.」，但依不同時態變化如下：

| 被動式 | 公式 | 說明 |
|---|---|---|
| 現在被動 | is / am / are + p.p. | be 動詞的現在式為 is / am / are，故現在被動的公式為 is / am / are + p.p. |
| 過去被動 | was / were + p.p. | be 動詞的過去式為 was / were，故過去被動的公式為 was / were + p.p. |
| 未來被動 | will be + p.p.<br><br>is / am / are<br>going to be + p.p. | 未來式的助動詞為 will，助動詞後方動詞需現原形，故未來被動的公式為 will be + p.p. 或者也可將助動詞 will 改成 is / am / are going to，由此得出，未來被動也可寫成 is / am / are going to be + p.p. |
| 現在完成被動 | has / have（助動詞）been + p.p. | 現在完成式　　 has / have + p.p.<br>+ 被動式　　　　　　　　 be + p.p.<br>―――――――――――――――<br>現在完成被動　has / have + been + p.p. |
| 過去完成被動 | had（助動詞）been + p.p. | 過去完成式　　 had + p.p.<br>+ 被動式　　　　　　　 be + p.p.<br>―――――――――――――――<br>過去完成被動　had + been + p.p. |
| 未來完成被動 | will have been + p.p. | 未來完成式　　 will have + p.p.<br>+ 被動式　　　　　　　　 be + p.p.<br>―――――――――――――――<br>未來完成被動　will have + been + p.p. |
| 現在進行被動 | is / am / are<br>being + p.p. | 現在進行式　　 is / am / are + Ving<br>+ 被動式　　　　　　　　 be + p.p.<br>―――――――――――――――<br>現在進行被動　is/am/are + being+ p.p. |
| 過去進行被動 | was / were<br>being + p.p. | 過去進行式　　 was / were + Ving<br>+ 被動式　　　　　　　　 be + p.p.<br>―――――――――――――――<br>過去進行被動　was / were + being + p.p. |
| 有助動詞的被動式 | 助動詞 be + p.p. | 助動詞後方的動詞需現原形，故含助動詞的被動式公式為：助動詞 + be + p.p. |

表格中同學們較困擾的「現在完成被動」等，公式其實不難背，只需用表格說明欄示範的「兩式相加法」即可得。這也說明了，對時態的基本認識是一

切的基礎囉。趕緊利用下方表格，檢驗自己是否已清楚了解被動式依不同時態所產生的變化吧。

■ 主動語態和被動語態的對照表

| 時態 | 主詞 | 動詞 | 受詞 |
|---|---|---|---|
| [主動]現在式 | She | buys | the novels. |
| 現在[被動]式 | The novels | (1) | by her. |
| [主動]過去式 | She | bought | the novels. |
| 過去[被動]式 | The novels | (2) | by her. |
| [主動]未來式 | She | will buy | the novels. |
| 未來[被動]式 | The novels | (3) | by her. |
| [主動]現在完成式 | She | has bought | the novels. |
| 現在完成[被動]式 | The novels | (4) | by her. |
| [主動]過去完成式 | She | had bought | the novels. |
| 過去完成[被動]式 | The novels | (5) | by her. |
| [主動]未來完成式 | She | will have bought | the novels. |
| 未來完成[被動]式 | The novels | (6) | by her. |
| [主動]現在進行式 | She | is buying | the novels. |
| 現在進行[被動]式 | The novels | (7) | by her. |
| [主動]過去進行式 | She | was buying | the novels. |
| 過去進行[被動]式 | The novels | (8) | by her. |
| [主動]含助動詞 | She | would buy | the novels. |
| 含助動詞[被動]式 | The novels | (9) | by her. |

解 (1) are bought (2) were bought (3) will be bought 或 are going to be bought (4) have been bought (5) had been bought (6) will have been bought (7) are being bought (8) were being bought (9) would be bought

## 小試身手：請選出正確解答

**01.** You might get a taste of the kawaii culture at this Hello Kitty namesake cafe, where everything from burger buns to soup bowls _____ like the mouthless cartoon cat.

(A) have shaped     (B) were shaped     (C) to be shap     (D) is shaped

> 解 你可在這家與 Hello Kitty 同名的餐廳裏，體驗到「萌」文化。所有東西，從漢堡包到湯碗，都被做成那隻無嘴貓的形狀。
>
> 關係副詞 where 帶出關係子句 where ... cat。單數主詞 everything，搭配單數動詞。每樣東西都「被塑形」，需搭配被動式，綜合以上，**D** 選項為正解。介係詞片語 from ... bowls，補充說明 everything 涵蓋的範圍，不會影響動詞。

**02.** Police have yet to press charges on the trek operator. They are now investigating whether the tragedy was an accident or _____.

(A) being prevented          (B) had been preventing

(C) could have been prevented       (D) was going to be prevented

> 解 警方尚未對旅行業者提起告訴。他們現在還在調查這場悲劇究竟是意外，或是可能可被避免。
>
> 間接問句 whether the tragedy was ... 的主詞 tragedy（悲劇），可以「被避免」，需搭配被動式。連接詞 or 連接兩個動詞，兩個動詞時態需對稱。從 was 可知，劃線處應為過去式。「could have + p.p.」可用於猜測之前可能發生的事情。綜合以上，**C** 選項為正解。

**03.** Trying to prevent cancer in the first place is a necessary complement to the advances in treatment; yet, what _____ to prevention is typically 2% of the overall budget.

(A) is allocated           (B) should have been allocating

(C) are going to allocate      (D) has allocated

> 解 極力預防癌症，與癌症療法的進步，兩者應相輔相成。然而，總預算中，一般僅百分之二被分配用於癌症預防。

從 is typically... 可知本句為「現在式」。複合關係代名詞 what 等於 the budget which，先行詞 (即主詞) the budget「被分配」，需搭配被動式。綜合以上，**A** 選項為正解。B、C、D 選項都不是被動式。

**04.** In the will, the rock star requested that his remains _____ to the country of Bali and cremated there in accordance with the Buddhist rituals.

(A) be taken　　　(B) had taken　　　(C) were being taken　　　(D) took

解 在這名搖滾明星的遺囑中，他要求他的遺體被帶往峇里島鄉間，並在那兒用佛教儀式進行火葬。

本題考點為特殊句型「要求」：request that S + (should) V 原。其中助動詞 should 常被省略，只剩下「動詞原形」。又 that 關係子句中的主詞 his remains (遺體)「被帶走」，需用被動式。綜合以上，**A** 選項為正解。

**05.** The nominations for the Oscars _____ on Thursday, and judging from its previous success, "The Danish Girl" seems likely to receive some more awards.

(A) would have  announced　　　　(B) will be announced
(C) is going to announce　　　　(D) have been announcing

解 奧斯卡獎的提名，將於星期四被宣布。從《丹麥女孩》之前的好戰績看來，這部片子似乎可再多贏得一些獎項。

主詞 the nominations (提名)「被宣布」，需搭配被動式。又從「可能得到 (likely to receive)」推知提名結果尚未公布，需搭配「未來式」。綜合以上，**B** 選項為正解。

**06.** Since two weeks ago, letters, which warn: "Whoever does not attend will be liable to questioning," _____ to shopkeepers and public sector workers, "inviting" them to "re-education" courses run by Islamic State.

(A) were distributed　　　　(B) have been distributed
(C) being distributed　　　　(D) is being distributed

解 從兩星期前開始，「邀請」大家參加由 IS 主辦的「再教育」課程的信件就已被發送給店家和公僕。信中警告大家：凡是沒參加的人可能得接受訊問。

since（自從）為「完成式」的記號。關係代名詞 which 所帶出來的關係子句 which...questioning 放在名詞後，補充說明 letters 的內容，為補述用的名詞子句，不會影響動詞，可略去不看。刪除 which 子句後，可看出複數主詞 letters「被分送」，需搭配複數「被動式」。綜合以上，**B** 選項為正解。

07. **The star player claims that the three-match suspension is too harsh since other players who committed similar fouls in the past _____ only one game.**

    (A) have suspended
    (B) to be suspended
    (C) had been suspending
    (D) were suspended

    解 明星球員宣稱禁賽三場太過嚴厲，因為以往犯規情節和他相似的人都只被禁賽一場。

    連接詞 since 帶出一個句子。關係子句從關係代名詞 who 開始，往後推，到劃線處（即第二個動詞）前結束。關係代名詞 who 帶出來的關係子句 committed... past 放在名詞 other players 後，為「形容詞子句」，不會影響動詞，可略去不看。請見下方句構分析：

    | since other players | who committed ... past | _____ only one game |
    |---|---|---|
    | 主詞 | 形容詞子句 | 動詞 |

    過去（in the past）犯規的球員，過去就「被禁賽」，需搭配「過去被動式」，**D** 選項為正解。

08. **Unless profound changes _____ oil consumption, early in the 2020s the world will be demanding more oil than it can produce.**

    (A) make to be lowered
    (B) will be made lowering
    (C) are made to lower
    (D) have made lower

    解 除非作出重大改變，降低油耗量，否則 2020 至 2030 前期，全世界對油的需求將超過產量。

    連接詞 unless 遇到未來式 will be demanding，unless 後方句的時態需改用「現在式」。後方句的主詞 changes「被做出來」，需搭配「被動式」。被動式後方的動詞，需搭配「to 動詞原形」。綜合以上，**C** 選項為正解。

**09.** As the massive snowstorm disrupts air traffic, passengers _____ expect significant delays and check their flight status before traveling to the airport.

(A) have advised to      (B) advise to be

(C) are being advised to      (D) would have been advising to

> 解 由於強烈暴風雪擾亂空中交通，搭乘飛機的旅客被建議將碰上班機嚴重誤點，且在動身前往機場前，應查明航班狀況。
>
> 從 disrupts 可知本句為「現在式」。passengers「被建議」應查明狀態，需搭配「被動式」。綜合以上，**C** 選項為正解。

**10.** To prepare for a new life in the US this July, I have eliminated all hobbies that _____ across borders, including my car and my piano. Hopefully, everything I own will fit in a carry-on by then.

(A) can't be easily carried      (B) haven't been easily carrying

(C) isn't easily being carried      (D) being easily carried

> 解 為了替今年七月即將在美國展開的新生活做準備，我除去那些不容易帶出國的心頭好，包括我的車子和鋼琴。希望屆時我所有的財產都可裝入一只手提行李。
>
> 從 have eliminated 可知本句用「現在式」。關係代名詞 that，代替前方的名詞 hobbies，喜歡的東西「被攜帶」，需搭配複數被動式。綜合以上，**A** 選項為正解。注意：關係子句裏的動詞應為完整動詞，即非 Ving / p.p. / to V 原。

**11.** Last year alone, tens of thousands of African elephants were killed to supply illegal ivory to markets throughout the world. Meanwhile, revenue generated from this bloody trade _____ war and terrorism in Africa.

(A) to be used to fueling      (B) was used to fuel

(C) would have used to fuel      (D) had been used to fueling

> 解 光去年一年，數以萬計的非洲象慘遭獵殺，以供應全球象牙交易黑市。同時，這血腥交易所產生的收入，被用來助長非洲的戰事和恐怖主義。
>
> meanwhile（同時）指的就是前一句的 last year，需搭配過去式。單數主詞 revenue（收入）「被使用」，需搭配單數被動式，且被動式後方的動詞得用「to 動詞原形」。綜合以上，**B** 選項為正解。切記勿將「被用來

...」be used to V 原，和「習慣 ...」be used to Ving 混為一談。

12. **Poverty in this country is both widespread and severe. Approximately 75 percent of its population _____ to live below the poverty line defined as an income that is insufficient to purchase daily necessities.**

    (A) is estimated                    (B) has estimated

    (C) have been estimating             (D) are being estimated

    > 解 國內普遍貧窮且狀況嚴重。國內人口約百分之 75 被預估生活在貧窮線下，按定義來說，就是收入不足以購買日常生活用品。
    >
    > 從 is both ... 可知本句為「現在式」。人口百分比是「被估算」出來的，需搭配被動式。又動詞單複數得視 of 後方的名詞 population 而定，和 75 percent 無關。單數主詞 population，搭配單數動詞。綜合以上，**A** 選項為正解。

13. **Doctors describe CTE as a disease that _____ with repeated brain trauma and common symptoms of it include memory loss, depression and progressive dementia.**

    (A) has associated                   (B) to be associated

    (C) is associated                    (D) associates

    > 解 醫師解釋了 CTE（慢性創傷性腦病變）。它是種和反覆腦創傷有關的疾病。常見症狀包括喪失記憶、沮喪憂鬱，和漸進式失智等。
    >
    > 從 describe / include 可知本句為「現在式」。關係代名詞 that，代替前方的名詞 disease。單數主詞 disease「被說和 ... 有關」，需搭配單數被動式。綜合以上，**C** 選項為正解。

14. **Experiments in the photography of moving objects _____ in both the United States and Europe well before 1900.**

    (A) were conducting                  (B) had been conducted

    (C) to be conducted                  (D) conducted

    > 解 拍攝移動中的物品的實驗，早在西元 1900 年之前就已在美國和歐洲被進行過了。
    >
    > 從 before 1900 可知，實驗比過去（西元 1900 年）還早發生，應用「過去

完成式」。主詞「拍攝移動物品的實驗」，重點在「實驗」，主詞 experiments 「被做」，需搭配被動式。綜合以上，**B** 選項為正解。

15. In science, a hypothesis needs to go through a lot of study and experimentations _____ a well-established theory.

(A) having labelled　　　　(B) will be labelled
(C) is labelled　　　　　　(D) to be labelled

解 在科學世界裡，「假說」需通過許多研究和實驗，才能被貼上「理論」這標籤，成為公認的理論。

從文意可知，「假說」通過許多實驗是「為了被貼上」理論這標籤。「不定詞」to 動詞原形，可用來表示「為了...」。假說「被貼上標籤」，需搭配被動式。綜合以上，**D** 選項為正解。

16. When one tuning fork _____ , the other tuning fork of the same frequency will also vibrate in resonance.

(A) will be stricken　　　　(B) is going to strike
(C) is struck　　　　　　　(D) has struck

解 當一支音叉被敲響時，另一支和它頻率相同的音叉，也將隨之震動，發出共鳴。

連接詞 when 遇到未來式 will also vibrate，when 後方句中的時態需改用「現在式」。又音叉「被敲擊」，需搭配被動式，綜合以上，**C** 選項為正解。

註 勿混淆以下兩個動詞的三態變化：(1) strike (v) 撞擊；strike – struck – struck / stricken (2) stick (v) 黏貼 / 插入；stick – stuck – stuck。

17. Eliminating problems by transferring the blame to others _____ as scapegoating and humans have a long history for it.

(A) have been referring to　　(B) is referred to
(C) are being referred to　　　(D) could have referred to

解 藉由怪罪別人來解決問題，就被稱為「找代罪羔羊」。這方法在人類歷史上由來已久。

從 have 可知本句為「現在式」。主詞「藉著 (by) ... 來解決問題」，重點

Unit 1
關係
代名詞

Unit 2
被動
語態

Unit 3
分詞
形容詞

Unit 4
分詞
構句

Unit 5
假設
語法

Unit 6
倒裝
句

Unit 7
間接
問句

Unit 8
特殊
動詞

Unit 9
主動詞
一致

Unit 10
對稱
結構

特別收錄
Unit 11
五回
試題

在「解決問題」(eliminating problems)。「1 個」動名詞 Ving 放句首當主詞，單數主詞，搭配單數動詞。這種解決問題的方式「被稱為」找代罪羔羊，需搭配被動式。綜合以上，**B** 選項為正解。

18. "I can't see the point of living," no matter how casually or jokingly said, may indicate suicidal thoughts and _____ seriously.

    (A) are being taken
    (B) should have taken
    (C) must be taking
    (D) needs to be taken

    解 「我不知道活著有什麼意思」，這句話無論是隨口說說，或半開玩笑地說，都可能暗示著說話者有自殺的想法，所以必須被認真看待。

    no matter ... said 為分詞構句。主詞為 "I can't see the point of living" 這一句話。單數主詞需搭配單數動詞。且這句話必須「被認真看待」，應搭配被動式。綜合以上，**D** 選項為正解。

19. Two years after she _____ the president of the Texas State Senate, Barbara Jordan campaigned successfully for a seat in the US Congress.

    (A) had chosen
    (B) was chosen
    (C) has been choosing
    (D) chose to be

    解 Barbara Jordan 獲選成為德州州議會議長兩年後，她競選成功，再下一城，取得國會議員席次。

    從 campaigned 可知本句為「過去式」。她「被選」為議長，需搭配被動式。綜合以上，**B** 選項為正解。

20. Though sea turtles will reach a very old age if left undisturbed by humans, so far it _____ how many years they can live in their natural habitats.

    (A) couldn't determine
    (B) hasn't been determined
    (C) wasn't determined
    (D) isn't going to be determined

    解 雖然若不受人為干擾，海龜將會很長壽。但是到目前為止，海龜在自然棲地可活幾年這問題尚未有定論。

    so far 需搭配「完成式」。虛主詞 it 指的是海龜可活幾年這件事。這件事需「被研究人員評定」，故搭配被動式。綜合以上，**B** 選項為正解。

# Unit 3　分詞當形容詞

Unit 1，我們已學會用「形容詞子句」來當形容詞。本單元，我們要介紹如何用現在分詞（即 Ving）和過去分詞（即 p.p.）來當形容詞。若形容的名詞，會主動執行動作，則用含「主動進行」意味的現在分詞來當形容詞；若形容的名詞，無法主動執行動作，則用含「被動」意味的過去分詞當形容詞。現在分詞（即 Ving）用於進行式，故帶有「主動進行」的意思，而過去分詞（即 p.p.）用於被動式，故帶有「被動」的意思。請見下方例句：

例 穿著舞獅表演服的舞者，逗樂了中國城的群眾。

### 形容詞子句的寫法

Dancers **who were dressed in lion costumes** entertained the crowds in Chinatown.

解 關係子句從關係代名詞開始，往後推，到第二個動詞 entertained 前結束。關係子句 who…costumes 放在名詞 dancers 後，為「形容詞子句」。

### 分詞當形容詞的寫法

Dancers **dressed in lion costumes** entertained the crowds in Chinatown.

解 從關係子句中的「過去被動式」were dressed 可知，若用分詞當形容詞時，應改成「被動」意味的 p.p. 形容詞 dressed。

例 去年，在英國申請庇護的人，僅半數取得難民身份。

### 形容詞子句的寫法

Last year, just half of those **who applied for asylum in the UK** were granted refugee status.

解 關係子句從關係代名詞開始，往後推，到第二個動詞 were granted 前結束。關係子句 who … UK 放在名詞 those (people) 後，為「形容詞子句」。

分詞當形容詞的寫法

Last year, just over half of those **applying for asylum in the UK** were granted refugee status.

> 解 從關係子句中的「過去式」applied 可知，用分詞當形容詞時，應改成表「主動進行」的 Ving 形容詞 applying。

例 無國界醫生組織裏的志工，都是全心投入救人的無名英雄。

形容詞子句的寫法

1. Volunteers in Doctors Without Borders are unsung heroes **who dedicate themselves to saving lives**.
2. Volunteers in Doctors Without Borders are unsung heroes **who are dedicated to saving lives**.

> 解 關係子句從關係代名詞開始，往後推，找不到第二個動詞，所以到句點為止。關係子句 who...lives 放在名詞 heroes 後，為「形容詞子句」。

分詞當形容詞的寫法

1. Volunteers in Doctors Without Borders are unsung heroes **dedicating themselves to saving lives**.
2. Volunteers in Doctors Without Borders are unsung heroes **dedicated to saving lives**.

> 解 句子 1 和句子 2 的意思完全相同，只是順應 dedicate 的用法，可用主動寫法「dedicate oneself to 名詞」，也可用被動寫法「be dedicated to 名詞」。句子 1，從關係子句中的「現在式」dedicate 可知，用分詞當形容詞時，應改成表「主動進行」的 Ving 形容詞 dedicating。句子 2，從關係子句中的「現在被動式」are dedicated 可知，用分詞當形容詞時，應改成「被動」意味的 p.p. 形容詞 dedicated。

**例** Nike 是一家強烈反對任何形式的歧視的公司。長久以來，他們始終捍衛同志權利。

形容詞子句的寫法

1. Nike, a company **which strongly opposes discrimination of any kind**, has long stood up for the rights of gays.
2. Nike, a company **which is strongly opposed to discrimination of any kind**, has long stood up for the rights of gays.

> **解** 關係子句從關係代名詞開始，往後推，到第二個動詞 has long stood up 前結束。關係子句 which...kind 放在名詞 company 後，為「形容詞子句」。

分詞當形容詞的寫法

1. Nike, a company **strongly opposing discrimination of any kind**, has long stood up for the rights of gays.
2. Nike, a company **strongly opposed to discrimination of any kind**, has long stood up for the rights of gays.

> **解** 句子 1 和句子 2 的意思完全相同，只是順應 oppose 的用法，可用主動寫法「oppose 名詞」，也可用被動寫法「be opposed to 名詞」。句 1，從關係子句的「現在式」opposes 可知，若用分詞當形容詞時，應改成表「主動進行」的 Ving 形容詞 opposing。句子 2，從關係子句中的「現在被動式」is opposed to 可知，若用分詞當形容詞時，應改成「被動」意味的 p.p. 形容詞 opposed。

## 小試身手：請選出正確解答

**01.** In the lecture, the professor points to Antarctica, a continent _____ peacefully among the international community, as a sign that we don't necessarily have to slice up land as if it were a giant pizza.

    (A) shared              (B) is shared

    (C) which has shared     (D) sharing

> **解** 課堂中，教授指著南極洲—1 個由國際社群和平共享的大陸。他用南極洲當作例子，說明我們不一定非得將土地當成巨大披薩般切割瓜分。
>
> 請見下方句構分析：
>
> … the professor points to Antarctica, a continent _____ … community, …
>             主詞      動詞             名詞     形容詞
>
> 從上方 1 個主詞和 1 個動詞可知句子結構已完整，故名詞 continent 後方應搭配 Ving 或 p.p. 形容詞。若用關係代名詞帶出來的關係子句當形容詞，則子句中需搭配完整的動詞，即非 Ving / p.p. / to V 原。continent「被國際社群分享」，需搭配表「被動」的 p.p. 形容詞 shared，**A** 選項為正解。若用關係子句當形容詞，則應寫成 a continent which (或 that) is shared (或 has been shared) …。

**02.** I figured a lunch with Bob would lead to another date, perhaps one _____ on a weekend and involved dinner. However, no such invitation arrived.

    (A) taking place           (B) that took place

    (C) was taken place       (D) taken place

> **解** 我猜和 Bob 的午餐可望帶來另一次約會，或許是發生在周末、含晚餐的約會。然而，事與願違。我沒收到這樣的邀請。
>
> 請見下方句構分析：
>
> I figured (that) a lunch with Bob would lead to …, one _____ and involved …
>                 主詞           動詞        名詞 形容詞子句
>
> 從上方 1 個主詞和 1 個動詞可知句子結構已完整。代名詞 one 代替名詞 one date。名詞 date 後方應搭配 Ving 或 p.p. 形容詞。若用關係代名詞帶出來的關係子句當形容詞，則子句中需搭配完整的動詞，即非 Ving / p.p. / to V 原。從 involved 後方有受詞 dinner 可知，involved 為動詞，所以 one 後方搭配的是形容詞子句，而非 Ving 或 p.p. 形容詞。連接詞

and 連接兩個動詞，時態需對稱，involved 為過去式動詞，故劃線處應為「關係代名詞 + 過去式動詞」。且片語「發生」take place 沒有被動式。綜合以上，**B** 選項為正解。若用分詞當形容詞，則應寫成 one taking place on the weekend and involving dinner。

**03.** **Belgian architect Vincent Callebaut has revealed ambitious plans for a series of underwater eco-villages _____ up to 20,000 people each in the future.**

(A) will be housed      (B) that are housed

(C) where it could house      (D) housing

解 比利時建築師 Vincent Callebaut 已宣布他的宏大計畫。他即將興建一系列可容納多達 2 萬人的水中生態聚落。

請見下方句構分析：

Callebaut has revealed … plans for … eco-villages _____ up to …
主詞 　　　 動詞 　　　 介係詞 　　 名詞 　　 形容詞

從上方 1 個主詞和 1 個動詞可知句子結構已完整，故名詞 eco-villages 後方應搭配 Ving 或 p.p. 形容詞。若用關係代名詞帶出來的關係子句當形容詞，則子句中需搭配完整的動詞，即非 Ving / p.p. / to V 原。villages 可「容納」2 萬人，應搭配表「主動進行」的 Ving 形容詞 housing，**D** 選項為正解。若用關係子句當形容詞，則應寫成：that / which will house …。that / which 為「物 / 主詞」性質的關代，代替前方的名詞 villages。從 in the future 可知，搭配未來式。

**04.** **Among a large number of pop culture icons _____ with so-called Bitchy Resting Face, Kristen Stewart and Victoria Beckham are named as prime examples.**

(A) said to be afflicted      (B) saying they afflict

(C) to say that they are afflicted      (D) that is said to be afflicting

解 在眾多據說為「臭臉」所苦的流行文化偶像中，Kristen Stewart（暮光之城的女主角）和 Victoria Beckham（球星貝克漢的老婆）被點名為頭號例子。

請見下方句構分析：

Among … pop culture icons _____ …, Kristen … are named as …
介係詞 　　 名詞 　　 形容詞 　　 主詞 　　 動詞

從上方 1 個主詞和 1 個動詞可知句子結構已完整，故名詞 pop culture

icons 後方應搭配 Ving 或 p.p. 形容詞。若用關係代名詞帶出來的關係子句當形容詞，則子句中需搭配完整的動詞，即非 Ving / p.p. / to V 原。icons「被人說是被臭臉折磨」，需搭配表「被動」的 p.p. 形容詞 said，和被動式「被折磨」be afflicted。綜合以上，**A** 選項為正解。若用關係子句當形容詞，則應寫成：that / who are said to be afflicted。當中 that / who 為「人 / 主詞」性質的關代，代替前方的名詞 a large number of pop culture icons。

註 「很多」a large number of Ns，搭配複數動詞。「… 的數字」the number of Ns，重點在 the number，故搭配單數動詞。

**05.** In the National Palace Museum, Chinese history is told through ceramics, bronze statues, jade carvings, calligraphy and other historical pieces, _____ to Chinese imperial families.

(A) many of which were belonged
(B) many belonged
(C) and many of what belonged
(D) many of them belonging

解 在故宮，中國歷史透過陶瓷製品、銅製雕像、玉石雕刻、書法和其他古物被訴說著。這些物品中，許多為皇室家族所有。

請見下方句構分析：

… Chinese history is told through ceramics, … pieces, _____ to …
　　　　主詞　　　　　　動詞　　介係詞

從上方 1 個主詞和 1 個動詞可知句子結構已完整，故代名詞 many (historical pieces) 後方應搭配 Ving 或 p.p. 形容詞。若用關係代名詞帶出來的關係子句當形容詞，則子句中需搭配完整的動詞，即非 Ving / p.p. / to V 原。動詞 belong to … 沒有被動式，可改成表「主動進行」的 Ving 形容詞 belonging，**D** 選項為正解。若用關係子句當形容詞，則可寫成：many of which belonged to …。which 為「物 / 受詞」性質的關係代名詞，代替前方的名詞 historical pieces。B 選項，is told / belonged 兩個動詞，代表兩個句子，需用 1 個連接詞或關代連接。逗號無法連接兩個句子。C 選項，連接詞或關係代名詞，二擇一，應改成：and many of them belonged 或 many of which belonged。

**06.** In most people, symptoms of Zika virus infection are mild, including fever, headache and possible pink eye. In fact, 80% of those _____ never know that they have the disease.

(A) contracting who
(B) are contracted
(C) contracted
(D) to contract

解 在大多數人身上，茲卡病毒感染的症狀，如：發燒、頭痛或可能有粉紅眼等，都很輕微。實際上，百分之 80 被感染的人，從不知道他們已罹病。

請見下方句構分析：

..., 80% of those _____ never know that ...

　　　　　主詞／名詞　　形容詞　　　　動詞

從上方 1 個主詞和 1 個動詞可知句子結構已完整，故主（名）詞 80% of those (people) 後方應搭配 Ving 或 p.p. 形容詞。若用關係代名詞帶出來的關係子句當形容詞，則子句中需搭配完整的動詞，即非 Ving / p.p. / to V 原。those (people)「被病毒感染」，需搭配表「被動」的 p.p. 形容詞 contracted，**C** 選項為正解。若用關係子句當形容詞，則可寫成：those who are contracted。who 為「人／主詞」性質的關代，代替前方的名詞 those (people)。從 know/ have 可知本句為現在式。

07. **Such countries as Germany and Norway _____ strong educational and social security systems now report the lowest belief rates in the world.**

(A) that features　　　　　　　　(B) have featured that

(C) where are featured　　　　　(D) featuring

解 像德國或挪威這些標榜穩固的教育和社會安全系統的國家，是目前全世界宗教信仰比例最低的國家。

請見下方句構分析：

Such ...and Norway _____ ... systems now report ...

　　　　　主詞／名詞　　　　形容詞　　　　　　動詞

從上方 1 個主詞和 1 個動詞可知句子結構已完整，故主（名）詞 such countries as Germany and Norway 後方應搭配 Ving 或 p.p. 形容詞。若用關係代名詞帶出來的關係子句當形容詞，則子句中需搭配完整的動詞，即非 Ving / p.p. / to V 原。原句為：countries feature strong educational ...，現在式動詞 feature 可改成表「主動進行」的 Ving 形容詞 featuring，**D** 選項為正解。若用關係子句當形容詞，則可寫成：countries which feature ... systems。which 為「物／主詞」性質的關代，代替前方的複數名詞 countries。A 選項，需將 features 改成 feature。

**08.** Air pollution _____ in homes, usually a by-product of cooking fires, kills around two million people annually.

(A) to be produced

(B) produced

(C) is producing

(D) that produces

> **解** 家裡製造出的空氣汙染（通常是柴火煮飯的副產品），每年害死近 2 百萬人。
>
> 請見下方句構分析：
>
> Air pollution _____ in homes, usually … fires, kills around …
> 主詞／名詞　　形容詞　　　　　　　　　同位格　　　動詞
>
> 從上方 1 個主詞和 1 個動詞可知句子結構已完整，故主（名）詞 air pollution 後方應搭配 Ving 或 p.p. 形容詞。若用關係代名詞帶出來的關係子句當形容詞，則子句中需搭配完整的動詞，即非 Ving／p.p.／to V 原。空污是「被製造出來的」，需搭配表「被動」的 p.p. 形容詞 produced，**B** 選項為正解。若用關係子句當形容詞，則可寫成：which／that is produced …。當中 which 為「物／主詞」性質的關係代名詞，代替前方的單數名詞 air pollution。

**09.** The stereotype of a butler as a lifelong position held by an older man is no longer the case. The average age of a newly _____ butler is 41, and 40% are women.

(A) employed

(B) employment where the

(C) employing

(D) employee whose

> **解** 將管家視為由年長男性所操持的終身職，這刻板印象早已不復存在。被雇用的新進管家，平均年齡為 41 歲，且當中百分之 40 為女性。
>
> 請見下方句構分析：
>
> The average age of a newly _____ butler is 41 …
> 主詞／名詞　　　　　　　　　　　　　　　動詞
>
> 從上方 1 個主詞和 1 個動詞可知句子結構已完整，故名詞 bulter 前方應搭配 Ving 或 p.p. 形容詞。管家「被雇用」，需搭配表「被動」的 p.p. 形容詞 employed，**A** 選項為正解。

**10.** **Unable to defend itself against competitors _____ with new products as well as technologies, the once prosperous company watches its profits erode, its best people leave, and its stock valuations tumble.**

(A) having armed　　(B) who are armed　(C) to have arms　　(D) arming

> 解 由於無法捍衛自己，抵禦挾新產品和新科技的眾多競爭對手，這家曾經生意興隆的公司，只好看著自家獲利逐漸流失，好員工出走，股價也暴跌。
>
> 請見下方句構分析：
>
> … against competitors _____ with …, the … company watches its profits …
>
> 　　　　　　 介係詞　　名詞　　　　　　　　　主詞　　　　　　動詞
>
> 從上方 1 個主詞和 1 個動詞可知句子結構已完整。名詞 competitors 後方應搭配 Ving 或 p.p. 形容詞。若用關係代名詞帶出來的關係子句當形容詞，則子句中需搭配完整的動詞，即非 Ving / p.p. / to V 原。從片語「A 具有 B 配備」：A be armed with B 可知，需用表「被動」的 p.p. 形容詞 armed。若用關係子句當形容詞，則可寫成：who are armed …，**B** 選項為正解。who 為「人 / 主詞」性質的關代，代替前方的複數名詞 competitors。A 和 D 選項都不是被動式，答題時可優先刪除。C 選項，arms (n) 武器，與文意不合。

**11.** **The company's garments, designed to evoke a romantic vision of English ladies _____ roses at their country manors, struck a chord with many women in the 1970s.**

(A) tending　　　　　　(B) to tend　　　　　(C) whose tending　(D) tended

> 解 這家公司的服飾，以喚起英國淑女在鄉間莊園照看玫瑰花的浪漫意象為設計主軸，因而在 1970 年代引發許多女性的共鳴。
>
> 請見下方句構分析：
>
> The company's garments, designed … ladies _____ roses …, struck …
>
> 　　　　　　　　　主詞　　　　　　　　　　　 名詞　　形容詞　　　　動詞
>
> designed … manors 為分詞構句。從上方 1 個主詞和 1 個動詞可知句子結構已完整。名詞 English ladies 後方應搭配 Ving 或 p.p. 形容詞。若用關係代名詞帶出來的關係子句當形容詞，則子句中需搭配完整的動詞，即非 Ving / p.p. / to V 原。女士們「照顧」玫瑰花，需搭配表「主動進行」的 Ving 形容詞 tending，**A** 選項為正解。若用關係子句當形容詞，則可寫成：who / that tended。who / that 為「人 / 主詞」性質的關代，代替前方的複數名詞 English ladies。時間點為 1970s，需搭配過去式。

12. In this world packed with advanced technologies, it is easy to forget that the most important tool _____ for knowledge acquisition is still the book.

(A) that is developing

(B) which had developed

(C) ever developed

(D) having

解 在這個充斥著先進科技的世界裡，人們很容易忘記，被研發出來且用於汲取知識的工具中，最重要的還是書。

請見下方句構分析：

… that the most important tool _____ … acquisition is still …

主詞 / 名詞　　　　　形容詞　　　　　　　動詞

關係代名詞 that 後方帶出了一個完整句子。從上方 1 個主詞和 1 個動詞可知句子結構已完整。主（名）詞 the most important tool 後方應搭配 Ving 或 p.p. 形容詞。若用關係代名詞帶出來的關係子句當形容詞，則子句中需搭配完整的動詞，即非 Ving / p.p. / to V 原。工具「被發展出來」，需搭配表「被動」的 p.p. 形容詞 developed，C 選項為正解。若用關係子句當形容詞，則應寫成：that was developed。先行詞中有最高級 the most important，只能用關代 that。that 為「物 / 主詞」性質的關代，代替前方的單數名詞 tool。且 tool 早被研發出來，需用單數過去被動式。

13. The news of 40-year-old frozen meat _____ to consumers leaves even the most seasoned experts in shock.

(A) that sold

(B) has been selling

(C) which selling

(D) sold

解 冷凍 40 年的肉，還被賣給了消費者，這新聞讓最老練的專家都大感震驚。

請見下方句構分析：

The news of…meat _____ to consumers leaves …

主詞　　　　　名詞　形容詞　　　　　　　動詞

從上方 1 個主詞和 1 個動詞可知句子結構已完整。名詞 meat 後方應搭配 Ving 或 p.p. 形容詞。若用關係代名詞帶出來的關係子句當形容詞，則子句中需搭配完整的動詞，即非 Ving / p.p. / to V 原。冷凍肉「被賣給消費者」，需搭配表「被動」的 p.p. 形容詞 sold，D 選項為正解。若用關係子句當形容詞，則應寫成：which / that is sold（或 has been sold）。which / that 為「物 / 主詞」性質的關代，代替前方的單數名詞 meat。

14. Thai police release a chilling CCTV of the suspect _____ into the shrine with a rucksack and then leave without it moments before the devastating blast.

(A) was seen walk
(B) seeing that walking
(C) seen to walk
(D) that saw to walk

解 泰國警方公布冷血錄影帶。影帶中，嫌犯被看見帶著背包走入廟宇，並在毀滅性爆炸前幾分鐘，沒背背包就離開。

請見下方句構分析：

Thai police release a chilling CCTV of the suspect _____ into ...
　　　主詞　　　　動詞　　　　　　　　　　　　　名詞　　　形容詞

從上方 1 個主詞和 1 個動詞可知句子結構已完整。名詞 suspect 後方應搭配 Ving 或 p.p. 形容詞。若用關係代名詞帶出來的關係子句當形容詞，則子句中需搭配完整的動詞，即非 Ving / p.p. / to V 原。嫌犯在影片中「被看見」，需搭配表「被動」的 p.p. 形容詞 seen。被動式後方動詞應為「to 動詞原形」。seen to walk ... and then (to) leave。連接詞 and，連接被看見的兩個動作。綜合以上，**C** 選項為正解。若用關係子句當形容詞，則應寫成：who / that was seen to walk。who / that 為「人 / 主詞」性質的關代，代替前方的單數名詞 suspect。

15. Cathy, who has a lung capacity of just 30% and requires significant medical attention, has donated "tens of thousands" of her own cells to labs _____ research on her disease and developing drugs.

(A) conducting
(B) which she conducts
(C) where conducting
(D) conducted

解 Cathy（她的肺容量只剩百分之 30，且需要許多醫療照護）已捐出自己數萬個細胞給研究她疾病和研發新藥的實驗室。

請見下方句構分析：

Cathy, who ... attention, has donated ... cells to labs _____ research ...
　主詞　　　　　　　　　　　　動詞　　　　　　　　　　名詞　形容詞

從上方 1 個主詞和 1 個動詞可知句子結構已完整。名詞 labs 後方應搭配 Ving 或 p.p. 形容詞。若用關係代名詞帶出來的關係子句當形容詞，則子句中需搭配完整的動詞，即非 Ving / p.p. / to V 原。labs「會做實驗」，需搭配表「主動進行」的 Ving 形容詞 conducting 和 developing。再用連接詞 and 連接兩個形容詞。綜合以上，**A** 選項為正解。若用關係子句當形容詞，則應寫成：that / which conduct ... and develop ...。that / which 為「物 / 主詞」性質的關代，代替前方的複數名詞 labs。

16. One of the important factors _____ to the evolution of the distinctive styles of traditional Chinese painting has been the materials used and their influence on artistic forms and techniques.

(A) to contribute
(B) contributing
(C) when they contribute
(D) which are contributed

解 造成中國傳統繪畫獨特風格演化的重要因素之一，就是使用的素材及這些素材對藝術形態和技巧的影響。

請見下方句構分析：

One of the … factors _____ to the … painting has been …
主詞　　　　　名詞　　形容詞　　　　　　　　　　動詞
從上方 1 個主詞和 1 個動詞可知句子結構已完整。名詞 factors 後方應搭配 Ving 或 p.p. 形容詞。若用關係代名詞帶出來的關係子句當形容詞，則子句中需搭配完整的動詞，即非 Ving / p.p. / to V 原。這一個因素「造成」中國繪畫的演化，需搭配表「主動進行」的 Ving 形容詞 contributing，B 選項為正解。若用關係子句當形容詞，則應寫成：which / that contributes (或 contribute)。which / that 為「物 / 主詞」性質的關代，代替前方的名詞 one (factor) 或 factors。片語「導致引發」contribute to N。

17. Diners couldn't help complaining about the restaurant's stomach-turning hygiene standards as they found one male chef's excessive sweat _____ into a sauce and another female chef's greasy long hair dangling over the lamb chop.

(A) that dripping
(B) which had dripped
(C) dripping
(D) dripped

解 當用餐者發現男廚師的淋漓汗水一直滴入醬汁裡，且另一個女廚師油膩膩的長髮還在羊排上晃來晃去時，他們忍不住抱怨餐廳令人反胃的衛生標準。

請見下方句構分析：

…as they found one male chef's … sweat _____ into a sauce …
主詞　動詞　　　　　　　　　　　名詞　　形容詞
連接詞 as 後方有 1 個主詞和 1 個動詞，由此可知句子結構已完整。這題的考點為「發現…」find + N + adj。名詞 sweat / long hair 後方都應搭配 Ving 或 p.p. 形容詞。汗「自動滴下」，需搭配表「主動進行」的 Ving 形容詞 dripping，C 選項為正解。長髮「自動掃過」，需搭配表「主動進

Unit 1
關係
代名詞

Unit 2
被動
語態

Unit 3
分詞
形容詞

Unit 4
分詞
構句

Unit 5
假設
語法

Unit 6
倒裝
句

Unit 7
間接
問句

Unit 8
特殊
動詞

Unit 9
主動詞
一致

Unit 10
對稱
結構

特別收錄
Unit 11
五回
試題

行」的 Ving 形容詞 dangling。

18. **I just got on a scary rollercoaster ride, with my head dizzy, my vision blurry and my heart _____ to my throat.**

   (A) jumping
   (B) that was jumped
   (C) jumped
   (D) to jump

   解 我剛剛才坐了一趟恐怖的雲霄飛車。搭的時候，我頭昏目眩、視力模糊、心臟還跳到喉嚨。

   請見下方句構分析：

   I just got on ... ride, with ... my heart _____ to my throat.
   主詞　動詞　　　　　　介係詞　　名詞　　形容詞
   從上方 1 個主詞和 1 個動詞可知句子結構已完整。這題的考點為句型「伴隨...而來的狀況」with + N + adj。名詞 my heart 會「自行跳動」，需搭配表「主動進行」的 Ving 形容詞 jumping，**A** 選項為正解。

19. **This campaign aims to raise money for those faced with _____ diseases. To learn how you can help or how you can receive help, please visit our website.**

   (A) life-threatening
   (B) life-threatened
   (C) threat-living
   (D) threat-lived

   解 這活動是為罹患威脅生命的疾病的病患募款。想知道如何貢獻一己之力，或怎樣才能獲得協助，請上我們的網站。

   請見下方句構分析：

   This campaign aims to raise ... for those faced with _____ diseases.
   　　　主詞　　　　　動詞　　　　　　　　介係詞 形容詞　　名詞
   從上方 1 個主詞和 1 個動詞可知句子結構已完整。名詞 diseases 前方應搭配 Ving 或 p.p. 形容詞。diseases「會威脅生命」，需搭配表「主動進行」的 Ving 形容詞 threatening。又「複合形容詞」= N-adj。綜合以上，**A** 選項為正解。

20. **The new act _____ effect before the end of March will also be applied to neighboring provinces that have suffered from severe air pollution.**

   (A) which is taken　(B) taking
   (C) takes　(D) taken

解 三月底生效的新法令，也將適用於為嚴重空污所苦的鄰近省份。

請見下方句構分析：

The new act _____ effect before the end of March will also be applied…
　　　　　主詞 / 名詞　　　　　　　　　　　　　　　　　　　　　動詞

從上方 1 個主詞和 1 個動詞可知句子結構已完整。名詞 the new standards 後方應搭配 Ving 或 p.p. 形容詞。若用關係代名詞帶出來的關係子句當形容詞，則子句中需搭配完整的動詞，即非 Ving / p.p. / to V 原。法案 (act)「本身就具備效力」，需搭配表「主動進行」的 Ving 形容詞 taking effect，**B** 選項為正解。若用關係子句當形容詞，則應寫成：which / that takes。which / that 為「物 / 主詞」性質的關代，代替前方的單數名詞 act。片語「生效」take effect，沒有被動式。

# Unit 4

分詞構句
## 4−1 基本款的分詞構句

■ 分詞構句的使用時機：

當兩個句子「主詞相同」時，為精簡句子，並變化句型，就可使用「分詞構句」。

■ 分詞構句形成步驟如下：

步驟1 確定兩句主詞相同。

步驟2 去掉連接詞。

步驟3 去掉「表原因」或「先發生」或「表條件」那句的主詞。若兩句看不出有以上三個明顯關係時，則將句意較不那麼重要的那句改成分詞構句。

步驟4 若去掉的主詞可主動執行該句的動作，則改成表「主動進行」的 Ving 分詞構句。若去掉的主詞無法執行該句的動作，則改成表「被動」的 p.p. 分詞構句。

步驟5 造否定的分詞構句時，將 not 或 never 放在 Ving 或 p.p. 分詞前即可。

例 因為 Mary 認為，就舒適度而言，摩托車遠比不上汽車，所以她偏好開車。

用兩個有「因果」關係的句子呈現：

句1 Mary prefers to drive.

句2 She thinks that a motorcycle is not comparable to a car in terms of comfort.

用連接詞連接兩句：

**Because she thinks** that a motorcycle is not comparable to a car in terms of comfort, Mary prefers to drive.

用「分詞構句」表達這個句子：

**Thinking** that a motorcycle is not comparable to a car in terms of comfort, Mary prefers to drive.

解 兩句主詞相同，都是 Mary，故可用「分詞構句」來精簡句子。去掉「表原因」那句的連接詞和主詞，thinks 為現式，需改成表「主動

進行」的 Ving 分詞構句 thinking ... comfort。分詞構句放句首時，記得打上逗號。若放句中，打不打逗號都可以。

例 朝敏捷的鹿射擊後，獵人隨即撿拾他的戰利品。

用兩個有「先後」關係的句子呈現：

句1 The hunter shot arrows at the swift deer.
句2 The hunter collected his reward afterward.

用連接詞連接兩句：

**After the hunter shot** arrows at the swift deer, the hunter collected his reward.

用「分詞構句」表達這個句子：

**Shooting** arrows at the swift deer, the hunter collected his reward afterward.

解 兩句主詞相同，都是 the hunter，故可用「分詞構句」來精簡句子。去掉「先發生」那句的連接詞和主詞，shot 為過去式，需改成表「主動進行」的 Ving 分詞構句 shooting ... deer。分詞構句放句首時，記得打逗號。若放句中，打不打逗號都可以。

註 shoot (v) 開槍射擊；shoot – shot – shot – shooting

例 若烹調得宜，豬排將會裏頭非常多汁，且外酥脆。

用兩個句子呈現，其中一句是另一句成立的條件：

句1 The pork chop will be cooked properly.
句2 The pork chop will be incredibly juicy on the inside and crispy on the outside.

用連接詞連接兩句：

**If the pork chop is cooked** properly, the pork chop will be incredibly juicy on the inside and crispy on the outside.

解 連接詞 if 遇到「未來式」will be，緊接在 if 後方的動詞需改用「現在式」is cooked。

用「分詞構句」表達這個句子：

**Cooked** properly, the pork chop will be incredibly juicy on the inside and crispy on the outside.

> 解 兩句主詞相同，都是 the pork chop，故可用「分詞構句」來精簡句子。去掉「表條件」那句的連接詞和主詞。is cooked 為現在被動式，需改成表「被動」的 p.p. 分詞構句 cooked properly。分詞構句放句首時，記得打逗號。若放句中，打不打逗號都可以。

■ 否定的分詞構句

> 例 今天早上我覺得很不舒服，所以我打電話請病假。

用兩個有「因果」關係的句子呈現：

句1 I didn't feel well this morning.
句2 I called in sick.

用連接詞連接兩句：

**Because I didn't feel** well this morning, I called in sick.

用「分詞構句」表達這個句子：

**Not feeling** well this morning, I called in sick.

> 解 兩句主詞相同，都是 I，故可用「分詞構句」精簡句子。去掉表「原因」那句的連接詞和主詞。 didn't feel 為否定的過去式，需改成「否定的」、表「主動進行」的 not Ving 分詞構句 not feeling ... morning 為止。分詞構句放句首時，記得打逗號。若放句中，打不打逗號都可以。

## 小試身手：請選出正確解答

**01.** _____ **with Bruce Lee, he not only dresses himself in Chinese garb like Lee's but turns himself into an expert in martial arts.**

(A) Obsessed (B) Obsessing

(C) To be obsessed (D) Obsession

> 解 因為迷戀李小龍，他不只穿著李小龍般的唐裝，更讓自己成了武術專家。
>
> 人的情緒都是被外在事物引發，需搭配被動式。片語「迷戀」be obsessed with N。原句為：he is obsessed with Bruce Lee / he not only dresses ...。兩句主詞相同，都是 he，可用分詞構句。is obsessed 為現在被動式，可改成表被動的 p.p. 分詞構句 obsessed with Bruce Lee，**A** 選項為正解。

**02.** **The World Health Organization has called the explosive spread of the Zika virus in the Americas a "public health emergency of international concern,"** _____ **as many as 4 million people could be infected with it in the next year.**

(A) estimating (B) is estimated

(C) which estimates (D) estimated

> 解 預估明年將有多達 400 萬人感染茲卡病毒後，世界衛生組織已將茲卡病毒在美洲的爆炸性擴散稱為足以引發國際關切的公共健康緊急事件。
>
> 原句為：the WHO has called ... / the WHO estimates as many as ...。兩句主詞相同，都是 the WHO，可用分詞構句。estimates 為現在式，可改成表主動進行的 Ving 分詞構句 estimating...year，**A** 選項為正解。

**03.** _____ **itself the "first luxury cruise ship on land," the resort offers everything you'd experience on a luxury cruise ship, except seasickness.**

(A) Call (B) To call (C) Being called (D) Calling

> 解 這個渡假勝地自稱是陸地上最奢華的郵輪。它提供了你在豪華郵輪上可享受的一切，除了暈船以外。
>
> 原句為：the resort calls itself ... / the resort offers everthing ...。兩句

主詞相同，都是 the resort，可用分詞構句。calls 為現在式，可改成表主動進行的 Ving 分詞構句 calling ... on land，**D** 選項為正解。

**04.** His songs, such as "Changes," and "Modern Love," are anthemic hits, _____ constantly on the radio and inspiring generations of musicians.

(A) which are playing　　　　(B) playing

(C) played　　　　　　　　　(D) to play

解 他的歌，如：Changes 和 Modern Love，都是像國歌般的暢銷歌曲。他的歌常被廣播播放，且啟發了世世代代的音樂家。

原句為：his songs ... are ... hits / his songs are played constantly ...。兩句主詞相同，都是 his songs，可用分詞構句。are played 為現在被動式，可改成表被動的 p.p. 分詞構句 played ... musicians，**C** 選項為正解。

註 句中還有另一個分詞構句。原句為：his songs ... are ... / his songs inspires generations of ...。inspires 為現在式，可改成表主動進行的 Ving 分詞構句 inspiring ... musicians。

**05.** The world's highest glass-bottomed bridge, stretching 375 m and _____ above the the Zhangjiajie Grand Canyon, is capable of holding up to 800 people at once.

(A) perched　　　(B) locating　　　(C) stood　　　(D) Setting

解 這座世界最高的玻璃橋，長 375 公尺，且位在張家界大峽谷的上方。這座橋一次可容納多達 800 人通行。

原句為：the ... bridge is perched（或 is located / stands / is set）... / the ... bridge is capable of ...。兩句主詞相同，都是 the bridge，可用分詞構句。動詞「位於...」分兩組。第一組：sit / stand / lie 得用主動寫法，可改成表主動進行的 Ving 分詞構句，故 C 選項應改成 standing。第二組：situate / locate / set / perch（棲息）得用被動寫法，可改成表被動的 p.p. 分詞構句，故 B 選項應改成 located，D 選項應改成 set（set - set - set）。綜合以上，**A** 選項為正解。

註 句中還有另一個分詞構句。原句為：the bridge stretches... / the bridge is capable of ...。stretch（延伸）多長是這座橋本身的特質，且 stretches 為現在式，得用表主動進行的 Ving 分詞構句 stretching 375 m。

**06.** Blood has a long road to travel: The blood vessels in the human body, _____ end to end, would measure about 100,000 km.

(A) to lay　　　　(B) having lain　　(C) laid　　　　(D) lying

解　血液運輸，長路漫漫。若將人體血管擺放出來，頭尾相接，人體血管測量起來約 10 萬公里。

原句為：the blood vessels ... are laid end to end / the blood vessels ... would measure ...。兩句主詞相同，都是 the blood vessels，可用分詞構句。are laid 為現在被動式，所以得用表被動的 p.p. 分詞構句 laid end to end，**C** 選項為正解。

註　注意分辨以下三個動詞的三態變化：(1) lay (v) 放；lay –laid – laid – laying (2) lie (v) 躺；lie – lay – laid – lying (3) lie (v) 說謊；lie – lied – lied – lying。

**07.** The extensive fabric collection, _____ back to the 10th century B.C., sheds a new light on the fashion in the days of King David's kingdom.

(A) to date　　　　(B) being dated　　(C) dating　　　　(D) dated

解　這為數眾多的織品收藏，可回溯至公元前 10 世紀。這些收藏品讓我們對大衛王時期王國中的流行有了嶄新的了解。

原句為：the ... collection dates back ... / the ... collection sheds a new light ...。兩句主詞相同，都是 the extensive fabric collection，可用分詞構句。dates 為現在式，可改成表主動進行的 Ving 分詞構句 dating ... B.C.，**C** 選項為正解。片語「回溯至 ...」有三種寫法： go back to 時間 / date back to 時間 / be traced back to 時間。

**08.** _____ to sales manager recently, Tom will oversee the newspaper's advertising staff.

(A) Promoted　　　　　　　(B) To be promoted
(C) That promoting　　　　　(D) Promoting

解　Tom 最近被擢升為行銷經理。Tom 將監管報社的廣告部門。

原句為：Tom has been promoted to sales ... / Tom will oversee ...。兩句主詞相同，都是 Tom，可用分詞構句。又 has been promoted 為現在完成被動式，可改成表被動的 p.p. 分詞構句 promoted ... recently，**A** 選項為正解。

**09.** Not everything goes as _____ when it comes to turning clever paper designs into real-life nuclear power plants.

(A) expecting
(B) to expecting
(C) it has expected
(D) expected

> 解 當討論到將巧妙的書面設計轉換成真實的核電廠時，並非一切都會如預期般進行。
>
> 原句為：not everything goes as everything is expected。連接詞 as 意指「就像」。兩句主詞相同，都是 everything，可用分詞構句。is expected 為現在被動式，可改成表被動的 p.p. 分詞構句 as expected。寫分詞構句時，也可留下連接詞 as。綜合以上，**D** 選項為正解。

**10.** Prices in Brisbane are affordable _____ to those in many large cities. Order a flat white and a pastry from a cafe there, and you'll typically pay no more than $4.40.

(A) compared
(B) to compare
(C) which they are compared
(D) comparing

> 解 相較於其他大都市，布里斯本的物價很合理。在那裏的咖啡店，點一杯加牛奶的濃縮咖啡和一份糕點，一般而言，你要付擔的費用不會超過美金 4.4 元。
>
> 原句為：prices in Brisbane are affordable … / prices in Brisbane are compared to those (prices) …。兩句主詞相同，都是 prices，可用分詞構句。are compared 為現在被動式，可改成表被動的 p.p. 分詞構句 compared … cities，**A** 選項為正解。

**11.** The festival, _____ on Valentine's Day evening, features luminaries and legends working in the music industry for 50 years.

(A) taking place
(B) occurred
(C) which held
(D) hosting

> 解 慶典將於情人節傍晚舉行。慶典上有縱衡音樂界 50 年的名人大咖和傳奇人物參與演出。
>
> 原句為：the festival takes place（或 occurs / happens / is held / is hosted）… / the festival features …。兩句主詞相同，都是 the festival，可用分詞構句。takes place 和 occurs 為現在式，可改成表主動進行的 Ving 分詞構句 taking place ... evening，**A** 選項為正解。B 選項應該成 occurring。C 選項有關係代名詞，需搭配完整動詞，應改成 which is held。

Unit 1 關係代名詞
Unit 2 被動語態
Unit 3 分詞形容詞
Unit 4 分詞構句
Unit 5 假設語法
Unit 6 倒裝句
Unit 7 間接問句
Unit 8 特殊動詞
Unit 9 主動詞一致
Unit 10 對稱結構
特別收錄
Unit 11 五回試題

「物／主詞性質」的關係代名詞 which 代替前方的 the festival，單數主詞 the festival，搭配單數被動式 is held。D 選項，is hosted 為現在被動式，可改成表被動的 p.p. 分詞構句 hosted … evening。

12. Fin whales are the second-largest mammals on the planet, _____ only by the blue whale.

    (A) preceded            (B) which might be preceding

    (C) having preceded      (D) preceding

解 長鬚鯨是地球上第二大哺乳類動物。長鬚鯨只被藍鯨領先。

原句為：fin whales are the second-largest … ／ fin whales are preceded only by …。兩句主詞相同，都是 fin whales，可用分詞構句。are preceded 為現在被動式，可改成表被動的 p.p. 分詞構句 preceded … whale，**A** 選項為正解。

13. _____ with a disruption in business conditions, those companies freeze; they're caught like the deer in the headlights

    (A) Confronting          (B) A confront

    (C) Confronted          (D) To confront

解 這些公司面臨商場上的亂流時，僵住了，不知所措。它們就像被車頭燈照到的鹿一般驚恐。

原句為：those companies are confronted with … ／ those companies freeze …。兩句主詞相同，都是 those companies，可用分詞構句。are confronted 為現在被動式，可改成表被動的 p.p. 分詞構句 confronted… conditions，**C** 選項為正解。片語「面對」有以下三種寫法：(1) face N ／ confront N ／ encounter N。(2) be faced with N ／ be confronted with N (3) have an encounter with N。改成分詞構句分別為：(1) facing N ／ confronting N ／ encountering N… (2) faced with N ／ confronted with N… (3) having an encounter with N…。

14. _____ to be seated separately on an airplane, Amy and Tony asked a stranger if they could switch seats with him.

    (A) Wanted not          (B) Never want

    (C) Having not wanted    (D) Not wanting

解 因為 Amy 和 Tony 不想在機上分開坐，所以他們問那個陌生人，是否可和他換座位。

原句為：Amy and Tony didn't want to be seated … / Amy and Tony asked …。兩句主詞相同，都是 Amy and Tony，可用分詞構句。didn't want…為否定的過去式，可改成否定的、表主動進行的 not Ving 分詞構句 not wanting … airplane，**D** 選項為正解。

15. **Tom, _____ by a taxi while _____, has been hospitalized in critical condition. What's worse, his wife has to pay for his pedestrian fine of $130.**

(A) having struck; being jaywalked      (B) who struck; he jaywalked

(C) struck; jaywalking      (D) striking; he has jaywalked

解 Tom 擅自穿越馬路時，被計程車撞了。Tom 狀況危急，已住院治療。更糟的是，他老婆還必須支付他行人違規的罰款一美金 130 元。

原句為：Tom was struck by a taxi while he jaywalked… / Tom has been hospitalized…。兩句主詞相同，都是 Tom，可用分詞構句。was struck 為過去被動式，可改成表被動的 p.p. 分詞構句 struck by a taxi。jaywalked 為過去式，可改成表主動進行的 Ving 分詞構句 jaywalking。綜合以上，**C** 選項為正解。分詞構句從 struck…jaywalking 為止。

註 注意以下兩個動詞的三態變化：(1) strike (v) 撞擊；strike – struck – struck / stricken (2) stick (v) 突出 / 黏貼；stick – stuck – stuck。

16. **Though the authority preaches about the significance of seatbelt use, fifty percent of people fail to buckle up, _____ that with airbags, seat belts are redundant.**

(A) and to think      (B) which is thought

(C) thinking      (D) thought

解 雖然當局奮力宣傳使用安全帶的重要性，百分之 50 的人沒繫安全帶，他們認為有了安全氣囊，安全帶是多餘的。

原句為：fifty percent of people fail … / fifty percent of people think that …。兩句主詞相同，都是 people，可用分詞構句。think 為現在式，可改成表主動進行的 Ving 分詞構句 thinking … redundant，**C** 選項為正解。

17. **Fun run is currently in vogue, _____ to all levels, from competitive race enthusiasts to casual runners who enjoy chances to stretch their muscles and legs.**

    (A) appealing                    (B) which is appealed
    (C) is attractive                 (D) attracted

    > 解 目前，趣味公益路跑正夯。趣味公益路跑吸引了各等級的跑者，從熱愛激烈競賽的跑者，到喜歡利用機會伸展筋骨的業餘跑者皆有。
    >
    > 原句為：fun run is... / fun run appeals to all levels (或 attracts all levels / is attractive to all levels)。兩句主詞相同，都是 fun run，可用分詞構句。appeal to / attract 為現在式，可改成表主動進行的 Ving 分詞構句 appealing to / attracting all levels，**A** 選項為正解。動詞「吸引」的用法如下：A 吸引 B：A attract B / A appeal to B / A be attractive to B = B 被 A 吸引：B is attracted to A。

18. **_____ crushing defeat in the election, the ruling party could no longer afford to ignore minorities, nor could they risk alienating young voters.**

    (A) That suffering    (B) Suffered        (C) Suffering        (D) To suffer

    > 解 執政黨在選戰中遭逢慘敗後，執政黨再也無法忽略少數族群，也不能冒險疏遠年輕選民。
    >
    > 原句為：the ruling party suffered crushing ... / the ruling party could no longer afford...。兩句主詞相同，都是 the ruling party，可用分詞構句。suffered (遭受) 為過去式，可改成表主動進行的 Ving 分詞構句 suffering ... election，**C** 選項為正解。

19. **_____ through crowds celebrating New Year, the destructive blast transformed a delightful scene into a spectacle of utter chaos and horror.**

    (A) Ripped                        (B) Having been ripped
    (C) To rip                         (D) Ripping

    > 解 毀滅性的爆炸，迅速炸開慶祝新年的人群。爆炸將原本歡樂的景象變成了十足混亂和恐怖驚悚的場景。
    >
    > 原句為：the destructive blast ripped through crowds ... / the destructive blast transformed ...。兩句主詞相同，都是 the blast，可用分詞構

句。ripped（撕裂扯開）為過去式，可改成表主動進行的 Ving 分詞構句 ripping … Year，**D** 選項為正解。

20. **The new drug that promises to reduce artery-clogging cholesterol comes at an eye-popping price. _____ between skeptical doctors and cost-conscious insurers, it has barely sold.**

(A) Caught                           (B) Though catching

(C) Having caught                    (D) To catch

解 保證可降低引發動脈栓塞的膽固醇新藥，價格令人咋舌。新藥被卡在對藥心存懷疑的醫生，和對藥價斤斤計較的保險公司間，新藥乏人問津。

原句為：the new drug is caught between … / the new drug has barely sold。兩句主詞相同，都是 the new drug，可用分詞構句。is caught（被卡住）為現在被動式，可改成表被動的 p.p. 分詞構句 caught ... insurers，**A** 選項為正解。

# Unit 4

分詞構句
## 4-2 進階款的分詞構句

學習進階的變型分詞構句前，我們先複習一下如何寫出基本款的分詞構句吧！

■ 分詞構句形成步驟如下：

步驟1 確定兩句主詞相同。

步驟2 去掉連接詞。

步驟3 去掉「表原因」或「先發生」或「表條件」那句的主詞。若兩句看不出有以上三個明顯關係時，則將句意較不那麼重要的那句改成分詞構句。

步驟4 若去掉的主詞，可主動執行該句的動作，則改成表「主動進行」的 Ving 分詞構句。若去掉的主詞，無法執行該句的動作，則改成表「被動」的 p.p. 分詞構句。

步驟5 造否定的分詞構句時，將 not 或 never 放在 Ving 或 p.p. 分詞前即可。

穩固了對分詞構句的了解後，接下來我們來看看分詞構句的兩種變型吧。

■ 分詞構句 [ 變型 1] 形成步驟如下：

步驟1 確定兩句主詞相同。

步驟2 保留連接詞。常被保留的連接詞有： if、when、while、(al)though 等。

步驟3 去掉連接詞那句的主詞。

步驟4 若去掉的主詞，可主動執行該句的動作，則改成表「主動進行」的 Ving 分詞構句。若去掉的主詞，無法執行該句的動作，則改成表「被動」的 p.p. 分詞構句。

由上可知，變型 1 和基本分詞構句的差別在於：保留連接詞。請見下方例句：

例 當我男友被問到他過去的戀情時，我男友閃躲我的問題。

用兩個句子呈現：

句1 My boyfriend is asked about his past relationships.

句2 My boyfriend dodges my questions.

用連接詞連接兩句

**When my boyfriend is asked** about his past relationships, my boyfriend dodges my questions.

用分詞構句 [ 變型 1 ] 表達這個句子：

**When asked** about his past relationships, my boyfriend dodges my questions.

> 解 兩句主詞相同，都是 my boyfriend，可用分詞構句。is asked 為現在被動式，可改成表被動的 p.p. 分詞構句 asked … relationships。連接詞 when 可去除，也可保留。

■ 分詞構句 [ 變型 2 ] 形成步驟如下：

兩個句子即便主詞不同，也可硬寫成分詞構句。

步驟 2 去掉連接詞。

步驟 3 保留兩句不同的主詞。將句意較不那麼重要的那句改成分詞構句。

步驟 4 分詞構句那句的主詞，若可主動執行該句的動作，則改成表「主動進行」的 Ving 分詞構句。若主詞無法執行該句的動作，則改成表「被動」的 p.p. 分詞構句。

由上可見，變型 2 和基本分詞構句的差別在於：保留兩句不同的主詞。請見下方例句：

> 例 當我在人群面前發言時，我的心跳得飛快，且我的聲音無法克制地顫抖。

用兩個句子呈現：

句 1 I speak in front of a crowd.

句 2 My heart races fast and my voice uncontrollably shakes.

用連接詞連接兩句

When I speak in front of a crowd, **my heart races** fast and **my voice** uncontrollably **shakes**.

用分詞構句 [ 變型 2 ] 表達這個句子：

I speak in front of a crowd, **my heart racing** fast and **my voice** uncontrollably **shaking**.

> 解 這兩個句子的主詞 I / my heart / my voice 雖然不同，但還是能硬寫成分詞構句。由於「心跳飛快」和「聲音顫抖」是伴隨公開談話而來的狀況，所以將 I speak... 當成主要句，而 my heart...and my voice...改成分詞構句。保留主詞 my heart / my voice。原句中，races / shakes 都是現在式，可改成表主動進行的 Ving 分詞構句 racing... / ...shaking。分詞構句從 my heart...shaking 為止。

# Unit 4

**分詞構句**
**4-3 易和分詞構句搞混的概念：**
**祈使句、動名詞、不定詞**

■ 祈使句

祈使句可用來表達「懇求你」、「命令你」、「禁止你」。因為主詞都是「你」，所以可省略主詞不寫，這也使得祈使句成為唯一可沒有主詞的句型。肯定的祈使句以「動詞原形」開頭，而否定祈使句則以「Don't + 動詞原形」開頭。通常，分辨祈使句和分詞構句的關鍵在於「連接詞」。請見下方例句：

例 早點到考場，然後你就會有時間複習你的筆記。

**Arrive** at the test site early, **and you will have** time to review your notes.

解 從沒有主詞，直接以「動詞原形」開頭可知 arrive at the test site early 為「祈使句」。主詞 you，加上動詞 will have，構成了另一個句子。再用連接詞 and 銜接兩個句子。

例 因為我早到考場，我有時間複習我的筆記。

**Arriving** at the test site early, I have time to review my notes.

解 原句為：I arrive at ... / I have time ...。兩句主詞相同，都是 I，可用分詞構句。arrive 為現在式，可改成表主動進行的 Ving 分詞構句 arriving...early。

例 不要在外面待太晚，否則媽媽會生你的氣。

**Don't stay** out too late, **or Mom will get** mad at you.

解 從沒有主詞，直接以「Don't + 動詞原形」開頭可知 Don't stay out too late 為「否定的祈使句」。主詞 Mom，加上動詞 will get，構成了另一個句子。再用連接詞 or（否則）銜接兩個句子。

■ 動名詞

動名詞 Ving，聽起來像動詞，但實際詞性卻為「名詞」，所以可放在句首當主詞，或放在動作後當受詞。分辨句首 Ving 究竟是動名詞，還是表主動進行的 Ving 分詞構句，關鍵在於「逗號」。有逗號的是分詞構句，沒逗號的則是動名詞當主詞。請見下方例句：

例 你努力，然後你就會成功。

**Working** hard, you will succeed.

> 解 因為 Working hard 後方有逗號，所以 Working 就是表主動進行的 Ving 分詞。原句為：If you work hard, you will succeed。兩句主詞相同，都是 you，可用分詞構句。work 為現在式，可改成表主動進行的 Ving 分詞構句 working hard。

例 努力是成功的關鍵之一。

**Working** hard is one of the keys to success.

> 解 因為 Working hard 後方沒有逗號，所以為動名詞當主詞。「1 個」動名詞當主詞，單數主詞，搭配單數動詞 is。

例 大峽谷廣闊無邊，這使得用單一照片就想捕捉全景這件事變得近乎不可能。

The vastness of the Grand Canyon makes **capturing** the entire landscape in one single photo nearly impossible.

> 解 句型「使...變得...」make + N (capturing ... photo) + adj (impossible)。動名詞 capturing 放在 make 後方，成了受詞。

■ 不定詞

不定詞「to 動詞原形」，或進一步延伸出的「in order to 動詞原形」和「so as to 動詞原形」，都可傳達「為了 ...」之意。而「not to 動詞原形」、「in order not to 動詞原形」和「so as not to 動詞原形」都可表示「為了不 ...」。當中「so as (not) to 動詞原形」，不可放句首。

例 我努力讀書是為了考好。

I study hard **(in order) to do** well on the test.

例 為了不想吵醒睡覺的小嬰兒，夫妻倆輕聲低語。

**Not to wake** the sleeping baby, the couple spoke in whispers.

## 小試身手：請選出正確解答

**01.** If your dad discovers a new dent in his car each time you've borrowed it, _____ when he questions your competence as a driver.

(A) don't be surprised

(B) not surprising

(C) not to be surprised

(D) never surprise

解 假如你爸發現，每次借你車，車子都會有新的凹洞，那麼當他質疑你身為駕駛人的能力時，你也別驚訝。

**考點：祈使句。**請見下方句構分析：

If your dad discovers … it, _____ when he questions …

連接詞 1　　句子 1　　　句子 2 連接詞 2　　句子 3

兩個連接詞，可銜接三個句子，所以正解應該是一個句子。唯一可以不用寫主詞的句子，就是用動詞原形，或 don't + 動詞原形開頭的「祈使句」。且人的情緒（如：驚訝）是被外在事物引發的，需用「被動式」be + p.p.。綜合以上，**A** 選項為正解。

**02.** Friction or constant contact between skin and clothing can cause acne problems. Therefore, _____ to looser-fitting clothes made of cotton, and you should soon start to see an improvement in your skin.

(A) switching

(B) switched

(C) switch

(D) to switch

解 皮膚和衣服的摩擦，或持續接觸，可能引發青春痘的問題。因此，改穿棉製的寬鬆衣服，很快地你應該就可看出膚況改善了。

**考點：祈使句。**請見下方句構分析：

_____ to looser-fitting … cotton, and you should soon start … your skin

句子 1　　　　　　　　連接詞　　　　　　　句子 2

連接詞 and 可連接兩個句子。句子 1 缺動詞，可見劃線處就是動詞。而唯一可不用寫主詞的句子就是用動詞原形，或 don't + 動詞原形開頭的「祈使句」。**C** 選項為正解。clothes「被用棉做出來」，made 為表被動的 p.p. 形容詞。

**03.** The fatal accident happened when the driver made an abrupt change _____ the highway exit.

(A) to avoid missing

(B) which avoided missing

(C) avoided to miss　　　　　　　(D) avoiding to miss

> 解 當駕駛人為避免錯過高速公路出口而突然轉彎時，致命的車禍就發生了。
>
> **考點：不定詞**
>
> 從文意可知，change 是「為了避免」錯過出口，需用不定詞「to 動詞原形」來表示「為了…」。avoid 後方需搭配 Ving。綜合以上，**A** 選項為正解。

04. _____ if he ate the doughnut, my little brother gave me a flat denial. Yet, since his face was covered with powdered sugar, what he said seemed ridiculous.

(A) When asked　　(B) To ask　　(C) Ask　　　　(D) Asking

> 解 當我弟被問到他是否吃了甜甜圈時，他堅決否認。但是因為他的臉上滿是糖粉，他說的話似乎很荒謬。
>
> **考點：分詞構句 [ 變型 1 ]**
>
> 原句為：my little brother was asked … / my brother gave me …。兩句主詞相同，都是 my little brother，可用分詞構句。was asked 為過去被動式，可改成表被動的 p.p. 分詞構句 when asked … doughnut。寫分詞構句時，也可保留連接詞 when，**A** 選項為正解。

05. _____ your exposed skin with a long-sleeved shirt and pants is a classic tip to prevent mosquito bites, but it's not always realistic when it's really hot outside.

(A) Cover　　　　(B) That Covering　　(C) Covering　　(D) Covered

> 解 穿長袖長褲來遮蓋露出來的皮膚，是防蚊子叮咬的典型秘訣，但當戶外天氣真的很熱時，這秘訣不一定實用。
>
> **考點：動名詞當主詞**。請見下方句構分析：
>
> _____ your … bites, but it's not always … outside.
> 　　　句子 1　　　　連接詞　　　　句子 2
>
> 進一步分析句子 1：
>
> _____ your exposed … pants is　　a classic tip …
> 　　　　　主詞　　　　　　　動詞
>
> 句子的基本架構為：主詞 + 動詞 + ( 地點 / 時間 )。可見動詞 is 之前的那

一串字就是主詞。動名詞 Ving 可當主詞，故 **C** 選項為正解。名詞 skin 前方的 exposed 為表被動的 p.p. 形容詞，意指「被露出來的」皮膚。片語「用 B 來覆蓋 A」cover A with B。

**06.** **All the butterfat _____ from milk, the remainder is called skim milk.**

(A) removed　　　(B) to be removed　　(C) that removes　　(D) removing

> 解　所有牛奶中的乳脂都被去除後，剩下的部份就被稱為脫脂奶。
>
> **考點：分詞構句 [ 變型 2 ]**
>
> 原句為：After all the butterfat is removed from milk, the remainder is called skim milk.。兩個句子的主詞 all the butterfat / the remainder 雖然不同，但還是能硬寫成分詞構句。首先，保留兩句不同的主詞 all the butterfat。is removed 為現在被動式，可改成表被動的 p.p. 分詞構句 all the butterfat removed from milk，**A** 選項為正解。B 選項，不定詞「to 動詞原形」，表示「為了...」。所有乳脂為了要被去除 ...，文意怪怪的。

**07.** **_____ on intuition rather than proper analysis often contributes to failure, particularly in complicated situations where there are a lot of factors at play.**

(A) Relied　　　　(B) To be reliable　　(C) That relies　　　(D) Relying

> 解　依賴直覺，而非妥適的分析，常導致失敗，尤其在有許多因素交互影響的複雜狀況中。
>
> **考點：動名詞當主詞。**請見下方句構分析：
>
> <u>_____ on intuition ... analysis</u> <u>often contributes</u> to failure ...
> 　　　　　　主詞　　　　　　　　　　　動詞
>
> 句子的基本架構為：主詞 + 動詞 + （地點 / 時間）。可見動詞 contributes 之前的那一串字就是主詞。動名詞 Ving 可當主詞，故 **D** 選項為正解。B 選項，雖然不定詞「to 動詞原形」也可以當主詞，但 reliable（值得信賴的）不合文意，應改成 reliant（依賴的）。C 選項，兩個動詞 relies / contributes，算兩個句子，可用關係代名詞連接，劃線處就是關係代名詞。但關係子句（_____ relies on intuition rather than analysis），缺主詞，文法錯誤。

**08.** **Though sea turtles will reach a very old age _____ undisturbed by humans, so far it hasn't been determined how many years they can live in their natural habitats.**

(A) when they leave      (B) to be left

(C) if left      (D) leaving

解 雖然若海龜不受人類打擾的話,海龜可活到很老。但到目前為止,它們在自然棲地裏可活幾年仍是未定數。

**考點:分詞構句[變型1]/ leave 的用法**

原句為:sea turtles will reach .... / if sea turtles are left undisturbed ...。兩句主詞相同,都是 sea turtles,可用分詞構句。are left 為現在被動式,可改成表被動的 p.p. 分詞構句 if left...humans。寫分詞構句時,也可保留連接詞 if,故 **C** 選項為正解。

註 片語「讓 N ...」leave + N + adj。...,humans leave the sea turtles undisturbed 改成被動語態,即成題目中的句子:..., the sea turtles are left undisturbed by humans。

**09.** _____ **fuel, we need infrastructure such as an extensive pipeline network in place as soon as possible.**

(A) In order to export      (B) Exported

(C) Exporting      (D) Export

解 為了出口燃油,我們需要讓四通八達的油管網絡等公共設施儘快就定位。

**考點:不定詞**

fuel 和 we need 之間沒有連接詞,可見 fuel 部分不是一個句子,所以不是祈使句。又從句意可知,需要鋪設好輸油管是「為了輸出」燃油。不定詞「(in order) to 動詞原形」表示「為了 ...」,**A** 選項為正解。C 選項,輸出燃油時 (exporting),油管應該早就鋪設好了,而非需要油管,文意不合。

**10.** _____ **harshly to Alice, an overly sensitive teen, in that she's simply too vulnerable to withstand any criticism and pressure.**

(A) No speaking      (B) Don't speak

(C) Not to speak      (D) Never spoken

解 對 Alice 這個過度敏感的少女,說話不要太嚴厲,因為她太脆弱,無法承受任何批評和壓力。

考點：祈使句。請見下方句構分析：

_____ harshly to Alice, an overly sensitive teen, in that she is ...

　　　句子 1　　　　　　　　　　　　　　　　　　　　連接詞　句子 2

連接詞 in that（因為）連接兩個句子。句子 1 缺動詞，可見劃線處就是動詞。唯一可以不用寫主詞的句子，就是用動詞原形，或 don't + 動詞原形開頭的「祈使句」，**B** 選項為正解。

11. **All the evidence _____, the jury retreated to a room to deliberate, discuss and debate so as to reach a unanimous verdict.**

(A) presenting　　　(B) presented　　　(C) is present　　　(D) to present

解 所有的證據都被提出來後，為達成一致的判決，陪審團退到房間來深思、討論和辯論。

考點：分詞構句 [ 變型 2 ]

原句為：After all the evidence was presented, the jury retreated to a room...。兩個句子的主詞 all the evidence / the jury 雖然不同，但還是能硬寫成分詞構句。首先，保留兩句不同的主詞 all the evidence。was presented 為過去被動式，可改成表被動的 p.p. 分詞構句 all the evidence presented，**B** 選項為正解。

註 present (v) 提出呈現 (adj) 出現的 / 在場的 (n) 禮物。

12. **A Rangers birthday cake, which reveals the team's signature green and white colors _____, becomes an online hit.**

(A) to be cut　　　(B) if they cut　　　(C) when cut　　　(D) cutting

解 當遊騎兵隊的生日蛋糕被切開時，蛋糕露出他們隊的招牌顏色—綠和白。這蛋糕在網路上大紅。

考點：分詞構句 [ 變型 1 ]

關係代名詞 which 代替前方的名詞 cake。原句為：a Rangers birthday cake reveals...colors if（或 when）a Rangers birthday cake is cut。兩句主詞相同，都是 a Rangers birthday cake，可用分詞構句。is cut 為現在被動式，可改成表被動的 p.p. 分詞構句 when cut。寫分詞構句時，也可保留連接詞 when，故 **C** 選項為正解。

註 cut (v) 切；cut - cut - cut。

**13.** Extremely hostile to abortion, voters here demand that the government make _____ pregnancy illegal.

(A) terminated　　　　　　　　　(B) to terminate

(C) terminating　　　　　　　　　(D) terminate

> 解 這裡的選民極度反對墮胎。這裡的選民要求政府讓終止懷孕變成違法。
>
> **考點：動名詞當受詞 / make 的用法**
>
> 句型「讓 N …」make + N (_____ pregnancy) + adj (illegal)。由此可知劃線部分應為動名詞 Ving，**C** 選項為正解。

**14.** Several of his companies _____ through bankruptcy, he has accumulated ample experiences of negotiating with creditors.

(A) gone　　　　(B) that go　　　　(C) to have gone　　　　(D) going

> 解 因為他的好幾家公司都經歷過破產，所以他已經累積了許多和債權人協商的經驗。
>
> **考點：分詞構句 [ 變型 2 ]**
>
> 原句為：Because several of his companies went through bankruptcy, he has accumulated ample experiences of negotiating with creditors.。兩個句子的主詞 several of his companies / he 雖然不同，還是能硬寫成分詞構句。首先，保留兩句不同的主詞 several of his companies。went 為過去式，可改成表主動進行的 Ving 分詞構句 several of his companies going through bankruptcy，**D** 選項為正解。

**15.** _____ any troublemakers in the festival, we'll have police officers in plain clothes and uniform carry out patrols.

(A) To deter　　　　　　　　　(B) Deterred

(C) Having been deterred　　　　(D) Deter

> 解 為了遏止有人在慶典中惹是生非，我們將請便衣刑警和制服刑警同時巡邏。
>
> **考點：不定詞**
>
> 從文意可知，警察巡邏 (carry out patrols) 是「為了遏止」搗蛋的人 (troublemakers)。不定詞「to 動詞原形」表示「為了…」，**A** 選項為正解。

16. Alzheimer's, an incurable disease, stealthily transforms James into a withered man stranded in a nursing home, all his aspirations for the future _____.

    (A) to discontinue

    (B) discontinuing

    (C) will be discontinued

    (D) discontinued

    解 阿茲海默症，一種不治之症，偷偷地將 James 變成了一個生命凋零、受困在安養院的人。他對未來的所有渴望都被 ( 阿茲海默症 ) 終止了。

    考點：分詞構句 [ 變型 2 ]

    原句為：Alzheimer's ... transforms ... / all his aspirations...are discontinued。兩個句子的主詞 Alzheimer's / all his aspirations 雖然不同，還是能硬寫成分詞構句。保留兩句不同的主詞 all his aspirations。are discontinued 為現在被動式，可改成表被動的 p.p. 分詞構句 all his aspirations for the future discontinued，D 選項為正解。

17. Electricity was a known phenomenon in Franklin's days although not completely _____.

    (A) understood

    (B) to understand

    (C) for understanding

    (D) had understood

    解 在 Franklin 的時代，雖然「電」仍未被全然了解，但「電」已是眾所皆知的現象。

    考點：分詞構句 [ 變型 1 ]

    原句為：Electricity was ..., although electricity wasn't completely understood。兩句主詞相同，都是 electricity，可用分詞構句。wasn't completely understood 為否定的過去被動式，可改成表否定、被動的 not p.p. 分詞構句 although not completely understood。寫分詞構句時，也可保留連接詞 although，A 選項為正解。

18. As the temperature increases, the chemical reactions that drive the spoilage accelerate. That's why _____ foods in the refrigerator or freezer helps to slow down the rotting process.

    (A) putting

    (B) it puts

    (C) would putting

    (D) put

    解 當溫度增加時，驅動食物腐敗的化學反應也會加速。那就是為何將食物放在冰箱或冷凍庫有助於減緩腐敗的過程。

Unit 1
關係
代名詞

Unit 2
被動
語態

Unit 3
分詞
形容詞

Unit 4
分詞
構句

Unit 5
假設
語法

Unit 6
倒裝
句

Unit 7
間接
問句

Unit 8
特殊
動詞

Unit 9
主動詞
一致

Unit 10
對稱
結構

特別收錄
Unit 11
五回
試題

> **考點：動名詞當主詞／間接問句**
>
> 間接問句的公式為：疑問詞（why）＋ 主詞（＿＿＿＿＿ foods … freezer）＋ 動詞（helps）…。由此可知，劃線部分應為動名詞 Ving，動名詞可當主詞，**A** 選項為正解。

19. **One batch of anti-cancer drugs was found to be counterfeit, ＿＿＿＿＿ a crucial component that interferes with cancer cell growth.**

   (A) missing                  (B) to miss

   (C) which has missed      (D) missed

> **解** 一批抗癌藥被發現是偽品，因為這些藥缺乏干擾癌細胞生長的重要成分。
>
> **考點：分詞構句**
>
> 原句為：One batch of … drugs was found … / one batch of … drugs missed a crucial component …。兩句主詞相同，都是 one batch of anti-cancer drugs，可用分詞構句。missed 為過去式，可改成表主動的 Ving 分詞構句 missing…growth，**A** 選項為正解。

20. **Though we've tried everything to stay in business, ＿＿＿＿＿ out of operation is a very bitter pill to swallow.**

   (A) forcing     (B) being forced     (C) a force which is  (D) forced

> **解** 雖然我們盡力想要繼續營業，但被迫關門大吉仍是我們必須吞下的苦藥（即不得不接受的事實）。
>
> **考點：動名詞當主詞**。請見下方句構分析：
>
> Though we have tried …, ＿＿＿＿＿ out of operation is a …
> 連接詞 主詞 1　動詞 1　　　　　　　　主詞 2　　　　動詞 2
> 句子的基本架構為：主詞 ＋ 動詞 ＋（地點／時間）。可見動詞 is 之前的那一串字就是主詞。動名詞 Ving 可當主詞。且關門是不得已、「被迫」的事，需搭配被動式。綜合以上，**B** 選項為正解。

# Unit 5

假設語法
## 5–1 連接詞 if 引導出來的假設語法

連接詞 if（假如）引導出來的假設語法，一向是考生們頭痛的句型。但只要記得「跳躍法」就可輕鬆學會。

■ 使用 if 句型的時機

　　if 句型非常實用，可用來預設「過去」、「現在」、「未來」發生的事。

■ 三種 if 假設句

1. 連接詞 if 放句首時，需打逗點。
2. if 針對「未來」做假設時，緊接在 if 後方的動詞需從「未來」往前跳一格，改用「現在式」，請見圖示。

過去完成式　　過去　　現在　　未來

針對「未來」做假設的公式：
If 主詞 1 + 動詞 1（現在式），主詞 2 + 動詞 2（未來式）.

例 假如明天天氣好，我們就去公園野餐。

**If** the weather **is** beautiful tomorrow, we **will go** on a picnic in the park.

> 解 If 針對「未來」tomorrow / will 做假設，緊接在 if 後方的動詞需從未來往前跳一格，改用「現在式」is。但逗號後，即便要去野餐也是明天的事，所以還是用未來式 will go。

3. if 針對「現在」做相反假設時，緊接在 if 後方的動詞需從「現在」往前跳一格，改用「過去式」，請見圖示。

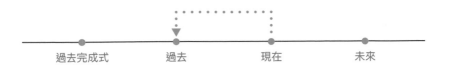

過去完成式　　過去　　現在　　未來

針對「現在」做相反假設的公式：

If 主詞 1 + 動詞 1（過去式），主詞 2 + 動詞 2（would 將會 / should 應該 / could 可以可能 / might 可能 + (not) + 動詞原形）.

需特別注意的是：和現在事實相反的 if 假設句中，be 動詞的過去式只能用「were」。若想加強語氣，還可去掉連接詞 if，將 were 移至句首。

例 假如我們辦公室有台咖啡機，我就可以每天早上煮咖啡了。

**If** there **were** a coffee machine in our office, I **could** then **make** coffee every morning.

> 解 從文意可知，現在辦公室裡沒有咖啡機。if 針對「現在」every morning 做相反假設，緊接在 if 後方的動詞需從現在往前跳一格，改用「過去式」。be 動詞在 if 句中的過去式只能用「were」。而句子 2 的動詞為「would / should / could / might + 動詞原形」。若想加強語氣，則可去掉連接詞 if，將 were 移至句首，即：
>
> **Were** there a coffee machine in our office, I **could** then **make** coffee every morning.

4. if 針對「過去」做相反假設時，緊接在 if 後方的動詞需從「過去」往前跳一格，改用「過去完成式」，請見圖示。

過去完成式　　過去　　現在　　未來

針對「過去」做相反假設的公式：

If 主詞 1 + 動詞 1 （過去完成式 had + (not) + p.p.），主詞 2 + 動詞 2 （would 將會 / should 應該 / could 可以可能 / might 可能 + (not) + have p.p.）

若想加強語氣，還可去掉連接詞 if，將過去完成式中的助動詞 had 移至句首。

例▶ 假如我那天沒生氣地說出那些傷人的話，我女友就不會和我分手了。

**If I had not said** those hurtful words in anger that day, my girlfriend **would not have broken up** with me.

> 解 從文意可知：我那天說了傷害我女友的話，所以我和我女友已經分手了。if 針對「過去」that day 做相反假設時，緊接在 if 後方的動詞需從過去往前跳一格，改用「過去完成式」had not said。而句子 2 的動詞為「would / should / could / might + have p.p.」。若想加強語氣，可去掉連接詞 if，將過去完成式中的助動詞 had 移至句首，即：
>
> **Had I not said** those hurtful words in anger that day, my girlfriend **would not have broken up** with me.

# Unit 5

假設語法
## 5–2 用於「間接問句」的疑問詞 if

很多同學會把連接詞 if（假如）和疑問詞 if（是否）的使用方式搞混了。了解 if 假設語法後，我們再來看看 if 間接問句的用法囉。

間接問句，又稱為名詞子句。公式為：疑問詞 + 主詞 + 動詞 +（地點 / 時間），常放在動詞後方當「受詞」，或放句首當「主詞」。間接問句中的疑問詞 if「是否⋯」，後方動詞不需跳躍，只要按句子發生的時間，寫出合適的時態即可。請見下方例句。粗體字即為「間接問句」：

例 我不知道 Andy 明天是否要來參加我的生日派對。

I don't know **if** **Andy** **will come** to my birthday party tomorrow.
　　　　　　疑問詞　主詞　　　動詞

> 解 疑問詞 if（是否），後方的動詞不需跳躍。句子發生時間為 tomorrow，故搭配未來式 will come。

例 時間將會證明市長當選人是否會在四年任期內兌現他的競選承諾。

Time will tell **if the mayor-elect** **will deliver** his election promises within his
　　　　　　　疑問詞　　　主詞　　　　動詞
**four-year term**.

> 解 if 子句放在動詞 tell 後方當受詞，應為「間接問句」，if 為疑問詞「是否」。if 間接問句中的動詞不需跳躍，而是依句中的時間點「未來四年內」（within his four-year term），搭配未來式 will deliver。

## 小試身手：請選出正確解答

**01.** You phone service will be disconnected if the payment _____ within 5 days.

(A) won't be received

(B) isn't received

(C) hasn't received

(D) wasn't receiving

> 解 假如我們在五天內沒收到你的繳款，你的電話將會被停話。
>
> if 針對「未來」will 做假設時，緊接在 if 後方的動詞需從未來往前跳一格，改用「現在式」。費用「被接收」，需搭配被動式。綜合以上，**B** 選項為正解。

**02.** Ten kilometers up in the sky, the winds of the jet stream are far stronger than those on the Earth's surface. If just 1% of this energy _____, it would be enough to power the entire world.

(A) were harvested

(B) would harvest

(C) has been harvesting

(D) is going to be harvested

> 解 空中十公里處，噴射氣流的強度，遠比地球表面的氣流強。假如能收集這能量的百分之一，就足以供電給全世界。
>
> 從文意可知，我們現在還無法收集高空氣流所產生的電力。if 針對「現在」are 做相反假設時，緊接在 if 後方的動詞需從現在往前跳一格，改用「過去式」。能量「被收集」，需搭配被動式。且 be 動詞在 if 假設句中的過去式只能用 were。綜合以上，**A** 選項為正解。

**03.** If you had followed the recipe, the cake _____ such a disaster.

(A) wouldn't have been

(B) might not be

(C) wasn't going to be

(D) hadn't been

> 解 假如你有照著食譜做，這蛋糕就不會一團糟了。
>
> 從 had followed 可知 if 針對「過去」做相反假設，公式如下：
>
> If 主詞 1 + 動詞 1（過去完成式 had (not) + p.p.），主詞 2 + 動詞 2(would / should / could / might (not) + have p.p.)。套公式，主詞 2 (the cake) + 動詞 2 (wouldn't have been) …。綜合以上，**A** 選項為正解。

Unit 1
關係
代名詞

Unit 2
被動
語態

Unit 3
分詞
形容詞

Unit 4
分詞
構句

Unit 5
假設
語法

Unit 6
倒裝
句

Unit 7
間接
問句

Unit 8
特殊
動詞

Unit 9
主動詞
一致

Unit 10
對稱
結構

特別收錄
Unit 11
五回
試題

**04.** **If an addict ＿＿＿＿ drugs, he will find his dopamine levels far lower than someone who has never taken drugs.**

(A) is stopping to use          (B) were stopped using

(C) stops using                 (D) would have stopped the use of

> 解 假如吸毒者停用毒品，他將會發現他的多巴胺指數遠低於從未嗑藥的人。
>
> if 針對「未來」will 做假設時，緊接在 if 後方的動詞需從未來往前跳一格，改用「現在式」。單數主詞 an addict，搭配單數動詞。且討論 addict (嗑藥者)「停用」藥物之後的狀況，需用 stop + Ving。綜合以上，**C** 選項為正解。

**05.** **Australian Aborigines believe that if Earth ＿＿＿＿ a voice, it would be like the deep, resonant drone of the didgeridoo.**

(A) is having                (B) would have had

(C) had                        (D) were

> 解 澳洲原住民相信，假如地球可發出聲音的話，將會是像 didgeridoo 那樣深沉宏亮的低鳴聲。
>
> 地球不會發出聲音。if 針對「現在」做相反假設時，緊接在 if 後方的動詞需從現在往前跳一格，改用「過去式」，**C** 選項為正解。

**06.** **Imagining themselves becoming wealthy beyond their wildest dreams, the students passionately talk about what they would do ＿＿＿＿ they ＿＿＿＿ in such a position.**

(A) were; x                 (B) had; been

(C) should; have been      (D) if; are

> 解 當想像自己變得意想不到地富有時，學生們熱烈地談論，假如他們在如此富有的狀況下會做些什麼事。
>
> 從 Imagining ...可推知，學生現在並不富有。if 針對「現在」做相反假設時，緊接在 if 後方的動詞需從現在往前跳一格，改用「過去式」。if 假設句中，be 動詞的過去式只能用「were」。為加強語氣，可去掉連接詞 if，將 were 移至句首。綜合以上，**A** 選項為正解。
>
> 請見下方句構分析：

if 假設句：

…what they would do **if they were in such a position**.

加強語氣版的假設句：

…what they would do **were they in such a position**.

07. **At that time, the anxious driver kept honking the horn fervently to warn you. You wouldn't have been hit if you _____ the music on so loud.**

    (A) wouldn't have had
    (B) don't have
    (C) hadn't had
    (D) wasn't had

    解 那時，著急的駕駛人一直猛按喇叭警告你。假如你沒將音樂開得那麼大聲，你就不會被撞了。

    從 wouldn't have been hit 可知 if 針對「過去」做相反假設，公式如下：

    If 主詞 1＋動詞 1（過去完成式 had (not)＋p.p.），主詞 2＋動詞 2（would / should / could / might (not)＋have p.p.）。套公式：if 主詞 1（you）＋動詞 1（hadn't had）…，**C** 選項為正解。

08. **In 2005, a scientist performed a study to see if peppermint's smell _____ motorists. He found that they became less agitated and more aware under the influence of peppermint.**

    (A) had affected
    (B) was affected
    (C) should have affected
    (D) affected

    解 科學家在 2005 進行了一項研究，觀察薄荷的味道對機車騎士是否有影響。他發現在薄荷影響下，騎士們變得沒那麼焦躁，且警覺性較高。

    if 子句放在動詞 see 後方當受詞，應為「間接問句」，if 為疑問詞「是否」。if 間接問句中的動詞不需跳躍，只要按研究發生的時間 2005 年，搭配過去式即可，**D** 選項為正解。

**09. She has written a thesis examining the common but somewhat absurd myth that food dropped on the floor will stay clean if it _____ up within five seconds.**

(A) has picked　　　　　　(B) picks

(C) would be picking　　　(D) is picked

> 解 她已經寫了一篇論文，檢視這個常見但有些荒謬的迷思：落地的食物將仍是乾淨的，假如在五秒內被撿起來的話。
>
> if 針對「未來」will stay 做假設，緊接在 if 後方的動詞需從未來往前跳一格，改用「現在式」。代名詞 it 代替 food，食物「被撿起」，需搭配被動式。綜合以上，**D** 選項為正解。

**10. In Britain, there are 200,000 deaths a year from heart attacks and strokes, many of which _____ if the conditions had been known about.**

(A) might have been avoided　　(B) would avoid

(C) have to be avoided　　　　　(D) were avoiding

> 解 在英國，每年有 20 萬人死於心臟病和中風。這些案例中，有許多是可避免的，假如人們對這些病症有所了解的話。
>
> 從文意可知，要避開的是心臟病和中風所引發的死亡。關係代名詞 which 代替前方的名詞 deaths。死亡「可以被避免」，應搭配被動式。從 had been known 可知 if 針對「過去」做相反的假設，公式如下：
>
> If 主詞 1 + 動詞 1（過去完成式 had (not) + p.p.），主詞 2 + 動詞 2（would / should / could / might (not) + have p.p.）。套公式：...，主詞 2（many of the deaths) + 動詞 2（might have been avoided），**A** 選項為正解。

**11. If it _____ so hard at this moment, you could all go outside and play football.**

(A) hadn't rained　　　　(B) weren't raining

(C) hasn't been raining　　(D) doesn't rain

> 解 假如現在雨沒下得這麼大，你們就可全部出去踢足球了。
>
> 從文意可知，現在正在下雨，所以無法踢球。if 針對「現在」at this moment 做相反假設時，緊接在 if 後方的動詞需從現在往前跳一格，改用「過去式」。又 if 假設句中，be 動詞的過去式只能用「were」。綜合以

上，**B** 選項為正解。

12. Voters will decide in November if physician-assisted suicide _____ for terminally ill patients who have six months or less to live.

    (A) is allowed

    (B) might allow

    (C) would have been allowing

    (D) will be allowed

    > 解 11 月，選民將決定醫生是否可協助存活期不超過六個月的絕症病患進行安樂死。
    >
    > if 子句放在動詞 decide 後方當受詞，應為「間接問句」，if 為疑問詞「是否」。if 間接問句中的動詞不需跳躍，而是按投票發生的時間點 will decide，搭配未來式。又 physician-assisted suicide（安樂死）「將被允許」，需搭配被動式。綜合以上，**D** 選項為正解。

13. Guests on today's show will discuss if so far the Muslims _____ negatively and unfairly, often as terrorists causing violence and chaos, by the media.

    (A) have been portrayed

    (B) are portraying

    (C) would have portrayed

    (D) may portray

    > 解 今晚節目裏，來賓將討論，截至目前為止，媒體對穆斯林的描繪是否是負面且失之公允。媒體通常將穆斯林形塑成引發混亂和暴力的恐怖份子。
    >
    > if 子句放在動詞 discuss 後方當受詞，應為「間接問句」，if 為疑問詞「是否」。if 間接問句中的動詞不需跳躍，而是以句中時間 so far 為準。so far（到目前為止），代表一段時間，得搭配完成式。又 Muslims「被媒體描繪」成恐怖份子，需搭配被動式。綜合以上，**A** 選項為正解。

14. If an icky item such as diapers_____ close to a non-icky item like cookies, consumers will perceive the latter as tainted. Ickiness, therefore, is contagious.

    (A) are displaying

    (B) will have displayed

    (C) is displayed

    (D) can display

    > 解 假如噁心的東西，如尿布，被擺在像餅乾這類不噁心的東西附近，消費者會將餅乾視為是被污染的。因此，噁心是會傳染的。

if 針對「未來」will 做假設，緊接在 if 後方的動詞需從未來往前跳一格，改用「現在式」。an item 才是句子的主詞，such as (比如說) 後方的 diapers 只是補充說明的例子。單數主詞 an item「被展示」，需搭配單數被動式。綜合以上，**C** 選項為正解。

15. If you uncontrollably _____ about your debut performance tomorrow, watching a comedy may be a welcome distraction that gives you a good laugh and helps you unwind.

(A) worry

(B) have been worrying

(C) will be worried

(D) worried

解 假如你為明天的首演擔心不已，那麼看部喜劇可能是轉移你注意力的好方法，讓你開懷大笑，協助你紓壓。

if 針對「未來」tomorrow 做假設，緊接在 if 後方的動詞需從未來往前跳一格，改用「現在式」。片語「擔心某事」有三種寫法：worry about N / be worried about N / express worries about N。綜合以上，**A** 選項為正解。

16. On my recent flight to New York, my annoying seatmate blasted a talk show on her phone, minus the earbuds. Had I had a set of earbuds with me, I _____ them to her.

(A) would have given

(B) had been given

(C) were giving

(D) could give

解 在我最近一次飛往紐約的航班上，討人厭的鄰座乘客用手機看脫口秀，音量震耳欲聾，且她沒用耳機。假如當時我有帶耳機，我就會給她。

從 Had I had 可知 if 針對「過去」做相反假設，公式如下：

If 主詞 1 + 動詞 1 (過去完成式 had (not) + p.p.)，主詞 2 + 動詞 2 (would / should / could / might (not) + have p.p.)。套公式：

If 主詞 1 (I) + 動詞 1 (had had) ...，主詞 2 (I) + 動詞 2 (would have given) ...

若想加強語氣，可去掉連接詞 if，將過去完成式中的助動詞 had 移至句首，即：Had I had ..., I would have given ...。綜合以上，**A** 選項為正解。

17. Compared with 25 percent of the public, ninety percent of the doctors surveyed say that they would not want CPR if they _____ into a deep coma.

(A) had slipped     (B) will slip     (C) are slipping     (D) slipped

> 解 相較於百分之 25 的民眾，百分之 90 接受調查的醫生表示，假如他們陷入重度昏迷，他們不希望被急救。
>
> 從文意可知，被調查的醫生現在還可表達意見 (say)，並未陷入昏迷。if 針對「現在」做相反假設時，緊接在 if 後方的動詞需從現在往前跳一格，改用「過去式」，**D** 選項為正解。

18. The police said in a statement, "If these allegations against Mr. Wang _____ out to be true, we are not going to rest until he is held accountable for his conducts."

(A) turned     (B) has turned     (C) is turning     (D) turn

> 解 警方在聲明中說到：假如這些對王先生的指控最後證明都是真的，我們將不會停止追查，直到他為他的行為負責為止。
>
> if 針對「未來」are not going to … 做假設時，緊接在 if 後方的動詞需從未來往前跳一格，改用「現在式」。又複數主詞 these allegations，需搭配複數動詞。綜合以上，**D** 選項為正解。

19. The police mentioned in yesterday's press conference, "We still can not confirm if the hostage really _____ as the human remains found in the car are burned beyond recognition."

(A) will be killed     (B) has been killed     (C) was killing     (D) kills

> 解 警方在昨天的記者會上提到：我們仍無法確認人質是否已遭殺害，因為車裡找到的遺骸被燒得面目全非，難以辨識。
>
> if 子句放在動詞 confirm 後方當受詞，應為「間接問句」，if 為疑問詞「是否」。if 間接問句中的動詞不需跳躍。先被殺害，才會有燒焦的遺骸。比「現在式」are burned 還早發生的動作需用「現在完成式」。人質「被殺害」，需搭配被動式。綜合以上，**B** 選項為正解。

**20.** _____ you a fish, one of the last birds you would want to see flying overhead would be a hungry osprey.

(A) Should      (B) Were      (C) If      (D) Wish

> 解 假如你是條魚的話,你最不希望看見在你頭頂飛翔的鳥類之一就是飢腸轆轆的魚鷹。
>
> 從文意可知,你永遠都不可能是條魚。if 針對「現在」做相反假設時,緊接在 if 後方的動詞需從現在往前跳一格,改用「過去式」。又 if 假設句中,be 動詞的過去式只能用「were」。為加強語氣,可去掉連接詞 if,將 were 移至句首。綜合以上,**B** 選項為正解。
>
> if 假設句:
>
> **If you were a fish**, one of the last birds you would want to see …
>
> 加強語氣版的假設句:
>
> **Were you a fish**, one of the last birds you would want to see …

# Unit 5

假設語法
## 5-3 其他由 if 延伸出的假設語法

學會了基本的 if 假設語法，接著再來看看如何使用由 if 延伸出的 as if、even if、if only、should 等來造假設句。其實只要牢記：緊接在連接詞 if（假如）後方的動詞需跳躍，就可輕鬆過關。

■ 連接詞 as if

連接詞 as if 意指「彷彿／好像」，多用於解釋或譬喻某事。as if 針對「現在」做譬喻時，as if 後方句的動詞需從現在往前跳一格，改用「過去式」，且 be 動詞在 as if 句中的過去式也只能用「were」。又 as if 針對「過去」做譬喻時，as if 後方句中的動詞需從過去往前跳一格，改用「過去完成式」。

例 我無法忍受 Amy 頤指氣使的態度。她表現得好像她是我老闆一樣，實際上她並不是。

I can't tolerate Amy's bossy attitude. She **acts as if** she **were** my boss, but in fact she isn't.

> 解 從 she isn't 可知 Amy 現在並非我老闆。as if 針對「現在」做譬喻時，緊接在 as if 後方的動詞需從現在往前跳一格，改用「過去式」。且 as if 句中，be 動詞的過去式只能用「were」。

但若 as if 後方句所譬喻的事情有可能會發生時，可用「直說法」，即依動作發生的時間點，搭配合適的時態即可。請見下方例句。

例 天空烏雲密佈。看起來好像快下雨了。

The sky is covered with black clouds. It looks **as if** it **is going to rain**.

> 解 從天空烏雲密佈推知有下雨的可能，所以 as if 後方句中的動詞不需跳躍。「快要下雨了」，故搭配未來式 is going to rain。

■ 連接詞 even if

連接詞 even if 意指「即使」，多用於文意轉折。even if 後方句的動詞也適用跳躍法。也就是說，遇「未來」，even if 後方句中的動詞需從未來往前跳一格，改用「現在式」。遇和「現在」相反的事實，則 even if 後方句中的動詞需從現在往前跳一格，改用「過去式」，且 even if 句中，be 動詞的過去式也只能用「were」。請見下方例句：

例〉即使他向我道歉，我也不會原諒他。

**Even if** he **apologizes** to me, I **won't forgive** him.

> 解 從文意可知，他還沒跟我道歉。就算他跟我道歉也是未來的事。even if 遇「未來」，緊接在 even if 後方的動詞需從未來往前跳一格，改用「現在式」。

例〉即使他是個瘋子，但蓄意誤傳他所說的話也是不合情理的。

**Even if** he **were** a lunatic, it **would stand** no reason to misreport what he has said on purpose.

> 解 從文意可知，他不是個瘋子。針對「現在」做相反陳述時，緊接在 even if 後方的動詞需從現在往前跳一格，改用「過去式」。且 even if 句中，be 動詞的過去式也只能用「were」。

■ 副詞 if only

副詞 if only 意指「但願 ... 就好」，後方句中的動詞也適用跳躍法。陳述和「現在」相反的事實，緊接在 if only 後方的動詞需從現在往前跳一格，改用「過去式」，且 be 動詞在 if only 句中的過去式也只能用「were」。而陳述和「過去」相反的事實時，緊接在 if only 後方的動詞需從過去往前跳一格，改用「過去完成式」。請見下方例句：

例〉我期中考沒考好。但願我之前努力一點就好。

I **didn't do** well on my midterm. **If only** I **had worked** harder.

> **解** 從 didn't do well 可看出事情發生過了，而我之前也不夠努力。if only 陳述和「過去」相反的事實時，句中的動詞從過去往前跳一格，改用「過去完成式」。

## ■ 助動詞 should

助動詞 should 除表示「應該 ...」外，也有「萬一」的意思，可用於假設未來可能發生的事，雖然發生機率很低，僅萬分之一。should 擺放的位置就是 if 的位置，用 should 取代 if 後，因為 should 為助動詞，句中動詞需用「原形」。請見下方例句：

**例** 萬一明天他來了，請他等一下。

用連接詞 if 來寫
**If** he **comes** tomorrow, please tell him to wait.

> **解** if 針對「未來」tomorrow 做假設時，緊接在 if 後方的動詞需從未來往前跳一格，改用「現在式」。

用助動詞 should 來寫
**Should** he **come** tomorrow, please tell him to wait.

> **解** 用 should 取代 if 後，因為 should 為助動詞，緊接 should 後方句中的動詞也應跟著現「原形」。和 if 那句相較，should 這句暗示著他明天出現的可能性很低。

# 小試身手：請選出正確解答

**01.** **Over the festive period, we give, we share and we care. Then why does it all have to stop so suddenly in January? If only Christmas spirit _____ 12 months, not 12 days.**

(A) will last      (B) lasts      (C) has lasted      (D) lasted

> 解 耶誕節慶期間，我們為他人付出、和他人分享，並關心他人。那麼為何一月時，一切都必須嘎然而止呢？但願耶誕節的精神可持續 12 個月，而非只有 12 天。
>
> 耶誕節不可能持續 12 個月，和「現在」事實相反。緊接在 if only 後方句中的動詞需從現在往前跳一格，改用「過去式」，**D** 選項為正解。

**02.** **Watching parkour participants in action is a lot like watching a team of acrobats. You may witness them walking along the side of a bridge as if _____ a balance beam.**

(A) you might have   (B) there is      (C) that had been   (D) it were

> 解 看著行進間的跑酷參加者，就很像看到一群雜技表演者。你可能目睹他們沿著橋邊走，彷彿走平衡木般。
>
> the side of a bridge (橋邊) 並非 a balance beam (平衡木)。as if 針對「現在」做相反譬喻時，緊接在 as if 後方的動詞需從現在往前跳一格，改用「過去式」，且 as if 句中，be 動詞的過去式只能用「were」，**D** 選項為正解。代名詞 it 意指 the side of a bridge。

**03.** **Rats have grown used to living off our scraps. It is unlikely that they will be able to survive long _____ we disappear.**

(A) even if      (B) were      (C) should      (D) had

> 解 老鼠已經習慣吃人類的殘餘物為生。萬一我們消失的話，他們也不太可能久活。
>
> 關係代名詞 that 帶出假設句。if 針對「未來」will be able 做假設，緊接在 if 後方的動詞需從未來往前跳一格，改用「現在式」，即：
>
> It is unlikely that they will be able to survive long **if we disappear**.

又因為這件事 unlikely，發生的可能性極低，所以也可用助動詞 should（萬一）造假設句。用 should 取代 if 後，因為 should 為助動詞，緊接 should 後方句中的動詞也應跟著現「原形」，即：

It is unlikely that they will be able to survive **should we disappear**.

綜合以上，**C** 選項為正解。

**04.** **Virtual reality refers to the computer technology used to create a simulated, three-dimensional world that a user can manipulate and explore while feeling as if he _____ in that world.**

(A) will be　　　(B) had been　　　(C) were　　　(D) is

解 虛擬實境指的是用來營造 3D 模擬世界的電腦科技。這項科技讓使用者可操控和探索虛擬世界，並覺得自己彷彿置身其中。

從文意可推知，消費者沒有置身 3D 模擬世界裡，和「現在」事實相反。故緊接在 as if 後方的動詞需從現在往前跳一格，改用「過去式」。且 as if 句中，be 動詞的過去式只能用「were」，**C** 選項為正解。

**05.** **If only I _____ more free time every day. Then, I can cook a delicious dinner and eat it with my family at a leisurely pace.**

(A) have　　　(B) had　　　(C) could have had　(D) had had

解 但願我每天有更多空閒時間就好。那麼，我就能煮一頓美味的晚餐，並和家人悠閒地共進晚餐。

從「但願我每天有更多時間」，可知我每天都沒空。if only 帶出和「現在」every day 相反的事，緊接在 if only 後方的動詞需從現在往前跳一格，改用「過去式」，**B** 選項為正解。

**06.** **A rat with damage to the amygdala will not freeze at all even if it _____ a cat. Moreover, it might even walk up to the sleeping cat and nibble on its ear.**

(A) had an encounter　　　　　(B) would have encountered
(C) encounters　　　　　　　　(D) will encounter with

解 杏仁核受損的老鼠，即便遇到貓時，也不會嚇呆。而且，它甚至還會走向睡貓，輕咬它的耳朵。

even if 遇「未來」will not freeze，緊接在 even if 後方的動詞需從未來往前跳一格，改用「現在式」。且 encounter N = have an encounter with N。綜合以上，**C** 選項為正解。

**07.** In a country where women are required by law to cover themselves in Islamic dress when in public, it's a huge bonus that inside this women-only hotel, they can move around uncovered as if they ＿＿＿＿ at home.

(A) are going to be　(B) had been　　　(C) are　　　　　(D) were

解 在這個依法律規定，女性於公開場合都應著伊斯蘭裝的國家裡，進到這家女性專屬的旅館卻可不穿罩袍、不帶頭紗、隨意走動，彷彿在自己家中一般，這真是一大好事。

從文意可知，她們在旅館而不在家。和「現在」事實 can move 相反，緊接在 as if 後方的動詞需從現在往前跳一格，改用「過去式」。且 as if 句中，be 動詞的過去式只能用「were」，**D** 選項為正解。

**08.** In the midst of territorial dispute between Israel and Syria, military action can be concentrated ＿＿＿＿ that age-old conflict escalate.

(A) should　　　　(B) if　　　　　　(C) were　　　　(D) had

解 在以色列和敘利亞為領土而爭議不休之際，萬一幾世紀以來的衝突節節高升的話，就可能會有密集的軍事行動。

can be 意指「可能會...」表猜測。由此可推知，if 針對「未來」做假設，if 後方句中的動詞需從未來往前跳一格，改用「現在式」，即：

...military action can be concentrated **if that age-old conflict escalates**.

若這件事發生可能性極低，也可用助動詞 should（萬一）來造假設句。用 should 取代 if 後，因為 should 為助動詞，緊接 should 後方句中的動詞也應跟著現「原形」，即：

...military action can be concentrated **should that age-old conflict escalate**.

題幹中的 escalate 為動詞原形，故 **A** 選項為正解。

**09.** The father of the suicide bomber who coordinated the attack told the media, "If I had known he would commit such brutal mass killings, I _____ him."

(A) would have killed

(B) would kill

(C) was killed

(D) have been killing

解 負責協調攻擊的那名自殺炸彈客的父親告訴媒體：假如我早知道他會犯下如此冷血殘忍的大屠殺，我就會先殺了他。

從 told the media 可知，自殺炸彈攻擊已發生，所以這名父親所說的話，是和「過去」相反的假設，公式如下：

If 主詞 1 + 動詞 1（過去完成式 had (not) + p.p.），主詞 2 + 動詞 2（would / should / could / might (not) + have p.p.）。套公式：If 主詞 1 (I) + 動詞 1 (had known) ..., 主詞 2 (I) + 動詞 2 (would have killed) ...，A 選項為正解。

**10.** Last night's earthquake was so strong that it almost seemed as if someone _____ up my armchair high into the air, then trying hard to throw me out of the chair.

(A) were to pick

(B) would have been picking

(C) had picked

(D) picked

解 昨晚的地震是如此地猛烈，似乎像是有人把我的扶手椅高舉空中，然後想盡辦法把我從椅子裡甩出來。

針對「過去」last night's earthquake 做譬喻，緊接在 as if 後方的動詞需從過去往前跳一格，改用「過去完成式」，C 選項為正解。

**11.** If the bacteria _____ the immune system, a problem more common among the malnourished rural poor in the South Asia, they will cause persistent fever, weight loss and if untreated, death.

(A) overwhelm

(B) is overwhelming

(C) had overwhelmed

(D) will overwhelm

解 假如細菌壓垮了免疫系統（這問題在南亞鄉村裡營養不足的窮人身上很常見），細菌將會引發持續高燒、體重減輕。又假如沒治療的話，還會造成死亡。

if 針對「未來」will cause 做假設時，緊接在 if 後方的動詞需從未來往前

跳一格，改用「現在式」。主詞 bacteria 為複數，需搭配複數動詞。綜合以上。**A** 選項為正解。

註 bacterium (n)（單數）細菌

12. In the search for your dream job, you need to ask yourself whether it is worth the financial risk and if you _____ more or at least the same amount of money as your current job.

(A) make (B) have made
(C) were making (D) will be making

解 當找尋你的夢幻工作時，你必須問自己是否值得為這份工作冒財務風險，且是否能賺得比現在的工作多，或至少差不多。

if 和 whether 子句放在動詞 ask 後方當受詞，應為「間接問句」，if / whether 為疑問詞「是否」。if 間接問句中的動詞不需跳躍，採直說法。從文意可知，拿「未來」從事 dream job 時賺的錢，和 current job 賺的錢做比較，需搭配未來式，**D** 選項為正解。

13. The critic mocks the actress for her fashion sense and her weight, saying that she looks as if she _____ triplets, one baby in front and two in her behind.

(A) had (B) was having
(C) has had (D) would have

解 評論家嘲笑該名女演員的時尚敏感度，以及她的體重。他說：她看起來好像身上背了三胞胎，一個放在前面，然後兩個在後面。

從文意可知，女演員只是體態豐腴，並沒帶著三胞胎，所以三胞胎這說法和「現在」looks 相反。緊接在 as if 後方的動詞需從現在往前跳一格，改用「過去式」，**A** 選項為正解。

14. I wouldn't wear high-heels, even if I _____ a pair for free right now. To me, they are torture devices disguised as fashion.

(A) were gotten (B) am getting (C) have got (D) got

解 即便我可免費獲得一雙高跟鞋，我也不會穿。對我而言，高跟鞋是偽裝成時尚象徵的折磨裝置。

從文意可知，我現在並沒有免費獲贈一雙鞋。even if 針對「現在」right now 做相反假設時，緊接在 even if 後方的動詞需從現在往前跳一格，改用「過去式」，**D** 選項為正解。

15. Because of the relative density of lava, _____ someone fall into a volcano, he will probably not be swallowed like a rock plopping into the water. Instead, he will land on top of the lava with a soft little hiss and then burst into flame.

(A) should          (B) if          (C) had          (D) wish

解 因為岩漿的相對密度，萬一某人掉到火山裡，或許他不會像石頭落入水中般被吞噬，反而會輕輕地、嘶地一聲落在岩漿表面，然後突然冒出火花。

想像掉到火山岩漿的狀況，故 if 針對「未來」will probably 做假設時，緊接在 if 後方的動詞需從未來往前跳一格，改用「現在式」：

..., **if** someone **falls** into a volcano, he **will** probably ....

因為這件事發生的機率極低，也可用助動詞 should（萬一）來造假設句。用 should 取代 if 後，因為 should 為助動詞，緊接 should 後方句中的動詞也應跟著現「原形」，即：

..., **should** someone **fall** into a volcano, he will probably...

綜合以上，**A** 選項為正解。

16. _____ for the substantial support and sponsorship from throughout the area, we would not have had such a successful festival.

(A) Were it not                  (B) Had it not been
(C) If it hasn't been             (D) If there wasn't

解 若不是因為有了這地區的大力支持和贊助，我們無法將慶典辦得如此成功。

從 would not have had 可知 if 針對「過去」做相反假設，公式如下：

If 主詞 1 + 動詞 1（過去完成式 had (not) + p.p.），主詞 2 + 動詞 2（would / should / could / might (not) + have p.p.）

套公式可得：

**If** it **had not been** for ..., we **would not have had** ....

加強語氣，可去掉連接詞 if，將過去完成式中的助動詞 had 移至句首，即：

**Had** it **not been** for ..., we **would not have had**....

Unit 1
關係
代名詞

Unit 2
被動
語態

Unit 3
分詞
形容詞

Unit 4
分詞
構句

Unit 5
假設
語法

Unit 6
倒裝
句

Unit 7
間接
問句

Unit 8
特殊
動詞

Unit 9
主動詞
一致

Unit 10
對稱
結構

特別收錄
Unit 11
五回
試題

綜合以上，**B** 選項為正解。

17. **If only I _____ to my parents. I wouldn't have to face the harsh consequences of my foolish actions now.**

　　(A) were listening 　　　　　(B) listen
　　(C) am going to listen 　　　(D) had listened

解 但願我之前有聽爸媽的話就好。我現在也不用面對我愚蠢行為所帶來的嚴峻的後果。

從文意可知，他之前沒聽爸媽建議，所以現在必須面對嚴重後果。if only 針對「過去」做相反假設時，緊接在 if only 後方的動詞需從過去往前跳一格，改用「過去完成式」，**D** 選項為正解。

18. **As if we _____ enough to worry about these days, now the World Health Organization is saying cellphones can produce cancer at the same level as the danger posed by lead or engine exhaust.**

　　(A) won't have 　　　　　(B) haven't had
　　(C) didn't have 　　　　　(D) aren't having

解 彷彿目前我們煩心的事還不夠多一樣，現在世界衛生組織說：手機引發癌症的危險程度和鉛或引擎廢氣相同。

從文意可知，我們煩心的事很多。和「現在」now / these days 相反，緊接在 as if 後方的動詞需從現在往前跳一格，改用「過去式」，**C** 選項為正解。

19. **The celebrity dad said, "I won't sell any exclusive photos of my newborn daughter even if I _____ a whopping price. I just don't want her to live under the media's microscope."**

　　(A) have offered 　　(B) were offering 　　(C) am offered 　　(D) will offer

解 明星老爸說：我將不會出售我剛出生的女兒的獨家照片，即便有人向我提出巨額收購價。我就是不願她生活在媒體顯微鏡般的檢視下。

even if 針對「未來」won't sell 做假設，even if 後方句中的動詞需從未來往前跳一格，改用「現在式」。又「媒體提供我錢」，即「我被媒體提供錢」，主詞 I 需搭配被動式。綜合以上，**C** 選項為正解。

20. When faced with a big challenge, I often hear this advice: Be more confident in yourself. What I think whenever I hear it is: If only it _____ that simple.

(A) has to be      (B) were            (C) will be            (D) had been

解 當面對大挑戰時，我常聽到這個建議：要對自己更有信心些。當我聽到這句話，我總想：但願有這麼簡單就好。

從文意可知，it 代替了「對自己更有信心」這件事。面臨重重挑戰時，這可沒那麼容易。if only 針對「現在」whenever I hear 做相反假設時，緊接在 if only 後方的動詞需從現在往前跳一格，改用「過去式」。且 be 動詞在 if only 句中的過去式也只能用「were」，B 選項為正解。

# Unit 6

倒裝句
## 6 –1 地方副詞，或介副詞放句首的倒裝句

句子的基本架構為：主詞＋動詞＋（地點）；而倒裝句的架構則是反過來：（地點）＋動詞＋主詞，藉由句形變化，加強語氣。本單元介紹的倒裝句分為三類：「地方副詞或介副詞放句首的倒裝句」、「否定副詞放句首的倒裝句」和「特殊倒裝句型」。

地方副詞或介副詞放句首時，需用倒裝句，句型結構如下：

地方副詞 / 介副詞 ＋ 動詞 ＋ 主詞

註 地方副詞或介副詞為首的倒裝句，句中不會出現助動詞喔！

請見下方例句：

例 小女孩去那裏了。（「那裏」為地方副詞）

正常句 The little girl goes there.
主詞　　　　動詞　地點

倒裝句 There goes the little girl.
地點　動詞　　　主詞

倒裝句 There　　she　　goes.
地點　代名詞當主詞　動詞

解 地方副詞「here」或「there」為首的倒裝句，若主詞為「代名詞」時，需將主詞往前提，放在「動詞前」。

例 兩名青少年從便利商店走出來。（「出便利商店」為介副詞）

正常句 Two teens walked out of the convenience store.
主詞　　　動詞　　　地點 / 介副詞

倒裝句 Out of the convenience store walked two teens.
地點 / 介副詞　　　動詞　　主詞

# Unit 6

倒裝句
## 6−2 否定副詞放句首的倒裝句

■ 否定副詞（/ 片語）放句首的倒裝句公式：

除「地方副詞 / 介副詞」為首的倒裝句，句中不會出現助動詞外，其它倒裝句將遵守以下基本結構：

- 否定副詞（/ 片語）＋ 助動詞 ＋ 主詞 ＋ 動詞原形（或 p.p.）…
- 否定副詞（/ 片語）＋ be 動詞 ＋ 主詞…

句中動詞為 be 動詞，就可直接放在主詞前。若句中動詞非 be 動詞，則需搭配助動詞，並將助動詞放在主詞前，同時，後方的動詞現原形。若這助動詞是完成（被動 / 進行）式的助動詞 has / have / had 時，主詞後方的動詞將保持 p.p. / been p.p. / been Ving 型態。

■ 常用的否定副詞（/ 片語）如下：

1. 絕不：never、by no means、under no circumstances、on no account、in no way

2. 幾乎不：seldom、little、rarely、hardly

3. 直到 … 才 …：not until
   註 連接詞 until 後方表時間的句子或副詞寫完後，才開始造倒裝，而非 until 後就緊接倒裝句。且 until 遇到「未來（時間）」，緊接在 until 後方的動詞需用「現在式」。

4. 再也不：no longer

5. 一 … 就 …：no sooner ＋ 句子 1 ＋ than ＋ 句子 2。其中「句子 1」需倒裝。
   即：No sooner ＋（現在 / 過去）完成式助動詞（has / have / had）＋ 主詞 1 ＋ p.p. …＋ than ＋ 主詞 2 ＋ 動詞 2（現在式 / 過去式）
   註 緊接在否定的 no sooner 後，句子 1 應寫成倒裝句。英文基本時態裡，「完成式」比「簡單式」早發生。由於句子 1 比句子 2 早發生，句子 1 的動詞需用完成式，句子 2 的動詞用簡單式。也就是說，若句子 2 為「現在式」，句子 1 則為「現在完成式」；同樣地，若句子 2 為「過去式」，句子 1 則為「過去完成式」。造倒裝時，將完成式中的助動詞 has / have / had 放在主詞前，主詞寫完，再續寫完成式的 p.p.。

6. 不只 ... 而且 ...：not only + 句子 1 , but + 句子 2。其中「句子 1」需倒裝。

即：Not only + be 動詞 1 + 主詞 1...+ but + 主詞 2 + 動詞 2

　　Not only + 助動詞 1 + 主詞 1 + 動詞原形 (或 p.p.) ... + but + 主詞 2 + 動詞 2

註 緊接在否定的 not only 後，第一句應為倒裝句。but also 連接第二句，句子的主詞一定要寫出來。

■ 請見下方否定副詞（/ 片語）為首的倒裝句例句：

例 她將絕對不會原諒你，若你劈腿的話。

正常句 She will never forgive you if you cheat on her.
倒裝句 **Never will she forgive** you if you cheat on her.

倒裝句公式 ▶ 否定副詞 + 助動詞 + 主詞 + 動詞原形...

> 解 否定副詞 never 放句首，需造倒裝句。forgive 不是 be 動詞，造倒裝句時要搭配助動詞。從「將不會原諒」可知應搭配未來式助動詞 will。if 針對「未來」做假設，if 後方句的動詞需從未來往前跳一格，改用「現在式」cheat。

例 我很少看到她這麼沮喪。

正常句 I seldom see her so upset.
倒裝句 **Seldom do I see** her so upset.

倒裝句公式 ▶ 否定副詞 + 助動詞 + 主詞 + 動詞原形...

> 解 否定副詞 seldom 放句首，需造倒裝句。see 不是 be 動詞，造倒裝句時要搭配助動詞 do，後方動詞 see 現原形。

例 直到她向我道歉，我才會跟她說話。

正常句 I won't talk to her until she apologizes to me.

解 從文意可推知：她還沒跟我道歉。連接詞 until 遇到「未來（時間）」will，緊接在 until 後方子句中的動詞需改用「現在式」apologizes。

倒裝句 <u>Not until she apologizes to me</u> **will I talk to her**.
　　　　　　　表時間的句子

倒裝句公式 ▶ 否定時間副詞 + 助動詞 + 主詞 + 動詞原形...

解 否定副詞 not until 放句首，需造倒裝句。但是需先將連接詞 until 後方表時間的句子 she apologizes to me 寫完後，才開始造倒裝。原句 won't 裡的 not 被抽出，和 until 一起搬到句首，倒裝時的助動詞的只剩 will，後方動詞 talk 現原形。

例 我以後再也不會說那些傷人的話了。

正常句 I will no longer say those hurtful words.
倒裝句 **No longer will I say** those hurtful words.

倒裝句公式 ▶ 否定副詞 + 助動詞 + 主詞 + 動詞原形...

解 否定副詞 no longer 放句首，需造倒裝句。say 不是 be 動詞，造倒裝句時要搭配助動詞，且從「以後」可知需用未來式助動詞 will，後方動詞 say 現原形。

例 她一進咖啡廳，大雨就傾盆而下 (bucket down)。

正常句 **As soon as** she **walked** into the café, the heavy rain **bucketed** down.

解 連接詞「一 ... 就 ...」as soon as 連接兩句時，第一句和第二句動詞時態需對稱。walked / bucketed 對稱，兩個都是過去式。唯一例外是當 as soon as 遇到「未來（時間）」時，緊接在 as soon as 後方句的動詞需改用「現在式」。

倒裝句
No sooner **had she walked** into the café than the heavy rain **bucketed** down.

<u>　　　　　　　　　　　　　　</u>　　　　　　　　　　<u>　　　　　　　　　</u>
句子 1 / 倒裝句　　　　　　　　　　　　　　句子 2

## 倒裝句公式 ▶

No sooner + <u>過去完成式助動詞 had + 主詞 1 + p.p.</u> ... than <u>主詞 2 + 過去式</u>

早發生的句子 / 倒裝句　　　　　　　　　　　晚發生的句子

> 解 先進咖啡廳，後下雨。否定的 no sooner 後，應接「早發生」的動作
> 「進咖啡廳」，且造倒裝句。than 後方接「晚發生」的動作「下雨」。
> 英文基本時態裡，「完成式」比「簡單式」早發生。若晚發生的動作
> 「下雨」用「過去式」，早發生的動作「進咖啡廳」就應寫成「過去完成
> 式」。造倒裝時，將過去完成式的助動詞 had 放在主詞 she 前，主
> 詞寫完，再續寫過去分詞 walked。

例 ▶ 他們不只拜訪了台北，還花了一星期探索花蓮。

正常句 They **not only visited** Taipei **but spent** one week exploring Hualien.

> 解 句型「不只 A ... 連 B ...」not only A but (also) B，A 和 B 的詞性、
> 動詞時態需對稱。如上句，visited 和 spent 對稱，都是過去式動
> 詞。

倒裝句 Not only **did they visit** Taipei, but they spent one week exploring Hualien.

<u>　　　　　　　　　　　　　　　　</u>　　　　<u>　　　　　　　　　　　　　　　</u>
句子 1 / 倒裝句　　　　　　　　　　　　句子 2

## 倒裝句公式 ▶

Not only + 助動詞 + 主詞 1 + 動詞原形 ... but 主詞 2 + 動詞 2

緊接在否定的 not only 後，句子 1「拜訪了台北」需寫成倒裝句。but 後方
的句子 2「花了一星期探索花蓮」，不用倒裝，但主詞 2 (they) 一定要寫出
來。visited 不是 be 動詞，造倒裝句時要搭配過去式助動詞 did，後方動詞
visit 現原形。

Unit 1
關係
代名詞

Unit 2
被動
語態

Unit 3
分詞
形容詞

Unit 4
分詞
構句

Unit 5
假設
語法

Unit 6
倒裝
句

Unit 7
間接
問句

Unit 8
特殊
動詞

Unit 9
主動詞
一致

Unit 10
對稱
結構

特別收錄

Unit 11
五回
試題

## 小試身手：請完成下列翻譯題 (藍色字就是需完成的倒裝句)

01. 不論你是 Kevin、Ashley、Mohammed 還是 Felicia，你的名字不只是你身分的重要一部分，也可能大大影響你未來成功與否。

Whether you're a Kevin, Ashley, Mohammed or Felicia, not only _____ _____ an important part of your identity, but _____ _____ your future success greatly.

> **解 倒裝句公式 ▶** Not only + be 動詞 + 主詞 1...but 主詞 2 + 動詞 2
>
> 緊接在否定的 not only 後，句子 1 需寫成倒裝句。but 後方的句子 2，不用倒裝。「是」為 be 動詞，造倒裝句時可直接放在主詞前，第一格：**is your name** 為正解。but 銜接第二句，句子的主詞一定要寫出來，為避免重複，建議用代名詞 it 來代替之前已提過的主詞 your name，後方續接現在式動詞 may impact，第二格：**it may (also) impact** 為正解。

02. 過去漫長的十年裡，特洛伊人堅信他們終於征服了希臘人。但他們幾乎不知道希臘人已有了另一個錦囊妙計。

In the past 10 long years, the Trojans firmly believed they had finally overcome the Greeks. However, little _____ that the Greeks had another trick up their sleeves.

> **解 倒裝句公式 ▶** 否定副詞 + 助動詞 + 主詞 + 動詞原形 ...
>
> 否定副詞 little (幾乎不) 放句首，後方需搭配倒裝句。從 firmly believed / had another 可知需搭配過去式。know 不是 be 動詞，造倒裝句時，需搭配助動詞 did，後方動詞現原形。**did they know** 為正解。

03. 風箏故事的來源就是 Franklin 的朋友—科學家 Joseph Priestley。從他開始，風箏故事有了生命，不斷地演變。但 Franklin 的風箏並沒在任何版本的故事中真地被閃電擊中。

The main source for the kite story is Franklin's friend, scientist Joseph Priestley. From there, the tale took on its own life. In no version of the story, yet, _____ by lightning.

Unit 1
關係
代名詞

Unit 2
被動
語態

Unit 3
分詞
形容詞

Unit 4
分詞
構句

Unit 5
假設
語法

Unit 6
倒裝
句

Unit 7
間接
問句

Unit 8
特殊
動詞

Unit 9
主動詞
一致

Unit 10
對稱
結構

解 **倒裝句公式** ▶ 否定副詞 + be 動詞 + 主詞 ...

否定副詞 in no version 放句首，後方需搭配倒裝句。從 took / depicted 等可知這件事發生於過去，且風箏「被閃電擊中」，需搭配過去被動式。造倒裝句時，be 動詞可直接放在主詞前，**was Franklin's kite really struck (或 stricken)** 為正解。

04. 絕不應該讓難民的弱勢（vulnerability）被用來當作剝奪他們基本權利的理由。難民們應該受保護，免於虐待、剝削和歧視。

Under no circumstances _____
as a reason to deny them their basic rights. They should be protected from abuse, exploitation and discrimination.

解 **倒裝句公式** ▶ 否定副詞 + 助動詞 + 主詞 + 動詞原形...

否定副詞 under no circumstances 放句首，後方需搭配倒裝句。難民的弱勢「被用來」當作可欺負他們的理由，需搭配被動式。句中有助動詞 should（應該），套公式：**should the vulnerability of the refugees be used** 為正解。

05. 主唱一躍上（hop）舞台，表演月球漫步（moon walk）時，歌迷們就陷入（erupt into）了瘋狂。

No sooner _____
_____ a frenzy.

解 **倒裝句公式** ▶
No sooner + 過去完成助動詞 had + 主詞 1 + p.p. ... than 主詞 2 + 過去式
　　　　　　早發生的句子 / 倒裝　　　　　　　　　　晚發生的句子
主唱先躍上舞台表演，歌迷才為之瘋狂。否定的 no sooner 後，應接「早發生」的動作「躍上舞台表演」，且造倒裝句。than 後方接「晚發生」的動作「歌迷瘋狂」。英文基本時態裡，「完成式」比「簡單式」早發生。若晚發生的動作「陷入瘋狂」用「過去式」，早發生的動作「躍上舞台表演」就應寫成「過去完成式」。套公式：**had the lead singer hopped onto the stage and performed moon walk than the audience erupted into** 為正解。

06. 你幾乎不能夠消除網路上關於你的負面評論，除非你在法庭上成功提起毀謗告訴，且取得法院命令。　註 能夠：be able to V 原

Rarely _____ those negative comments about you from the Internet unless you successfully sue in court for libel and get a court order.

> **解 倒裝句公式 ▶ 否定副詞 + be 動詞 + 主詞 …**
>
> 否定副詞 rarely（幾乎不）放句首，後方需搭配倒裝句。從 sue / get 可知本句為現在式。片語「能夠」be able to 動詞原形。造倒裝句時，將 be 動詞 are 放在主詞 you 前，**are you able to erase** 為正解。

07. 這些社工的許多努力背後是一個令人感到憤憤不平的 (bitter) 爭論—為何即便有全額健保的病患仍然受到癌症照護鉅額開銷的影響。

Behind enormous efforts of these social workers_____ over why even those patients with full healthcare insurance still get hit with extraordinary costs for cancer care.

> **解 倒裝句公式 ▶ 地方副詞 / 介副詞 + 動詞 + 主詞**
>
> 表地點的介副詞 behind … workers 放句首，可造倒裝句。單數主詞「一個爭論」，搭配單數 be 動詞。從 still get 可知，本句為現在式。套公式：**is a bitter dispute** 為正解。

08. 多數人直到他們失去健康時才了解健康的重要性。

Not until _____ the importance of it.

> **解 倒裝句公式 ▶ 否定時間副詞 + 助動詞 + 主詞 + 動詞原形 …**
>
> 否定詞 not until 放句首，後方需搭配倒裝句。但需先完成連接詞 until 後方表時間的句子「他們失去健康時」，將時間點說明清楚後，才開始造倒裝。understand 不是 be 動詞，造倒裝句時要搭配助動詞。套公式：**they lose their health will most people understand** 為正解。

09. 我們絕對不抱怨我們遊牧民族般的生活型態。身為旅遊部落客，我們知道自己多幸運，可不斷四處遊覽。

In no way _____ about our nomadic lifestyle. We, as travel bloggers, know just how lucky we are to be in a position to travel endlessly.

> 解 **倒裝句公式** ▶ 否定副詞 + 助動詞 + 主詞 + 動詞原形 …
>
> 否定副詞 in no way 放句首，後方需搭配倒裝句。complain 不是 be 動詞，造倒裝句時要搭配助動詞。從 know / we are 可知，本句為現在式。套公式：**do we complain** 為正解。

10. 不只食物已準備好了，連餐桌都已擺設完成 (lay)。

Not only _____,

but _____

> 解 **倒裝句公式** ▶ Not only + 助動詞 + 主詞 1… but 主詞 2 + 動詞 2
>
> 緊接在否定詞 not only 後，句子 1「食物已準備好了」需寫成倒裝句。but 後方的句子 2「餐桌都已擺設完成」，不用倒裝，但主詞 2 (餐桌) 一定要寫出來。從「已」推知需用「完成式」。食物「被準備」、餐桌「被擺設」，需搭配被動式。所以造倒裝句時，將現在完成被動式的助動詞 has，放在主詞 the food 前。套公式：**has the food been prepared / the table has been laid** 為正解。
>
> 註 lay (v) 擺放；lay – laid – laid – laying

11. 她一升官 (promote) 就開始表現得很高傲 (arrogantly)。她似乎以「那真蠢！」或「你是個頭腦簡單、四肢發達的人」這一類的話來貶低他人為樂。

No sooner _____
_____. She seems to take delight in putting down others with phrases like "that's stupid" or "you're a bozo."

> 解 **倒裝句公式** ▶
>
> No sooner + 現在完成式助動詞 has + 主詞 1 + p.p. … than 主詞 2 + 現在式
> <u>　　　　早發生的句子 / 倒裝　　　　</u>　　　<u>　　晚發生的句子　　</u>
>
> 先升官，後高傲。否定的 no sooner 後，應接「早發生」的動作「被拔擢

Unit 1
關係
代名詞

Unit 2
被動
語態

Unit 3
分詞
形容詞

Unit 4
分詞
構句

Unit 5
假設
語法

Unit 6
倒裝
句

Unit 7
間接
問句

Unit 8
特殊
動詞

Unit 9
主動詞
一致

Unit 10
對稱
結構

特別收錄
Unit 11
五回
試題

升官」，且造倒裝句。than 後方接「晚發生」的動作「表現高傲」。英文基本時態裡，「完成式」比「簡單式」早發生。若晚發生的動作「表現高傲」用「現在式」，早發生的動作「被拔擢升官」就應寫成「現在完成被動式」。套公式：**has she been promoted than she begins to act arrogantly** 為正解。

12. 車禍不只粉碎 (shatter) 了她成為舞者的夢想，也讓她往後的人生蒙上了陰影 (cast a shadow over N)。

Not only _____ her dream of becoming a dancer, but _____ a shadow over the rest of her life.

> 解 **倒裝句公式** ▶
>
> Not only + 助動詞 + 主詞 1 + 動詞原形...but 主詞 2 + 動詞 2
>
> 緊接在否定的 not only 後，句子 1「車禍粉碎夢想」需寫成倒裝句。but 後方的句子 2「車禍讓人生蒙上陰影」，不用倒裝，但主詞 2 (the accident) 一定要寫出來。從文意可知車禍已發生，得用「過去式」。shatter 不是 be 動詞，造倒裝句時需搭配「助動詞」。第一格，套公式：**did the accident shatter** 為正解。but 銜接第二句，為避免重複，建議用代名詞 it 來代替之前已提過的主詞 the accident。第二句，套公式：**it cast** 為正解。
>
> 註 cast (v) 投 / 丟；cast – cast – cast – casting。

13. 我一放開繩子，那些氣球就往上飛 (go up)，高升入空。

As soon as I let go of the string, up _____, high into the sky.

> 解 **倒裝句公式** ▶ 地方副詞 / 介副詞 + 動詞 + 主詞
>
> 表地點的介副詞 up 放句首時，後方造倒裝句，但不會出現助動詞。let 可能是現在式或過去式，套公式：**go those balloons** 或 **went those balloons** 都是正解。

14. 直到這家餐廳提升食材、環境還有員工的衛生，我才會去那用餐。

Not until _____

_____ dine there.

解 **倒裝句公式** ▶ 否定時間副詞 + 助動詞 + 主詞 + 動詞原形…

否定詞 not until 放句首，後方需搭配倒裝句。但需先完成連接詞 until 後方表時間的句子「餐廳提升食材、環境還有員工衛生」。將時間點說明清楚後，才開始造倒裝。dine 不是 be 動詞，造倒裝句時要搭配助動詞，而去用餐是等餐廳改善後才會做的事，可搭配「未來式」。連接詞 until 遇到「未來（時間）」will，緊接在 until 後方句中的動詞需改用「現在式」。套公式：**the restaurant improves the hygiene of their ingredients, environment and employees will I** 為正解。

15. 我一星期都沒睡好。我覺得筋疲力竭。我幾乎不能睜開我的眼睛。註 能夠 can

Not having proper sleep for one week, I am feeling exhausted. Barely _____
_____.

解 **倒裝句公式** ▶ 否定副詞 + 助動詞 + 主詞 + 動詞原形…

否定副詞 barely（幾乎不）放句首，後方需搭配倒裝句。從 am feeling 可知本句為現在式。片語「讓某人 / 某物…」keep + N + adj。keep 不是 be 動詞，造倒裝句時要搭配助動詞。套公式：**can I keep my eyes open** 為正解。

16. 多年來，這名超級馬拉松（ultramarathon）選手從沒停止練習，即便他的腳又腫又痛。

For so many years, never _____
practice for one single day, even if his feet are swollen and sore.

解 **倒裝句公式** ▶ 否定副詞 + 助動詞 + 主詞 + p.p….

否定副詞 never 放句首，後方需搭配倒裝句。從 for so many years 可知，一段時間，應搭配「現在完成式」。套公式：**has this ultramarathon runner stopped** 為正解。

17. 玩當紅遊戲「寶可夢」時，一名少年十分驚恐地發現河岸邊躺著一具身首異處且被砸爛的屍體。

While playing the now popular game, "Pokemon Go," a teenage boy was utterly shocked and terrified to discover that on the river bank _____ _____, mutilated and battered.

> **解 倒裝句公式** ▶ 地方副詞 / 介副詞 + 動詞 + 主詞
>
> 關係代名詞 that 帶出了一個以地方副詞 on the river bank 為首的倒裝句。地點為首的倒裝句，句中為 1 字動詞，不會出現助動詞。從 was 可推知本句應用「過去式」。套公式：**lay a dead body** 為正解。
>
> **註** lie (v) 躺；lie – lay – lain – lying。屍體「被弄得支離破碎」、「被重擊砸爛」，需搭配表被動的 p.p. 形容詞 mutilated / battered。

18. 番薯 (sweet potatoes) 不只富含纖維質 (fiber)，而且有低的升糖指數。這意味著番薯消化得慢，食用後可讓你長時間有飽足感。

Not only_____, but _____a low glycemic index. This means they are digested slowly and will keep you feeling satiated long after your meal.

> **解 倒裝句公式** ▶ Not only + be 動詞 + 主詞 1 ... but 主詞 2 + 動詞 2
>
> 緊接在否定的 not only 後，句子 1「番薯富含纖維質」需寫成倒裝句。but 後方的句子 2「番薯有低升糖指數」，不用倒裝，但主詞 2 (sweet potatoes) 一定要寫出來。說明番薯的特質，需用「現在式」。片語「富含」be rich in N。造倒裝句時，be 動詞放在主詞 sweet potatoes 前。第一格，套公式：**are sweet potatoes rich in fiber** 為正解。but 銜接第二句，為避免重複，建議用代名詞 they 來代替之前已提過的主詞 sweet potatoes。第二句，套公式：**they have** 為正解。

19. 未取得原本版權擁有者的許可時，你絕對不能複製他的圖像到你的網站上。

Without obtaining the permission of the original rights owner, on no account _____ his images onto your own website.

> **解 倒裝句公式** ▶ 否定副詞 + 助動詞 + 主詞 + 動詞原形...

否定片語 on no account 放句首，後方需搭配倒裝句。copy 不是 be 動詞，造倒裝句時要搭配助動詞。助動詞「能夠」即 can。套公式：**can you copy** 為正解。

20. 直到調查完成，警方才會針對這宗致命的校園槍擊案做出評論。

Not until ＿＿＿＿＿＿＿＿＿＿＿＿＿＿＿＿＿＿＿＿＿＿＿

comments on this fatal campus shooting.

解 **倒裝句公式** ▶ 否定時間副詞 + 助動詞 + 主詞 + 動詞原形...

否定詞 not until 放句首，後方需搭配倒裝句。但需先完成連接詞 until 後方表時間的句子「調查被完成」，將時間點說明清楚後，才開始造倒裝。「做評論」(make comments on N) 不是 be 動詞，造倒裝句時要搭配助動詞。又評論是等調查完成後才會做的事，可搭配「未來式」。連接詞 until 遇到「未來 (時間)」will，緊接在 until 後方子句中的動詞需改用「現在式」。套公式：**the investigation is finished will the police make** 為正解。

# Unit 6

倒裝句
## 6－3 其他特殊倒裝句句型

這節要討論的特殊倒裝句句型涵蓋：so、such 為首的「如此地...以致於...」倒裝句、only 為首的倒裝句、表附和的倒裝句，以及比較級 than 後方的倒裝句。

■ so、such 為首的「如此地 ... 以致於 ...」倒裝句

「如此地 ... 以致於 ...」句型中的 so、such 放句首時，緊接 so、such 後方的句子需寫成倒裝句，但關代 that 後方句則不需倒裝。so、such 倒裝句公式如下：

- So + 形容詞 + be 動詞 + 主詞 1 + that + 主詞 2 + 動詞 2
- Such + be 動詞 + 主詞 1 + that + 主詞 2 + 動詞 2

so、such 後方倒裝句中的動詞都是「be 動詞」。原本 such 後方應搭配名詞，但因主詞也是名詞，所以乾脆 such 後方名詞省略，等到寫主詞時再一次寫齊。請看下方例句：

例 Jack 是如此地驚訝，以致於他根本說不出話來。

正常句　　Jack was so surprised that he couldn't say a word.

倒裝句 1　So surprised　was　he　that he　couldn't say a word.
　　　　　　形容詞　　　動詞 1　主詞 1　　主詞 2　　動詞 2

倒裝句 2　Such was　his surprise　that he　couldn't say a word.
　　　　　　動詞 1　　主詞 1　　　　主詞 2　　　動詞 2

解 Jack 覺得如此驚訝，所以驚訝這心情是他所擁有的，故用 his surprise 來當 such 倒裝句的主詞。

■ only 搭配副詞、副詞子句或片語為首的倒裝句

only（只要 ...）可搭配副詞、副詞子句或片語，如：only after、only then、only when、only by Ving、only in this way 等放句首，得造倒裝句，遵守基本倒裝句公式：

- Only 副詞 + 助動詞 + 主詞 + 動詞原形（或 p.p.）

- Only 副詞 + be 動詞 + 主詞 ...

若 only 後方搭配是的和時間相關的連接詞，如：when 或 after 等，需先完成連接詞 when 或 after 後方表時間的句子，將時間點說明清楚後，才開始造倒裝句。

請見下方例句：

例 只有當你去的時候我才會去。

> 正常句 I will go only when you go.

> 解 連接詞 when 遇到「未來」will，緊接在 when 後方句中的動詞需改用「現在式」。

> 倒裝句 Only when you go will I go.

> 倒裝句公式 ▶ Only when 表時間的句子 + 助動詞 + 主詞 + 動詞原形...

> 解 造倒裝句時，需寫完連接詞 only when 後方表時間的句子「只有當你去的時候」，將時間點說明清楚後，才開始造倒裝。go 不是 be 動詞，造倒裝句時要搭配助動詞。且從文意看來，這個句子是用來預設以後的狀況，可搭配未來式助動詞 will。

例 蝙蝠只有在晚上才會離開洞穴。

> 正常句 Bats leave their caves only at night.

> 解 蝙蝠的習性，幾乎不太會改變，故用「現在式」。

> 倒裝句 Only at night do bats leave their caves.

> 倒裝句公式 ▶ Only + 時間副詞 + 助動詞 + 主詞 + 動詞原形...

> **解** 造倒裝句時，需先寫完表時間的副詞「只有在晚上時」，將時間點說明清楚後，才開始造倒裝。leave 不是 be 動詞，造倒裝句時，可搭配現在式助動詞 do。

**例** 只有藉著努力唸書你才可能考好。

正常句　You are able to do well on the test only by studying hard.

> **解** 介係詞「藉著」by，後方需搭配動名詞 Ving

倒裝句　Only by studying hard are you able to do well on the tests.

倒裝句公式 ▶ Only by Ving ... + be 動詞 + 主詞...

> **解** 先將「藉著...」方法，即「藉著努力讀書」寫完後，才開始造倒裝。片語「能夠」be able to 動詞原形。造倒裝句時，be 動詞可直接放在主詞前。

■ 附和前一句的「也」/「也不」倒裝句

附和肯定句的「也」，共有兩種寫法：副詞 so，後方需搭配倒裝句。或副詞 too 放句尾，too 前方打上逗號。附和否定句的「也不」，也有兩種寫法：副詞 neither 後方搭配「去掉 not」的倒裝句，避免雙重否定。或副詞 either 放句尾，either 前方再打上逗號。

□ 附和句的公式如下：

**附和肯定句**

- 肯定句，and 主詞 + be 動詞 / 助動詞 , too
- 肯定句，and so + be 動詞 / 助動詞 + 主詞

**附和否定句**

- 否定句，and 主詞 + be 動詞 / 助動詞 + not, either
- 否定句，and neither + be 動詞 / 助動詞 + 主詞

□ 造附和句時，需特別注意以下幾個原則：

1. 若前方句子使用 be 動詞，附和句就會跟著使用 be 動詞。若前方句子使用助動詞，那麼附和句就會跟著使用助動詞。若前方句子使用一般動詞，那麼附和句就搭配和前一句一般動詞相同時態的助動詞。助動詞後方不需將和第一句重複的動詞原形或過去分詞寫出來。總結來說，附和句中，動詞部分的處理原則和「造簡答句」相同，寫到 be 動詞／助動詞為止。

2. neither（也不）後方的倒裝句，不能有 not，因為要避免兩個否定合起來變成肯定。而附和否定句的 either 則不受此規範，因為 either 前方有逗號，將 not 和 either 隔開，這樣就不會造成因為雙重否定而反轉語義的情形。

例▶ 你肚子很餓，而我也是。

正常句  You are hungry and **I am, too**.

> 解 「你肚子很餓」為肯定句，附和時，可用肯定的副詞「也」too。第一句用 be 動詞寫成，too 附和句也跟著用 be 動詞，並在 too 前方打上逗號。

倒裝句  You are hungry, and **so am I**.

> 解 「你肚子很餓」為肯定句，附和時，也可用肯定的副詞「也」so，但 so 後方句需「倒裝」。第一句用 be 動詞寫成，so 倒裝句也跟著用 be 動詞，並將 am 放在主詞 I 前。

例▶ Alice 已經取得街頭藝人證照，而我也是。

正常句  Alice has got a street performer permit and **I have, too**.

> 解 「Alice 已取得...」為肯定句，附和時，可搭配肯定的副詞「也」too。第一句用現在完成式助動詞 has 寫成，too 附和句也跟著用現在完成式助動詞，主詞 I，搭配 have，並在 too 前方打上逗號。

倒裝句 Alice has got a street performer permit and **so have I**.

> 解 「Alice 已取得...」為肯定句，附和時，也可搭配副詞「也」so，但 so 後方句需「倒裝」。第一句用現在完成式助動詞 has 寫成，故 so 倒裝句也跟著用現在完成式助動詞，並將助動詞 have 放在主詞 I 前。

注意：Alice has got a street performer permit, and so have I got...（x）

> 解 將過去分詞 got 寫出來是錯誤的。so 倒裝句，動詞部分的處理原則和「造簡答句」相同，寫到 be 動詞 / 助動詞為止。

例 Jack 在退休五年內破產，而我也是。

正常句 Jack went broke within five years of retirement, and **I did, too**.

> 解 「Jack 破產」為肯定句，附和時，可搭配肯定的副詞「也」too。第一句用過去式 went 寫成，too 附和句用過去式助動詞 did，取代重複的動詞 went。並在 too 前方打上逗號。

倒裝句 Jack went broke within 5 years of retirement, and **so did I**.

> 解 「Jack 破產」為肯定句，附和時，也可搭配副詞「也」so，但 so 後方句需「倒裝」。第一句用過去式動詞 went 寫成，故 so 倒裝句則搭配過去式助動詞 did，用助動詞 did 取代重複的動詞 went。並將助動詞 did 放在主詞 I 前。

注意：Jack went broke within five years of retirement, and so did I go broke....（x）

> 解 將動詞 go broke 寫出來是錯誤的。so 倒裝句，動詞部分的處理原則和「造簡答句」相同，寫到 be 動詞 / 助動詞為止。

例 我不想讓焚化爐在這興建，其他當地居民也是。

正常句 I didn't want the incinerator to be built here, and **other local residents didn't, either**.

解 「我不想...」為否定句，附和時，需搭配否定的副詞「也不」either。第一句用過去式助動詞 didn't 寫成，either 附和句也跟著用過去式助動詞 didn't，並在 either 前方打上逗號。

倒裝句 I didn't want the incinerator to be built here, and **neither did other local residents**.

解 「我不想...」為否定句，附和時，也可搭配副詞「也不」neither，但 neither 後方句需「倒裝」。第一句用否定的過去式助動詞 didn't 寫成，neither 倒裝句雖然也跟著用過去式助動詞，但需去除 not，以避免 neither didn't 合起來變成肯定。接著將過去式助動詞 did 放在主詞 other local residents 前。

注意：I didn't want the incinerator to be built here, and neither didn't other local residents want............................................. (x)

解 將動詞 want 寫出來是錯誤的。neither 倒裝句，動詞部分的處理原則和「造簡答句」相同，寫到 be 動詞 / 助動詞為止。neither 倒裝句出現 not，也是錯的。neither（也不），加上 not，雙重否定會造成語意反轉。但 either 則不受此規範，因為 either 前方有逗號，將 not 和 either 隔開，就不會混淆語意。

例 我還沒完成我的歷史報告，而 Jane 也是。

正常句 I haven't finished my history report, and **Jane hasn't, either**.

解 「我還沒...」為否定句，附和時，需搭配否定的副詞「也不」either。第一句用現在完成式助動詞 haven't 寫成，either 附和句也跟著用現在完成式助動詞。主詞 Jane，搭配現在式助動詞 hasn't，並在 either 前方打上逗號。

倒裝句 I haven't finished my history report, and **neither has Jane**.

> 解 「我還沒...」為否定句，附和時，也可搭配副詞「也不」neither，但 neither 後方句需「倒裝」。第一句用現在完成式助動詞 haven't 寫成，neither 倒裝句雖然也跟著用現在完成式助動詞，但需去除 not，以避免 neither hasn't 合起來變成肯定。接著將現在完成式助動詞 has 放在主詞 Jane 前。

注意：I haven't finished my history report, and neither hasn't Jane
finished……（x）

> 解 將動詞 finished 寫出來是錯誤的。neither 倒裝句，動詞部分的處理原則和「造簡答句」相同，寫到 be 動詞 / 助動詞為止。neither 倒裝句裏出現 not，也是錯的。neither（也不），加上 not，雙重否定會造成語意反轉。但 either 則不受此規範，因為 either 前方有逗號，將 not 和 either 隔開，就不會混淆語意。

■ 比較用的 as / than 倒裝句

常出現在原級裡的 as，表「一樣... / 就像...」之意，放句首時，後方需倒裝。而比較級 than 後方的句子，一般採直說法，但若想加強語氣，則可寫成倒裝句。

□ as / than 帶出來的倒裝句公式如下：

- ..., as + be 動詞 / 助動詞 + 主詞
- ... than + be 動詞 / 助動詞 + 主詞

□ 造 as / than 倒裝句時，需特別注意以下幾個原則：

若前方句子使用 be 動詞，那麼 as / than 倒裝句就會跟著使用 be 動詞。若前方句子使用助動詞，那麼 as / than 倒裝句就會跟著使用助動詞。又若前方句子使用一般動詞，那麼 as / than 倒裝句就搭配和前一句一般動詞相同時態的助動詞。總結起來，as / than 倒裝句中，動詞部分的處理原則和「造簡答句」相同，寫到 be 動詞 / 助動詞為止。請見下方例句：

例 假如被丟入水中的話,熊會游泳,狗也一樣。

If thrown into water, bears can swim, **as can dogs**.
= If thrown into water, bears can swim, **and dogs can, too**.
= If thrown into water, bears can swim, **and so can dogs**.

> 解 as 表「一樣 ... / 就像 ...」之意,放句首時,後方需倒裝。前方句子使用了助動詞 can,故 as 後方的倒裝句也沿用助動詞 can。助動詞 can 放在主詞 dogs 前,造倒裝句。

注意:If thrown into water, bears can swim, as can dogs swim.... (x)

> 解 將動詞原形 swim 寫出來是錯誤的。as 倒裝句,動詞部分的處理原則和「造簡答句」相同,寫到 be 動詞 / 助動詞為止。

例 研究顯示,父母比小孩看更多電視。

The study shows that parents watch more TV **than their children do**.
= The study shows that parents watch more TV **than do their children**.

> 解 比較級 than 後方的句子,可採直說法,但若想加強語氣,則可寫成倒裝句。前方句子使用了現在式動詞 watch,故 than 後方句子就需搭配現在式助動詞。複數主詞 children,搭配現在式助動詞 do。用助動詞 do 取代重複的動詞 watch, 避免重複累贅。若想加強語氣,可將助動詞 do 放在主詞 their children 前,造倒裝句。

注意:The study shows that parents watch more TV
　　　 than do their children watch ... (x)
　　　 than watch their children ........ (x)

> 解 將動詞 (原形) watch 寫出來是錯誤的。than 倒裝句,動詞部分的處理原則和「造簡答句」相同,寫到 be 動詞 / 助動詞為止。

## 小試身手：請完成下列翻譯題 （藍色字就是需完成的倒裝句）

01. 我們覺得如此的不滿 (annoyance) ，以致於我們拒絕和他們進一步合作。

Such _____ we refuse to cooperate with them further.

> **解** 倒裝句公式 ▶ Such + be 動詞 + 主詞 1 + that + 主詞 2 + 動詞 2
>
> 「我們覺得不滿」，不滿這情緒是我們的，故 **is our annoyance that** 為正解。

02. 身為發明家，Franklin 創造了許多大家迫切需要，且目前仍在使用的物品。雙焦眼鏡是他大受歡迎的發明品，而避雷針也是。

As an inventor, Franklin created many much-needed items that are still in current use today. Bifocals are a popular invention of his, _____ _____ the lightning rod.

> **解** 倒裝句公式 ▶ and so + be 動詞 / 助動詞 + 主詞
>
> 避雷針「也是」Franklin 的發明品。附和肯定句的「也」，有 so / too 兩種寫法，但 too 只能放句尾。從句尾沒看到 too 可知本句是用副詞 so 寫成的，so 後方需搭配倒裝句。第一句使用現在式 be 動詞 are，那麼 so 附和句就會跟著使用現在式 be 動詞。單數主詞 lightning rod，搭配單數 be 動詞 is，套公式：**and so is** 為正解。也可寫成 as is。

03. 只有當病患同意 (consent) 將他的醫療紀錄和其他特定的 (specific) 醫療照護單位分享時，醫院才能透露 (disclose) 他的醫療資訊。

Only when _____ _____ his treatment information.

> **解** 倒裝句公式 ▶ Only when 表時間的句子 + 助動詞 + 主詞 + 動詞原形
>
> only 放句首，需造倒裝句，但得先寫完連接詞 when 後方表時間的句子「當病患同意 ...」，將時間點說明清楚後，才能開始倒裝。disclose 不是 be 動詞，造倒裝句時得搭配助動詞。套公式：**a patient consents to**

share his medical records with other specific healthcare providers can a hospital disclose 為正解。

Unit 1
關係
代名詞

Unit 2
被動
語態

Unit 3
分詞
形容詞

Unit 4
分詞
構句

Unit 5
假設
語法

Unit 6
倒裝
句

Unit 7
間接
問句

Unit 8
特殊
動詞

Unit 9
主動詞
一致

Unit 10
對稱
結構

特別收錄
Unit 11
五回
試題

04. 受鑽油計畫影響的海豹和鯨魚為數不少，而這計畫對環境的衝擊也不小。

The numbers of seals and whales affected by the oil drilling plan are not small, _____.

解 倒裝句公式 ▶ and neither + be 動詞 / 助動詞 + 主詞。

鑽油計畫對環境的衝擊「也不」小。附和否定句的「也不」，有 either / neither 兩種寫法，但副詞 either 只能放句尾，從句尾沒看到 either 可知本句是用副詞 neither 寫成的。neither 後方需搭配倒裝句。第一句使用現在式 be 動詞 are，那麼 neither 附和句就會跟著使用現在式 be 動詞。單數主詞 its impact，搭配單數現在式 be 動詞 is。套公式：**and neither is its impact on the environment** 為正解。也可用複數寫：**and neither are its impacts on the environment**。

註 neither 倒裝句中不可出現 not，雙重否定會造成語意反轉。its 指 the plan's。

05. 只有當你給我們更大的 (deeper) 折扣時，我們才有可能接受這宗交易。

Only if _____
_____ accept this deal.

解 倒裝句公式 ▶ Only if 表條件的句子 + 助動詞 + 主詞 + 動詞原形

only 放句首，需造倒裝句，但先寫完 if 條件子句後，才能開始倒裝。accept 不是 be 動詞，造倒裝句時得搭配助動詞。接受交易是「未來」的事，if 針對「未來」做假設，緊接在 if 後方的動詞從未來往前跳一格，改用「現在式」。倒裝時，將助動詞 will 放在主詞前。套公式：**you give us deeper discounts will we possibly** 為正解。若用片語「可能」be likely to 動詞原形，那麼造倒裝句時，就需將 be 動詞 are 放在主詞前。套公式：**you give us deeper discounts are we likely to** 也是正解。

06. 專業體育的風險逐漸升高，而支付給運動員的錢也節節高升。

The stakes in professional sports are rising, _____
_____ paid to athletes.

> **解** 倒裝句公式 ▶ and so + be 動詞 / 助動詞 + 主詞
>
> 支付給運動員的錢「也」上升。附和肯定句的「也」，有 so / too 兩種寫
> 法，但 too 只能放句尾。從句尾沒看到 too 可知本句是用副詞 so 寫成的。
> so 後方需搭配倒裝句。第一句使用現在式 be 動詞 are，那麼 so 附和句
> 就會跟著使用現在式 be 動詞。單數主詞 the money，需搭配單數現在
> 式 be 動詞 is。套公式：**and so is the money** 為正解。
>
> **註** paid 為表被動的 p.p. 形容詞。

07. 馬鈴薯可煮、可烤、可炸，是種多變的蔬菜。更棒的是，馬鈴薯還能比其它
作物更迅速地做成營養的食物。（用倒裝句寫）

Boiled, baked or fried, the potato is a versatile vegetable. What's better, it
also produces nutritious food quicker than _____.

> **解** 倒裝句公式 ▶ ... than + be 動詞 / 助動詞 + 主詞
>
> 為了加強語氣，than 後方可搭配倒裝句。than 前方句使用現在式動詞
> produces，那麼 than 後方的倒裝句就需搭配現在式助動詞。套公式：
> **do other crops** 為正解。
>
> **註** than 倒裝句，動詞部分的處理原則和「造簡答句」相同，寫到 be 動詞 /
> 助動詞為止。

08. 天氣是如此地惡劣（nasty），以致於我們八天的巴黎之旅大多在室內度過。

So _____ we spent most of
our time indoors during our eight-day trip to Paris.

> **解** 倒裝句公式 ▶ So + 形容詞 + be 動詞 + 主詞 1 + that + 主詞 2 + 動詞 2
>
> so 放句首時，so 後方句需倒裝，但是關代 that 後方句則不需倒裝。從
> spent 可知，本句需用過去式。套公式：**nasty was the weather that**
> 為正解。

09. 你必須用使用者名稱和密碼來驗證你的身分。只有在那時，才能被給予 (grant) 管道 (access) 來登入該購物網站。

A username and password must be used to verify your identity. Only then _____ to log on to the shopping website.

> 解 倒裝句公式 ▶ Only then + be 動詞 + 主詞 + p.p.
>
> 主詞 the access 是「被給予」的，需搭配被動式。套公式：**is the access granted** 為正解。或 **can you be granted the access** 也可。

10. 這些雇主對員工是如此地苛刻 (harsh)，以致於罷工變得相當頻繁。

So _____ strikes become quite frequent.

> 解 倒裝句公式 ▶ So + 形容詞 + be 動詞 + 主詞 1 + that + 主詞 2 + 動詞 2
>
> so 放句首時，so 後方句需倒裝，但關代 that 後方句則不需倒裝。從 become 可知本句應用現在式。複數主詞 employers，搭配複數現在式 be 動詞 are。套公式：**harsh are the employers on their employees that** 為正解。

11. 公司有動機雇用打工族，因為五個臨時員工做一份工作，遠比一個正職 (full-time) 員工做那份工作來得便宜多了。（用倒裝句寫）

Companies have an incentive to use part-time workers because five people working the same position on a part-time basis are much less expensive than _____.

> 解 倒裝句公式 ▶ ... than + be 動詞 / 助動詞 + 主詞
>
> 為了加強語氣，than 後方可搭配倒裝句。than 前方句使用現在式 be 動詞 are，那麼 than 後方的倒裝句就需搭配現在式 be 動詞。單數主詞「一名正職員工」，搭配單數現在式 be 動詞 is。員工自己會工作，可搭配強調「主動進行」的 Ving 形容詞 doing。套公式：**is a full-time employee doing that job** 為正解。

Unit 1
關係
代名詞

Unit 2
被動
語態

Unit 3
分詞
形容詞

Unit 4
分詞
構句

Unit 5
假設
語法

Unit 6
倒裝
句

Unit 7
間接
問句

Unit 8
特殊
動詞

Unit 9
主動詞
一致

Unit 10
對稱
結構

特別收錄
Unit 11
五回
試題

12. 只有藉著忽略發明家愛迪生對世界的諸多貢獻，才可能簡潔扼要地概述他的一生。

Only _____
a brief summary of the life of Thomas Edison possible.

> **解 倒裝句公式 ▶ Only by Ving ... + be 動詞 + 主詞...**
>
> 介係詞「藉著」by，後方需搭配動名詞 Ving。整個句子缺動詞，故補上「be 動詞」。單數主詞 a brief summary，搭配單數 be 動詞 is。套公式：**by ignoring his numerous contributions to the world is** 為正解。

13. 彗星 (comet) 鮮少 (rarely) 肉眼可見，以致於每當這種彗星出現時，總能吸引來自世界各地的天文迷。

So _____
when one is, it never fails to draw astronomy fans from all over the world.

> **解 倒裝句公式 ▶ So + 副詞 + be 動詞 + 主詞 1 + that + 主詞 2 + 動詞 2**
>
> 從 fails 可知本句應用現在式。加強形容詞 invisible（看得見的）得用副詞 rarely（鮮少 / 幾乎不）。so 放句首時，後方句需倒裝，但關代 that 後方句則不需倒裝。套公式：**rarely is a comet visible to the naked eye that** 為正解。代名詞 one，代替 a comet。

14. 我們向前聯合國主席 Kofi Annan 致意。他處理事情時的冷靜和堅定將永遠被記得，他的專注投入也會被記得。

We pay tribute to Kofi Annan, the former UN chief. His calm and resolute approach to matters will always be remembered, _____
_____ his commitments.

> **解 倒裝句公式 ▶ and so + be 動詞 / 助動詞 + 主詞**
>
> 專注投入「也」被記得。附和肯定句的「也」，有 too / so 兩種寫法，但副詞 too 只能放句尾。從句尾沒看到 too 可知本句是用副詞 so 寫成的。so 後方需搭配倒裝句。第一句使用助動詞 will，那麼 so 附和句就會跟著使用助動詞 will。套公式：**and so will** 為正解。

15. 我同意，而我女友也一樣 (as)：我們不是藉由找到完美的人而愛上彼此，而是藉著學會如何將不完美的人視為完美。

I agree, _____, that we come to love each other not by finding a perfect person, but by learning to see an imperfect person perfectly.

> **解** 倒裝句公式 ▶ ..., as + be 動詞 / 助動詞 + 主詞
>
> 常出現在原級裡的 as，表「一樣 ... / 就像 ...」之意，放句首時，後方需倒裝。前方句使用現在式動詞 agree，後方倒裝句需搭配現在式助動詞。單數主詞 my girlfriend，搭配單數現在式助動詞 does。套公式：**as does my girlfriend** 為正解。

16. 黃金這類的貴金屬很罕見，創意和想像力等某些 (certain) 個人特質，在電影產業也很罕見。

Precious metals like gold are rare, _____ _____, including originality and imagination in the film business.

> **解** 倒裝句公式 ▶ and so + be 動詞 / 助動詞 + 主詞
>
> 從 are 可知本句應用現在式。創意等「也」罕見。附和肯定句的「也」，有 so / too 兩種寫法，但 too 只能放句尾。從句尾沒看到 too 可知本句是用副詞 so 寫成的。so 後方需搭配倒裝句。第一句使用現在式 be 動詞 are，那麼 so 附和句就會跟著使用現在式 be 動詞。複數主詞 certain personal characteristics，搭配複數現在式 be 動詞 are。套公式：**and so are certain personal characteristics** 為正解。

17. 解譯古文字的專家提到：印度文明的手稿 (script) 比其他文明 (civilization) 的手稿更難解譯。

Experts deciphering ancient written languages mention that the Indus civilization's script is more difficult to decode than _____ _____.

> **解** 倒裝句公式 ▶ ... than + be 動詞 / 助動詞 + 主詞
>
> 關係代名詞 that，帶出一個句子。為了加強語氣，than 後方可搭配倒裝句。than 前方句使用現在式 be 動詞 is，那麼 than 後方的倒裝句就需搭

配現在式 be 動詞。複數主詞「其他文明的手稿」，搭配複數現在式 be 動詞 are。在有比較性的句子中，重複的複數名詞 scripts，也可用代名詞 those 來代替。套公式：**are those**（或 **the scripts**）**of other civilizations** 為正解。

18. 當青少年體重增加時，他們體內的脂肪分布將會改變，他們的骨骼和肌肉比例（proportion）一樣也會改變。（用 as 寫）

When adolescents gain weight, the amount and distribution of fat in their bodies will change, _____

_____.

解 倒裝句公式 ▶ ..., as + be 動詞 / 助動詞 + 主詞

常出現在原級裡的 as，表「一樣 ... / 就像 ...」之意，放句首時，後方需倒裝。由於前方句使用了助動詞 will，as 後方倒裝句也會跟著使用 will。套公式：**as will the proportion of their bones and muscles** 為正解。

註 as 倒裝句，動詞部分的處理原則和「造簡答句」相同，寫到 be 動詞 / 助動詞為止。

19. 唯有藉由將合法買菸年齡提高到 21 歲，我們才能有效減少青少年抽菸人數。

Only _____

_____ we able to effectively reduce the number of teenagers smoking.

解 倒裝句公式 ▶ Only by Ving ... + be 動詞 / 助動詞 + 主詞...

介係詞「藉著」by，後方需搭配動名詞 Ving。整個句子缺動詞（able 為形容詞），故補上「be 動詞」。套公式：**by raising the legal age of cigarette purchase to 21 (years old) are** 為正解。

20. 先被注射新藥，才暴露在致命放射線下的老鼠，可能比其他未經治療的（untreated）動物存活久些。

Mice injected with the new drug before being exposed to lethal radiation were more likely to survive longer than _____

_____.

解 倒裝句公式 ▶ ... than + be 動詞 / 助動詞 + 主詞

為了加強語氣，than 後方可搭配倒裝句。than 前方句使用過去式 be 動詞 were，那麼 than 後方的倒裝句也會跟著使用過去式 be 動詞。複數主詞「其他未經治療的動物」，搭配複數過去式 be 動詞 were。套公式：**were other untreated animals** 為正解。

註 動物「未被治療」，故搭配表被動的 p.p. 形容詞 untreated。老鼠「被注射」，故搭配表被動的 p.p. 形容詞 injected。

# Unit 7　間接問句和名詞片語

「間接問句」是包含在句子裡的問句，用於在句中提問，屬名詞子句。因為間接問句為「問句」，故以「疑問詞」開頭，又間接問句也是「句子」，故需有「主詞」和「動詞」。綜合以上：

間接問句的公式 ▶ 主要句 + 間接問句 (= 疑問詞 + 主詞 + 動詞 ...)

**使用間接問句時，需注意的事項如下：**

1. 句尾標點符號得和主要句一致。若主要句為「直述句」如：“I don't know ...”，句尾就打句號。若主要句為「問句」如：“Do you know ...?”，句尾就打問號。請見下方例句：

   例 我不知道她現在在哪。

   I don't know where　she　is　now.
   <u>　　　　　　　　　　 疑問詞　主詞　動詞 ... = 間接問句</u>

   解 句尾標點符號以主要句 I don't know 為準，故搭配句號。

2. **翻譯不會翻出來的、沒意思的助動詞 do、does、did，不會出現在間接問句中。除了上述三個助動詞以外，有意思的助動詞都要保留，如 will、should、could、完成式的助動詞 have 等。請見下方例句：**

   例 你知道你的薪水都花去哪兒了嗎？

   句1 Do you know it?
   句2 Where does your salary go?

   用間接問句合併兩句：
   Do you know where your salary goes?
   <u>　　　　　　　　　疑問詞　　　主詞　　　動詞 ... = 間接問句</u>

> **解** 第一句為主要句。代名詞 it 指的就是第二句。第二句成了要併入第一句的間接問句。去掉沒意思的助動詞 does 時，從 does 可知間接問句的時態應為「現在式」。且句尾標點符號以主要句 Do you know ... 為準，搭配問號。

3. 疑問詞「是否 ...」if / whether 帶出來的間接問句。

if 除了當連接詞「假如」，造假設句外，也可當疑問詞「是否」，帶出間接問句。連接詞「假如」if 帶出假設句，句中動詞需用跳躍式寫法，而疑問詞「是否」if / whether 帶出間接問句，句中動詞則按句子發生時間，搭配相對應的時態即可。請見下方例句：

> **例** 沒人知道她明天是否會出席她前男友的婚禮。

No one knows if / whether she will attend her ex-boyfriend's wedding tomorrow.
　　　　　　　疑問詞　主詞　動詞　... = 間接問句

> > **解** if / whether 為疑問詞「是否」，帶出了間接問句。間接問句 = 疑問詞 + 主詞 + 動詞。因句中的時間點為 tomorrow，故搭配「未來式」。句尾標點符號以主要句 No one knows ... 為準，搭配句號。

4. 間接問句放句首當「主詞」

間接問句就是名詞子句，除可放動詞後當「受詞」外，也放句首當「主詞」，使用時需注意主詞和動詞單複數需一致。請見下方例句：

> **例** 我姐姐何時才要去日本，這件事尚無定論。

When my sister will leave for Japan is undecided.
疑問詞　　主詞　　　動詞　　... = 間接問句

When my sister will leave for Japan is undecided.
　　　　間接問句當主詞　　　　　　　動詞

> **解** 「一個」間接問句放句首當主詞。單數主詞，搭配單數動詞 is。

5. 間接問句的「疑問詞」，同時也是「主詞」時

間接問句 = 疑問詞 + 主詞 + 動詞 ...。所以當間接問句的疑問詞，同時也是主詞時，疑問詞後方應直接接動詞。疑問詞 who / what / which 當主詞時，視為「第三人稱單數」，應搭配單數動詞。請見下方例句：

例 當時天色很暗。我看不清**現場發生什麼事了**。

It was dark then. I couldn't see clearly <u>what</u> <u>was happening</u> on the scene.
　　　　　　　　　　　　　　　疑問詞 + 主詞　　　動詞　　　... = 間接問句

> 解 what 既是疑問詞，也是主詞，則 what 後方直接接動詞。what 疑問詞當主詞時，視為「第三人稱單數」，故搭配單數動詞 was happening。句尾標點符號以主要句 I couldn't see ... 為準，搭配句號。

6. 間接問句可精簡成「名詞片語」

間接問句就是名詞子句，可進一步精簡成「名詞片語」，公式為「疑問詞 + to 動詞原形」。但注意，並非所有間接問句都可簡化成名詞片語，可簡化的通常是內含助動詞的間接問句。**注意：「if / why 間接問句」無法改成名詞片語**。請見下方例句：

例 我不知道**我該如何處理這個問題**。

I don't know how 　 I 　 should deal with this problem.
　　　　　　　　疑問詞　主詞　　　動詞　　　... = 間接問句
I don't know how 　 to deal with this problem.
　　　　　　　　疑問詞　 to 動詞原形 ... = 名詞片語

> 解 疑問詞 how 帶出來的間接問句，內含助動詞，可進一步精簡成由「疑問詞 + to 動詞原形」組成的名詞片語。標點符號仍以主要句 I don't know ... 為準，搭配句號。

例 請比較下方兩句的意思

I can't remember **what I said in my witness statement**. (間接問句)
我不記得我之前說了什麼證詞。

I can't remember **what to say in my witness statement**. (名詞片語)
我不記得要說什麼當證詞。

> 解 從上方例句可知,若將不含助動詞的間接問句硬改成名詞片語,
> 可能會改變語意。將含助動詞的間接問句,精簡成名詞片語,語
> 意才會相同。

## 小試身手：請完成下列翻譯題（藍色字就是需完成的倒裝句）

**01.** 目前為止，還不清楚是否這名女子為自殺還是被謀殺。

So far, it hasn't been clear _____

_____.

> **解** 間接問句的公式 ▶ 疑問詞＋主詞＋動詞 …。
>
> 套公式：**whether**（疑問詞）**the woman**（主詞）**committed suicide**（動詞1）**or was murdered**（動詞2）為正解。疑問詞「是否是 A 還是 B」**whether A or B**，帶出了 A「自殺」和 B「被謀殺」兩個動詞，兩動詞時態需對稱，因事件已發生，故用過去式。且「被謀殺」，需搭配過去被動式。

**02.** 眼週的毛孔不會產生油脂。這解釋了為什麼那個區域的皮膚從不會出油 (greasy)。

The pores around the eyes don't produce oil. This explains _____

_____.

> **解** 間接問句的公式 ▶ 疑問詞＋主詞＋動詞…。
>
> 套公式：**why**（疑問詞）**the skin in that area**（主詞）**is**（動詞）**never greasy** 為正解。句中 greasy 為形容詞，故需搭配 be 動詞。從 explains 可知本句為現在式。單數主詞 skin，搭配單數現在式 be 動詞 is。

**03.** 我坐在書桌前，毫無頭緒地想著英文作文該寫什麼主題，這英文作文其實一個月前早該交了。

Sitting at the desk, I aimlessly thought about _____

_____,

which was long due one month ago.

> **解** 間接問句的公式 ▶ 疑問詞＋主詞＋動詞 …。
>
> 套公式：**what topic**（疑問詞）**I**（主詞）**should write**（動詞）**for my English composition** 為正解。

04. 我爸跑來坐在我旁邊，而最初幾分鐘，我們只聽見一陣沉默。正當我好奇著接下來會突然冒出 (pop up) 什麼話題 (topic) 時，我終於聽見他說話了。
註 以「be going to V 原」表達 "接下來將會"。

My dad came to sit beside me. At the first few minutes, what we heard was silence. Right as I wondered _____
_____, I heard him speak.

解 間接問句的公式 ▶ 疑問詞 + 主詞 + 動詞 ...。

套公式：**what topic ( 疑問詞 / 主詞 ) was going to pop up ( 動詞 ) next** 為正解。what topic 既是疑問詞也是主詞，後方直接接動詞。從 wondered 可知本句應為過去式。單數主詞 subject，搭配單數過去式 be 動詞 was going to...。

05. Sue 記得她去上班前明明有鎖門。她不知道竊賊 (burglar) 如何闖進 (break into) 她家，偷走珠寶 (jewelry) 和大筆現金。

Sue remembered locking the door before going to work. She didn't know ___
_____
_____.

解 間接問句的公式 ▶ 疑問詞 + 主詞 + 動詞...。

套公式：**how ( 疑問詞 ) the burglar ( 主詞 ) broke into her house ( 動詞 1 ) and got away with ( 或 stole away) jewelry and a large amount ( 或 sum ) of cash ( 動詞 2 )** 為正解。從 remembered / didn't know 可知本句應寫成過去式 broke / got。Jewelry 和 cash 都是不可數名詞。

06. 當被問到她是否後悔她的選擇時，她的回答讓許多人感到驚訝。她說：我沒有什麼好後悔的。人生總是充滿各式各樣不同的經驗。

When she was asked _____,
her answer surprised many people. She said, "I have nothing to regret. Life is always full of diverse experiences."

解 間接問句的公式 ▶ 疑問詞 + 主詞 + 動詞...。

套公式：**whether / if**（疑問詞）**she**（主詞）**regretted**（動詞）**her choices** 為正解。從 was asked / surprised 可知本句應寫成過去式 regretted。

07. 若你花一輩子關注他人對你的看法如何，那麼你會不會忘記自己真實的面貌（即：你是誰）？

If you spend your whole life concentrating on_____,

will you then forget _____?

**解** 間接問句的公式 ▶ 疑問詞 + 主詞 + 動詞 ...。

套公式：**what**（疑問詞）**others**（主詞）**think of**（或 **planned** / 動詞）**you** 為第一格正解。他人對你的看法為「名詞」，故用「疑問詞」what 來問，而非 how。再套公式：**who**（疑問詞）**you**（主詞）**really are**（動詞）為第二格正解。

08. 嫌犯家中找到的筆電，提供警方許多關於嫌犯如何規劃與執行這宗攻擊案的關鍵細節。

The notebook found in the suspect's house offered the police many details about _____.

**解** 間接問句的公式 ▶ 疑問詞 + 主詞 + 動詞...。

套公式：**how**（疑問詞）**he**（主詞）**plotted**（或 **planned** / 動詞 1）**and executed**（或 **carried out** / 動詞 2）**this attack** 為正解。從 offered 可知本句應寫成過去式。

09. 考古學家發現混雜著五名慘遭謀殺的孩童遺骸和可食用的蝸牛肉的罐子。這驚人發現讓考古學家好奇究竟是什麼讓米諾安人 (the Minoans) 表現地如此野蠻兇殘 (savagely)。

The alarming discovery of the remains of five murdered children in a jar along with edible snails led the archeologists to wonder _____

_____.

**解** 間接問句的公式 ▶ 疑問詞 + 主詞 + 動詞 ...。

套公式：**what**（疑問詞 + 主詞）**might have caused**（動詞）**the Minoans**

**to act so savagely** 為正解。what 既是疑問詞也是主詞，後方直接接動詞。猜測之前發生過的事，可用 might have p.p.。cause 的用法：cause + 受詞 + to 動詞原形。

Unit 1
關係
代名詞

Unit 2
被動
語態

Unit 3
分詞
形容詞

Unit 4
分詞
構句

Unit 5
假設
語法

Unit 6
倒裝
句

Unit 7
間接
問句

Unit 8
特殊
動詞

Unit 9
主動詞
一致

Unit 10
對稱
結構

特別收錄
Unit 11
五回
試題

10. 選民是否相信政府正竭力 (do one's best) 解決經濟問題，可能會反映在投票狀況上。

_____

will likely be reflected in the polling booth.

> 解 間接問句的公式 ▶ 疑問詞 + 主詞 + 動詞...。
>
> 套公式：**Whether / If (疑問詞) voters (主詞) believe (或 are convinced /動詞) that the government is doing its best to solve the economic issues** 為正解。間接問句放句首當主詞。

11. 警方之所以重新調查 1997 年那場讓黛安娜王妃香消玉殞的車禍，是為了檢驗王妃之死是否為意外 (accidental)，或是否某種陰謀讓 (have) 她遇害。

The investigation into the 1997 car crash that killed Princess Diana was reopened to examine _____,
or_____.

> 解 間接問句的公式 ▶ 疑問詞 + 主詞 + 動詞...。
>
> 王妃已死，這句需用過去式。套公式：**whether / if (疑問詞) her death (主詞) was (動詞) accidental** 為第一格正解。再套公式：**whether / if (疑問詞) some kind of conspiracy (主詞) had (動詞) her killed** 為第二格正解。使役動詞 have，後方受詞 her「被殺」，故搭配表被動的過去分詞 killed。

12. 姓氏可透露關於這些人家可能來自於哪裡的線索。比如說，若某人的姓氏字尾為 stein，那麼很可能他的祖先是從德國來的。而以 Mc 為首的姓氏，則祖先可能為愛爾蘭籍。

Surnames might reveal some clues as to _____
_____. For instance, a person whose surname ends with "stein" will likely have forefathers from Germany and a name beginning with "Mc" has Irish ancestors.

> **解** 間接問句的公式 ▶ 疑問詞 + 主詞 + 動詞...。
>
> 套公式：where（疑問詞）families（主詞）may have come from（動詞）為正解。猜測過去可能發生的事情可用 may（或 might）have + p.p.。

13. 種植和處理作物時所耗費的能源，可能讓生質燃料變得和石化燃料一樣具汙染性。汙染程度就視栽種了什麼，且如何處理 (process) 這作物而定。

    Energy used in farming and processing the crops can make biofuels as polluting as fossil fuels, depending on ＿＿＿＿＿＿＿＿＿＿＿＿＿＿ and ＿＿＿＿＿＿＿＿＿＿＿＿＿＿＿＿＿＿＿.

    > **解** 間接問句的公式 ▶ 疑問詞 + 主詞 + 動詞...。
    >
    > 從 can make 可知本句為現在式。套公式：what（疑問詞 + 主詞）is grown（動詞）為第一格的正解。what 既是疑問詞也是主詞，後方直接接動詞。what 當主詞時，視為第三人稱單數，且穀物「被種植」，故搭配單數現在被動式 is grown。再套公式：how（疑問詞）the crop（或 it / 主詞）is processed（動詞）為第二格的正解。句中 it 代替的是前一句被種植的 what (crop)。this crop「被處理」，需搭配單數現在被動式 is processed。

14. 老師心中暗想，她必須做的不只是告訴小孩種族偏見是不理性的。她必須想出一個讓她的學生可深切體認到歧視究竟是像什麼，感覺起來如何，且對他們可能有什麼影響的方法。

    The teacher thought to herself that she had to do more than simply tell children racial prejudice was irrational. She needed to come up with a way of letting her students find out for themselves, deeply, ＿＿＿＿＿＿＿＿＿＿＿＿＿＿, ＿＿＿＿＿＿＿＿＿＿＿＿＿＿, and＿＿＿＿＿＿＿＿＿＿＿＿＿＿ ＿＿＿＿＿＿＿＿＿＿＿＿＿＿.

    > **解** 間接問句的公式 ▶ 疑問詞 + 主詞 + 動詞...。
    >
    > 從 came 可知本句為過去式。套公式：what（疑問詞）discrimination（主詞）was（動詞）like 為第一格的正解。再套公式：how（疑問詞）it（主詞）felt（動詞）為第二格的正解。又套公式：what effect(s)（疑問詞）it（主詞）might have（動詞）on them 為第三格的正解。第二格和第三格，代名詞 it 代替 discrimination。代名詞 them 代替 children。

15. 放療過程中，癌細胞附近的健康細胞也可能被放射線殺死，這就是為什麼放射科醫師 (radiologist) 必須盡可能精準地瞄準 (target) 腫瘤 (tumor)。

In the radiotherapy process, healthy cells may be killed alongside cancer cells, which is_____.

> **解** 間接問句的公式 ▶ 疑問詞 + 主詞 + 動詞...。
>
> 從 is 可知本句為現在式。套公式：**why（疑問詞）radiologists（主詞）need to target（動詞）the tumors as precisely as possible** 為正解。

16. 治癒癌症將費時多久尚無定論（用間接問句當主詞來造句），但政府倡議投資創新癌症研究這舉動著實令人振奮。畢竟了解如何阻止人們讓自己暴露 (expose) 在癌症危機下（用名詞片語造句）是防癌的第一步。

_____
is anyone's guess, but the government initiatives to invest in innovative cancer research are encouraging. After all, understanding_____
_____is the first step towards prevention.

> **解** 間接問句的公式 ▶ 疑問詞 + 主詞 + 動詞 …
>
> 名詞片語的公式 ▶ 疑問詞 + to 動詞原形。
>
> 第一格套公式：**How long（疑問詞）it（主詞）will take（動詞）to cure cancer** 為正解。事情「花」時間，需用動詞 take。1 句間接問句當「主詞」，單數主詞，搭配單數動詞 is anyone's guess。第二格套公式：**how（疑問詞）+ to prevent（to 動詞原形）people from exposing themselves to cancer risks** 為正解。片語「阻止 … 做 …」prevent N from Ving；片語「將...暴露在...之下」expose N to N。「1 個」動名詞 understanding 放句首當主詞，單數主詞，搭配單數動詞 is。

17. 在如何成為「網紅」這堂課上，學生的成績不是由考試決定，而是要看學生的網頁在線上社群可吸引多少關注而定。

In a class on how to become "Internet Famous," students' grades are determined not by tests but by_____

_____.

> **解** 間接問句的公式 ▶ 疑問詞 + 主詞 + 動詞 ...。
>
> 從 are 可知本句為現在式。套公式：**how much attention**（疑問詞）**their web pages**（主詞）**can attract**（動詞）**in the online community** 為正解。

18. 陪審團是否認為這是預謀 (premediate) 犯罪，這足以造成一級謀殺和二級謀殺之別，所以這真是生死攸關的事。

_____

is the difference between a second- and first-degree murder charge, so it's a matter of life and death.

> **解** 間接問句的公式 ▶ 疑問詞 + 主詞 + 動詞 ...。
>
> 從 is 可知本句為現在式。套公式：**Whether**（疑問詞）**a jury**（主詞）**thinks**（動詞）**( that ) a crime is premediated** 為正解。罪刑「被預謀構思出來」，需搭配被動式。1 句間接問句當「主詞」，即單數主詞，搭配單數動詞 is the difference...。

19. 人生裡，真正重要的事不在於你發生什麼事了，而在於你如何因應那些發生在你身上的事。

Life is not about _____,

but about_____.

> **解** 間接問句的公式 ▶ 疑問詞 + 主詞 + 動詞...。
>
> 從 is 可知本句為現在式。套公式：**what**（疑問詞 + 主詞）**happens**（動詞）**to you** 為第一格正解。「某人發生 ... 事了」的寫法為：事 happen to 人。what 既是疑問詞也是主詞，後方直接接動詞。what 當主詞時，視為第三人稱單數，搭配單數動詞 happens。再套公式：**how**（疑問詞）**you**（主詞）**deal**（動詞）**with it** 為第二格正解。代名詞 it 代替前一句所說的，發生在你身上的事。

20. 我們得到多少睡眠，大大影響我們的生活。睡太多讓我們沒精打采，但是睡太少會造成我們的心情變差，注意力也下滑。

_____ affects us greatly. Too much sleep makes us lethargic while sleeping too little causes our mood and concentration to suffer.

---

解 間接問句的公式 ▶ 疑問詞 + 主詞 + 動詞 ...。

從 affects 可知本句為現在式。套公式：**How much sleep** ( 疑問詞 ) **we** ( 主詞 ) **get** ( 動詞 ) 為正解。1 句間接問句當「主詞」，單數主詞，則搭配單數動詞 affects。

# Unit 8

### 特殊動詞：使役動詞、感官動詞、連綴動詞
## 8-1 使役動詞

使役動詞 have、make、get 意指「使、讓、叫」，多用於差遣或命令他人。使役動詞後方動詞的形態，會隨受詞是否可執行動作而變。have、make 後的受詞若「可執行」後方動作，則搭配「動詞原形」或「not 動詞原形」。相反地，若 have、make 後的受詞「無法執行」後方動作，則搭配表被動的「過去分詞」或「not 過去分詞」。而 get 後的受詞若「可執行」後方動作，則搭配「to 動詞原形」或「not to 動詞原形」。相反地，若 get 後的受詞「無法執行」後方動作，也是搭配表被動的「過去分詞」或「not 過去分詞」。請見下方圖示：

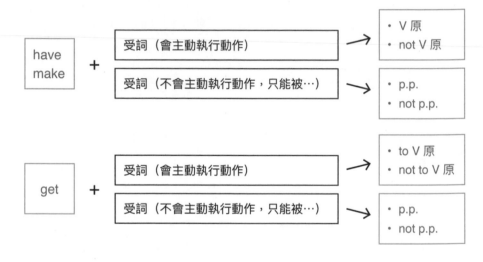

例 我不想去補習，但是我媽叫我去。

句1 I don't want to go to cram school, but my mom **makes** me **go**.
句2 I don't want to go to cram school, but my mom **has** me **go**.
句3 I don't want to go to cram school, but my mom **gets** me **to go**.

> 解 使役動詞 makes、has 後方受詞 me 可執行 go 這動作，故搭配「動詞原形」go。使役動詞 gets 後方受詞 me 可執行 go 這動作，故搭配「to + 動詞原形」to go。

例 Mark 叫他兒子幫他洗車。Mark 讓他的車子被洗。

句1 Mark **has** his son **wash** his car. Mark **has** his car **washed**.
句2 Mark **makes** his son **wash** his car. Mark **makes** his car **washed**.
句3 Mark **gets** his son **to wash** his car. Mark **gets** his car **washed**.

> 解 前半句，使役動詞 has、makes 後方受詞 his son 可執行 wash 這動作，故搭配「動詞原形」wash。而使役動詞 gets 後方受詞 his son 可執行 wash 這動作，故搭配「to 動詞原形」to wash。後半句，使役動詞 has、makes、gets 後方受詞 his car「被洗」，故搭配表被動的「過去分詞」washed。

例 你越快把回家作業寫完，你就有越多可自行支配的空閒時間。

The sooner you **have** / **get** your homework **done**, the more leisure time you will have at your disposal.

> 解 使役動詞 have、get 後方受詞 your homework「被做」，故搭配表被動的「過去分詞」done。

例 去年，老師叫 Mary 帶領科展計畫，而不是我。

句1 Last year, the teacher **had** / **made** Mary **lead** the science fair project instead of me.
句2 Last year, the teacher **got** Mary **to lead** the science fair project instead of me.

> 解 使役動詞 had、made 後方受詞 Mary 可執行 lead 這動作，故搭配「動詞原形」lead。使役動詞 got 後方受詞 Mary 可執行 lead 這動作，故搭配「to 動詞原形」to lead。

# Unit 8

特殊動詞：使役動詞、感官動詞、連綴動詞
## 8-2 感官動詞

感官動詞包含「感覺」feel，五官中的「看」see、watch、look at 和「聽」hear、listen to，再加上「注意到」notice，共 7 個。感官動詞後方動詞的形態，會隨受詞是否可執行動作而變。若感官動詞後的受詞「可執行」後方動作，則搭配「動詞原形」或「動詞 ing」。相反地，若感官動詞後的受詞「無法執行」後方動作，則搭配表被動的「過去分詞」。請見下方圖示：

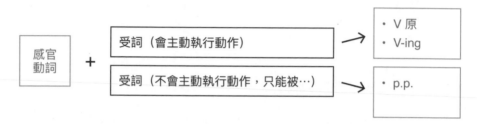

例 我之前就已聽過這對夫妻互相飆罵和大吼大叫許多次，但這回那女子淒厲的尖叫聲讓我下床一探究竟。

> 句1 I have **heard** the couple **swearing** and **yelling** at each other many times, but this time the woman's shrill scream leads me to get out of my bed and see what is happening.
> 句2 I have **heard** the couple **swear** and **yell** at each other many times, but this time the woman's shrill scream leads me to get out of my bed and see what is happening.

> 解 感官動詞 have heard 後方受詞 the couple 可主動執行 swear 和 yell 這兩個動作，可搭配動詞原形 (swear / yell) 或動詞 ing (swearing / yelling)，兩個動詞形態要一致。swear / yelling，就是錯誤寫法。

例 根據目擊證人的說法，他聽見兩聲槍聲，然後看到女孩的屍體被包裹在床單裡帶走。

According to the witness, he heard two gun shots and later **saw** the girl's body **wrapped** up in a bed sheet and **taken** away.

> 解 感官動詞 saw 後方的受詞 the girl's body「被包裹」和「被帶走」，故搭配帶被動意味的過去分詞 wrapped / taken。

## Unit 8　特殊動詞：使役動詞、感官動詞、連綴動詞
### 8-3 連綴動詞

連綴動詞和「感覺」、「五官」、「似乎」及「轉變」有關。常見的連綴動詞共 11 個：feel（感覺起來）、look（看起來）、smell（聞起來）、taste（嚐起來）、sound（聽起來）、seem / appear（似乎是 …）、get / become / turn / grow（變成）。

大致說來，連綴動詞後需搭配「形容詞」，詳細用法如下：

- feel / look / smell / taste / sound + 形容詞
- feel / look / smell / taste / sound + 介係詞 like（像）+ 名詞
- get / become / turn / grow + 形容詞
- seem / appear + 形容詞
- seem / appear + to 動詞原形
- seem / appear + that + 主詞 + 動詞

例 A: 這餅乾聞起來及嚐起來如何？ B: 它們聞起來香，嚐起來美味。

A: How do the cookies smell and taste?
B: They smell good and taste delicious.

> 解 疑問詞「如何」how，可問出「形容詞」good 和 delicious。連綴動詞 smell 和 taste 後方應搭配形容詞，而非副詞，因為真正香和美味的是餅乾，而非聞和嚐這兩個動作。修飾「名詞」餅乾，需用形容詞。

例 A: 這香水聞起來如何？ B: 它聞起來很特別，有珍珠奶茶的味道。

句1 A: How does the perfume smell?
　　 A: What does the perfume smell like?
句2 B: It smells special, like pearl milk tea.

> 解 疑問詞「如何」how，可問出「形容詞」special，而非副詞，因為真正聞起來特別的是香水，而非聞這個動作。修飾「名詞」香水，需用形容詞。而疑問詞「像什麼」what...like，可問出「名詞」pearl milk tea。介係詞 like 後方需搭配名詞。

# Unit 8

特殊動詞：使役動詞、感官動詞、連綴動詞
## 8-4 釐清易搞混的動詞用法

■ 比較「使役動詞」get 和「連綴動詞」get 的用法

> **例** 你讓會議準時開始的秘訣是什麼呢？

What are your best tips for **getting** a meeting **started** on time?

> **解** 使役動詞「讓」get，後方受詞 a meeting「被開始」，需搭配含被動意味的過去分詞 started。

> **例** 當有人又問起他剛剛才回答過的問題時，Henry 就變得很生氣。

Henry **got** very **annoyed** when someone asked him a question that he had just answered.

> **解** 連綴動詞「變得」get，後方需搭配「形容詞」。情緒相關的形容詞，ed 結尾形容人，而 ing 結尾形容事物。

■ 比較「感官動詞」look at 和「連綴動詞」look 的用法

> **例** Alice 開心地看著他兒子玩著玩具。

Alice **looked** happily **at** her son **play / playing** with the toy.

> **解** 感官動詞「看」looked at，後方受詞 her son 可執行 play 這動作，故搭配 play 或 playing。修飾動詞 looked at，需用副詞 happily。

> **例** 他對周遭發生的事看起來很漠然。

He **looked indifferent** to what was happening around him.

> **解** 連綴動詞「看起來」looked，後方需搭配形容詞 indifferent。

## 小試身手：請完成下列翻譯題

Unit 1
關係
代名詞

Unit 2
被動
語態

Unit 3
分詞
形容詞

Unit 4
分詞
構句

Unit 5
假設
語法

Unit 6
倒裝
句

Unit 7
間接
問句

Unit 8
特殊
動詞

Unit 9
主動詞
一致

Unit 10
對稱
結構

特別收錄

Unit 11
五回
試題

**01.** One type of orchid in New Guinea smells _____ than a rotting corpse. To the flies that pollinate it, though, the terrible odor smells _____.

(A) fouler; like a delicious meal      (B) more foully; deliciously

(C) to be foul; more deliciously      (D) more foul; to be a delicious meal

> 解 新幾內亞有種蘭花聞起來比腐屍還臭。但對為它授粉的蒼蠅而言，這可怕的味道聞起來像一頓美味大餐。
>
> **考點：連綴動詞**
>
> 連綴動詞 smell，後方需搭配「形容詞」或「介係詞 like（像）＋ 名詞」。且 than 為比較級的記號，需將形容詞 foul 改為比較級 fouler。**A** 選項為正解。

**02.** Anne doesn't speak French very fluently, but she manages to make herself _____ in most situations.

(A) to understand      (B) understood

(C) understanding      (D) that is understood

> 解 Anne 法文說得不流利，但她想辦法讓自己在大多數情境下可被了解。
>
> **考點：使役動詞**
>
> 使役動詞 make，後方受詞 Anne，想讓自己「被了解」，故搭配表被動的過去分詞 understood，**B** 選項為正解。

**03.** A hospital can disclose treatment information only when a patient consents to have it _____ with another specific health-care provider.

(A) to share      (B) be sharing      (C) shared      (D) share

> 解 只有當病患同意將他的醫療資訊和某特定醫療照護機構分享時，醫院才能透露那些訊息。
>
> **考點：使役動詞**
>
> 使役動詞 have，後方受詞 it（即：treatment information）「被分享」，需搭配表被動的過去分詞 shared，**C** 選項為正解。

**04.** The biggest event of the football season is the Super Bowl. People throw parties, munching on buffalo wings and pizza, as they watch the two best teams _____ off for the title.

(A) squared      (B) to square      (C) that squaring      (D) square

> 解 美式足球季的最大盛事就是超級盃。人們辦派對，邊啃雞翅和披薩，邊看兩強隊摩拳擦掌，爭奪勝隊頭銜。
>
> **考點：感官動詞**
>
> 感官動詞 watch，後方受詞 two best teams 可執行 square off (準備迎戰) 這動作，需搭配「動詞原形」或「動詞 ing」，**D** 選項為正解。

**05.** There was so much noise at the wedding banquet that I shouted all the time to have myself _____.

(A) to hear      (B) hearing      (C) hear      (D) heard

> 解 婚宴上如此嘈雜，以致於我老是得扯開嗓子才能讓自己的聲音被聽見。
>
> **考點：使役動詞**
>
> 我大聲說話是為了讓 (have) 我自己「被聽見」，需搭配表被動的過去分詞 heard，**D** 選項為正解。

**06.** Allen's life _____ lead of his father's and grandfather's before him—private schools, a top-ranked medical school and a career as a great plastic surgeon.

(A) seems certain to follow      (B) certainly seems following

(C) seems to following certain      (D) seems certainly follow

> 解 Allen 的生活似乎一定會照他父執輩們的指引，一路從私校、頂尖醫學院，到進入職場，成為出色的整形醫師。
>
> **考點：連綴動詞**
>
> 連綴動詞 seem，可搭配「形容詞」或「to 動詞原形」，**A** 選項為正解。

**07.** The majority of the city council appeared _____ the pleas of the public to make the community safer. They simply sat there poker-faced, inattentive to comments about infrastructure issues such as crumbling sidewalks and poor lighting.

Unit 1
關係
代名詞

Unit 2
被動
語態

Unit 3
分詞
形容詞

Unit 4
分詞
構句

Unit 5
假設
語法

Unit 6
倒裝
句

Unit 7
間接
問句

Unit 8
特殊
動詞

Unit 9
主動詞
一致

Unit 10
對稱
結構

特別收錄
Unit 11
五回
試題

(A) unmovingly

(B) that was unmoved by

(C) to be unmoved by

(D) unmoving

> 解 大多數市議會成員似乎對大眾增進社區安全的請願無動於衷。他們坐著，擺張撲克臉，對崩壞的人行道或照明欠佳等公設問題漫不在乎。
>
> **考點：連綴動詞**
>
> 連綴動詞 appeared，後方需搭配「形容詞」或「to 動詞原形」。從 inattentive（不關心的）可知，議會成員「不被感動」，得用表被動的 p.p. 形容詞，或 to 被動式。綜合以上，形容詞 unmoved by 和 to be unmoved by 都對，**C** 選項為正解。

08. **Those bed-ridden patients are highly prone to lose their muscle strength and then become _____ to stand.**

(A) too weak

(B) so weakly as

(C) so weakening as

(D) weakly enough

> 解 那些臥床的病患很可能喪失肌力，然後變得太虛弱，以致於無法站立。
>
> **考點：連綴動詞**
>
> 連綴動詞 become，後方需搭配「形容詞」。從 lose…strength 可知病患太虛弱，以致於無法站立了。「too + 形容詞 + to 動詞原形」太…以致於無法…。綜合以上，**A** 選項為正解。

09. **One of Amy's most formidable talents is to get her husband _____ what she wants by having him _____ it his idea.**

(A) to do; think

(B) do; to think

(C) done; thinking

(D) doing; thought

> 解 Amy 最驚人的本事之一，就是她有辦法叫他老公順她意做事，卻又讓老公認為一切都是他自己的主意。
>
> **考點：使役動詞**
>
> 使役動詞 get，後方受詞 her husband 可執行 do 這動作，故搭配「to 動詞原形」to do。又使役動詞 have，後方受詞 her husband 可執行 think 這動作，故搭配「動詞原形」think。綜合以上，**A** 選項為正解。

10. _____ these ideas may sound, they can just be the ones that change the world.

    (A) How insanely
    (B) However insane
    (C) What insane
    (D) Whatever insanity

> 解 無論這些點子聽起來有多瘋狂，它們可能就是改變世界的契機。
>
> **考點：連綴動詞**
>
> 連綴動詞 sound，後方需搭配「形容詞」insane。連接詞「無論如何...」no matter how + 形容詞，且 no matter how 三字合起來可變成 however。綜合以上，**B** 選項為正解。

11. If you see yourself _____ by evil spirits in a dream, it means that you are suffering from overwhelming stress or depression.

    (A) to be possessed
    (B) be possessive
    (C) possessed
    (D) possessing

> 解 若你夢見自己被惡靈附身，這代表你正承受巨大的壓力或極度抑鬱。
>
> **考點：感官動詞**
>
> 感官動詞 see，後方受詞 yourself「被惡靈附身」(by evil spirits)，需搭配表被動的過去分詞 possessed，**C** 選項為正解。

12. I spent $40 to get this coat _____ to fit my narrow shoulders, the most I had ever spent on a single piece of clothing.

    (A) to tailor
    (B) tailoring
    (C) be tailored
    (D) tailored

> 解 我花了美金 40 元，讓這件外套被修改，好配合我的窄肩。這是我花在單件服飾上最大的一筆費用。
>
> **考點：使役動詞**
>
> 使役動詞 get，後方受詞 this coat「被修改」，需搭配表被動的過去分詞 tailored，**D** 選項為正解。

13. Pushing my way through a bush, I stepped on something round and almost fell. There was a loud hiss, and I felt something first _____ against me and sink its jaws into my boot.

(A) slapping      (B) was slapped      (C) to slap      (D) slap

> 解 奮力在樹叢間推進時，我踩到某個圓圓的東西，差點跌倒。巨大嘶嘶聲後，我覺得某個東西先是打了我一下，接著利牙刺進我的靴子。
>
> **考點：感官動詞**
>
> 感官動詞 felt，後方受詞 something（某生物）可執行 slap（拍打）和 sink its jaws（咬）這兩個動作，故搭配「動詞原形」或「動詞 ing」。從 sink 可知，為求對稱，劃線處也應為動詞原形，**D** 選項為正解。

14. **The candidate's irritating sniffle at the presidential debate makes him _____ he was fighting off a cold with cocaine.**

    (A) to sound that            (B) sound like
    (C) sounding like that       (D) sounded

> 解 候選人在總統辯論會上討人厭的吸鼻聲，讓他聽起來好像他想藉吸食古柯鹼來擊退感冒一般。
>
> **考點：使役動詞 / 連綴動詞**
>
> 使役動詞 makes，後方受詞 him 可執行 sound 這動作，需搭配「動詞原形」sound。連綴動詞 sound，後方可搭配「形容詞」或「介係詞 like（像）+ 名詞」，從名詞子句 (that) he ... cocaine 可知這裏的用法為：like + N。綜合以上，**B** 選項為正解。

15. **Mary looked _____ at my report card and raised her eyebrows as if in disbelief. She seemed quite _____.**

    (A) close; astonishing          (B) closely; astonishment
    (C) closely; astonished         (D) close; to astonish

> 解 Mary 仔細地看著我的成績單，還揚起她的眉毛，彷彿不可置信般。她似乎相當驚訝。
>
> **考點：連綴動詞**
>
> 修飾一般動詞 look at，需用副詞 closely。連綴動詞 seem，後方需搭配「形容詞」，且和情緒相關的形容詞，ed 結尾形容人，ing 結尾形容事物。副詞 quite（非常地）加強劃線處的形容詞。綜合以上，**C** 選項為正解。

16. In all the cities in his empire, Alexander the Great put up statues that made him _____, and paintings that showed him fearlessly leading his army on the battlefield.

(A) look powerful　　　　　　　　(B) looking powerfully

(C) looked at power　　　　　　　(D) to look at powerfully

> 解 亞歷山大大帝在國內所有城市豎立起讓他看來強悍有力的雕像，以及描繪他無懼地領軍上戰場的繪畫。
>
> **考點：使役動詞／連綴動詞**
>
> 使役動詞 made，後方受詞 him 可執行 look（看起來）這動作，故搭配「動詞原形」look。連綴動詞 look，後方可搭配「形容詞」。綜合以上，**A** 選項為正解。

17. I saw a hawk _____ in the sky and then swooping down rapidly before it dived into the water to attack its prey.

(A) hovered　　(B) to hover　　(C) hovering　　(D) hover

> 解 我看見一隻鷹在空中盤旋，然後在潛入水中攻擊獵物前，迅速向下俯衝。
>
> **考點：感官動詞**
>
> 感官動詞 saw，後方受詞 hawk（鷹）可執行 hover（盤旋）／swoop（向下俯衝）這兩個動作，需搭配「動詞原形」或「動詞 ing」。為了和 swooping 對稱，劃線處也應為動詞 ing，**C** 選項為正解。

18. Click the link below to hear original versions of those timeless tracks _____ on tonight's show.

(A) to be performing　　　　　　(B) that performed

(C) performing　　　　　　　　　(D) performed

> 解 按下方連結，就可聽到今晚節目中這些經典曲目的原版演出。
>
> **考點：感官動詞**
>
> 感官動詞 hear，後方受詞 timeless tracks（經典歌曲）「被演出」，需搭配表被動的過去分詞 performed，**D** 選項為正解。

19. **A recent research shows that personality _____ to play a more important role in the types of music you enjoy than your gender, age or cultural background.**

(A) appears

(B) to have become

(C) makes

(D) getting

> 解 最近的研究顯示，個性似乎在影響你喜歡的音樂類型上，比性別、年齡或文化背景等因素扮演更重要的角色。
>
> **考點：連綴動詞**
>
> 關係代名詞 that 帶出一個句子。句中主詞為 personality，劃線處應為單數動詞，所以可刪除 B、D 選項。連綴動詞 appears，後方需搭配「to 動詞原形」或「形容詞」，**A 選項為正解**。C 選項，makes 後方一定要有受詞。

20. **The gangsters got teens _____ on drugs and then made them _____ drugs for quick cash.**

(A) to hook; peddling

(B) hook; to peddle

(C) hooked; peddle

(D) hooking; peddled

> 解 幫派讓青少年吸毒成癮，然後逼他們賣毒，好快速賺一筆。
>
> **考點：使役動詞**
>
> 使役動詞 got，後方受詞 teens「被毒品 (drugs) 勾引 (hook)」，需搭配表被動的過去分詞 hooked。使役動詞 made，後方受詞 them (即 teens) 可執行 peddle (販售) 這動作，需搭配「動詞原形」peddle。綜合以上，**C 選項為正解**。

# Unit 9 主動詞單複數一致

「主動詞單複數一致」是英文檢定考試和升學考試中常見的考點，也是大家在翻譯或寫作時常犯錯的項目。以下為常考題型和解題要領。

■ 以 Ving 為首的句子

首先，需區分句首的 Ving 究竟是「動名詞」，還是表主動進行意味的「形容詞」。若 Ving 為動名詞，放句首當主詞時，得視動名詞數量來決定動詞單複數。若 Ving 為形容詞，則視後方名詞單複數來決定動詞單複數。請見下方例句：

例 騎腳踏車不只有趣，且為我們帶來許多好處，包括減少體脂肪和協助對抗憂鬱症等。

**Riding** bikes **is** not only fun but **brings** many great benefits which include reducing body fat and helping combat depression.

> 解 「騎腳踏車」為一件事，riding 為動名詞，放句首當主詞。1 個動名詞代表一件事，單數主詞，搭配單數動詞 is / brings。關係代名詞 which 代替了前方的複數名詞 benefits，故搭配複數動詞 include。

例 規律運動和吃均衡飲食都是健康的關鍵。

**Taking** regular exercise and **having** a well-balanced diet **are** the keys to good health.

> 解 「做運動」和「吃均衡飲食」為兩件事，riding 和 having 都為動名詞，放句首當主詞。兩個動名詞代表兩件事，複數主詞，搭配複數動詞 are。

例 不及格的成績暗示著 Tom 缺乏了解課程資料所需的能力或努力。

**Failing grades indicate** that Tom lacks the required ability or effort to comprehend the course material.

> 解 主詞「不及格的成績」，重點在「成績」。複數主詞 grades，搭配複數動詞 indicate。形容詞 failing 意指「不及格的」。

■ 用 or 或 nor 連接主詞時

用 or 或 nor 連接主詞時，動詞單複數和靠近的主詞一致。請見下方例句：

例 被認為該為做出如此糟糕的決策負責的，不是我，就是 Amy。

**Either** Amy **or I am** held accountable for making such poor decisions.

> 解 「不是 A 就是 B」，either A (Amy) or B (I) 放句首當主詞時，動詞靠近 B (I)，故以 I 為主，搭配 be 動詞 am。

例 被認為該為做出如此糟糕的決策負責的，不是我，就是 Amy 嗎？

**Is either Amy or** I held accountable for making such poor decisions?

> 解 「不是 A 就是 B」，either A (Amy) or B (I) 放句首當主詞時，動詞靠近 A (Amy)，故以 Amy 為主，搭配 be 動詞 is。

例 Jack 和我都不喜歡僵屍片。片中的血腥場面把我們嚇壞了。

**Neither** Jack **nor I am** fond of zombie movies. The blood and gore in the films scares us stiff.

> 解 「既不是 A 也不是 B」，即 A 和 B 兩者都不是。neither A (Jack) nor B (I) 放句首當主詞時，動詞靠近 B (I)，故以 I 為主，搭配 be 動詞 am。

■ 動詞單複數視後者 (B) 而定的句型

1. 「不是 A 而是 B」：主詞 (Not A but B) + 動詞 (以 B 為主)

例 被認為該為做出如此糟糕的決策負責的，不是你，而是 Amy。

**Not** you **but Amy is** held accountable for making such poor decisions.

> 解 「不是 A 而是 B」not A (you) but B (Amy) 當主詞時，以 B (Amy) 為主，故搭配 be 動詞 is。

2. 「不只是 A 連 B 都 ...」：主詞 (not only A but (also) B) + 動詞 (以 B 為主)

例 不只你，連 Amy 都被認為該為做出如此糟糕的決策負責。

**Not only** you **but Amy is** held accountable for making such poor decisions.

> 解 「不只是 A 連 B 都 ...」not only A (you) but B (Amy) 當主詞時，以 B (Amy) 為主，故搭配 be 動詞 is。

■ 動詞單複數視前者 (A) 而定的句型

1. 「A, 包括 B」：主詞（A, including B,）+ 動詞（以 A 為主）

例 班上的每個人，包括我，對即將到來的大學入學考試感到緊張萬分。

**Everyone** in the class, including me, **is** very nervous about the forthcoming college entrance exam.

> 解 A (Everyone in the class) , including B (me) 當主詞時，以 A (Everyone in the class) 為主，單數主詞 everyone，故搭配單數 be 動詞 is。

2. 「A, 加上 / 和 B」：主詞（A, with / together with / along with / as well as B,）+ 動詞（以 A 為主）

例 我，加上 Amy，對即將到來的大學入學考試都感到緊張萬分。

I, as well as Amy, **am** very nervous about the forthcoming college entrance exam.

> 解 A (I) , as well as B (Amy) 當主詞時，以 A (I) 為主，故搭配 be 動詞 am。

3.「A, 同位格 B,」: 主詞 (A , 同位格 B,) + 動詞 (以 A 為主)

> 例 我，一名行程緊湊的高三生，對即將到來的大學入學考試感到緊張萬分。

I, a senior with a tight schedule, **am** nervous about the forthcoming college entrance exam.

> 解 A (I) , 同位格 B (a senior with a tight schedule) 當主詞時，I 和 a senior 是同一個人。同位格 a senior...schedule 補充說明用，不會影響動詞，故動詞以 A (I) 為主，搭配 be 動詞 am。

■ 主詞為「百分比或分數 of ...」時

當主詞為「百分比或分數 of ...」時，動詞單複數視 of 後方名詞的單複數而定。若 of 後方的名詞為單數，則搭配單數動詞；若 of 後方的名詞為複數，則搭配複數動詞。請見下方例句：

> 例 只有百分之一的受訪者同意該名候選人在邊界築高牆的提案。

Only one percent of **the respondents agree** with the candidate's proposal to build a great border wall.

> 解 當主詞為「百分比 of ...」時，動詞單複數視 of 後方名詞的單複數而定。of 後方的名詞 the respondents 為複數，故搭配複數動詞 agree。

> 例 地球表面的三分之二被水覆蓋。

Two-thirds of **the earth's surface is covered** by water.

> 解 當主詞為「分數 of ...」時，動詞單複數視 of 後方名詞的單複數而定。of 後方的名詞 the earth's surface 為單數，故搭配單數動詞 is covered。

■ 主詞為「數量詞 of ...」時

當主詞為「數量詞 of ...」，若 of 後方的名詞為可數名詞時，則動詞單複數視數量詞單複數而定；若 of 後方的名詞為不可數名詞時，則永遠搭配單數動詞。請見下方例句：

例 最棘手，但也最常見的求職面試問題之一就是：你最大的缺點是什麼？

**One** of the toughest, and most common, job interview questions **is** perhaps what your greatest weakness is.

> 解 當主詞為「數量詞 of ...」時，of 後方名詞 question 為可數名詞，則動詞單複數視前方數量詞而定。題中，數量詞 one 為單數，故搭配單數動詞 is。

例 我大部分的空閒時間都用來打線上遊戲。

**Most** of my leisure **time is spent** (in) playing online games.

> 解 當主詞為「數量詞 of ...」時，of 後方的名詞 time 為不可數名詞，則永遠搭配單數動詞，和數量詞多寡無關。

■ 其它結構裡包含「of」的主詞

除上述「百分比、分數、數量詞 of ...」這些和數字相關的主詞外，其它含介係詞 of 的主詞，文意重心均為 of 前方的名詞，故動詞單複數視 of 前方名詞的單複數而定。

例 恐龍大滅絕的主因始終眾說紛紜。

The main **cause** of the mass extinction of dinosaurs **has been** much **disputed**.

> 解 主詞「恐龍滅絕的主因」，重點在「主因」。cause 為單數，故搭配單數動詞 has been much disputed。

例 豐富的課外活動讓我們成了台北市最炙手可熱的高中。

**The abundance** of extracurricular activities **makes** us Taipei's most sought-after high school.

> 解 主詞「課外活動的充足豐富」，重點在「充足豐富」。abundance 為單數，故搭配單數動詞 makes。

■ 主詞後面跟著很長的形容詞或補述詞時

遇這類題目時，需先分析句子，找出以「名詞 + 形容詞」結構所寫成的主詞。若主詞結構中的名詞為單數，或不可數名詞，則搭配單數動詞。若主詞結構中的名詞為複數，則搭配複數動詞。若主詞後，緊接著用兩個逗號包夾住的補述詞時，為簡化句子結構，建議刪除補述詞，再依主詞單複數，搭配相對應動詞。

例 介於 HIV 病毒感染和 AIDS 症狀浮現的那段時間就是所謂的潛伏期。

**The time** between infection with the HIV viruses and the onset of AIDS symptoms **is** known as the latent period.

> 解 請見下方句構分析：
>
> The time between infection ... AIDS symptoms is known as ...
> 　　　　　　　　主詞　　　　　　　　　　　　動詞
> The time between infection ... AIDS symptoms is known as ...
> 　名詞　　　　　介係詞片語　　　　　　　動詞
> 主詞結構中的名詞 the time 為單數，則搭配單數動詞 is。

例 強震後，他旗下企業之一所經營的八所學校被變成了避難所。

After the massive earthquake, **eight schools** operated by one of his businesses **are turned** into temporary shelters.

> 解 請見下方句構分析：
>
> After...earthquake, eight schools operated...businesses are turned into...
> 　　時間　　　　　名詞　　　　　形容詞　　　　　動詞
>
> 八所學校「被企業經營」。operated 為 p.p. 形容詞。因主詞結構中的名詞 eight schools 為複數，故搭配複數動詞 are turned。

例 神風特攻隊在執行自殺任務前寫給摯愛家人的那些信件，目前存放在和平會館裡。

**The letters**, which kamikaze pilots wrote to their loved ones before embarking on the suicide missions, **are** currently **housed** in the Peace Museum.

> 解 句子結構分析如下：
>
> The letters, which kamikaze ... missions, are ... housed ...
> 　主詞　　　　補述用的子句　　　　　　動詞
>
> 英文的逗號相當於中文的括號，括號裏的文字都是補充說明用的。為簡化句子結構，先刪除由兩個逗號包夾住的補述詞。複數主詞 the letters，搭配複數動詞 are housed。

■ 關係子句中的動詞

「主詞」性質的關係代名詞，引導出後方子句。 而句中動詞的單複數，需視關係代名詞代替的先行詞單複數而定。其他性質的關係代名詞所帶出的子句，句中動詞單複數，則視子句中的主詞單複數而定。請見下方例句：

例 骨髓檢驗包含抽取脊髓液。這在診斷白血病時，可能是必要的程序。

**A bone marrow test, which involves** extracting fluid from the marrow, may be necessary for diagnosing leukemia.

解 「主詞」性質的關係代名詞 which，代替了前方的名詞 a bone marrow test。關係子句的主詞 a bone marrow test 為單數，故搭配單數動詞 involves。

例 當光線進入照相機，遇到底片，就會讓包覆底片的表面物質感光。

When light enters a camera, it strikes the film, whose **coated surface reacts** to the light.

解 所有格性質的關係代名詞 whose，意指 the film's。關係子句的主詞 the film's … surface 為單數，故搭配單數動詞 reacts。

例 美國對委內瑞拉強加經濟制裁，這件事情必然會讓兩國緊繃的關係愈形劍拔弩張。

**The US imposes financial sanctions on Venezuela, which is** bound to dramatically escalate tension between the two countries.

解 「主詞」性質的關係代名詞 which，代替了前方 The US imposes … Venezuela 這 1 個句子，這 1 件事。故單數主詞，搭配單數動詞 is。片語「註定… / 必然 …」be bound to V 原。

例 這些受害者被迫在這家銀行開戶。這些戶頭後來都被詐騙集團用來洗錢。

These victims were forced under threat to open **accounts** in this bank **which were** then **used** for money laundering by the scam artists.

解 「主詞」性質的關係代名詞 which，代替了前方的名詞 accounts in this bank。銀行裡的帳戶，重點在「帳戶」。關係子句的主詞 accounts 為複數，故搭配複數動詞 were used。

## 小試身手：請選出正確解答

**01.** As walkers continue to jaywalk and risk their lives as well as the safety of others, the number of pedestrian casualties _____.

(A) are on the increase

(B) have been increased

(C) increasing

(D) increases

> 解 當行人持續闖越馬路，冒著危害自己生命和他人安全的風險時，行人的傷亡人數增加了。
>
> 主詞「行人傷亡人數的數字」，重點在「數字」。the number 為單數，故搭配單數動詞 increases，**D** 選項為正解。

> 註 「... 的數目」the number of 複數可數名詞，文意重點在 the number，故搭配單數動詞。「很多」a (large / great) number of 複數可數名詞，搭配複數動詞。而「一些」a number of 複數可數名詞，也是搭配複數動詞。

**02.** There are two indications that the Greek medical system, once one of the best in Europe, _____ on the verge of collapse: a drug shortage and a healthcare brain drain.

(A) has been　　(B) to be　　(C) being　　(D) are

> 解 有兩個指標，一是藥物短缺，二是健康照護人才的流失，都顯示曾是全歐最棒的希臘醫療系統，目前已在崩解的邊緣。
>
> 關係代名詞 that 帶出了關係子句，請見下方句構分析：
>
> …that the Greek medical system, once one of the best in Europe, _____ on…
>
> 　　　主詞　　　　　　　　　　同位格補述用　　　　　　　動詞
>
> 為精簡句子，先刪除由兩個逗號包夾住的補述用同位格。單數主詞 the Greek medical system，搭配單數動詞 has been，**A** 選項為正解。

**03.** This 140-centimeter tall robot waiter, integrated with sensors, navigation hardware and user interface technology, _____ to hold and serve up to 7 kilograms of food or beverage.

(A) able　　(B) have the ability　(C) is able　　(D) enables

Unit 1
關係
代名詞

Unit 2
被動
語態

Unit 3
分詞
形容詞

Unit 4
分詞
構句

Unit 5
假設
語法

Unit 6
倒裝
句

Unit 7
間接
問句

Unit 8
特殊
動詞

Unit 9
主動詞
一致

Unit 10
對稱
結構

特別收錄

Unit 11
五回
試題

解 這 140 公分高的機器人服務生，內有感應器、導航硬體和使用者介面科技。他能夠支撐和將七公斤重的食物或飲料端上桌。請見下方句構分析：

This…waiter, integrated with sensors … technology, _____ to hold …
　　主詞　　　　　　　　　　分詞構句　　　　　　　動詞

原句為：the robot waiter is integrated（併入）with sensors … / the robot waiter is able to hold … ，兩句主詞相同，都是 the robot waiter，可用「分詞構句」。integrated … technology 就是「分詞構句」。為精簡句型，先刪除分詞構句。單數主詞 this … robot waiter，搭配單數動詞 is able，**C** 選項為正解。A 選項，able 為形容詞。D 選項，動詞 enable 的用法為：enable 人 to 動詞原形。

**04.** About 40 percent of the food grown and sold in America _____ out. Wasting food not only weighs on people's conscience but drains their wallet.

(A) to be thrown　　(B) have thrown　　(C) is thrown　　(D) throws

解 約百分之 40 在美國種植和販售的食物被丟棄。浪費食物不只讓人們良心不安，也會榨乾他們的錢包。

主詞為「百分比 of …」時，動詞單複數視 of 後方名詞的單複數而定。of 後方的名詞 the food 為單數，故搭配單數動詞。且食物「被丟棄」，需搭配被動式。綜合以上，**C** 選項為正解。食物「被種」和「被賣」，grown 和 sold 都是表被動的 p.p. 形容詞。請見下方句構分析：

About 40 percent of the food grown and sold in America _____ out…
　　　主詞 / 名詞　　　　　　　形容詞　　　　　　　　　動詞

**05.** Cutting-edge science that can reveal details of our past and confirm theories _____ our understanding of both the world that is long gone and how it has shaped our lives today.

(A) helps　　　　(B) to help　　　　(C) have helped　　(D) helping

解 揭露我們人類過往的細節和認證理論的先進科學，幫助我們了解早已灰飛煙滅的世界，以及過往的世界如何形塑我們今天的生活。

請見下方句構分析：

Cutting-edge science that can reveal…theories _____ our understanding…
　　主詞 / 名詞　　　　　　形容詞子句　　　　　　動詞

關係子句從關係代名詞開始，can reveal 和 confirm 已用連接詞 and

處理過，視為一組動詞，再往後推，到第二個動詞（劃線處）前結束。
關係子句 that … theories 放在名詞 science 後，為「形容詞子句」。為精
簡句子，可先刪除 that 形容詞子句。單數主詞 cutting-edge science，
搭配單數動詞 helps，**A** 選項為正解。

**06.** The presence of oxygen and moisture _____ the growth of microorganisms that contribute to the deterioration of nutrients, flavors, and colors within foods.

(A) that enhance　　(B) have enhanced　(C) to enhance　　(D) enhances

解 氧和水分的出現，促進了破壞食物營養素、風味和色澤的微生物的生長。

主詞「氧和水分的出現」，重點在「出現」。單數主詞 the presence，搭
配單數動詞 enhances，**D** 選項為正解。

**07.** China, as well as the US and Vietnam, _____ unhappy about Mr. Ma's trip to the Taiping Island, claiming that it has "undisputable authority" over islands in the South China Sea.

(A) which are　　(B) is　　　　(C) have been　　(D) being

解 中國，以及美國和越南，都對馬先生的太平島之行感到不滿。中國宣
稱，毫無疑問地，中國擁有南海諸島的管轄權。

A (China), as well as B (the US and Vietnam) 當主詞時，以 A(China)
為主，搭配單數動詞 is，**B** 選項為正解。

**08.** The historic shipwreck, which lies in the mud of Devon's coasts and is visible to the public when the tides are right, _____ for its potential to shed light on the key period of English maritime history.

(A) has been protected　(B) protecting　　(C) are protected　　(D) protects

解 這艘古老的沈船卡在 Devon 岸邊的淤泥中。若潮汐合適時，大家就可看
見它。這些殘骸已受保護，因為它能讓人們多了解英國航海歷史的關鍵
時期。請見下方句構分析：

The historic shipwreck, which … the tides are right, _____ for its …
　　　主詞　　　　　　　　補述用的名詞子句　　　　動詞
兩個逗號包夾住的 which 子句，放在名詞 shipwreck 後，當補述用的「名
詞子句」。為精簡句子，可先刪除 which 子句。單數主詞 the historic

shipwreck，應搭配單數動詞。沈船需「被保護」，故搭配被動式。綜合以上，**A** 選項為正解。

Unit 1
關係
代名詞

Unit 2
被動
語態

Unit 3
分詞
形容詞

Unit 4
分詞
構句

Unit 5
假設
語法

Unit 6
倒裝
句

Unit 7
間接
問句

Unit 8
特殊
動詞

Unit 9
主動詞
一致

Unit 10
對稱
結構

特別收錄
Unit 11
五回
試題

**09.** **Though being able to immediately generate an income after graduation _____ like an appealing thought, I still think high school graduates should attend college first.**

(A) to sound

(B) sounds

(C) which might sound

(D) sounding

> 解 雖然「畢業後立即可有收入」這想法聽起來很吸引人，我還是認為高中畢業生應該先上大學。請見下方句構分析：
>
> Though being able … graduation _____ like…thought, I still …
> 連接詞　　　　主詞 1　　　　動詞 1
>
> 動名詞 being 放句首當主詞。1 個動名詞，代表一件事。單數主詞 being，應搭配單數動詞，**B** 選項為正解。

**10.** **Neither you nor Mary _____ successful in landing a high-paying job because you don't equip yourselves with the knowledge and skills needed to adapt to the ever-changing job market.**

(A) are going to

(B) being

(C) seem to be

(D) is

> 解 你和 Mary 都沒能成功找到高薪的工作，因為你們都不具備適應這變化萬千的就業市場的知識與技能。
>
> 「既不是 A 也不是 B」neither A (you) nor B (Mary) 放句首當主詞時，動詞靠近 B (Mary)，故以 B (Mary) 為主，搭配 be 動詞 is，**D** 選項為正解。

**11.** **Even though most of the milk produced in the US _____ with vitamin D, around 33 percent of Americans still suffer from vitamin D deficiency.**

(A) to be fortified

(B) are fortifying

(C) is fortified

(D) fortifies

> 解 雖然大多數美國出產的牛奶都有添加維他命 D，但約百分之 33 的美國人還是飽受維他命 D 不足之苦。
>
> 當主詞為「數量詞 of …」時，動詞單複數視 of 後方名詞的單複數而定。of 後方的名詞 the milk 為不可數名詞，永遠為單數，需搭配單數動詞。且牛奶「被加了」維生素，需搭配被動式。綜合以上，**C** 選項為正解。

12. Employees in my company, without exception, _____ imperative to observe a code of ethics: Don't poach each other's clients.

   (A) has to be          (B) are          (C) to be          (D) is

   > 解 我公司裡的員工，毫無例外地，都必須遵守 1 條道德守則：不可互挖客戶。
   >
   > 主詞「公司裡的員工」，重點為「員工」。複數主詞 employees，搭配複數動詞 are，B 選項為正解。

13. The snowman those naughty boys spend hours building _____ into a monstrous giant, twenty feet tall and hideously misshapen.

   (A) is grown          (B) have grown          (C) grows          (D) growing

   > 解 那些頑皮的男孩花了數小時打造而成的雪人，長成了 20 英呎高、面目可憎且奇形怪狀的龐然大物。請見下方句構分析：
   >
   > The snowman (that) those naughty boys...building _____ into a monstrous...
   > 主詞 / 名詞　　　　　　形容詞子句　　　　　　動詞
   >
   > 關係子句從關係代名詞開始，往後推，到第二個動詞 (即劃線處) 前結束。關代 that 帶出來的關係子句 (that) those … building 放在名詞 snowman 後，為形容詞子句。形容詞子句不會影響動詞，為精簡句型，可先刪除。單數主詞 the snowman，搭配單數動詞 grows (成長)，C 選項為正解。A 選項，grow (成長) 沒有被動式。grow (種植) 才有被動式。

14. When it comes to mediating a dispute, finding common ground between both parties _____ crucial, but it can be better to find new ground. In other words, Sally may want X and Joe may want Y, but the best solution could be Z.

   (A) to be          (B) which are          (C) have been          (D) is

   > 解 當談論到調解紛爭時，尋求兩方的共同點是很重要的，但若能找到新立基點就更好了。換句話說，Sally 可能想要 X，而 Joe 可能想要 Y，但最好的排解歧異的方法可能是 Z。請見下方句構分析：
   >
   > …finding…both parties _____ crucial, but　it　can be…
   > 主詞 1　　　　　　動詞 1　　　　　連接詞 主詞 2　動詞 2
   >
   > 動名詞 finding 放句首當主詞。1 個動名詞，代表一件事，單數主詞，應搭配單數動詞，故 D 選項為正解。

15. **Acids are chemical compounds that, in water solution, _____ a sharp taste and the ability to turn certain blue vegetable dyes into red.**

(A) have      (B) includes      (C) containing      (D) are

> 解 酸類是化學化合物。在水溶液中，酸類有強烈的味道，且能讓某些藍色植物染料變紅。
>
> 主詞性質的關係代名詞 that，代替前方的名詞 compounds。複數主詞 compounds 需搭配複數動詞。compounds「有」強烈的味道，而非「是」強烈的味道。綜合以上，**A** 選項為正解。

16. **This is our last post, but don't fret, faithful readers! None of the content that has appeared on this website _____. Links will persist, and past coverage should be easily found through search.**

(A) to get lost               (B) is being lost

(C) are missing               (D) would have been missed

> 解 這是我們最後一則 po 文。但是忠實的讀者們，別擔心！出現在這個網站上的任何內容都不會消失。除了站上連結將續留外，透過搜尋也可輕鬆找到之前的報導。請見下方句構分析：
>
> None of the content that has appeared on this website _____.
>    主詞 / 名詞            形容詞子句            動詞
>
> 關係子句從關係代名詞開始，往後推，到第二個動詞（即劃線處）前結束。關係代名詞 that 帶出來的關係子句 that has ... website，放在名詞 content 後，為形容詞子句。形容詞子句不會影響動詞，為精簡句型，可先刪除。當主詞為「數量詞 of ...」時，因為 of 後方的名詞 the content 為不可數名詞，視為單數，故搭配單數動詞。且內容是「被弄丟的」，需搭配被動式。綜合以上，**B** 選項為正解。「弄丟 / 不見」：be（或 get）lost = be missing。

17. **All marble is composed of crystals of the minerals calcite or dolomite, which, when pure, _____ perfectly white.**

(A) to be      (B) it has been      (C) are      (D) is

> 解 所有大理石都是由方解石或白雲石等礦物質結晶所組成。這些結晶，當無雜質時，是純白色的。
>
> 主詞性質的關係代名詞 which，代替了前方的名詞 crystals of the

minerals ...。主詞「礦物質的結晶」，重點在「結晶」。複數主詞 crystals，搭配複數動詞 are，**C** 選項為正解。

18. **Only one species of modern bird, the South American Hoatzin, _____ claws on its wings as did prehistoric birds.**

(A) has      (B) have been      (C) having      (D) had

> 解 只有一種現代鳥類—麝雉—和史前鳥類一樣，翅膀上有爪子。
>
> 請見下方句構分析：
>
> Only one species of modern bird, the South American Hoatzin, _____ claws...
> <u>主詞</u>     <u>補充說明的同位格</u>     <u>動詞</u>
> 為精簡句子，先刪去兩個逗號包夾住、補述用的同位格。單數主詞 one species of（1 種）...，應搭配單數動詞。「現代的」（modern）鳥類應搭配現在式。綜合以上，**A** 選項為正解。
>
> 註 species 單複數同型，需從前方數字判斷 species 的單複數。一種 ...：a species of 單數名詞；四種 ...：four species of 複數名詞。

19. **Joan is one of those creative, animated teachers whose cheerful energy _____ even the most reluctant pupil into learning.**

(A) luring      (B) are lured      (C) have lured      (D) lures

> 解 Joan 是那些有創意且活力充沛的老師之一。那些老師的歡樂活力甚至能誘使不愛念書的學生投入學習。
>
> 所有格性質的關係代名詞 whose，代替了 teachers'。關係子句裡，主詞「老師們的能量」teachers' energy，重點在「能量」。單數主詞 energy，搭配單數動詞 lures，**D** 選項為正解。

20. **When it comes to most bird species, the young, more often than not, _____ totally dependent on parental care after hatching.**

(A) are      (B) have      (C) being      (D) has been

> 解 當談論到多數鳥類時，幼鳥常在孵化後，完全仰賴鳥爸媽的照顧。
>
> 「the＋形容詞」代表全體，視為複數。複數主詞 the young，搭配複數動詞。be 動詞才能接後方形容詞 dependent。綜合以上，**A** 選項為正解。B 選項 have，後方需搭配名詞。

# Unit 10 | 對稱結構

英文是個相當重視結構對稱與平衡的語言。對等連接詞如：and 或 not only ... but ... 等，左右兩方詞性、時態或名詞單複數都應對稱。

請見下方例句：

例 當談論到薪資協商時，氣沖沖地闖入老闆辦公室，並威脅著要辭職，很達成令你滿意的結果。

句1 When it comes to salary negotiation, **storming** into your boss's office and **threatening** to quit will rarely give you the desirable outcome.

句2 When it comes to salary negotiation, **to storm** into your boss's office and **to threaten** to quit will rarely give you the desirable outcome.

> 解 **考點：結構對稱。**請見下方句構分析：
>
> 動名詞 (Ving) 和不定詞 (to V 原) 都可當主詞。為促成對稱，有兩種寫法：
>
> ..., storming into ... office and threatening to quit will rarely give you ...
>  <u>主詞</u> <u>動詞</u>
> 連接詞 and 連接兩個動名詞 storming 和 threatening，當主詞。 storming / threatening 詞性、結構對稱。
>
> ..., to storm into ... office and to threaten to quit will rarely give you ...
>  <u>主詞</u> <u>動詞</u>
> 連接詞 and 連接兩個不定詞 to storm 和 to threaten，當主詞。to storm / to threaten 詞性、結構對稱。

例 人生的價值不在於活多久，而在於我們如何運用活著的時光。

The value of life lies not **in the length of days** we live but **in the use** we make of them.

> 解 **考點：結構、詞性對稱。** 請見下方句構分析：
>
> ... lies **not** in the length of days ... **but** in the use ...
> <u>　　　 介係詞 + 名詞 　　　　　　　　　 介係詞 + 名詞</u>
>
> 「不是 A 而是 B」not A but B，A、B 詞性和形式需對稱。句中的 A 和 B 都是「介係詞 + 名詞」。
>
> 註 名詞 days 後方的 we live，和名詞 use 後方的 we make of them 都是「形容詞子句」。

例 專業品酒師必須仰賴味覺、視覺和嗅覺來評定酒的品質。

A professional taster must count on **taste**, **sight**, and **smell** to determine the quality of a wine.

> 解 **考點：詞性對稱。** 請見下方句構分析：
>
> ... on　taste,　sight,　**and**　smell　to determine ...
> <u>　 介係詞 名詞 1　名詞 2　　　　 名詞 3</u>
>
> 介係詞 on 後方必須搭配名詞，且為遵守對稱原則，對等連接詞 and 左右共銜接了三個名詞。

例 線上教育讓學生可超越時間和空間的障礙，且全心投入學習。

Online education allows students **to transcend** time and space barriers and **be** fully engaged in learning.

> 解 **考點：詞性的對等。** 請見下方句構分析：
>
> ... allows students to transcend ... barriers **and** (to) be ... engaged in...
> <u>　　　　　　 to V 原 1　　　　　　　　　　　 to V 原 2</u>
>
> 「讓某人做某事」allow 人 to 動詞原形。連接詞 and 連接線上教育讓學生可達成的兩件事：「超越」障礙，和「全心」學習。to transcend / to be engaged in 詞性、形式對稱。
>
> 註 「to V 原 1」和「to V 原 2」可共用一個 to，故「to V 原 2」的 to 可略去不寫。

**例** 核危機讓饕客敬海鮮而遠之。有些高檔的日本餐廳不只回報生意驟減七成，還被迫歇業。

The nuclear crisis scares diners off seafood. Some high-end Japanese restaurants not only **reported** business plummeting by 70 percent but **were forced** to close down.

---

**解 考點：詞性、時態對等。**請見下方句構分析：

… **not only** reported  business … **but** were forced …
　　　　　　 動詞 1　　　　　　　　　　　 動詞 2

「不只 A，連 B 都…」not only A but (also) B，A、B 詞性和形式需對稱，reported 和 were forced 都是過去式動詞。

---

**例** 這個小鎮的自然資源包括肥沃的土地、礦物沉積、蔥鬱的森林和多元的野生動物。

The natural resources of this town include **fertile lands, mineral deposits, thick forests,** and **diverse wildlife populations.**

---

**解 考點：詞性、結構對稱。**請見下方句構分析：

…include fertile lands, mineral deposits, thick forests, **and** diverse…populations.
　　　　 名詞 1　　　　 名詞 2　　　　 名詞 3　　　　　　 名詞 4

為遵守對稱原則，連接詞 and 連接了 4 個「形容詞 + 複數名詞」當受詞。

---

## 小試身手：請選出正確解答

**01.** **A study suggests that a switch to perennial grains could help increase yields by making crops more weather-resistant, using less water, and _____ soil erosion, thanks to their deeper roots.**

(A) reduce      (B) reductive      (C) reducing      (D) reduced

> 解 研究顯示，轉種多年生的穀物有助於增加產量。因為這些多年生作物的根扎得深，讓作物較能抵抗氣候變化，較不耗水，也能減少土壤侵蝕。
>
> **考點：詞性／結構對稱。**請見下方句構分析：
>
> … by   making …, using less water, **and** _____ soil erosion …
> 　　　介係詞 動名詞 1　　動名詞 2　　　　　　　　動名詞 3
> 介係詞 by 後方需搭配（動）名詞。為遵守對稱原則，連接詞 and 左右共連接了三個「動名詞」(Ving)，**C** 選項為正解。

**02.** **The award-winning playwright's dramas are all marked by their witty and _____ plots.**

(A) tightly woven                (B) weave tight
(C) woven tight                (D) tightly weaving

> 解 機智幽默且緊密交織的劇情就是這個得獎劇作家的戲劇特色。
>
> **考點：詞性對稱。**請見下方句構分析：
>
> … marked by their witty and _____ plots.
> 　　　　介係詞　　形容詞 1　　形容詞 2
> 介係詞 by 後方需搭配「名詞」。名詞 plots 前可搭配形容詞。為遵守對稱原則，連接詞 and 左邊是形容詞 witty，右邊也需搭配「形容詞」。劇情「被編劇寫得緊密交織」，需搭配表被動的 p.p. 形容詞 woven。加強形容詞 woven 需用副詞。綜合以上，**A** 選項為正解。
>
> 註 weave (v) 編織；weave – wove – woven – weaving。

**03.** **Ironically, a lawmaker who voted to heavily clamp down on drunk driving was arrested yesterday for driving under the influence of alcohol _____ to take the breath test.**

(A) and declining                (B) which had declined

(C) declined

(D) to decline

Unit 1
關係
代名詞

Unit 2
被動
語態

Unit 3
分詞
形容詞

Unit 4
分詞
構句

Unit 5
假設
語法

Unit 6
倒裝
句

Unit 7
間接
問句

Unit 8
特殊
動詞

Unit 9
主動詞
一致

Unit 10
對稱
結構

特別收錄

Unit 11
五回
試題

> **解** 諷刺地，投票贊成強力取締酒駕的立委，昨天卻因酒駕和拒絕吹氣檢測而遭逮捕。
>
> **考點：詞性對稱。**請見下方句構分析：
>
> … was arrested for　driving … alcohol　_____　to take … test
>
> 　　　　　　　介係詞　動名詞 1　　　連接詞 + 動名詞 2
>
> 從文意可推知，這名立法委員被逮捕是因為「酒駕」和「拒絕呼氣檢測」。介係詞 for（因為）後方需搭配「（動）名詞」。為遵守對稱原則，對等連接詞 and（和）左邊為動名詞 driving，右邊劃線處也應為「動名詞」。綜合以上，**A** 選項為正解。

**04.** **Manufacturing industries are usually located in areas where there are abundant natural resources, efficient transportation systems, _____, and large populations.**

(A) the climate is desirable

(B) desirable climates

(C) a desire for the mild climate

(D) desired to enjoy the mild climate

> **解** 製造業通常位在自然資源豐富、交通便捷、氣候宜人和人口眾多的地區。
>
> **考點：詞性 / 結構對稱。**請見下方句構分析：
>
> are abundant…resources, efficient…systems, _____, **and** large populations.
>
> 　　　形容詞 1+ 名詞 1　　　形容詞 2+ 名詞 2　　　　　　形容詞 4+ 名詞 4
>
> 為遵守對稱原則，對等連接詞 and 左右共銜接了四組「形容詞 + 複數名詞」，**B** 選項為正解。

**05.** **Since middles have neither the attention enjoyed by the first-borns nor _____, they become experts at negotiation and compromise.**

(A) the privileges of the last-borns

(B) had by the privileges of the last-borns

(C) have the privileges of the last-borns

(D) the last-borns who have the privileges

> **解** 排行中間的小孩，既得不到老大所享有的關注，也沒有老么的特權，因此他們成了協商和折衝妥協的專家。

考點：詞性 / 結構對稱。請見下方句構分析：

… have **neither** the attention enjoyed by the first-borns **nor** _____
　　　　　　　名詞　　　　　　　　　形容詞　　　　　　　　名詞

「既不是 A 也不是 B」neither A nor B，A 和 B 兩者時態、詞性和結構需對稱。neither 後方搭配名詞 the attention，nor 後方也應搭配名詞，A 選項為正解。attention「被享有」，需搭配表被動的 p.p. 形容詞 enjoyed。D 選項雖然也是名詞，但文意不通，因為 middles (排行中間的小孩) 不會 have the last-borns (老么)。

06. The real difficulty lies not so much in developing novel ideas _____ from old ones. Going against popular thinking can be tricky, whether you are a businessman bucking company tradition or a teen refusing to follow the fashion trend.

(A) that escape　　　　　　　　　(B) as to escape

(C) as in escaping　　　　　　　　(D) than escaping

解 真正的困難不在於發展新點子，而在於跳脫舊思維。不隨波逐流可能是很困難的，不論你是抵制公司傳統的生意人，還是拒絕追隨時尚潮流的青少年。

考點：形式結構對稱。請見下方句構分析：

… **not so much** in developing novel ideas _____ from …
　　　　　　　　in + 動名詞　　　　　　　　as in + 動名詞

片語「在於 …」lie in N。連接詞「與其說是 A，還不如說是 B」not so much A as B，A、B 時態、詞性和形式要對稱。A 為「in + 動名詞」，為遵守對稱原則，B 也應為「in + 動名詞」，C 選項為正解。

07. Text messages now outrank phone calls as the dominant form of communication among Millennials, who feel sending a line convenient and _____.

(A) giving someone a ring somehow intrusive

(B) gave someone a somehow intrusive ring

(C) someone to give a somehow intrusive ring

(D) to give someone a ring was intrusive

解 簡訊現已超越打電話，成為千禧世代最主要的溝通形式。千禧世代覺得發簡訊很方便，而打電話有些打擾人。

考點：形式結構對稱。請見下方句構分析：

… Millennials, who feel sending a line convenient **and** _____.
動名詞　　　　　　形容詞　　　動名詞＋形容詞

「覺得…如何」feel + N + adj。為遵守對稱原則，連接詞 and 左邊為「動名詞 + 形容詞」，右邊劃線處也應為「giving someone a ring (動名詞) + intrusive (形容詞)」，A 選項為正解。

08. The ancient Egyptians believe firmly in life after death. Thus, they learned how to preserve the body well by drying it out, oiling and then _____ the body in linen.

(A) how to wrap　　(B) wrapping　　(C) they wrap　　(D) wrapped

解 古埃及人堅信有來生。因此，他們學會了如何藉乾燥屍體、抹油和用亞麻包裹屍體來妥善保存大體。

考點：詞性 / 結構對稱。請見下方句構分析：

… well by drying it out, oiling **and** then _____ the body …
介係詞　動名詞1　　動名詞2　　　　動名詞3

從文意可知，古埃及人藉由三道程序來保存屍體。介係詞 by (藉著) 後方需搭配 (動) 名詞。為遵守對稱原則，連接詞 and 左右共連接了三個「動名詞」，B 選項為正解。

09. The talented actor has no difficulty _____ his lines quickly and successfully bringing a scripted character to life.

(A) memorizing
(C) that memorizing

(B) to memorize
(D) with memorization

解 這個有天分的男演員毫無困難地迅速背誦台詞，且成功地演活了劇本中的角色。

考點：詞性、結構對稱。請見下方句構分析：

… has no difficulty (in) _____ his lines … **and** … bringing … to life.
動名詞1　　　　　　　　　　　　動名詞2

男演員毫無困難地執行兩件事：背台詞，和演活角色。片語「沒困難」have no difficulty (in) Ving。片語中的介係詞 in 可省略不寫，但後方需搭配動名詞。為遵守對稱原則，連接詞 and 右邊為動名詞 bringing，左邊劃線處也應為「動名詞」，A 選項為正解。

10. **Window treatments, furniture arrangements and _____ all contribute to the overall impression of a room.**

    (A) color combinations                 (B) combining colors

    (C) combine with colors to            (D) colors which

> **解** 窗戶的處理、家具的擺設和配色都可形塑房間給人的整體印象。
>
> **考點：詞性、結構對稱。** 請見下方句構分析：
>
> Window treatments, furniture arrangements and _____ all contribute to …
>                 主詞                       動詞
> Window treatments, furniture arrangements **and** _____ all contribute to …
>     名詞 1           名詞 2         名詞 3     動詞
>
> 主詞就是名詞。為遵守對稱原則，連接詞 and 連接了三個複數名詞當主詞，且結構上都為「名詞 + 名詞」，**A** 選項為正解。D 選項，由於句中只有一個動詞 contribute，所以不需要關係代名詞。

11. **Artificial reefs, scattered all over, from 15 to hundreds of feet of water, _____ fish with food and shelter but enhance fishing opportunities for anglers.**

    (A) not to provide                  (B) which provides

    (C) not only provide               (D) providing

> **解** 人造珊瑚礁散佈各處，從 15 英呎到幾百英呎深的水域。它們不只為魚類提供食物和庇護所，也為垂釣者增加許多釣魚的機會。
>
> **考點：詞性、時態、結構對稱。** 請見下方句構分析：
>
> Artificial reefs, scattered all over, from … water, _____ fish…but enhance…
>     主詞          分詞構句         地點       動詞 1         動詞 2
> 「不只是 A，連 B 都 …」not only A but (also) B，A 和 B 兩者時態、詞性要對稱。B 為現在式動詞 enhance，劃線處應為「not only + 現在式動詞」，**C** 選項為正解。原句為：artificial reefs provide fish … / artificial reefs are scattered all over …。兩句主詞相同，都是 artificial reefs，可用「分詞構句」。人造珊瑚礁「被散佈」，需搭配表被動的 p.p. 分詞構句：scattered all over。

12. **I opened the container with leftovers from my favorite meal and my nostrils _____ with a disgusting odor that killed my appetite in a matter of seconds.**

(A) had assaulted　(B) were assaulted　(C) assaulting　(D) assaulted

解 這容器裝有我最愛的那餐的剩菜。當打開它時，我的鼻孔被一股噁心的味道襲擊，幾秒鐘內，我就胃口全失。

**考點：動詞時態對稱。**請見下方句構分析：

I　opened　the container ... **and** my nostrils _____ with ...
主詞 1　動詞 1　　　　　　　　　　主詞 2　　動詞 2

連接詞 and 連接兩個句子，兩個句子的動詞時態應對稱。and 左邊為過去式動詞 opened，右邊劃線處也應為過去式動詞。鼻孔「被氣味襲擊」，應搭配被動式。綜合以上，**B** 選項為正解。

13. **To start every day right, _____ these expert-approved dietary guidelines and make sure to have breakfast within two hours of waking.**

(A) following　　(B) to follow　　(C) followed by　　(D) follow

解 為了讓每天都有正確的開始，你應遵守這些專家同意的飲食守則，且務必在醒來兩小時內享用早餐。

**考點：結構對稱。**請見下方句構分析：

... _____ these ... guidelines **and** make sure to have ...
祈使句 1　　　　　　　　　　祈使句 2

「following 或 to follow guidelines」不會開啟每一天 (to start every day right)，不是主詞。從沒有主詞，可推知 ... these ... guidelines 應為祈使句。肯定的祈使句以「動詞原形」開頭。連接詞 and 連接兩個祈使句，**D** 選項為正解。

14. **_____ your subway seat to a pregnant woman or volunteering in an orphanage is a gesture of goodwill.**

(A) That yield　　(B) To yield　　(C) Yielding　　(D) Yield

解 將捷運座位讓給孕婦，或到孤兒院當志工，都是善意的表現。

**考點：詞性、結構對稱。**請見下方句構分析：

_____ your subway seat ... or volunteering ... orphanage is a gesture ...
主詞　　　　　　　　　　　　　　　　　　　　動詞

180

_____ your subway seat ... **or** volunteering ... orphanage is a gesture ...
動名詞 1                                           動名詞 2                              動詞

主詞就是 (動) 名詞。為遵守對稱原則，連接詞 or 右邊為動名詞 volunteering，左邊劃線處也應為動名詞，**C** 選項為正解。用 or 連接主詞時，動詞單複數和靠近的主詞一致。動詞靠近 volunteering 這 1 件事，故搭配單數動詞 is。

15. **More than we probably want to admit, we sometimes are secretly pleased or take glee in seeing our rivals stumble or _____ a crushing defeat.**

(A) suffered      (B) suffer      (C) in suffering      (D) suffering

解 我們常不願承認，當看到對手犯錯或遭逢慘敗時，我們有時會暗自竊喜或幸災樂禍。

**考點：詞性、結構對稱。請見下方句構分析：**

... seeing our rivals stumble **or** _____ a crushing defeat
感官動詞                          動詞原形 1    動詞原形 2

從文意可知，看見對手「犯錯」，或看見對手「遭逢」慘敗。感官動詞 see 後方受詞 our rivals 可執行 stumble / suffer 這兩個動作，需搭配「動詞原形」或「動詞 ing」。為遵守對稱原則，連接詞 or 左邊為動詞原形 stumble，右邊劃線處也應為動詞原形，**B** 選項為正解。C 選項，喜歡慘敗 (take glee in suffering ...)，文意不通。

16. **The flight cancellation and _____ dilute his joy to embark on a trip to New York.**

(A) wait impatiently at the airport      (B) long dreary airport wait
(C) how dreary the wait at the airport is      (D) so long the wait that

解 航班取消和在機場漫長無聊的等待，稀釋他對展開紐約之旅的興奮之情。

**考點：詞性對稱。請見下方句構分析：**

The flight cancellation and _____ dilute his joy ...
             主詞                   動詞
The flight cancellation **and** _____ dilute his joy ...
        名詞 1              名詞 2    動詞

主詞就是名詞。為遵守對稱原則，連接詞 and 左邊為名詞 the flight

cancellation，右邊劃線處也應為名詞，**B** 選項為正解。wait (v)(n) 等待，在此當名詞用。

17. **John is notorious for his bad temper. Every time when he loses a game, he either unleashes a volley of abuse and anger at the umpire _____ the racket.**

(A) as well as smashes (B) instead of smashing

(C) , nor does he smash (D) or smashes

解 John 的壞脾氣惡名昭彰。每當他輸了比賽，他要不找裁判出氣，連珠炮地咒罵，不然就是把球拍摔爛。

**考點：詞性、結構對稱。**請見下方句構分析：

… **either** unleashes … umpire _____ the racket
　　　　　動詞 1　　　　　　　　　or + 動詞 2

「不是 A 就是 B」either A or B，A 和 B 兩者時詞性和結構要對稱。A 為第三人稱單數的現在式動詞 unleashes，劃線處也應為「or + 第三人稱單數的現在式動詞」，**D** 選項為正解。

18. **The bill, which allows guns at colleges, is heralded as a big victory by gun rights advocates, but criticized by many professors as disturbing, _____, and simply unnecessary.**

(A) offensively (B) total ignorance (C) irresponsible (D) mischief

解 允許槍隻進入大學的法案，被持槍權的擁護者譽為大勝利，但是卻被許多教授評為令人不安、不負責任和簡直沒必要。

**考點：詞性對稱。**請見下方句構分析：

… criticized … as disturbing, _____, **and** simply unnecessary.
　　動詞 2　　　　　　形容詞 1　　形容詞 2　　　　　　　　形容詞 3

從文意可知，這法案被評為 …，後方用三個形容詞來形容這法案。為遵守對稱原則，連接詞 and 左右共連接了三個形容詞，**C** 選項為正解。

19. **Wealth will be squandered, power will change hands, _____. Only beauty and creativity are immortal.**

(A) in which life will wither (B) with life withering

(C) and life itself will wither (D) not to mention withering life

解 財富會揮霍殆盡，權力會換手，且生命會凋零枯萎。只有美和創意不死。

**考點：結構對稱。**請見下方句構分析：

Wealth will be squandered, power will change hands, _____.

<u>句子 1</u>　　　　　　　<u>句子 2</u>　　　　<u>and 句子 3</u>

題目中已出現兩個未來式的句子並列，卻尚未出現連接詞。因此可推知，為遵守對稱原則，劃線處應為「連接詞 + 一個未來式的句子」，**C** 選項為正解。

20. The new study published last month presented valuable insights into and _____ the complex issues of global warming and climate change.

(A) comprehensive analyses of

(B) comprehensively analyzing

(C) they comprehensively analyzed

(D) analyzes to comprehend

解 上個月公布的新研究，對全球暖化和氣候變遷等複雜議題提出了寶貴的洞察力和詳盡的分析。

**考點：結構對稱。**請見下方句構分析：

... presented valuable insights into and _____ the ... issues ...

<u>動詞</u>　　<u>名詞 1</u>　　<u>介係詞</u>　<u>名詞 2 + 介係詞</u>

從文意可知，這研究提出了「洞察力」和「分析」。為遵守對稱原則，連接詞 and 左邊為「名詞 + 介係詞」，右邊劃線處也應為「名詞 + 介係詞」。介係詞 into / of 後方都是搭配名詞 the complex issues。綜合以上，**A** 選項為正解。B、D 選項，動詞時態沒對稱，都應改成過去式 analyzed。C 選項，應將代名詞 they，改成 it，代替 the new study。

# Unit 11

**01.** You can eat your way to fabulous skin. Consuming fruits and vegetables rich in antioxidants _____ your skin stay radiant, supple, and blemish-free.

(A) helps      (B) to help      (C) that help      (D) help

> 解 你可「吃」出好膚質。吃富含抗氧化物的蔬果，可幫助你的皮膚保持有光澤、飽滿且沒斑點。
>
> **考點：主動詞一致。**請見下方句構分析：
>
> Consuming fruits and vegetables rich in antioxidants _____ your skin...
> <u>主詞</u>      <u>形容詞</u>      <u>動詞</u>
> 動名詞 consuming 放句首當主詞。1 個動名詞，代表一件事，單數主詞，搭配單數動詞，**A** 選項為正解。

**02.** The study is believed to be the first analysis to account for how the disease progresses in a patient and the ways _____ it can spread.

(A) that      (B) in which      (C) how      (D) where

> 解 據說，這是第一個分析解釋這個疾病在病患身上的病程，以及它的擴散方式的研究。
>
> **考點：關係代名詞。**請見下方句構分析：
>
> ... account for how ... patient and the ways _____ it can spread.
> <u>動詞 1</u>   <u>名詞 1（間接問句）</u>   <u>名詞 2</u>   <u>關代</u>   <u>動詞 2</u>
> 連接詞 and 連接兩個名詞。account for / can spread 兩個動詞，代表兩個句子，故劃線部分應為具連接句子功能的關係代名詞。將先行詞 the ways 放回後方 it can spread 這句子排排看，得出：it（即 the disease）can spread in（用）the ways，由此可知需用「物 / 受詞性質」的關係代名詞 which，但因關係代名詞只能代替名詞 the ways，無法代替介係詞 in，故答案應為 in which，**B** 選項為正解。關係代名詞 in which 帶出來的關係子句 it can spread 放在名詞 ways 後方，為「形容詞子句」。

**03.** One 10-minute phone call is probably not enough to completely alleviate South Korea's anxiety about whether the US under Trump will truly come to its defense _____ anything unthinkable happen.

(A) if      (B) were      (C) until      (D) should

> **解** 一通十分鐘的電話，或許不足以完全緩和南韓的焦慮。他們對於萬一難以想像的局勢發生時，川普領導下的美國是否會協防南韓感到惶惶不安。
>
> **考點**：should 假設語法
>
> 從文意「任何令人不敢想像的事」（anything unthinkable）可知，這句是針對「未來」做假設。若用 if 假設語法，緊接在 if 後方的動詞需從未來往前跳一格，改用「現在式」，即：
>
> … whether the US **will** come to its defense **if** anything unthinkable **happens**.
>
> 也可用助動詞 should（萬一）取代 if 造假設句。should 的位置就是 if 的位置，但需留意助動詞 should 後方要搭配動詞原形，即：
>
> … whether the US will come to its defense **should** anything unthinkable **happen**.
>
> 由上可知，**D** 選項為正解。

**04.** I would die of boredom listening to Professor Brown _____ a stuffy lecture in a dreadfully monotone voice.

(A) delivered      (B) and delivering      (C) to deliver      (D) deliver

> **解** 聽 Brown 教授用極其單調平板的聲音來講解沉悶的課程，可能讓我無聊而死。
>
> **考點**：感官動詞
>
> 感官動詞 listen to，後方受詞 Professor Brown 可執行 deliver（發表）課程，需搭配「動詞原形」或「動詞 ing」，**D** 選項為正解。

**05.** Our country needs strong, capable political leaders during such tumultuous times. However, _____ it has instead is a succession of political scandals and a president lawmakers have voted to remove.

(A) that      (B) either      (C) no wonder      (D) what

解 在如此動盪的時刻，我們國家需要有能耐的強硬領導人。然而，我們國家有的卻是一連串的政治醜聞，和一個已被立委投票罷免的總統。

**考點：關係代名詞，**

has / is 兩個動詞，代表兩個句子，故劃線部分應為具連接句子功能的關係代名詞。關係代名詞前無先行詞，故答案不是 that 就是 what。關係子句 it（即 our country）has「意思不完整」，我們的國家有甚麼呢？故 **D** 選項為正解。複合關係代名詞 what 帶出來的關係子句 what it has 放在句首當主詞，屬「名詞子句」。

06. _____ about my previous salary in yesterday's interview, I dodged this tricky question by giving my target salary range instead.

(A) Having asked　　(B) When asked　　(C) To ask　　(D) Asking

解 當昨天面試被問到我之前的薪水時，我藉著點出我的目標薪水來閃躲這個棘手的問題。

**考點：分詞構句 [ 變形 1 ]**

面試時，我「被考官問」，應搭配被動式。原句為：when I was asked about my previous salary … / I dodged this tricky question…。兩句主詞相同，都是 I，可用分詞構句。was asked 為過去被動式，需改成表被動的 p.p. 分詞構句 when asked … interview。寫分詞構句時，也可保留連接詞 when，**B** 選項為正解。

07. The people surveyed picked fresh-brewed coffee as the smell they'd most like to wake up to. Hardly_____, considering the poll was conducted for coffee roasters.

(A) was that an coincidence　　　(B) an coincidence that was

(C) will it be seen as an coincidence　　(D) happened an coincidence

解 受訪者選出現煮咖啡為他們早晨醒來最想聞到的味道。有鑑於那是為咖啡商而做的調查，那結果幾乎不是個巧合。

**考點：倒裝句**

否定副詞 hardly 放句首，後方需搭配倒裝句，公式為：Hardly + be 動詞（was）+ 主詞（that）…，或 Hardly + 助動詞 + 主詞 + 動詞原形 …。從 was conducted 可知，劃線處應為過去式。綜合以上，**A** 選項為正解。C 選項應改成：was it seen as an coincidence。

**08.** Rapid increase in tuition fees _____ low-income students, in particular, from enrolling, making higher education less and less accessible to those from disadvantaged background.

(A) is deterred

(B) have been deterred

(C) has deterred

(D) deter

> 解 學費飛漲特別阻礙低收入家庭的學生註冊就讀。對於弱勢背景的學生而言，高等教育越來越遙不可及。
>
> **考點：主動詞一致**
>
> 主詞「學費的快速增加」，重點為「增加」。單數主詞 increase，搭配單數動詞。片語「遏阻某人做某事」deter 人 from Ving。綜合以上，**C** 選項為正解。A、B 選項都是被動式，漲學費「被阻礙」，不合文意。

**09.** In German myth, mermaids called nixes are flat-out evil. They use music to lure men into their river to drown them, similar to the sweet-voiced sirens _____ in Homer's work.

(A) depicting

(B) who have depicted

(C) to be depicted

(D) depicted

> 解 德國神話故事中，美人魚又稱為水妖，是非常邪惡的。和荷馬作品中聲音甜美的女海妖相似，他們用歌聲誘惑男子進入河中，好將他們溺死。
>
> **考點：分詞當形容詞。請見下方句構分析：**
>
> They use music ...them, similar to the...sirens _____ in ...
> 　主詞 動詞　　　　　　　　　　　　介係詞　　　名詞
>
> 從上方 1 個主詞和 1 個動詞可知句子結構已完整，故名詞 sirens 後方應搭配 Ving 或 p.p. 形容詞，若用關係代名詞帶出來的關係子句當形容詞，則子句中需搭配完整的動詞，即非 Ving / p.p. / to V 原。sirens「被 Homer 在故事中描述」，應搭配表被動的 p.p. 形容詞 depicted，**D** 選項為正解。若用關係子句當形容詞，則應寫成 sirens who（或 that）have been depicted ...。關係代名詞 who 代替前方的名詞 sirens。複數主詞 sirens，搭配複數動詞 have been depicted。

**10.** There are, however, still some concerns that the agreement will be difficult to enforce despite it _____ a broadly warm welcome.

(A) being given

(B) is given

(C) will give

(D) giving

Unit 1
關係
代名詞

Unit 2
被動
語態

Unit 3
分詞
形容詞

Unit 4
分詞
構句

Unit 5
假設
語法

Unit 6
倒裝
句

Unit 7
間接
問句

Unit 8
特殊
動詞

Unit 9
主動詞
一致

Unit 10
對稱
結構

特別收錄
Unit 11
五回
試題

解 儘管這協定贏得廣泛熱烈的歡迎，但是仍然對它有些顧慮，擔心它將會很難施行。

**考點：介係詞 / 被動式**

介係詞 despite 後方需搭配名詞。且 it（即：the agreement）「受 / 被給」歡迎，需搭配被動式。綜合以上，**A** 選項為正解。

11. **I regret marching along on a parallel track with my son _____ chances of intersecting with his life.**

(A) and losing　　　(B) therefore lose　　(C) to lose　　　　(D) lost

解 我後悔走上一條和我兒子平行的路，失去和他的人生有交集的機會。

**考點：對稱。**請見下方句構分析：

I regret marching … son _____ chances …
　　　　動名詞 1　　　連接詞 + 動名詞 2

從文意可知，我後悔的事有兩件：走上和兒子平行的路 / 失去機會。regret 後方需加「(動) 名詞」。為遵守對稱原則，連接詞 and 連接兩個「動名詞」Ving，**A** 選項為正解。B 選項，副詞 therefore 無法連接 regret / lose 這兩個動詞，需用連接詞才行。

12. **To deter any troublemakers in the festival, we'll have police officers in plain clothes and uniform _____ out patrols.**

(A) to carry　　　　　　　　　　(B) carrying
(C) who are carried　　　　　　　(D) carry

解 為遏阻好事者在慶典裏滋事，我們將派便衣和制服刑警執行巡邏。

**考點：使役動詞**

使役動詞 have，後方受詞 police officers 會執行 (carry out) 勤務，需搭配「動詞原形」，**D** 選項為正解。

13. **_____ is happening far faster than that through natural factors, but the result is equally destructive.**

(A) The losses of a human habitat

(B) The human-caused habitat loss

(C) The habit losses caused by people

(D) The loss-causing human habitat

> 解 人類引發的棲地流失遠比自然因素引發的快多了，但結果是兩者同樣具毀滅性。
>
> **考點：分詞當形容詞 / 複合形容詞 / 主動詞一致**
>
> 主詞「人類引發的棲地流失」，重點為「流失」。單數主詞 loss，才能搭配單數動詞 is。複合形容詞 = N – 分詞形容詞（Ving / p.p.）。因為 habitat loss「被人類引發」，需搭配表被動的 p.p. 形容詞。綜合以上，**B** 選項為正解。A 和 C 選項，複數主詞 losses，無法搭配單數動詞 is。D 選項，引發損失的棲地，文意不通。

14. **March 11th marks the five-year anniversary of the disaster at the nuclear power plant, _____ reactors melted down following an earthquake-driven tsunami.**

    (A) where      (B) which      (C) if      (D) as though

> 解 3 月 11 號就是核電廠災難的五周年紀念日。地震引發海嘯後，電廠反應爐熔毀。
>
> **考點：關係代名詞**
>
> marks / melted down 兩個動詞，代表兩個句子，故劃線部分應為具連接句子功能的關係代名詞。將先行詞 the nuclear power plant 放回後方句 reactors … tsunami 排排看，得出：reactors in the nuclear power plant melted down following …，由此可知需用「物 / 受詞性質」的關代 which。但因關係代名詞只能代替名詞 the nuclear power plant，無法代替介係詞 in，故答案應為 in which，或代替地點的關係副詞 where。綜合以上，**A** 選項為正解。關係子句從關係副詞開始，往後推，找不到第二個動詞，所以到句點為止。關係副詞 where 帶出關係子句 reactors … tsunami，放在名詞 the nuclear power plant 後方，補充說明核電廠的狀況，為「名詞子句」。

15. **_____ was premeditated can be the difference between a second- and first-degree murder charge, so it's a matter of life and death.**

    (A) If a jury had thought that a crime      (B) Why does a jury think a crime

    (C) Whether a jury thinks a crime      (D) A jury thinks how a crime

> 解 陪審團認為犯罪究竟是預謀與否，可能造成一級和二級謀殺起訴的差別，所以陪審團的想法攸關生死。

Unit 1
關係
代名詞

Unit 2
被動
語態

Unit 3
分詞
形容詞

Unit 4
分詞
構句

Unit 5
假設
語法

Unit 6
倒裝
句

Unit 7
間接
問句

Unit 8
特殊
動詞

Unit 9
主動詞
一致

Unit 10
對稱
結構

特別收錄
Unit 11
五回
試題

考點：**間接問句當主詞**。請見下方句構分析：

... was premediated can be the difference between ...
　　　　　主詞　　　　　　　　　動詞

間接問句就是名詞子句，可放句首當主詞。間接問句的公式為：疑問詞 + 主詞 + 動詞 ...。套公式：whether（疑問詞）a jury（主詞）thinks（動詞）(that) a crime was ...。關係代名詞 that 帶出關係子句 a crime was premediated，放在動詞 thinks 後方，當受詞。綜合以上，**C** 選項為正解。A 選項，過去完成式 had thought 比過去式 was premediated 早發生，文意為：犯人預謀犯罪前，陪審團早已想到了，文意不合。

**16.** Alice feels awkward _____ in social situations. She would like to get rid of her shyness and become more outgoing.

(A) and puts　　　　(B) whenever put　　(C) to put　　　　(D) putting

**解** 每當身處社交情境，Alice 就覺得笨拙尷尬。她想要去除害羞，變得活潑外向些。

考點：**分詞構句〔變形 1〕**

原句為：Alice feels awkward whenever Alice is put in social...。兩句主詞相同，都是 Alice，可用分詞構句。is put 為被動寫法，需用表被動的 p.p. 分詞構句 when put...situations。寫分詞構句時，也可保留連接詞。綜合以上，**B** 選項為正解。

**17.** The wealthy family enjoys a luxury lifestyle _____ anyone struggling to make ends meet.

(A) which resents　　　　　　　(B) so as to resent being
(C) that is resented by　　　　　(D) resenting

**解** 這富有的家庭，過著被任何掙扎過日子的人所憤恨的奢華生活方式。

考點：**分詞當形容詞 / 形容詞子句 / 被動式**。請見下方句構分析：

The wealthy family enjoys a luxury lifestyle _____ anyone struggling...
　　　主詞　　　　　動詞　　　　名詞　　　　　形容詞　　　　　形容詞

從上方 1 個主詞和 1 個動詞可知句子結構已完整，故名詞 a luxury lifestyle 後方應搭配 Ving 或 p.p. 形容詞，若用關係代名詞帶出來的關係子句當形容詞，則子句中需搭配完整的動詞，即非 Ving / p.p. / to V 原。奢華的生活方式「被窮人怨恨」，應搭配表被動的 p.p. 形容詞 resented by ...。從 enjoys 可知本句為「現在式」。 若用關係子句當形容詞，則應

寫成 a luxury lifestyle which（或 that）is resented by ...。關係代名詞 that 代替前方的名詞 a lifestyle。單數主詞 a lifestyle，搭配單數現在被動式 is resented by ...，**C** 選項為正解。A、D 選項意思為：奢華生活怨恨掙扎求生的人，文意不通。

18. **The amount of counterfeit US dollars _____ from circulation so far has more than doubled, from $103 million to $261 million, over recent three years.**

(A) that remove　　(B) whose removal　(C) removed　　　　(D) removing

解 到目前為止，流通的美金中，被移除的假鈔金額從 1 億零 3 百萬元上升至 2 億 6 千 1 百萬元。過去三年來，已增加超過兩倍。

**考點：分詞當形容詞。**請見下方句構分析：

The amount of counterfeit US dollars _____ from circulation…has…doubled
<u>　　　　主詞／名詞　　　　</u>　　<u>形容詞</u>　　　　　　　<u>動詞</u>

從上方 1 個主詞和 1 個動詞可知句子結構已完整，故主（名）詞 the amount of ... dollars 後方應搭配 Ving 或 p.p. 形容詞。若用關係代名詞帶出來的關係子句當形容詞，則子句中需搭配完整的動詞，即非 Ving／p.p.／to V 原。dollars「被移除」，需用表被動的 p.p. 形容詞，**C** 選項為正解。若用關係子句當形容詞，則應寫成：... dollars which／that have been removed ... so far。關係代名詞 which／that 為「物／主詞」性質的關係代名詞，代替前方的複數名詞 US dollars。B 選項，關係子句 whose removal ... so far，缺動詞，文法錯誤。

19. **Studies show that major life milestones previously reserved for 20-somethings, such as getting married, buying a home and starting a family, _____ later in life.**

(A) are taking place　　　　　　　(B) taken place
(C) has been occurred　　　　　　(D) to occur

解 研究顯示，先前專為 20 多歲的年輕人預留的人生里程碑，如：結婚、買房、成家，都延後發生。

**考點：主動詞一致。**請見下方句構分析：

...major life milestones previously reserved..., such as...a family, _____ later...
　　<u>主詞</u>　　　　　<u>形容詞</u>　　　<u>milestone 的例子</u>　<u>動詞</u>
複數主詞 life milestones，搭配複數動詞。「發生」沒有被動式。綜合以上，**A** 選項為正解。人生里程碑「被預留」，故搭配表被動的 p.p. 形容詞 reserved。

20. **Every August, the Perseid meteor shower provides sky watchers in the Northern Hemisphere with a phenomenal show, if _____.**

(A) it permitted

(B) the weather permitting

(C) they are permitting

(D) to be permitted

> 解 每年 8 月，若天氣許可的話，Perseid 流星雨會為北半球的天文愛好者提供一場絕美的秀。
>
> **考點：分詞構句 [ 變形 2 ]**
>
> 原句為：... the Perseid meteor shower provides...a phenomenal show if the weather permits。兩個句子的主詞 the Perseid meteor shower / the weather 雖然不同，還是能將 if 那句硬寫成分詞構句。首先，保留不同的主詞 the weather。permits 為現在式，應改成表主動進行的 Ving 分詞構句 the weather permitting。寫分詞構句時，也可保留連接詞 if。綜合以上，**B** 選項為正解。

21. **Ninety percent of the doctors in the study say they would not want CPR _____ in a coma, compared with 25 percent of the public.**

(A) if they had been　(B) unless being　(C) were they　(D) to be

> 解 研究中，百分之 90 的醫生說，若他們陷入昏迷，他們不想進行 CPR 急救。相較下，百分之 25 的社會大眾持相同看法。
>
> **考點：假設語法**
>
> 百分之 90 受訪的醫生還會 say，現在並沒有昏迷，也沒做 CPR。if 針對「現在」做相反假設時，緊接在 if 後方的動詞從現在往前跳一格，改用「過去式」。又 be 動詞在 if 句中的過去式只能用 were。即：
>
> ... they would not want CPR **if** they **were** in a coma...
>
> 也可去掉 if，並將 were 放句首，改成加強語氣版的假設語法，即：
>
> ... they would not want CPR **were** they in a coma
>
> 由上可知，**C** 選項為正解。B 選項，連接詞 unless 後方需加句子，即：主詞 + 動詞。being in a coma 為名詞。

22. **For some Muslim women, wearing the veil is a religious duty and an act of piety. It represents neither submission to men _____ to the secular world.**

(A) but to resist

(B) nor resistance

(C) and doesn't resist

(D) or resists

解 對有些回教女性而言，戴面紗是種宗教義務，及虔敬的表現。戴面紗既不代表屈從男性，也不意味著抗拒世俗。

**考點：對稱。** 請見下方句構分析：

…respresnts **neither** submission… **nor** _____ to …

名詞 1　　　　　　　　名詞 2

「既不是 A 也不是 B」neither A nor B，A 和 B 兩者時態、詞性和結構要對稱。由上方分析可知，劃線處應為「nor + 名詞」，**B** 選項為正解。

23. The average human head has 100,000 hair follicles, _____ is able to produce 20 individual hairs during a person's lifetime.

    (A) and none of it

    (B) most of what

    (C) each of which

    (D) few of them

解 人們頭上平均有 10 萬個毛囊。在人的一生中，每個毛囊都能製造 20 根頭髮。

**考點：關係代名詞 / 主動詞一致**

has / is 兩個動詞，代表兩個句子，故劃線部分應為具連接句子功能的關係代名詞。將先行詞 hair follicles 放回後方句 is able…lifetime 排排看，得出：單數數量詞 of the hair follicles is able to….lifetime，由此可知需用「物 / 受詞性質」的關係代名詞 which，且搭配單數數量詞。C 選項中的 each（每一），就符合後面單數動詞 is 的要求，**C** 選項為正解。

24. A few doors down from his office _____ the creamy, Italian building, built by wealthy Jewish merchants in 1906.

    (A) is located　　(B) stands　　(C) situated　　(D) lie

解 離他辦公室幾戶之遙，有棟由富有的猶太商人於 1906 年所興建的乳白色義式建築。

**考點：倒裝句。** 請見下方句構分析：

A few doors down from his office _____ the creamy, Italian building, built…

地方副詞　　　　　　　　　動詞　　　　主詞　　　　分構

地方副詞放句首時，需用倒裝句，公式為：地方副詞 + 1 字動詞 + 主詞。單數主詞 the…building，需搭配單數動詞。動詞「位在…」，sit / stand / lie 為主動寫法，可用 1 字呈現，故 **B** 選項為正解。其他如：locate / situate / set / perch 需用被動寫法 be + p.p.，無法用 1 字呈現，所以非

正解。D 選項，應改成 lies。

25. **Cancer has always been a costly disease. Recent studies have documented patients' financial distress, from reduced income to _____ savings or even bankruptcy.**

(A) depletion　　(B) depleting　　(C) depleted　　(D) deplete

解 癌症始終是個所費不貲的疾病。最近的研究已記錄了病患財務困頓的狀況，從收入減少，到耗盡存款，或甚至破產。

**考點：分詞當形容詞**

Recent studies have documented…, from … to _____ savings …
　　　　　　主詞　　　　　　　　動詞　　　　　　介係詞　形容詞　名詞

從上方 1 個主詞和 1 個動詞可知句子結構已完整，故名詞 savings 前方應搭配 Ving 或 p.p. 形容詞。由於 savings「被耗盡」，應搭配表被動的 p.p. 形容詞，C 選項為正解。

26. **Since violent crimes by teens peak around 3pm on school days, experts reckon that after-school activities will be a better way of keeping youths out of troubles and _____ hobbies for a lifetime.**

(A) to help the development of　　　(B) that helps them to develop
(C) helping them develop　　　　　(D) helps developing

解 由於青少年在周間所犯下的暴力犯罪於下午三點達到高峰，教育專家認為課後活動是避免青少年闖禍，幫助他們發展可持續一輩子的嗜好的好方法。

**考點：對稱。**請見下方句構分析：

…after-school activities will be a…way of　keeping … and _____ …
　　　　主詞　　　　　　　　動詞　　　　　介係詞 動名詞 1　　　　動名詞 2

介係詞 of 後方需搭配「名詞」。為遵守對稱原則，連接詞 and 左邊為動名詞 keeping，右邊劃線處也應為動名詞。help 後方可搭配「(to) 動詞原形」。綜合以上，C 選項為正解。

27. **Billie Holiday's reputation as a great jazz-blues singer _____ on her ability to give emotional depth to her songs.**

(A) to rest　　(B) resting　　(C) are rested　　(D) rests

解 身為藍調爵士歌手，Billie Holiday 的名聲建立在她賦予歌曲情感深度的能力。

**考點：主動詞一致**

主詞「身為藍調爵士歌手的名聲」，重點為「名聲」。單數主詞 reputation，應搭配單數動詞，**D** 選項為正解。

28. **Successive droughts caused herds of livestock to perish, _____.**

    (A) left farmers to feel devastating
    (B) leaving farmers devastated
    (C) which left farmers devastating
    (D) have left farmers devastated

解 連續乾旱造成大批牲畜死亡，讓農場主人傷透心。

**考點：分詞構句／分詞當形容詞**

原句為：droughts caused herds … / droughts left farmers…。兩句主詞相同，都是 droughts，可用分詞構句。left 為過去式，需改成表主動進行的 Ving 分詞構句 leaving farmers devastated。句型「讓某人／某物…」leave + N + adj。farmers 的心「被乾旱蹂躪摧毀」，需搭配表被動的 p.p. 形容詞 devastated。綜合以上，**B** 選項為正解。

29. **Alice has a history of depression. She has been working very hard to keep it at bay, but it seems to have recurred, with symptoms of disturbed sleep, _____ and unexplained pains.**

    (A) to have lost appetite
    (B) losing appetite
    (C) loss of appetite
    (D) loses appetite

解 Alice 有憂鬱症病史。雖然她一直奮力控制自身的憂鬱症，但憂鬱症似乎已復發，伴隨著睡不安穩、沒胃口、沒來由的疼痛等症狀。

**考點：對稱。**請見下方句構分析：

… it seems …, with symptoms of … sleep, _____ and … pains
　主詞 動詞　　　　　　　　　介係詞　名詞1　名詞2　　　名詞3

介係詞 of 後方需搭配「名詞」。為遵守對稱原則，連接詞 and 左右共連接了三個名詞，**C** 選項為正解。若選 B 選項，of 後方應有三個 Ving。

30. **Patients should not be left in the dark. They deserve the peace of mind and the right to know whether the doctors _____ they entrust their life are qualified.**

(A) for which       (B) x       (C) to whom       (D) whoever

> 解 病患不應被蒙在鼓裡。他們應該要能安心，且有權了解他們託付性命的醫生是否為合格醫生。
>
> **考點：關係代名詞**
>
> entrust / are qualified 兩個動詞，代表兩個句子，故劃線部分應為具連接句子功能的關係代名詞。將先行詞 doctors 放回後方句 they entrust their life 排排看，得出：they (指 patients) entrust their life to the doctors，由此可知需用「人 / 受詞性質」的關係代名詞 whom，又關代只能代替名詞 the doctors，無法代替介係詞 to，答案應為 to whom，**C** 選項為正解。關係子句從關係代名詞開始，往後推，到第二個動詞 are 前結束。關係代名詞 to whom 帶出來的關係子句 to whom they entrust their life 放在名詞 doctors 後方，為「形容詞子句」。

31. **A refund or exchange for garments with price tags attached _____ within 35 days of purchase with a valid receipt.**

(A) to process            (B) can be processed
(C) have processed      (D) processing

> 解 購買日起算 35 天內，只要衣服價格標完整，且附上收據，即可辦理退款或換貨。
>
> **考點：被動式。**請見下方句構分析：
>
> A refund or exchange for garments with price tags attached _____ ...
>       主詞              介係詞  名詞    形容詞   動詞
> or 連接主詞時，動詞單複數以靠近的主詞為準。主詞「退換衣服」，重點為「退換」。單數主詞 exchange，搭配單數動詞。且退換貨「被處理」，應搭配被動式。綜合以上，**B** 選項為正解。

32. **Seldom _____ floor bidding once the hammer has fallen, although he can do so at his discretion if he thinks an error has occurred.**

(A) will an auctioneer re-open      (B) an auctioneer reopens
(C) reopened an auctioneer         (D) an autioneer's reopening of

解 一旦成交槌落下後，拍賣官很少重啟拍賣，即便若他認為有失誤時，他可斟酌重拍。

**考點：倒裝句**

否定副詞 seldom 放句首，後方需搭配倒裝句。reopen 不是 be 動詞，造倒裝句時需搭配助動詞。倒裝句公式為：seldom + 助動詞 + 主詞 + 動詞原形。if 針對「未來」做假設，if 後方的動詞才會改用現在式 thinks。所以倒裝句需搭配未來式助動詞 will，**A** 選項為正解。

33. The town residents want to see buildings such as this _____ to their former glory instead of being lost in the mist of time, but the reality is not so simple.

   (A) restored      (B) restoring      (C) to restore      (D) restore

解 鎮上居民想看建築物都像這棟一樣恢復到它們往日的光榮，而非迷失在時間迷霧中，但是實務上這可沒那麼容易。

**考點：感官動詞**

感官動詞 see，後方受詞 buildings「被恢復往日面貌」，需搭配表被動的「過去分詞」restored，**A** 選項為正解。

34. Most living things would disappear from the earth within a few years _____ to an abrupt end.

   (A) were photosynthesis to come      (B) for photosynthesis that comes
   (C) if photosynthesis had come      (D) despite photosynthesis coming

解 若光合作用突然中止，多數生物將在幾年內陸續從地球消失。

**考點：假設語法**

由文意可知，光合作用 (photosynthesis) 目前並沒有中止。if 針對「現在」做相反假設時，緊接在 if 後方的動詞從現在往前跳一格，改用「過去式」。又 be 動詞在 if 句中的過去式只能用 were。即：

Most living things would disappear … **if** photosynthesis **were** to come …

也可去掉 if，並將 were 放句首，改成加強語氣版的假設語法，即：

Most living things would disappear **were** photosynthetis to come …

由上可知，**A** 選項為正解。D 選項，介係詞 despite (雖然 / 儘管) 後方加名詞為正確用法，但是文意不對。「可能」be to V 原＝be (supposed) to V 原。

Unit 1
關係
代名詞

Unit 2
被動
語態

Unit 3
分詞
形容詞

Unit 4
分詞
構句

Unit 5
假設
語法

Unit 6
倒裝
句

Unit 7
間接
問句

Unit 8
特殊
動詞

Unit 9
主動詞
一致

Unit 10
對稱
結構

特別收錄
Unit 11
五回
試題

**35.** Kids actually love to help out around the house, as it empowers them and bolsters their self-esteem. They take pride in feeling _____ within the family.

(A) they need to be  (B) needed　　　(C) their needs　　　(D) needy

> 解 實際上，小孩喜歡幫忙做家事，因為家事賦予他們權力，增強他們的自尊。他們對於被家人需要感到引以為豪。
>
> **考點：連綴動詞 / 分詞當形容詞**
>
> 連綴動詞 feel 後方應搭配「形容詞」。they（即 kids）對「被需要」感到引以為豪，應搭配表被動的 p.p. 形容詞 needed，**B** 選項為正解。needy (adj) 窮困的。

**36.** _____ couples with and without children, researchers found that the rate of the decline in relationship satisfaction is nearly twice as steep for couples who have children as for childless couples.

(A) Compared　　　(B) To compare　　　(C) Comparing　　　(D) Compare

> 解 比較有小孩和沒小孩的夫妻後，研究人員發現，前者夫妻關係滿意度的下滑幅度約為後者的兩倍。
>
> **考點：分詞構句**
>
> 原句為：researchers compared couples ... / researchers found...。兩句主詞相同，都是 researchers，可用分詞構句。又 compared 為過去式，可改成表主動進行的 Ving 分詞構句 comparing ... children，**C** 選項為正解。

**37.** Due to Joe's mental health issues, the commanding officer strongly recommended _____ from the military.

(A) him discharging　　　　　(B) that he be discharged
(C) he had discharged　　　　(D) him to discharge

> 解 因為 Joe 的心理健康問題，指揮官強烈建議他從軍隊退役。
>
> **考點：被動式 / 特殊句型**
>
> 從文意可知，因為健康問題，Joe「被除役」，需用被動式。特殊句型：建議 (recommend) / 命令 / 要求 / 堅持 + that S + (should) V 原。助動詞 should 常被省略，只剩下動詞原形。綜合以上，**B** 選項為正解。

**38.** _____ on a number of factors, including fabric, dye and your personal feelings on hygiene.

(A) How are jeans laundered depending

(B) That jeans should be laundered depends

(C) Whether to launder the jeans, it is dependent

(D) How often jeans should be laundered is dependent

> 解 牛仔褲該多常洗，視許多因素而定，如：織品、染料，以及你個人對衛生的感受等。
>
> 考點：間接問句當主詞 / 主動詞一致。請見下方句構分析：
>
> _____ … on …, including fabric, … on hygiene.
> 　主詞　　動詞　　　介係詞　　　名詞
>
> 「視…而定」意味著這件事尚無定論，還是個問題，需搭配間接問句，而非關係子句。間接問句就是名詞子句，可放句首當主詞。間接問句的公式為：疑問詞 + 主詞 + 動詞 …。套公式：how often（疑問詞）jeans（主詞）should be laundered（動詞）。1 間接問句放句首當主詞，單數主詞，需搭配單數動詞 is。綜合以上，**D** 選項為正解。

**39.** During this holiday season, no sooner _____ their hankies after seeing "Manchester by the Sea" than they were awash again during "Loving."

(A) movie goers dried and fluffed

(B) dried and fluffed movie goers

(C) had movie goers dried and fluffed

(D) would movie goers dry and fluff

> 解 休假旺季，看完 *Manchester by the Sea* 的觀眾才剛晾乾手帕，就又被 *Loving* 感動到熱淚盈眶。
>
> 考點：倒裝句
>
> 先看 *Manchester by the Sea*，後又被 *Loving* 感動。否定的 no sooner 後，應接早發生的動作「看 *Manchester by the Sea*」，且造倒裝句。than 後方接晚發生的動作「被 *Loving* 感動」，不用倒裝。英文基本時態裡，「完成式」比「簡單式」早發生。晚發生的動作「被 *Loving* 感動」用「過去式」，早發生的動作「看 *Manchester by the Sea*」就應寫成「過去完成式」。
>
> 套公式：No sooner + 動詞 1（過去完成式的助動詞 had）+ 主詞 1 + p.p. …+ than + 主詞 2 + 動詞 2（過去式）。套公式，**C** 選項為正解。

**40.** Ben values punctuality a lot. He would definitely have arrived at the press conference on time _____.

(A) if he doesn't have a flat tire

(B) should he not have a flat tire

(C) had he not had a flat tire

(D) if there weren't a flat tire

> 解 Ben 很強調準時。若不是他的車子爆胎，他絕對會準時抵達記者會。
>
> **考點：假設語法**
>
> 從 would have arrived 可知 if 針對「過去」做相反假設，公式如下：
>
> If 主詞 1 + 動詞 1（過去完成式 had (not) + p.p.），主詞 2 + 動詞 2（would / should / could / might (not) + have p.p.）
>
> 套公式：He would definitely have arrived … **if** he **had not had** a flat tire.
>
> 也可去掉 if，並將過去完成式的助動詞 had 放句首，改成加強語氣版的假設語法，即：
>
> He would definitely have arrived … **had** he **not had** a flat tire.
>
> 由上可知，**C** 選項為正解。

41. The largest ice-free region in Antarctica is a windswept, frozen desert _____ rugged terrain looks as if it belongs on Pluto rather than our planet.

   (A) to which　　(B) when　　(C) that　　(D) whose

> 解 南極洲最大的無冰區就是狂風吹襲的冰凍荒漠。荒漠崎嶇的地形，彷彿像是冥王星上的景象，而非地球上的地貌。
>
> **考點：關係代名詞**
>
> is / looks 兩個動詞，代表兩個句子，故劃線部分應為具連接句子功能的關係代名詞。將先行詞 desert 放回後方句 rugged…planet 排排看，得出：the desert's rugged terrain looks…planet，由此可知需用「物 / 所有格性質」的關係代名詞 whose，**D** 選項為正解。關係子句從關係代名詞開始，往後推，looks / belongs 兩動作已用連接詞 as if 處理過，視為一組動詞。找不到第二個動詞，所以到句點為止。關係代名詞 whose 帶出來的關係子句 rugged…planet 放在名詞 desert 後方，為「形容詞子句」。

42. The authority said they could not confirm _____ as the human remains in the car were burned beyond recognition.

   (A) whether the Taliban leader really had been killed

   (B) that the Taliban leader had been really killed

   (C) how was the Taliban leader killed

   (D) why the Taliban leader were killed

**解** 當局說他們無法確認 Taliban 領導人是否已身亡，因為車子裏的遺體已燒到面目全非，無法辨識。

**考點：間接問句**

從「無法確認」可知這件事仍是個問題，故 confirm 後方接的是間接問句，而非關係子句。間接問句的公式為：疑問詞＋主詞＋動詞…。套用公式可得：whether（疑問詞）the Taliban leader（主詞）really had been killed（動詞）。綜合以上，**A** 選項為正解。D 選項，遺體燒到面目全非，和領導人為何遇害無關。

43. For women who are pregnant or are trying to conceive, travel to areas where Zika infection is spreading now _____.

    (A) have been avoided            (B) should be avoided
    (C) and avoiding                 (D) to avoid

> **解** 那些懷孕中或準備懷孕的婦女，應避免前往 Zika 感染擴散的疫區。
>
> **考點：被動式。**請見下方句構分析：
>
> ... travel to area where Zika infection is spreading now _____
> 　主詞　　名詞　　　　　　形容詞子句　　　　　　動詞
>
> 單數主詞 travel 需搭配單數動詞。又旅遊這件事應「被避免」，需搭配被動式。綜合以上，**B** 選項為正解。關係子句從關係副詞開始，往後推，到第二個動詞（即劃線處）前結束。關係副詞 where 帶出來的關係子句 Zika...now 放在名詞 area 後方，為「形容詞子句」。

44. Russian novelist and philosopher Leo Tolstoy puts it well, "What counts in making a happy marriage _____ how you deal with incompatibility.

    (A) is not how compatible you are but
    (B) are that you are compatible and
    (C) is not only compatible but
    (D) compatible with

> **解** 蘇俄小說家及哲學家 Leo Tolstoy 說得好，擁有幸福婚姻的重點不在於你們有多處得來，而在於你們如何因應彼此間的衝突。
>
> **考點：對稱／主動詞一致／間接問句。**請見下方句構分析：
>
> What counts in ... marriage _____ ...
> 　關係子句當主詞　　　　　　　動詞

1 個關係子句放句首當主詞，單數主詞，搭配單數動詞。「不是 A 而是 B」not A but B，A 和 B 兩者時態、詞性和結構要對稱。B（how you deal ...）為間接問句，那麼 A 也應為間接問句。間接問句的公式為：how compatible（疑問詞）+ you（主詞）+ are（動詞）。綜合以上，**A** 選項為正解。C 選項，「不只 A 連 B 都...」not only A but B，A 和 B 兩者時態、詞性和結構要對稱，形容詞 compatible 和間接問句 how you deal with incompatibility 不對稱。

45. So _____ that their parents often have to force them to break for sports and meals.

(A) serious addiction to electronics the children have

(B) become the children addicted to electronics

(C) are electronics addictive to the children

(D) addicted to electronics are the children

解 孩子們對電子產品如此著迷，以致於他們的爸媽常需強迫他們休息一下，做做運動或吃個飯。

**考點：倒裝句**

So 為首的倒裝句公式如下：

So + 形容詞 + be 動詞 + 主詞 1 + that + 主詞 2 + 動詞 2

套公式：So + addicted to ...（形容詞）+ are（be 動詞）+ the children（主詞 1），**D** 選項為正解。

46. One in 10 people who decided in advance to donate their organs _____. His families refuse to allow this to happen despite their dead relative's wishes.

(A) has his wishes block      (B) have their wishes to block

(C) is having his wishes blocked      (D) to have their wishes blocking

解 10 個事先決定器捐的民眾中，就有 1 個無法如願。儘管死者希望器捐，他的家人卻拒絕促成此事。

**考點：使役動詞 / 主動詞一致。** 請見下方句構分析：

One in ten people who decided ... organs _____.
    主詞             形容詞子句        動詞

主詞「10 人當中有 1 個」，重點為「1 個」。單數主詞 one，搭配單數動

詞。使役動詞 have 後方的受詞 wishes「被阻擋」，需搭配表被動的「過去分詞」blocked。綜合以上，C 選項為正解。關係子句從關係代名詞開始，往後推，decided / donate 已用不定詞 (to V 原) 處理過，視為一組動詞，所以到第二個動詞 ( 即劃線處 ) 前為止。關係代名詞 who 帶出來的關係子句 decided... organs 放在名詞 people 後方，為「形容詞子句」。

47. Archaeologists digging at the historic Parson Smith house in Windham have unearthed artifacts _____ back to the 18th century.

(A) which trace　　(B) gone　　(C) to be traced　.　(D) dating

解 在 Windham 鎮上古老的 Parson Smith 家挖掘的考古學家，已挖出可回溯到 18 世紀的工藝品。

考點：分詞當形容詞。請見下方句構分析：

Archaeologists digging...Windham have unearthed artifacts _____ back...
　　主詞　　　　　　　形容詞　　　　　　動詞　　　　名詞　　形容詞

從上方 1 個主詞和 1 個動詞可知句子結構已完整，故名詞 artifacts 後方應搭配 Ving 或 p.p. 形容詞，若用關係代名詞帶出來的關係子句當形容詞，則子句中需搭配完整的動詞，即非 Ving / p.p. / to V 原。片語「往回追溯至...時」有三個寫法：date back to 時間 / go back to 時間 / be traced back to 時間。改成形容詞也有三解：dating / going / traced，D 選項為正解。若用關係子句當形容詞，則應寫成 artifacts which (或 that) date / go / are traced back to ...。「物 / 主詞性質」的關係代名詞 which，代替前方的複數名詞 artifacts。

48. At high altitude, sleeping becomes difficult, _____ simple bodily functions like digesting food.

(A) and so are　　(B) as do　　(C) and neither is　　(D) nor does

解 身處高海拔時，睡眠變得困難，如消化食物等簡單的身體功能也變得困難。

考點：附和用的倒裝句

身體功能的運作「也」變得困難。附和肯定句的「也」，共有 so / too 兩種寫法，但 too 只能放句尾。從句尾沒看到 too 可知本句是用副詞 so 寫成的。so 後方需搭配倒裝句，公式為：and so + be 動詞 / 助動詞 + 主詞。前方句使用現在式一般動詞 becomes，故後方倒裝句需搭配現在式助動詞。複數主詞 bodily functions 搭配現在式助動詞 do。套公式得出：and so do，也可寫成 as do，B 選項為正解。

49. **What ultimately ended the Great Depression was WWII. Had the US not entered the war, the 1940 unemployment rate of 14% _____ far further.**

(A) might be risen
(B) had been rising
(C) would have risen
(D) was risen

> 解 第二次世界大戰終結了經濟大蕭條。若美國沒有參戰，1940 年的失業率將從百分之 14 再進一步往上攀升。
>
> **考點：假設語法 / 主動詞一致**
>
> 由文意可知，美國 1940 年參戰了，所以才能終結經濟大蕭條。if 針對「過去」(1940 年) 做相反假設，公式如下：
>
> If 主詞 1 + 動詞 1 (過去完成式 had (not) + p.p.)，主詞 2 + 動詞 2（would / should / could / might (not) + have p.p.)
>
> 套公式：If the US had not entered the war, the 1940 unemployment rate of 14% would have risen far further.
>
> 綜合以上，**C** 選項為正解。
>
> 註 rise (上升) 沒有被動式，三態變化為：rise – rose – risen – rising。

50. **Before being considered an employee, all candidates had to fill out a questionnaire that asked tricky questions so as to assess _____ to the company.**

(A) whether will they be loyal
(B) that they are loyal
(C) why to be loyal
(D) if they could be loyal

> 解 在獲選為正式員工前，所有求職者必須填寫一份問卷。為評估求職者是否會為公司效忠，這份問卷問了許多棘手的問題。
>
> **考點：間接問句 / 名詞片語**
>
> 從 assess (評估) 可知尚無定論，還有問題。所以 assess 後方應接間接問句，而非關係子句。間接問句的公式為：疑問詞 + 主詞 + 動詞...。套公式：if (疑問詞 - 是否) they (主詞) could be loyal (動詞)，**D** 選項為正解。C 選項不正確，因為 if / why 間接問句無法改成名詞片語 (to 動詞原形)。

Unit 1
關係
代名詞

Unit 2
被動
語態

Unit 3
分詞
形容詞

Unit 4
分詞
構句

Unit 5
假設
語法

Unit 6
倒裝
句

Unit 7
間接
問句

Unit 8
特殊
動詞

Unit 9
主動詞
一致

Unit 10
對稱
結構

特別收錄
Unit 11
五回
試題

# Unit 11

特別收錄：五回試題
## 第二回試題

**01.** One of the silly dress codes that requires all students to tuck in their shirts _____ a source of conflict between teachers and students. I do hope the school could abolish it.

(A) has long been　(B) to be　　　(C) have had　　　(D) are

> **解** 要求所有學生紮襯衫這項愚蠢的服儀規定，長久以來就是師生衝突的來源。我非常希望學校能廢除這法規。
>
> 考點：主動詞一致。請見下方句構分析：
>
> One of the silly dress codes that requires ... shirts _____ a source...
> 主詞　　　　　　　　　　形容詞子句　　　　　　動詞
> 當主詞為「數量詞 of ...」時，of 後方名詞 codes 為可數名詞，則動詞單複數視前方數量詞而定。單數主詞 one，搭配單數動詞 has long been，A 選項為正解。關係子句從關係代名詞開始，往後推，requires / tuck 已用不定詞 (to V 原) 處理過，視為一組動詞，所以到第二個動詞 (即劃線處) 前為止。關係代名詞 that 帶出來的關係子句 requires ... shirt 放在名詞 dress codes 後方，為「形容詞子句」。

**02.** India _____ made news as the citizens of Delhi choked on polluted air, is taking steps to ban new combustion-driven cars within a decade.

(A) whose　　　　(B) that　　　　(C) , when　　　(D) , which

> **解** 當德里市民因空污而窒息時，印度也上了新聞。印度現正採取步驟，十年內將禁止新的汽柴油驅動汽車。
>
> **考點：關係代名詞**
>
> made / is taking 兩個動詞，代表兩個句子，故劃線部分應為具連接句子功能的關係代名詞。將先行詞 India 放回後方句 made new ... air 排排看，得出：India made news ... air，由此可知連接兩句時需用「物 / 主詞性質」的關係代名詞 which，又 India 只有一個，關代前方需打逗號。綜合以上，**D** 選項為正解。關係子句從關係代名詞開始，往後推，made / choked 已用連接詞 as 處理過，視為一組動詞。找不到第二個動詞，所以到斷句用的逗點為止。關係代名詞 which 帶出來的關係子句 made ... air 放在名詞 India 後方，補充說明 India 的狀況，為「名詞子句」。B

選項，關代 that 前方不可打逗號。

**03.** **Counterfeit products have caused us a great loss in sales and damaged our _____ brand reputation.**

(A) hardly-earning          (B) earning-hard

(C) hard-earned            (D) earned-hardly

解 山寨貨已造成我們巨大的銷售損失，也損害我們辛苦贏得的品牌聲譽。

**考點：分詞當形容詞 / 複合形容詞**。請見下方句構分析：

Counterfeit products have caused … and damaged our_____brand reputation…
         主詞                  動詞

從上方 1 個主詞和 1 個動詞可知句子結構已完整，故名詞 brand reputation 前方應搭配 Ving 或 p.p. 形容詞。名聲是「被掙來的」，應搭配表被動的 p.p. 形容詞 earned。且加強形容詞，需用副詞，故在 earned 前方在加上副詞 hard（辛苦地）。綜合以上，**C** 選項為正解。D 選項，hardly (adv) 幾乎不，不合文意。

**04.** **When _____ inevitable parenting challenges, mothers with lower confidence and more parenting stress give up more quickly.**

(A) encountering          (B) having an encounter

(C) facing with             (D) faced

解 當遇到無法避免的育兒挑戰時，低自信心且承受較多育兒壓力的媽媽比較快投降。

**考點：分詞構句**

原句為：when mothers face / are faced with / encounter / have an encounter with inevitable parenting challenges, mothers … give up … 。兩句主詞相同，都是 mothers，可用分詞構句。face / encounter / have an encounter with 為現在式，可改成表主動進行的 Ving 分詞構句，即：when facing / encountering / having an encounter with … challenges。are faced with 為被動式，可改成表被動的 p.p. 分詞構句，即：when faced with…challenges。綜合以上，**A** 選項為正解。

206

**05.** If your friend is heartbroken about a recent break-up, holding off on gushing about your new love _____ the most thoughtful thing to do.

(A) being      (B) are going to be    (C) to have been     (D) is

> 解 假如你的朋友因最近分手而心碎時，克制自己，別喜孜孜地談論你的新歡就是最體貼的事。
>
> 考點：主動詞一致。請見下方句構分析：
>
> If    your friend   is ..., holding off ... love _____ the ...
> 連接詞    主詞 1    動詞 1      主詞 2      動詞 2
> 連接詞 if 連接兩個句子。動名詞 holding off ... 放句首當主詞。1 個動名詞，代表一件事，單數主詞，需搭配單數動詞 is，**D** 選項為正解。

**06.** Your employer might terminate your employment without notice if you _____ guilty of improper conducts such as resume fraud or sexual harassment.

(A) had found      (B) are found      (C) will be found      (D) find

> 解 假如你因為如：履歷造假或性騷擾等不當行為而被定罪時，你的雇主可能無預警地中止雇用你。
>
> 考點：假設語法 / 被動式
>
> 這句意在說明未來雇主可以解雇員工的狀況。if 針對「未來」做假設，緊接在 if 後方的動詞需從未來往前跳一格，改用「現在式」。你「被發現」有不良行為，才會被解雇，需搭配被動式。綜合以上，**B** 選項為正解。

**07.** Heavy snowfall disrupted air traffic, leaving hundreds of passengers either stranded in the airport or _____ for alternatives.

(A) scrambling      (B) to scramble      (C) scrambled      (D) scramble

> 解 大雪擾亂空中交通，讓數百名乘客困在機場，或手忙腳亂地尋求替代方案。
>
> 考點：對稱。請見下方句構分析：
>
> ..., leaving hundreds of passengers **either** stranded...**or** _____ for...
>              名詞               形容詞 1     形容詞 2
> 「讓...覺得...」leave + N + adj。且「不是 A 就是 B」either A or B。A 和

B 詞性需對稱，stranded（被困著）為表被動的 p.p. 形容詞，劃線部份也應為形容詞。passengers 可執行 scramble（手忙腳亂）這動作，應搭配表主動進行的 Ving 形容詞，**A** 選項為正解。

**08.** Currently, treatment is limited to interferon therapy, _____ 50 percent of patients will respond. For those with liver failure, transplantation holds the only hope.

(A) now that      (B) where      (C) whose      (D) to which

解 治療方法目前僅限於干擾素療法。百分之 50 的病患將對此有反應。而對於那些肝衰竭的病患，移植則是他們唯一的希望。

**考點：關係代名詞**

is limited / will respond 兩個動詞，代表兩個句子，故劃線部分應為具連接句子功能的關係代名詞。將先行詞 therapy 放回後方句 50 percent...respond 排排看，得出：50 percent of the patients will respond to the therapy，由此可知需用「物／受詞性質」的關係代名詞 which，但因關係代名詞只能代替名詞 the therapy，無法代替介係詞 to，答案應為 to which，**D** 選項為正解。關係子句從關係代名詞開始，往後推，找不到第二個動詞，所以到句點為止。關係代名詞 to which 帶出來的關係子句 50 percent...respond，放在名詞 therapy 後方，補充說明干擾素療法，為「名詞子句」。

**09.** Implicit racial biases might be more destructive than overt racial discrimination because the former _____ harder to spot, and therefore harder to combat.

(A) is      (B) be
(C) was used to being      (D) are

解 隱晦的種族偏見，可能比外顯的種族歧視更具毀滅性，因為前者比後者更難看清，因此也更難擊退。

**考點：主動詞一致**

連接詞 because 帶出句子，句中的主詞「前者」the former（即 implicit racial biases），為複數主詞，需搭配複數動詞，**D** 選項為正解。

Unit 1 關係代名詞
Unit 2 被動語態
Unit 3 分詞形容詞
Unit 4 分詞構句
Unit 5 假設語法
Unit 6 倒裝句
Unit 7 間接問句
Unit 8 特殊動詞
Unit 9 主動詞一致
Unit 10 對稱結構
特別收錄
Unit 11 五回試題

10. The textile pieces, most _____ of wool but some of linen, shed the first light on fashion in the days of King David's kingdom.

(A) making

(B) of them are made

(C) of what is made

(D) made

> 解 這些織品碎片，大多數為羊毛，但有些是亞麻布。它們讓我們對大衛王時期，王國裏的時尚流行有初步的了解。
>
> **考點：分詞當形容詞。** 請見下方句子分析：
>
> The textile pieces, most _____ of wool ..., shed the first ...
>       主詞      名詞          動詞
>
> 從上方 1 個主詞和 1 個動詞可知句子結構已完整，故名詞 most（即：most textile pieces）後方應搭配 Ving 或 p.p. 形容詞。若用關係代名詞帶出來的關係子句當形容詞，則子句中需搭配完整的動詞，即非 Ving / p.p. / to V 原。織品「被用羊毛做成」，需搭配表被動的 p.p. 形容詞 made of，**D** 選項為正解。若用關係子句當形容詞，則應寫成 most of which were made of ...。most of which 代替前面的名詞 most of the textile pieces，複數主詞，搭配複數動詞。

11. When Portuguese explorers introduced peanuts to Africa early in the sixteenth century, they _____ into Africa's agriculture.

(A) were quickly adopted

(B) are quickly adopting

(C) would have been quickly adopted

(D) adopted

> 解 16 世紀初期，當葡萄牙探險家將花生引進非洲時，花生很快就被非洲農業接納採用。
>
> **考點：被動式 / 對稱**
>
> they（即 peanuts）「被非洲接納採用」，需搭配被動式。從 introduced 可知本句應為過去式。綜合以上，**A** 選項為正解。C 選項，完成式比過去式早發生，即：先被接納採用，後引進，不合文意。

12. As new and old rivals step up their strategies, Netflix, the streaming giant, faces _____ competitive pressure and threats to its subscriber base.

(A) with grown

(B) that grows

(C) growing

(D) to grow

> 解 當新舊對手紛紛強化他們的戰略時，線上串流巨頭 Netflix 面臨日益增長的競爭壓力。對手對其訂閱人數的威脅也與日俱增。

考點：分詞當形容詞。請見下方句構分析：

... Netflix, the streaming giants, faces ＿＿＿＿ ... pressure ...
主詞　　　　　　同位格　　　　　　動詞　　　　　　名詞

從上方 1 個主詞和 1 個動詞可知句子結構已完整，故名詞 pressure 前方應搭配 Ving 或 p.p. 形容詞。壓力會「自動增長」，需用表主動進行的 Ving 形容詞 growing，**C** 選項為正解。片語「面對」face N = be faced with N。

13. It was premature to discuss how much the drug would cost, because it has neither gone through clinical trials ＿＿＿＿.

(A) or approved by the FDA

(B) nor FDA had approved it

(C) nor been approved by the FDA

(D) and FDA's approval

解 現在討論藥的價格還言之過早，因為它根本還沒通過臨床試驗，也沒得到食品藥物管理局的認可。

考點：對稱 / 被動式。請見下方句構分析：

... it　has **neither** gone through ... trials ＿＿＿＿ ...
主詞 動詞 1　　　　　　p.p.　　　　　　nor + 動詞 2-p.p.

「既不是 A 也不是 B」neither A nor B，A 和 B 詞性需對稱。gone 為過去分詞，劃線部份也應為過去分詞。主詞 it（指 drug）需「被 FDA 認可」，故搭配被動式 has been approved。和 gone 共用 has，故剩下 been approved。綜合以上，**C** 選項為正解。

14. The themes that this award-winning author deals with in her novel are universal, ＿＿＿＿ much of the human condition such as the meaning of life.

(A) encompass

(B) and emcompasses

(C) encompassing

(D) encompassed

解 得獎作家在她的小說中所處理的主題是普遍常見的，包含許多人生處境，如：人生的意義。

考點：分詞構句。請見下方句構分析：

The themes that this ... author deals ... novel are universal, ＿＿＿＿ ...
主詞　　　　　　　　形容詞子句　　　　　　動詞

原句為：the themes ... are universal / the themes encompass much of ...。兩句主詞相同，都是 the themes，可用分詞構句。encompass 為現在式，可改成表主動進行的 Ving 分詞構句 encompassing ... life，**C** 選項為正解。A 選項，無法用逗號連接 are / encompass 這兩個動詞。

210

B 選項，複數主詞 the themes，需搭配複數動詞，B 選項應改為 and encompass。

15. **With the oath of office _____, the president made his inaugural speech and pledged to make his administration the most transparent in history.**

   (A) taken      (B) to be taken      (C) that is taken      (D) taking

   解 宣誓就職後，總統隨即發表就職演說，誓言讓他的執政成為歷史上最公開透明的。

   考點：分詞當形容詞。請見下方句構分析：

   With　the oath of office _____, the president made ...
   　介係詞　　　名詞　　　　形容詞　　　主詞　　　動詞
   從上方 1 個主詞和 1 個動詞可知句子結構已完整。句型「伴隨...而來的狀況」with +N + adj。名詞 the oath of office 後方需搭配 Ving 或 p.p. 形容詞。就職誓言「被總統說」，應用表被動的 p.p. 形容詞，**A** 選項為正解。C 選項，is taken / made 時態不對稱。

16. **It is widely known in the supermarket industry that _____ on the shelves either sends sales through the roof or makes them never really reaches their full potential.**

   (A) how products are positioned      (B) how should products position
   (C) positioning what products      (D) where to position products

   解 超市產業都知道商品如何上架陳列足以讓銷售量一飛沖天，又或讓商品永遠無法完全發揮它們的潛力。

   考點：間接問句當主詞 / 主動詞一致。請見下方句構分析：

   ... that _____ on the shelves either sends　sales ...
   　　　　　主詞　　　　　　　　　　　動詞
   關係代名詞 that 帶出一個句子。1 個間接問句放句首當主詞，單數主詞，搭配單數動詞 sends。間接問句的公式為：疑問詞 + 主詞 + 動詞 ...。套用公式：how（疑問詞）products（主詞）are positioned（動詞），**A** 選項為正解。D 選項，句中的 shelves 已回答 where 這問題了，文法錯誤。

17. Not until the 1970s ＿＿＿＿＿ without passing through the inspection of the Comics Magazine Association of America.

(A) comic books had been published

(B) published comic books

(C) were comic books able to be published

(D) publishing comic books was

解 直到 1970 年間，漫畫書才能不經美國漫畫雜誌協會的審核就出版。

**考點：倒裝句**

否定詞 not until 放句首，後方需搭配倒裝句。但需先將時間點說明清楚後，才開始造倒裝。not until 為首的倒裝句公式為：Not until … + be 動詞 + 主詞…。comic books「被出版」，需搭配被動式。1970s 需用過去式。套公式，C 選項為正解。B、D 選項應改成：were comic books published。

18. Some people claim that placing a ring of flowers on the grave keeps the dead firmly below the ground where they belong, and ＿＿＿＿＿ them from wandering among the living.

(A) preventing　　(B) prevents　　(C) to prevent　　(D) prevent

解 有些人宣稱，將花環放在墳墓上可讓死者穩居地下，避免他們在人間遊蕩。

**考點：對稱／主動詞一致。**請見下方句構分析：

… that placing … on the grave keeps …, and ＿＿＿＿＿ them …
　　　　　　主詞　　　　　　　動詞 1　　　　　　動詞 2

關係代名詞 that 帶出一個句子。從文意可知，放花的功能有兩個，一個是讓死者留在地下，一個是避免他們回到人間。連接詞 and 連接兩個動詞，兩個動詞時態需對稱。1 個動名詞 placing，代表一件事，單數主詞，搭配單數現在式動詞 keeps 和 prevents。綜合以上，B 選項為正解。

19. The emergency room is packed with sick children, three ＿＿＿＿＿ into a single bed.

(A) that have squeezed　　　　(B) squeeze

(C) to be squeezing　　　　　(D) squeezed

Unit 1
關係
代名詞

Unit 2
被動
語態

Unit 3
分詞
形容詞

Unit 4
分詞
構句

Unit 5
假設
語法

Unit 6
倒裝
句

Unit 7
間接
問句

Unit 8
特殊
動詞

Unit 9
主動詞
一致

Unit 10
對稱
結構

特別收錄
Unit 11
五回
試題

解 急診室擠滿病童，三個孩子被擠在一張病床上。

**考點：分詞構句 [ 變形 2 ]**

原句為：the emergency room is packed … / three (kids) are squeezed …。兩句的主詞 the emergency room / three kids 雖然不同，還能硬寫成分詞構句。首先，保留兩句不同的主詞 three。原句中 are squeezed 為被動式，需改成表被動的 p.p. 分詞構句 squeezed … bed。綜合以上，**D** 選項為正解。

**20.** Consumers might not deem household cleaning products as dangerous substances, while many of them can do harm to health, particularly if _____ improperly.

    (A) using       (B) to be used     (C) they use     (D) used

解 消費者可能不會將家裏的清潔用品視為危險物質，然而這些清潔用品中，許多對健康有害，尤其若使用不當的話。

**考點：分詞構句 [ 變形 1 ] / 被動式**

原句為：… many of them (即 household cleaning products) can do harm to health, … if they (即 household cleaning products) are used improperly。兩句主詞相同，都是 household cleaning products，可用分詞構句。are used 為被動式，應改成表被動的 p.p. 分詞構句 if used improperly。寫分詞構句時，也可保留連接詞 if。綜合以上，**D** 選項為正解。C 選項，應改成 if they ( 即 cleaning products) are used。若 they 指 consumers 的話，use 後方應接受詞 cleaning products。

**21.** _____ money from the register leads to the cashier's dismissal.

    (A) Being caught stealing       (B) Catching to steal
    (C) Caught to be stealing       (D) To catch stealing

解 被抓到偷收銀機的錢，導致收銀員被解雇。

**考點：被動式 / 動名詞當主詞**。請見下方句構分析：

_____ …the register leads to …
   主詞         動詞

「被抓到偷錢」才會促成解雇，由此可知，需用被動式。動名詞可放句首當主詞，故答案應為 being p.p.。綜合以上，**A** 選項為正解。不定詞放句首也可當主詞，但是 D 選項應改成：To be caught stealing。

22. **Cattle that have access to sunlight and are allowed to graze or exercise in open pastures require less medication than _____ in jam-packed, filthy feedlots.**

    (A) do those raised
    (B) those are raised
    (C) raising those
    (D) require those to raise

    > 解 能享受日照，且被允許在空曠草原吃草或活動的牛隻，比起那些養在擁擠骯髒的牛圈裏的同伴，較不需要藥物治療。
    >
    > **考點：倒裝句 / 分詞當形容詞。**請見下方句構分析：
    >
    > Cattle that have ... in open pasture require ...than _____ ...
    >   主詞　　　　　形容詞子句　　　　動詞
    > 比較級 than 後方的句子，可採直說法，但若想加強語氣，也可寫成倒裝句。than 帶出來的倒裝句公式為：... than + be 動詞 / 助動詞 + 主詞。前方句使用現在式動詞 require，那麼 than 倒裝句需搭配現在式助動詞。句中，草原吃草的牛 (cattle) 和那些圈養的牛做對比 (those cattle)，複數主詞 those (cattle)，搭配現在式助動詞 do。主詞 / 名詞 those 後方可搭配形容詞。牛「被養」，故搭配表被動的 p.p. 形容詞 raised。綜合以上，**A** 選項為正解。C 選項，cattle 和 raising those (cattle) 非同性質的事，無法做比較。
    >
    > 註 cattle 為複數名詞。

23. **National quarantine of travelers _____ to Zika virus is neither appropriate or feasible. It might not have any meaningful impact on the spread of the disease but would result in negative consequences on tourism and commerce.**

    (A) are exposed　　(B) who expose　　(C) exposed　　(D) exposing

    > 解 對暴露在茲卡病毒下的遊客進行全國性的檢疫隔離，既不妥適，也不可行。這對疾病擴散不會有任何有意義的影響，卻會為旅遊和商業貿易帶來負面後果。
    >
    > **考點：分詞當形容詞。**請見下方句構分析：
    >
    > National ... travelers _____ to Zika virus is ...
    >   主詞　　　　形容詞　　　動詞
    > 從上方 1 個主詞和 1 個動詞可知句子結構已完整，故名詞 travelers 後方應搭配 Ving 或 p.p. 形容詞。若用關係代名詞帶出來的關係子句當形 e 容詞，則子句中需搭配完整的動詞，即非 Ving / p.p. / to V 原。travelers「被暴露在病毒威脅下」，應搭配表被動的 p.p. 形容詞 exposed，**C** 選項

Unit 1
關係
代名詞

Unit 2
被動
語態

Unit 3
分詞
形容詞

Unit 4
分詞
構句

Unit 5
假設
語法

Unit 6
倒裝
句

Unit 7
間接
問句

Unit 8
特殊
動詞

Unit 9
主動詞
一致

Unit 10
對稱
結構

特別收錄
Unit 11
五回
試題

為正解。若用關係子句當形容詞，則應寫成 travelers who（或 that）are exposed ...。「人 / 主詞性質」的關代 who / that 代替前面的複數名詞 travelers。

24. Suppose a cosmetic company develops a new facial cream. To test it, researchers will apply the chemical agents in the cream to lab animals' skin and eyes, feed it to them, _____ its vapors.

(A) having them to breathe

(B) have them breathing

(C) and to have them breathed

(D) and have them breathe

解 假設有家化妝品公司發展出一種新的面霜。為檢測面霜，研究人員會將面霜裏的化學物質塗在實驗室動物的皮膚和眼睛上，餵給動物吃，並讓它們吸入化學物質的蒸氣。

考點：使役動詞 / 對稱。請見下方句構分析：

..., researchers will apply ..., feed it to them _____ its vapors.
　　　主詞　　　　動詞 1　　　 動詞 2　　　　 連接詞 + 動詞 3

為遵守對稱原則，需靠連接詞連接三個未來式動詞，三個動詞共用助動詞 will 後，都為「動詞原形」。使役動詞 have，後方受詞 them（即 animals）自己會 breathe，故搭配「動詞原形」。綜合以上，D 選項為正解。

25. Slavery violated the promise of equality in the Declaration of Independence and _____ on injustice and cruelty.

(A) founded　　　　(B) to found　　　　(C) was founded　　　　(D) founding

解 蓄奴違反獨立宣言中人人平等的承諾，且它是建立在不公義和殘忍的基礎之上。

考點：被動式

Slavery violated ... and _____ on injustice ....
　　主詞　　動詞 1　　　　　動詞 2

單數主詞 slavery「被建立（found）」在不公益的基礎上，需搭配單數被動式。連接詞 and 連接兩個動詞，兩個動詞時態需對稱，從 violated 可知劃線處也應為過去式。綜合以上，C 選項為正解。

26. The same approach used to build bendable aircraft wings could also create robotic arms and legs _____ shapes could bend continuously along their entire length rather than just having a fixed number of joints.

(A) that         (B) whatever      (C) whose        (D) where

> 解 用於建造可彎曲的機翼的方法，也可用來打造機器人的手腳，讓機器人手腳的形狀可順著全長持續彎曲，而非只有固定數量的關節而已。
>
> **考點：關係代名詞**
>
> create / could bend 兩個動詞，代表兩個句子，故劃線部分應為具連接句子功能的關係代名詞。將先行詞 arms and legs 放回後方句 shapes... joints 排排看，得出：the arms' and legs' shapes could bend ...，由此可知需用「物 / 所有格性質」的關係代名詞 whose，**C** 選項為正解。關係子句從關係代名詞開始，往後推，找不到第二個動詞，所以到句號為止。關係代名詞 whose 帶出來的關係子句 shapes could bend...joints 放在名詞 arms and legs 後，為「形容詞子句」。

27. Subjected to extremely high pressure and intense heat, graphite changes into the substance _____ diamond.

(A) that is commonly referred to as      (B) commonly referring to

(C) which commonly refers as      (D) and commonly refers to

> 解 受極度高壓和強熱的影響，石墨變成常被稱為鑽石的這種物質。
>
> **考點：被動式 / 主動詞一致 / 分詞當形容詞。**請見下方句構分析：
>
> ..., graphite changes into the substance _____ diamond.
>        主詞     動詞               形容詞
>
> 從上方 1 個主詞和 1 個動詞可知句子結構已完整。名詞 substance 後方應搭配 Ving 或 p.p. 形容詞，若用關係代名詞帶出來的關係子句當形容詞，則子句中需搭配完整的動詞，即非 Ving / p.p. / to V 原。substance 「被稱為鑽石」，應搭配表被動的 p.p. 形容詞 referred to as。若用關係子句當形容詞，則應寫成 substance which（或 that）is referred to as ...。「物 / 主詞性質」的關係代名詞 which / that 代替前方的 substance。單數主詞 substance，搭配單數 / 主動式動詞，**A** 選項為正解。片語「把 A 稱做 B」refer to A as B，套公式：people refer to the substance as diamond = the substance is referred to as diamond (by people)。另一個易混淆的片語，「意指 ...」refer to N。

**28.** Based on this survey, if a retailer _____ customer credit card information hacked or stolen, more than half of the customers say they would return to using only cash at the checkout.

(A) will have      (B) had had      (C) should have      (D) has

> 解 根據這個調查，若零售商讓消費者的信用卡資訊被駭或被偷，超過一半的消費者說，他們將回歸只使用現金結帳。
>
> 考點：假設語法 / 使役動詞
>
> 這句意在用一個假設性的、未發生情境（即：若信用卡被駭）來探問消費者的意向。if 針對「未來」做假設，緊接在 if 後方的動詞需從未來往前跳一格，改用「現在式」。單數主詞 a retailer，搭配單數現在式動詞，D 選項為正解。使役動詞 has，後方受詞 credit card information「被駭 / 被偷」，故搭配表被動的「過去分詞」hacked or stolen。

**29.** The city government received approximately 240 submissions, _____ the public for suggestions on changing the name of the avenue.

(A) when asking      (B) and then asked    (C) asked      (D) to ask

> 解 當就更換路名一事尋求大家建議時，市政府收到大約 240 個投書。
>
> 考點：分詞構句
>
> 原句為：The city government received approximately... / the city government asked the public ...。兩句主詞相同，都是 the city government，可用分詞構句。asked 為過去式，需搭配表主動進行的 Ving 分詞構句 when asking... avenue。寫分詞構句時，也可保留連接詞 when。綜合以上，A 選項為正解。B 選項，順序顛倒，應先徵詢市民意見，才會收到市民投書。

**30.** Not until scientific ways of excavating, recording and preserving the ancient burial sites were developed _____ damage done to archaeological artefacts and remains greatly _____.

(A) could; reduce                  (B) to reduce; x

(C) was; reduced                  (D) have reduced; x

> 解 直到挖掘、記錄和保存古埋葬場的科學方法被發展出來，我們對考古藝品和遺骸、遺跡的損傷才得以大大降低。
>
> 考點：倒裝句 / 主動詞一致。請見下方句構分析：

Not until scientific ways…developed _____ damage done to…remains…

    時間         be 動詞   主詞        形容詞

否定詞 not until 放句首，後方需搭配倒裝句。但需先將時間點說明清楚後，才開始造倒裝。時間點用句子寫成：scientific ways of … sites（主詞）+ were developed（動詞）。not until 為首的倒裝句公式為：Not until … + be 動詞 + 主詞 + p.p. …。damage 為不可數名詞，視為單數。單數主詞 damage「被減少」，故搭配單數被動式 was + p.p.。套公式，**C** 選項為正解。損害是「被做出來的」，done 為表被動的 p.p. 形容詞。

31. **While it _____ with some serious outcomes that must be addressed, the Zika virus does not spread in a way that makes quarantine something worth consideration.**

(A) has been associated         (B) associates

(C) would have associated      (D) is associating

解 雖然茲卡病毒和某些必須解決的嚴重後果有關，但它並未擴大到讓隔離檢疫變成值得考慮的事。

**考點：被動式**

it（即 the Zika virus）「被認為和 … 有關」，需搭配被動式。連接詞 while 連接兩個動詞，兩動詞時態需對稱，does not spread 為現在式，劃線處也應為現在式。綜合以上，**A** 選項為正解。

32. **The artist suggests using the walls of the MRT station as a screen _____ high-definition videos of distant national parks are projected.**

(A) on which     (B) whose     (C) when     (D) what

解 藝術家建議利用捷運車站的牆壁當作螢幕，並將遠方國家公園的高解析影片投射在上方。

**考點：關係代名詞**

suggests / are projected 兩個動詞，代表兩個句子，故劃線部分應為具連接句子功能的關係代名詞。將先行詞 screen 放回後方句 high-definition…are projected 排排看，得出：high-definition videos…are projected on the screen，由此可知需用「物／受詞性質」的關係代名詞 which。關代只能代替名詞 the screen，無法代替介係詞 on，故答案為 on which，**A** 選項為正解。關係子句從關係代名詞開始，往後推，找不到第二個動詞，所以到句點為止。關係代名詞 on which 帶出來的關係子句 high-definition…are projected 放在名詞 screen 後，為「形容詞子句」。

218

**33.** Those apartment buildings destroyed in the strong earthquake last year _____ in violation of the government's building codes.

(A) to be constructed          (B) contructed

(C) had been constructed       (D) contructing

> 解 去年在強震中被摧毀的公寓大樓是在違反政府建築法規之下興建而成的。
>
> **考點：被動式。** 請見下方句構分析：
>
> Those apartment buildings destroyed…last year _____ in violation of…
>       主詞                               形容詞         動詞
>
> 主詞 apartment buildings 是「被建造出來的」，需搭配被動式。且先建造公寓大樓，之後大樓才被摧毀。英文時態中，「完成式」比「簡單式」早發生。比過去式 (last year) 還早發生，需用「過去完成式」。綜合以上，**C** 選項為正解。apartment buildings「被摧毀」，後方應搭配表被動的 p.p. 形容詞 destroyed。

**34.** It's no surprise that kids of all ages can get addicted to their electronic toys. That's because every text that a kid sends or receives, every Facebook "like," and every point scored during a video game _____ the feel-good chemical, dopamine.

(A) to create      (B) have created      (C) creating      (D) creates

> 解 各年齡層的孩子都對他們的電子玩具上癮，我們對這一點都不感到驚訝。這是因為每則孩子所發送或接收的簡訊，每個臉書上的讚，和電玩得到的每一分，都會產生讓人覺得開心的化學物質 – 多巴胺。
>
> **考點：主動詞一致。** 請見下方句構分析：
>
> every text that a kid … receives, every …"like," and every point scored … _____
>   主詞 1         形容詞          主詞 2            主詞 3    形容詞    動詞
>
> 連接詞 because 帶出一個句子。句中主詞裏都有 every (每一)，故即便有三個主詞，也一律視為「單數」，搭配單數動詞，**D** 選項為正解。

**35.** The case is very grave as the ex-president has demonstrated acts of power abuse by getting companies _____ money and infringing on the freedom of corporate management.

(A) giving        (B) given        (C) that are given     (D) to give

**解** 這個案子很嚴重，因為前總統已表現出濫權的行為，唆使公司給錢，並違反企業管理的自由。

**考點：使役動詞**

使役動詞 getting，後方受詞 companies 能執行 give money 這動作，故搭配「to + 動詞原形」，**D** 選項為正解。介係詞 by（藉著）後方需搭配動名詞。遵守對稱原則，連接詞 and 連接兩個動名詞 getting / infringing，指出總統濫權的兩個例子。

36. **Thomas Alva Edison once revealed that his inventions _____ in a flash of inspiration but evolved slowly from his previous works.**

    (A) sprang to life not        (B) did not spring to life
    (C) not only springing to life       (D) were not only sprung

**解** Thomas Alva Edison 曾經透露，他的發明並非靈光乍現下就活絡了起來，而是從他之前的作品慢慢演進而成的。

**考點：對稱。** 請見下方句構分析：

... that his inventions _____ in a flash of inspiration **but** evolved ...
　　　　　　　　主詞　　　　　　動詞 1　　　　　　　　　　　　　　　動詞 2
關係代名詞 that 帶出一個句子。「不是 A 而是 B」not A but B，A 和 B 詞性、時態需對稱。evolved 為過去式動詞，劃線處也應為過去式動詞，**B** 選項為正解。D 選項，inventions（創作發明）自己會活起來，也有生命力會自行演進，應用主動語態，而非被動式。

37. **_____ the arrest warrant for Ms. Park, who was formally removed from office on March 10th, _____, prosecutors will have up to 20 days to continue investigations and file charges against her.**

    (A) Were; issued          (B) If; is issued
    (C) Should; issue        (D) That; will be issued

**解** Park 小姐三月 10 日正式被撤職。假如逮捕她的拘票被發出，檢察官最多將有 20 天可持續調查和對她提告。

**考點：假設語法**

從 will have 可知 if 針對「未來」做假設，緊接在 if 後方的動詞需從未來往前跳一格，改用「現在式」。單數主詞 the arrest warrant「被發出」，應搭配單數現在被動式，**B** 選項為正解。解題時，建議先精簡句型，刪除兩

個逗號包夾住、補充說明 Ms. Mark 狀況的名詞子句 who...March 10th。

38. **As cabins become more crowded and seats shrink, passengers on board a flight _____ to use headphones as a courtesy to other travelers when listening to any device.**

(A) are encouraged

(B) will be encouraging

(C) has encouraged

(D) encourage it

解 由於機艙變得越來越擁擠，座位也縮小，當聽任何裝置時，機上的乘客被鼓勵使用耳機，這對其他乘客也是種禮貌。

**考點：主動詞一致。**請見下方句構分析：

As cabins become ..., passengers on board a flight _____ to use...

　　　　　主詞1　動詞1　　　　主詞2　　　　形容詞　　　動詞2

複數主詞 passengers「被鼓勵」使用耳機，需搭配複數被動式。句首的連接詞 as 連接兩個動詞，兩個動詞時態需對稱。become 為現在式，劃線部份也應為現在式。綜合以上，**A** 選項為正解。B、C、D 選項都是主動語態，後方需有受詞。片語「鼓勵 ... 做 ...」encourage N to V 原。D 選項，代名詞 it 代替 a flight，文意不通。

39. **Einstein is reported to have said: If only I had known. I _____ a watchmaker. Apparently, he was remorseful for his role in facilitating the development of the atom bomb that has forever changed the world.**

(A) should have become

(B) became

(C) would become

(D) was to become

解 據說，Einstein 曾說：但願我早知道，我應該成為製錶師才對。顯然，他對自己在促進原子彈發展上所扮演的角色感到後悔。原子彈永遠改變了世界。

**考點：假設語法**

從 if only I had known 可知 if only 針對「過去」做相反假設。副詞 if only 後方句，文法操作方式和 if 相同。if 針對「過去」做相反假設的公式如下：

If 主詞1 + 動詞1（過去完成式 had (not) + p.p.），主詞2 + 動詞2（would / should / could / might (not) + have p.p.）

套公式可知，**A** 選項為正解。should have p.p. 意指「過去該做卻沒有做」。

**40.** Offering wine or coffee in bookstores is an ongoing effort by physical retailers to attract consumers, though some wonder _____ them from closing their doors.

(A) that beverages are saving     (B) if beverages are saving

(C) whether can beverages save     (D) what has saved

> 解 在書店裏供應酒或咖啡，是實體零售商為吸引顧客所持續做出的努力。雖然有些人好奇這些飲品是否可拯救店家，使它們免於關門噩夢。
>
> **考點：間接問句**
>
> 從 wonder（好奇）可知仍心存疑問，後方應搭配間接問句，而非關係子句。間接問句的公式為：if（疑問詞）+ beverages（主詞）+ will save（動詞）…。綜合以上，**B** 選項為正解。疑問詞 if（是否）後方的動詞不須跳躍，搭配和語意相對應的時態即可。

**41.** Rarely _____ to meet the candidates running for office in person, so they ultimately rely on information from the Internet or TV to decide for whom to vote.

(A) do voters get     (B) get voters

(C) voters gotten     (D) voters who get

> 解 選民很少見到競選公職的候選人本人，所以他們最後都靠網路或電視上的訊息來決定投票給誰。
>
> **考點：倒裝句**
>
> 否定副詞 rarely（幾乎不）放句首，後方需搭配倒裝句。連接詞 so 連接兩個動詞，兩個動詞時態需對稱，rely 為現在式，劃線部份也應為現在式。get 不是 be 動詞，造倒裝句時需搭配「助動詞」。倒裝句公式：rarely + 助動詞 + 主詞 + 動詞原形。套公式，**A** 選項為正解。

**42.** Canada was overwhelmed by a surge of illegal immigrants who poured across the border to seek asylum. The public couldn't help wondering _____ people to enter Canada unlawfully.

(A) whether to accord them full refugee benefits and to encourage

(B) that according them full refugee benefits actually has encouraged

(C) how will according them full refugee benefits actually encourage

(D) if according them full refugee benefits actually encourages

Unit 1 關係 代名詞

Unit 2 被動 語態

Unit 3 分詞 形容詞

Unit 4 分詞 構句

Unit 5 假設 語法

Unit 6 倒裝 句

Unit 7 間接 問句

Unit 8 特殊 動詞

Unit 9 主動詞 一致

Unit 10 對稱 結構

特別收錄 Unit 11 五回 試題

解 加拿大已被跨越邊界、尋求庇護的大批非法移民給壓垮了。大家不禁好奇，給予他們全套難民優惠是否會鼓勵人們非法進入加拿大。

**考點：間接問句 / 動名詞 / 主動詞一致**

從 wondering（好奇）可知仍心存疑問，後方應搭配間接問句，而非關係子句。間接問句的公式為：if（疑問詞）+ according...benefits（主詞）+ encourages（動詞）...。動名詞 according 放句首當主詞。1 個動名詞，代表一件事，單數主詞，搭配單數動詞 encourages。綜合以上，**D** 選項為正解。疑問詞 if（是否）後方的動詞不須跳躍。A 選項，whether...to encourage people to enter Canada illegally（是否鼓勵人們非法進入加拿大），文意不通。accord (v) 給予。

43. **According to a video posted on Twitter, everyone onboard looked _____ while the security forcibly removed and dragged a passenger off the overbooked flight.**

    (A) appalling　　(B) appallingly　　(C) appalled　　(D) to appall

解 根據 Twitter 上的影片，當警衛暴力地將一名乘客拖離超賣的班機時，機上的每個人看起來都很驚恐。

**考點：連綴動詞**

連綴動詞 looked，後方需搭配「形容詞」或「like + 名詞」。情緒動詞 appall（驚恐）改成的形容詞，ed 結尾形容人，ing 結尾形容事物。綜合以上，**C** 選項為正解。

44. **Precious metals such as gold are scare and limited, _____: Originality and imagination are rare goods in the film business.**

    (A) and some personal attributes do, too.
    (B) nor do some personal attributes
    (C) and so are some personal attributes
    (D) but some personal attributes aren't, either

解 如黃金等貴金屬是稀有且限量的，某些個人特質也是。創意和想像力在電影產業中就是稀有商品。

**考點：附和用的倒裝句**

某些個人特質（如：imagination）「也是」稀有限量的（rare goods）。附和肯定句的「也」，共有 so / too 兩種寫法。第一句使用現在式 be 動詞，那

麼 so / too 附和句就會跟著使用現在式 be 動詞。複數主詞 some personal attributes，需搭配複數 be 動詞 are。若用 too 來附和，應寫成：and some personal attributes are, too.。若用 so 來附和，so 後方需搭配倒裝句，公式為：and so + be 動詞 + 主詞。套公式：and so are some personal attributes。綜合以上，**C** 選項為正解。

Unit 1
關係
代名詞

Unit 2
被動
語態

Unit 3
分詞
形容詞

Unit 4
分詞
構句

Unit 5
假設
語法

Unit 6
倒裝
句

Unit 7
間接
問句

Unit 8
特殊
動詞

Unit 9
主動詞
一致

Unit 10
對稱
結構

特別收錄
Unit 11
五回
試題

45. **The witness said that she saw an ambulance _____ to the crash scene and the victim with multiple gunshots soon _____ away to the hospital.**

(A) rushing; took　　(B) rushed; taking　　(C) rushing; taken　　(D) rush; take

解 目擊者說，他看見救護車趕到車禍現場，然後受多重槍傷的被害者很快地就被送到醫院。

**考點：感官動詞**

感官動詞 saw 後方第一個受詞 ambulance 可執行 rush（迅速運送）這動作，故可搭配「動詞原形」或「動詞 ing」。第二個受詞 the victim「被帶走」，故搭配表被動的過去分詞。綜合以上，**C** 選項為正解。

46. **Ever since the video of passengers dragged from the overbooked plane went viral, the airline has come under scathing criticism for how it handled the situation, from its insistence that paying customers give up seats to _____.**

(A) use violence frequently by the security officers
(B) the level of violence used by security officers
(C) the security officers use violence frequently
(D) be used by violent security officers

解 自從乘客被拖離超賣的班機的影片快速傳開來後，航空公司就因處理機位超賣的方式，從它堅持付費的乘客必須放棄座位，到安全警衛使用暴力的程度，而飽受嚴厲批評。

**考點：對稱。** 請見下方句構分析：

..., from its insistence　　that paying...seats　　to　　_____.
　　介係詞　　名詞　　　子句補充說明 insistence　介係詞　名詞

「從 A 到 B」from A to B，A 和 B 對稱，都是名詞。名詞 violence「被使用」，故後方搭配表被動的 p.p. 形容詞 used，**B** 選項為正解。C 選項為句子，the security officers（主詞）+ use（動詞）...。介係詞 to 無法銜接句子。A 選項，客戶付錢是為了使用暴力，文意不合。

**47.** **Job hopping doesn't look good on your resume, and you need to be ready to justify your short employment stints with an explanation of _____ for the new job you are interviewing for.**

(A) why are you qualified

(B) what make you a better candidate

(C) how you did to accumulate the needed experiences

(D) how all your experiences have prepared you

> 解 跳槽換工作，在履歷上看起來並不討喜。你必須準備好為自己的短命工作辯護，並解釋為何你的經歷已讓你為你面試的這份新工作做好了萬全準備。
>
> **考點：間接問句**
>
> 間接問句的公式為：how（疑問詞）+ all your experiences（主詞）+ have prepared（動詞）…，**D** 選項為正解。A 選項應改為：why（疑問詞）+ you（主詞）+ are qualified（動詞）。B 選項，what 既是疑問詞也是主詞，且 what 當主詞時，應視為第三人稱單數，需改成：what makes you…。C 選項，did what 而非 did how，名詞才能當受詞，故應改成：what you did to…。

**48.** **_____ the insurer _____ to detect the insurance fraud earlier, the beneficiary, who hired two gunmen to murder her husband, wouldn't have had the slightest chance to collect his life insurance benefits which are worth 90 million dollars.**

(A) Had; been able

(B) If; has been able

(C) Should; be able

(D) Was; able

> 解 若保險公司能夠早點察覺這宗保險詐欺案，那個雇用兩名槍手來謀殺丈夫的受益人，根本沒機會領取她丈夫值 9 千萬的壽險金。
>
> **考點：假設語法**
>
> 從 wouldn't have had 可知 if 針對「過去」做相反假設，公式如下：
>
> If 主詞 1 + 動詞 1（過去完成式 had (not) + p.p.），主詞 2 + 動詞 2（would / should / could / might (not) + have p.p.）
>
> 套公式：**If** the insurer **had been able** to detect the insurance fraud earlier, the beneficiary…wouldn't have had the slightest chance to …
>
> 也可去掉 if，並將 had 放句首，改成加強語氣版的假設語法，即：
>
> **Had** the insurer **been able** to detect … earlier, the beneficiary …

由上可知，**A** 選項為正解。

49. While some people seem to be aware of their heart rhythms at all times, others have almost never felt their heart _____. Obviously, the latter group is less likely to complain of palpitations.

(A) like beats      (B) to beat      (C) beating      (D) beaten

> 解 雖然有些人似乎總能意識到他們的心律，但其他人幾乎從未感受到他們心臟的跳動。顯然，後者較不可能抱怨心悸的問題。
>
> **考點：感官動詞**
>
> 感官動詞 felt，後方受詞 their heart，可執行 beat（跳動）這動作，故搭配「動詞原形」或「動詞 ing」，**C** 選項為正解。

50. Campaign strategy is the ways _____ candidates attempt to manipulate money, the media attention and momentum to achieve the nomination.

(A) whose      (B) what      (C) in which      (D) how

> 解 活動策略就是候選人試著操控金錢、媒體關注和勢頭以贏得提名的方法。
>
> **考點：關係代名詞 / 複合關係代名詞 / 關係副詞**
>
> is / attempt 兩個動詞，代表兩個句子，故劃線部分應為具連接句子功能的關係代名詞。將先行詞 the ways 放回後方句 candidates attempt … nomination 排排看，得出：candidates attempt to manipulate money, …the nomination in（用）the ways，由此可知需用「物 / 受詞性質」的關係代名詞 which。但因為關係代名詞只能代替名詞 the ways，無法代替介係詞 in，故答案應為 in which，**C** 選項為正解。關係子句從關係代名詞開始，往後推，attempt / manipulate / achieve 都用不定詞（to V 原）處理過，視為一組動詞，由於找不到第二個動詞，所以到句點為止。關係代名詞 in which 帶出來的關係子句 candidates attempt … nomination 放在名詞 ways 後方，為「形容詞子句」。

# Unit 11

**特別收錄：五回試題**
**第三回試題**

**01.** When there are more passengers than seats on the flight, someone has to give up his seat. _____ will vary with a complicated seating hierarchy. Among the variables are when you bought the tickets and when you checked in.

(A) Who is that person

(B) The person is who

(C) Who that person is

(D) It is the person that

> 解 當班機上乘客比座位多時，就有人必須放棄座位。至於那人是誰，將隨複雜的座位分級而不同。其中兩個變因就是你何時買票及何時報到。
>
> **考點：間接問句。** 請見下方句構分析：
>
> _____ will vary with ...
> <u>主詞</u>　<u>動詞</u>
> 間接問句就是名詞子句，可放句首當主詞。間接問句的公式為：who（疑問詞）+ that person（主詞）+ is（動詞），**C** 選項為正解。

**02.** The criminal justice system here is still heavily reliant on confessions _____ forcefully through torture and ill-treatment to secure a conviction.

(A) obtaining

(B) to obtain

(C) that have obtained

(D) obtained

> 解 這裏的司法系統，仍相當依賴靠折磨和虐待強取的口供，來確保定罪。
>
> **考點：分詞當形容詞。** 請見下方句構分析：
>
> The criminal ... here is still ... reliant on confessions _____ forcefully ...
> <u>主詞</u>　　　<u>動詞</u>　　　　　　<u>名詞</u>　　<u>形容詞</u>
> 從上方 1 個主詞和 1 個動詞可知句子結構已完整，故名詞 confessions 後方應搭配 Ving 或 p.p. 形容詞。若用關係代名詞帶出來的關係子句當形容詞，則子句中需搭配完整的動詞，即非 Ving / p.p. / to V 原。由於 confessions「被強迫取得」，應用表被動的 p.p. 形容詞，**D** 選項為正解。若用關係子句當形容詞，則應寫成：confessions which（或 that）are obtained 或 have been obtained ...。「物 / 主詞性質」的關係代名詞 which / that 代替前方的名詞 confessions。複數主詞 confessions，搭配複數現在被動式。

**03.** This organization criticizes the university for failing to create an environment that "engages in diversity, equity and inclusion." Ironically, it is now demanding that a space _____ aside for use solely by students of certain skin color.

(A) sets      (B) to be set      (C) setting      (D) be set

解 這組織批評大學沒能創造出一個多元、平等、包容的環境。諷刺地，這組織現正要求學校撥出一個空間，專供特定膚色的學生使用。

考點：被動式 / demand 句型

特殊句型：建議、命令、要求 (demand)、堅持 that S + (should) V 原。當中，助動詞 should 常被省略，剩下「動詞原形」。space「被留作...用」，須搭配被動式。綜合以上，**D** 選項為正解。片語 set aside 指「留起來」。

**04.** Sipping one good cup of coffee is delightful, but the cumulative effects of drinking it all day _____ heartburn and insomnia.

(A) are      (B) has been      (C) to be      (D) is

解 啜飲一杯好咖啡令人開心，但是喝咖啡喝一整天，累積下來的影響就是胃灼熱和失眠。

考點：主動詞一致

連接詞 but 帶出一個句子。句中主詞「喝咖啡的影響」，重點為「影響」。複數主詞 effects，搭配複數動詞，**A** 選項為正解。

**05.** Among the list of the world's first discovered treasures in Australia this year was the oldest ground-edge stone axe, _____ discovery pushed back the aboriginal technology to 49,000 years ago.

(A) which      (B) when      (C) whose      (D) what

解 今年在澳洲發現的首批世界寶藏清單中，有把最古老的鋒利石斧。石斧的發現讓原住民科技可回溯至 4 萬 9 千年前。

考點：關係代名詞

was / pushed 兩個動詞，代表兩個句子，故劃線部分應為具連接句子功能的關係代名詞。將先行詞 axe 放回後方句 discovery...ago 排排看，得出：axe's discovery pushed ... ago，由此可知需用「物 / 所有格詞性質」的關係代名詞 whose，**C** 選項為正解。關係子句從關係代名詞開始，往

後推，找不到第二個動詞，所以到句點為止。關係代名詞 whose 帶出來的關係子句 discovery pushed…ago 放在名詞 axe 後方，補充說明 axe 帶來的影響，為「名詞子句」。

**06.** This two-disc set, _____ 310-minute viewing time, is the sequel to Anne of Green Gables, based on the treasured book by Lucy Maud Montgomery.

(A) made up of　　(B) composed of　　(C) constituting　　(D) comprising

> 解 這兩張 CD 組，共 310 分鐘，是 Anne 的綠色小屋的續集。全劇以 Lucy Maud Montgomery 最被珍藏的作品為本。
>
> **考點：分詞構句**
>
> 原句為：this two-disc set（小團體）constitutes 310-minute viewing time（大團體）… / this two-disc set is the sequel…。兩句主詞相同，都是 the two-disc set，可用分詞構句。constitutes 為現在式，可改成表主動進行的 Ving 分詞構句 constituting…time，**C** 選項為正解。310-minute viewing time（大團體）comprises / is composed of / is made up of this two-disc set（小團體），改成分詞構句分別為：comprising / composed of / made up of…time。A、B、D 選項，主詞都是 310-minute viewing time，和題目不合。

**07.** If the demand for 500,000 electric cars _____ in three years, Tesla, the most valuable automaker in the US, would find itself stuck with an extremely expensive battery factory it doesn't need.

(A) doesn't materialize　　　　　(B) hadn't materialized
(C) weren't materialized　　　　(D) won't be materialized

> 解 假如三年內電動車的需求未達 50 萬輛，堪稱美國最有價值的車商 Tesla 將發現自己受困於無用武之地的天價電池廠。
>
> **考點：假設語法**
>
> 從 in three years（未來 3 年內）可知 if 針對「未來」做假設，緊接在 if 後方的動詞需從未來往前跳一格，改用「現在式」。主詞「電動車的需求」，重點在「需求」。單數主詞 demand，搭配單數動詞。綜合以上，**A** 選項為正解。「實現某事」：事 materialize，不需用被動式。

**08.** The best practice of combating bias in Artificial Intelligence _____.
It requires a long-term research agenda for computer scientists,
sociologists, and psychologists.

(A) aren't working out

(B) still need to be worked out

(C) is still being worked out

(D) has worked out

> 解 打擊人工智慧偏見的最佳方法正被擬定中。這有賴電腦科學家、社會學家、心理學家長期研究。
>
> **考點：主動詞一致 / 被動式**
>
> 主詞「打擊偏見的最佳方法」，重點為「最佳方法」。單數主詞 practice，搭配單數的動詞。又方法「被擬定中」，需搭配被動式。綜合以上，**C** 選項為正解。B 選項應改成：still needs to be worked out。

**09.** When a passenger books a flight, the only way to get him _____ from the plane is through a voluntary system, by offering compensation on which they agree.

(A) remove　　(B) removing　　(C) to remove　　(D) removed

> 解 當乘客預訂班機時，唯一可讓他被從飛機移除的方法將是透過自願系統，提供雙方都同意的補償。
>
> **考點：使役動詞**
>
> 使役動詞 get，後方受詞 him「被從飛機移除」，需搭配表被動的「過去分詞」，**D** 選項為正解。

**10.** The Internet is a freely and highly accessible medium, _____ it is very easy to copy and republish material without thinking about copyright.

(A) why　　(B) when　　(C) which　　(D) where

> 解 網路是免費且很方便取得的媒介。在網路上，很容易在沒考慮到版權的狀況下，複製和重新發布訊息。
>
> **考點：關係代名詞**
>
> is / is 兩個動詞，代表兩個句子，故劃線部分應為具連接句子功能的關係代名詞。將先行詞 medium（媒介）放回後方句 it is ... copyright 排排看，得出：it is very easy to copy ... through the medium，由此可知需用「物 / 受詞性質」的關係代名詞 which，但因為關係代名詞只能代替名詞 the

medium，無法代替介係詞 through，故答案應為 through which，或代替地點的關係副詞 where。**D** 選項為正解。關係子句從關係副詞開始，is / copy / republish 三個動詞已用不定詞 (to V 原) 和連接詞 and 處理過了，應視為一組動詞。由於找不到第二個動詞，所以到句點為止。關係副詞 where 帶出來的關係子句 it is very … copyright 放在名詞 medium 後方，補充說明 the Internet 是怎樣的媒介，為「名詞子句」。

11. **Complicating coral recovery now is the fact that the bouts of bleaching are growing longer and more severe, while the _____ recovery periods are shorter and less frequent.**

    (A) much-needed

    (B) very-needing

    (C) need-driving

    (D) too-needy

    > 解 讓珊瑚復原變得更複雜的是：一波波的白化時間拉得愈來愈長，且狀況也愈形嚴重，同時，珊瑚極為需要的復原時間也變得越來越短，且較不頻繁。
    >
    > **考點：分詞當形容詞**。請見下方句構分析：
    >
    > …, while the _____ recovery periods are shorter …
    > 　　　　　　　主詞 / 名詞　　　　動詞
    >
    > 連接詞 while 帶出一個句子。從上方 1 個主詞和 1 個動詞可知句子結構已完整，故主 (名) 詞 recovery periods 前方應搭配 Ving 或 p.p. 形容詞。由於 recovery periods「被珊瑚需要」，應搭配表被動的 p.p. 形容詞 needed，且加強形容詞可用副詞 much，**A** 選項為正解。C 選項，recovery periods「被驅動」，應搭配表被動的 p.p. 形容詞 driven，但即便改成 need-driven (被需求所驅動的復原期)，還是文意不通。 D 選項，形容詞 needy 意指「貧窮的」，不合文意。
    >
    > 註 複合形容詞形成的公式有兩個：(1) N-adj (2) adv-adj。

12. **The number of employees filing retirement applications _____ short of previous projections. Fewer retirees mean lower pension costs.**

    (A) to fall　　　(B) are fallen　　　(C) falling　　　(D) falls

    > 解 提出退休申請的員工數，較原先預估少。越少退休的人，也意味著退休金的開銷較低。
    >
    > **考點：主動詞一致**。請見下方句構分析：
    >
    > The number of employees filing … applications _____ short of previous…
    > 　　　　主詞　　　　　　　　　　　　　　形容詞　　　動詞

主詞「員工的數量」，重點為「數量」。單數主詞 the number，搭配單數動詞，D 選項為正解。員工會主動提出申請，故搭配表主動進行的 Ving 形容詞 filing。

13. _____ together on social media but the whole online communities have become more ideologically unified, which prevents them from getting exposed to different kinds of information.

(A) The like-minded don't enjoy gathering

(B) Not only are the like-minded gathering

(C) Not merely gather the like-minded

(D) The like-minded not only have gathered

解 志同道合的人不只在社群媒體上集結，且整個線上社群在意識型態上也更趨團結。這讓他們無法暴露在不同訊息下。

考點：倒裝句

從文意可知，人們「不只」聚集在社群媒體上，而且同社群的人在意識型態上「也」更一致，需用連接詞「不只 A，而且 B」not only A but (also) B 銜接兩句，A 和 B 詞性和結構對稱。若將否定詞 not only 放句首，則需造倒裝句。套公式：Not only + be 動詞 (are) + 主詞 1 (the like-minded) … but + 主詞 2 (the whole online communities) + 動詞 2 (have become) …，B 選項為正解。「the + adj」代表全體，the like-minded 應視為複數。D 選項，動詞 have gathered 和句子 the whole online communities have become …，不對稱。C 選項應改成：Not merely do the like-minded gather。

14. The executive order, dubbed "Buy American, Hire American," is part of a history of government action _____ back to the Great Depression.

(A) dating (B) to go (C) that traces (D) gone

解 被暱稱為「買美國貨，雇用美國人」的這道執行令是政府行動史的一部份。政府行動史可回溯至經濟大蕭條時。

考點：分詞當形容詞。請見下方句構分析：

The executive order, dubbed …, is part of government action _____ …
　　主詞　　　　　分詞構句　動詞　　　　　　名詞

從上方 1 個主詞和 1 個動詞可知句子結構已完整，名詞 government action 後方應搭配 Ving 或 p.p. 形容詞。若用關係代名詞帶出來的關係子句當形容詞，則子句中需搭配完整的動詞，即非 Ving / p.p. / to V

原。片語「回溯至...時」go back to 時間 / date back to 時間 / be traced back to 時間，改成形容詞分別為 going / dating / traced，**A** 選項為正解。若用關係子句當形容詞，則應寫成：... government action which（或 that）goes / dates / is traced back to ...。「物 / 主詞性質」的關代 which / that 代替前面的 action。單數主詞 action，搭配單數動詞。

15. **The former president, who might face criminal charges over a corruption scandal, apologized to the public, before _____ prosecutors for 14 hours.**

A) his questioning

(B) being questioned by

(C) he had questioned

(D) was questioned by

解 可能因貪污醜聞而面臨刑事起訴的前總統，在被檢察官訊問 14 小時前，先向大眾道歉。

**考點：被動式**

從文意可知，可能面臨起訴的前總統要「被檢察官訊問」，需搭配被動式。又連接詞 before，後方接句子（S + V），即：...before he was questioned by prosecutors ...。介係詞 before，後方接（動）名詞，即：...before being questioned by prosecutors ...。綜合以上，**B** 選項為正解。

16. **Having a year or two head start makes a big difference, not only cementing Tesla's reputation as the leading electric car brand _____ Tesla to make further investments that help it stay one step ahead of rivals down the road.**

(A) and also positions

(B) but positioning

(C) to position

(D) which will position

解 早業界一兩年開始，結果可是大不同。這一兩年不只鞏固了 Tesla 電動車龍頭的名聲，也讓 Tesla 能夠做進一步投資，保持未來仍領先對手一步。

**考點：分詞構句 / 對稱**

原句為：having a...head start makes a big difference / having a head start not only cements Tesla's reputation ..., but positions（將 ... 放在適當位置）Tesla to make ...。兩句主詞相同，都是 having a ...head start 這件事，可用分詞構句。cements / positions 為現在式，可改成表主動進行的 Ving 分詞構句 cementing ... brand 和 positioning ... road。接著用連接詞來連接兩個 Ving 分詞構句，即：not only [ 分詞構句 1 ]

but [ 分詞構句 2 ]，形成對稱。綜合以上，**B** 選項為正解。

17. **Saving historical buildings has been an uphill battle in a place _____ doesn't have a formalized planning system, and _____ many public buildings have been swiftly privatized in deals.**

(A) which; where
(B) that; whose
(C) that; which
(D) where; that

> 解 在沒有正式規劃系統的地方，和許多公共建築都已在買賣中快速私有化的地區，拯救歷史建築是場苦戰。
>
> **考點：關係代名詞 / 關係副詞**
>
> has been / doesn't have 兩個動詞，代表兩個句子，故第一格應為具連接句子功能的關係代名詞。將先行詞 a place 放回後方句 doesn't have … system 排排看，得出：a place doesn't have a … system，由此可知需用「物 / 主詞性質」的關係代名詞 which。關係代名詞帶出來的關係子句 doesn't … system 放在名詞 place 後方，為「形容詞子句」。同樣地，has been / have been 兩個動詞，代表兩個句子，故第二格也應為具連接句子功能的關係代名詞。將先行詞 a place 放回後方句 many public buildings … in deals 排排看，得出：many public buildings have been privatized … in deals in a place，由此可知需用 in which，或代替地點的關係副詞 where。關係副詞帶出來的關係子句 many public buildings … deals 放在名詞 place 後方，為「形容詞子句」。接著再用連接詞 and 連接兩個形容詞子句。綜合以上，**A** 選項為正解。請見下方句構分析：

| Saving … building | has been | … a place | which … system, | and where … deals. |
|---|---|---|---|---|
| 主詞 | 動詞 | 名詞 | 形容詞子句 1 | 形容詞子句 2 |

18. **Currently, the annual real-estate fee is $825 for our apartment in Sweden. However, if we _____ the same property in the US now, our taxes would be $18,000 a year.**

(A) had owned
(B) owned
(C) are going to own
(D) own

> 解 目前，我們在瑞典的公寓，每年的房地產費為美金 825 元。然而，假如我們在美國擁有同樣這棟公寓的話，我們的稅金將高達一年美金 18000 元。
>
> **考點：假設語法**
>
> 由文意可知，敘事者目前住在瑞典，他們在美國並沒有房產。if 針對「現

Unit 1
關係
代名詞

Unit 2
被動
語態

Unit 3
分詞
形容詞

Unit 4
分詞
構句

Unit 5
假設
語法

Unit 6
倒裝
句

Unit 7
間接
問句

Unit 8
特殊
動詞

Unit 9
主動詞
一致

Unit 10
對稱
結構

特別收錄
Unit 11
五回
試題

在」now 做相反假設，緊接在 if 後方的動詞需從現在往前跳一格，改用「過去式」，**B** 選項為正解。

19. Estimates for the border wall construction so far have varied, with $12 billion at the low end and $15 billion as a more reasonable figure. With so many unknowns, it's difficult to say _____.

(A) who more accurate estimations offer

(B) whose price is right

(C) how much does the proposal cost

(D) how is the toal cost calculated

解 建造邊界高牆的預估費用，目前為止眾說紛紜，從最少美金 120 億，到比較合理的美金 150 億。伴隨這麼多未知數，很難說誰的開價才是正確的。

**考點：間接問句**

從 difficult to say 可知，仍有問題未解決，故 say 後方應接間接問句。間接問句的公式為：whose price（疑問詞 + 主詞）+ is（動詞）...，**B** 選項為正解。whose price 既是疑問詞也是主詞，單數主詞 price，搭配單數動詞 is。A 選項應改為：who（疑問詞 + 主詞）offers（動詞）more accurate estimations。who 既是疑問詞也是主詞。who 當主詞時，視為第三人稱單數，搭配單數動詞 offers。C 選項應改成：how much（疑問詞）+ the proposal（主詞）+ costs（動詞）。D 選項應改成：how（疑問詞）+ the total cost（主詞）+ is calculated（動詞）。

20. Years of teaching experiences reinforce my _____ belief that students would stay motivated and ask better questions when they are actively engaged in the learning process.

(A) firmly-holding （B) hold-firm
(C) long-held （D) holding-long

解 多年的教學經驗強化了我長久以來所抱持的信念：當學生積極投入學習的過程，他們將會動機滿滿，且提問較好的問題。

**考點：分詞當形容詞。**請見下方句構分析：

| Years of ... experiences | reinforce | my _____ | belief | that... |
|---|---|---|---|---|
| 主詞 | 動詞 | 形容詞 | 名詞 | |

從上方 1 個主詞和 1 個動詞可知句子結構已完整，故名詞 belief 前方應搭配 Ving 或 p.p. 形容詞。我的信念，意即信念「被我持有」，應搭配被

Unit 1
關係
代名詞

Unit 2
被動
語態

Unit 3
分詞
形容詞

Unit 4
分詞
構句

Unit 5
假設
語法

Unit 6
倒裝
句

Unit 7
間接
問句

Unit 8
特殊
動詞

Unit 9
主動詞
一致

Unit 10
對稱
結構

特別收錄
Unit 11
五回
試題

動意味的 p.p. 形容詞 held，且加強形容詞可用副詞 long，**C** 選項為正解。

21. I've had so many Syrian doctors _____ appeal letters to urge President Obama to intervene to break the siege of Aleppo and stop bombardments of hospitals.

    (A) written      (B) writing      (C) to write      (D) write

    解 我已經讓許多敘利亞醫師寫請願信來促請歐巴馬總統介入，打破 Aleppo 圍城攻擊，並停止轟炸醫院。

    **考點：使役動詞**

    使役動詞 have，後方受詞 doctors 可執行 write 這動作，故搭配表主動的「動詞原形」write，**D** 選項為正解。

22. By now, 80 brands have pulled their advertising from the show. It's hard to say how much of a blow this boycott would have been or how many brands would have returned _____ O'Reilly, the star host, _____ an apology for his misconduct.

    (A) were; issued          (B) should; be issued
    (C) if; issues             (D) had, issued

    解 到目前為止，80 個品牌已抽節目廣告。假如這節目的明星主持人 O'Reilly 之前就為他的不當行為道歉，還是很難說這聯合杯葛的殺傷力有多大，或多少品牌廣告會回流。

    **考點：假設語法**

    從 would have returned 可知 if 針對「過去」做相反假設，公式如下：

    If 主詞 1 + 動詞 1（過去完成式 had (not) + p.p.），主詞 2 + 動詞 2（would / should / could / might (not) + have p.p.）

    套公式：... how many brands would have returned **if** O'Reilly, the star host, **had issued** an apology for his misconduct

    也可去掉 if，並將 had 放句首，改成加強語氣版的假設語法，即：

    ... how many brands would have returned **had** O'Reilly, the star host, **issued** an apology for his misconduct

    由上可知，**D** 選項為正解。A 和 B 選項，主持人自己會發道歉聲明，所以不用被動式。

23. The US vice president, _____ recent strikes in Syria as signs of Trump's "resolve," flew to South Korea to warn Kim not to test Trump.

    (A) citing      (B) to cite      (C) who was cited    (D) cited

> 解 美國副總統引述敘利亞最近的空襲為 Trump 決心的標記。他還飛到南韓來警告 Kim 別測試 Trump。
>
> **考點：分詞構句**
>
> 原句為：the US vice president flew to South Korea / the US vice president cited recent strikes ...。兩句主詞相同，都是 the US vice president，可用分詞構句。cited 為過去式，可改成表主動進行的 Ving 分詞構句 citing ... resolve，**A** 選項為正解。

24. In 1990, while delayed on a train back to London, J.K. Rowling came up with the idea of a boy-wizard named Harry Potter. Before the ride was over, she had plotted out _____ would become the most popular children's books ever.

    (A) some of those    (B) whether they    (C) which      (D) what

> 解 1990 年，在返回倫敦的誤點火車上，J.K. Rowling 想出了名叫做 Harry Potter 的小男巫的點子。旅程結束前，她已勾勒出日後將成為史上最暢銷的童書的劇情。
>
> **考點：關係代名詞**
>
> had plotted out / would become 兩動詞，代表兩個句子，故劃線部分應為具連接句子功能的關係代名詞。關係代名詞前無先行詞，只有動詞 plotted out，故答案不是 that 就是 what。關係子句 ... would become ... ever，缺主詞，「意思不完整」，故 **D** 選項為正解。關係子句從複合關係代名詞開始，往後推，找不到第二個動詞，所以到句點為止。複合關係代名詞 what 帶出來的關係子句 would become ... ever 放在動詞 plotted out 後方當受詞，屬「名詞子句」。

25. The state senator used a racial slur and vulgar insults during a private conversation with two African-American colleagues. Several others at the scene of the exchange said they _____ witnesses.

    (A) could be called              (B) thought them
    (C) were regarded               (D) might see as

解 州議員在和兩名非裔美籍同事聊天時，用了種族歧視和粗俗的侮辱字眼。其他幾個在談話現場的人說，他們自己可以被稱為是目擊證人。

**考點：被動式**

從文意可知，they（即：several others at the scene）「被稱為」目擊證人，須搭配被動式。「把 A 稱為 B」call A B。套公式：They could call themselves witnesses. = They could be called witnesses.。綜合以上，**A** 選項為正解。「把 A 看作 B」think A (to be) B = think of A as B = regard A as B = see A as B。套公式：They thought themselves (to be) witnesses. = They thought of themselves as witnesses. = They regarded / saw themselves as witnesses.。換成被動式：They were thought (to be) witnesses = They were thought of as witnesses. = They were regarded / seen as witnesses.

26. **How long _____ dependent on a number of factors, including whether each side is willing to compromise to avoid loss in revenue and income.**

(A) does the possible strike last to be    (B) the possible strike is

(C) would the possible strike be           (D) the possible strike lasts is

解 可能的罷工將持續多久，視許多因素而定，包括勞資雙方是否願意妥協，以避免公司和個人的收入損失。

**考點：間接問句。**請見下方句構分析：

How long _____ _____ dependent on a number of factors, ...
　　　疑問詞　主詞 + 動詞　動詞　　　形容詞

一般句子的基本架構為：主詞 + 動詞 + (地點 / 時間)。所以劃線處應包含主詞和動詞。間接問句的公式為：疑問詞 + 主詞 + 動詞...。套公式可得：how long（疑問詞）+ the possible strike（主詞）+ lasts（動詞）。1 句間接問句 ( 即：名詞子句 ) 當主詞，單數主詞，搭配單數動詞 is。綜合以上，**D** 選項為正解。

Unit 1
關係
代名詞

Unit 2
被動
語態

Unit 3
分詞
形容詞

Unit 4
分詞
構句

Unit 5
假設
語法

Unit 6
倒裝
句

Unit 7
間接
問句

Unit 8
特殊
動詞

Unit 9
主動詞
一致

Unit 10
對稱
結構

特別收錄
Unit 11
五回
試題

27. Increasingly, job recruiters are relying on AI to take a first pass at résumés. However, if _____, AI can learn and act upon gender stereotypes in their decision-making.

   (A) leaving it to check
   (B) it is left checking
   (C) left unchecked
   (D) it leaves to be checked

> 解 招募者越來越倚賴人工智慧幫他們做初步履歷篩選。然而，若讓 AI 不被檢驗的話，AI 可能在做決策的過程中學習和表現出性別刻板印象。
>
> 考點：分詞構句 / 分詞當形容詞
>
> 句型「讓 N ...」leave + N + adj。套入句型：people leave AI unchecked = AI is left unchecked。AI「沒被檢驗」，應搭配表被動的 p.p. 形容詞 unchecked。原句為：... if AI is left unchecked, AI can learn ...。兩句主詞相同，都是 AI，可用分詞構句。is left 為被動式，可改成表被動的 p.p. 分詞構句 if left unchecked。寫分詞構句時，也可保留連接詞 if。綜合以上，**C** 選項為正解。

28. That a man with as flimsy of a relationship to the truth as Mr. Smith can win a presidential election _____ to show that lying is a winning strategy.

   (A) to go
   (B) going
   (C) which is going to
   (D) goes

> 解 像 Smith 先生這樣不顧真相的人也能贏得總統大選，這顯露出說謊是獲勝的策略。
>
> 考點：主動詞一致。請見下方句構分析：
>
> That a man with...can win a presidential election _____ to show...
> 　　　　關係子句當主詞　　　　　　　　　單數動詞
> 關係子句從關係代名詞 that 開始，往後推，到第二個動詞 (即劃線處) 前結束。1 句關係子句 that ... election 放句首當主詞，單數主詞，需搭配單數動詞，**D** 選項為正解。進一步分析主詞：
>
> That a man with as flimsy ... relationship ... as Mr. Smith can win ...
> 　　主詞 介係詞　形容詞　　　名詞　　　　　　　　　　動詞

29. Scientists are worried about how to keep the Sphinx from falling apart again. They have talked about constructing a wall around the Sphinx to protect it from the wind and sand, or perhaps \_\_\_\_\_ completely with a glass pyramid.

(A) having it covered        (B) have had it cover

(C) have it covering          (D) have its cover

解 科學家擔心如何讓獅身人面像不要再次四分五裂。他們已討論在獅身人面像周圍建造高牆，保護它免於風沙，或者也許可用一座玻璃金字塔將它完全覆蓋。

**考點：對稱／使役動詞。**請見下方句構分析：

They have talked about constructing …, or perhaps _____ …completely …
<u>  主詞  </u> <u>  動詞  </u> <u> 介係詞 </u> <u> 動名詞 1 </u>               <u> 動名詞 2 </u>

他們討論的事情有兩件：築高牆，和蓋玻璃金字塔。介係詞 about 後方需搭配（動）名詞。連接詞 or，左右兩邊須對稱，左邊為動名詞 constructing，右方劃線處也應為動名詞。使役動詞 have，後方受詞 it（即：Sphinx 獅身人面像）「被覆蓋」，故搭配表被動的「過去分詞」covered。綜合以上，**A** 選項為正解。如何保護獅身人面像還在討論中，所以不可能 Sphinx 已被玻璃金字塔覆蓋，不能用 B 選項完成式。

30. **Nonprofit charities have two distinct sets of "customers" who rarely cross paths: donors, who pay the bills, and the people they aim to serve, who _____ to deliver feedback on their satisfaction.**

(A) rarely to ask           (B) are rarely asked

(C) rarely asking them       (D) rarely ask

解 非營利的慈善機構有兩組不同的、幾乎不會有交集的「客戶」：付錢的捐助者，和慈善機構服務的對象。後者很少被要求反映他們對服務的滿意度。

**考點：被動式。**請見下方句構分析：

... the people (that) they aim to serve, who _____ to deliver...
   <u>  名詞  </u>       <u> 形容詞子句 </u>

句中的 they 指慈善機構。「人／主詞性質」的關係代名詞 who，代替前方的名詞 the people，即：慈善機構服務的對象。複數主詞 the people「被要求」給回應（deliver feedback），需搭配複數被動式。且關係子句裏應有完整動詞，而非 Ving／p.p.／to V 原。綜合以上，**B** 選項為正解。

31. **Orders placed on our site that meet a minimum order value of $75 pre-tax _____ eligible for free shipping.**

(A) being       (B) they are       (C) is going to be       (D) are

解 在我們網站上所下的訂單，若稅前滿美金 75 元，就符合免運的資格。

考點：主動詞一致。請見下方句構分析：

Orders placed ... our site that meet ... pre-tax _____ eligible ...
　　　　　主詞　　　　　形容詞　　　　　形容詞子句　　　　動詞

訂單「被訂下」，故主（名）詞 orders 後方應搭配表被動的 p.p. 形容詞 placed。關係子句從關係代名詞開始，往後推，到第二個動詞（即劃線處）前結束。關係代名詞 that 帶出來的關係子句 meet ... pre-tax，放在名詞 orders 後，為「形容詞子句」。刪除不會影響動詞的形容詞 placed 和 that 形容詞子句後，可看出複數主詞 orders，應搭配複數動詞 are，**D** 選項為正解。

32. The never-ending din of trade wars shows no sign of abating, and _____ the pessimism on profits.

(A) neither does　　(B) as shows　　(C) neither haven't　(D) so are

解 無止盡的貿易戰喧鬧聲似乎沒有減弱的跡象，對獲利的悲觀也沒有稍減。

考點：附和用的倒裝句

悲觀想法「也沒」削減。附和否定句的「也不」，有 either / neither 兩種寫法，但副詞 either 只能放句尾。從句尾沒看到 either 可知本句是用副詞 neither 寫成的。neither 後方需搭配倒裝句，公式為：and neither + be 動詞 / 助動詞 + 主詞。由於第一句使用現在式動詞 shows，那麼 neither 附和句需用現在式助動詞。主詞「對獲利感到悲觀」，重點在「悲觀」。單數主詞 pessimism，搭配現在式助動詞 does。套公式，**A** 選項為正解。

33. While the weather pattern, _____ to El Niño events, is abnormal, crop yields do not seem to be severely affected.

(A) whose link　　　　　　　　(B) which it links
(C) linking　　　　　　　　　 (D) linked

解 雖然和聖嬰現象相關的天氣型態是不正常的，作物產量似乎沒受到嚴重影響。

考點：分詞構句 / 分詞當形容詞

原句為：the weather pattern is abnormal... / the weather pattern is linked to El Nino events。the weather pattern 不會主動去牽關連（link），需

搭配被動式。兩句主詞相同，都是 the weather pattern，可用分詞構句。
is linked 為被動寫法，應改成表被動的 p.p. 分詞構句 linked...events，D 選項為正解。

Unit 1
關係
代名詞

Unit 2
被動
語態

Unit 3
分詞
形容詞

Unit 4
分詞
構句

Unit 5
假設
語法

Unit 6
倒裝
句

Unit 7
間接
問句

Unit 8
特殊
動詞

Unit 9
主動詞
一致

Unit 10
對稱
結構

特別收錄
Unit 11
五回
試題

34. **Fox News has paid off victims to settle several high-profile sexual harassment scandals. It's managed to minimize exposure by requiring arbitration rather than lawsuits and _____ gag orders on the women as part of the settlement.**

   (A) is imposed （B) has been imposed

   (C) by imposing （D) imposing of

   解 為解決幾起高知名度的性騷擾醜聞，Fox 新聞付錢給被害者。為減少醜聞的曝光度，Fox 新聞設法藉著要求仲裁私了，而非打官司，並對被害女性下封口令，做為和解的一部份。

   **考點：對稱。**請見下方句構分析：

   It has managed ... by requiring ... and _____ gag orders ...
   主詞　　動詞　　　　介係詞 + 動名詞　　（介係詞）+ 動名詞
   從文意可知，減少性騷擾醜聞曝光的方法有兩個，一個是藉著仲裁私了，另一個是藉著下封口令。連接詞 and 連接這兩個方法，兩個方法的寫法需對稱，都用介係詞「藉著」(by) +（動）名詞，C 選項為正解。Fox News 主動對被害女性強加（impose）封口令，故包含被動式的 A、B 選項都是錯的。D 選項，意思會變成：為減少醜聞曝光，Fox 新聞藉著仲裁私了，而不是官司和強加的封口令，文意不合，下封口令也是私了的方法之一。

35. **If Fox News had responded promptly and effectively to complaints of harassment, it _____ thorough investigations as well as protected employees from retaliation and serial harassers.**

   (A) would have conducted （B) was conducted

   (C) might have been conducted （D) had to conduct

   解 假如 Fox 新聞之前對性騷擾的抱怨做出立即且有效的反應的話，它就會徹查，保護員工不被報復，並遠離性騷擾慣犯。

   **考點：假設語法**

   從 had responded 可推知，if 針對「過去」做相反假設，公式如下：

   If 主詞 1 + 動詞 1（過去完成式 had (not) + p.p.），主詞 2 + 動詞 2（would / should / could / might (not) + have p.p.）

it（即 Fox 新聞台）可主動做 (conduct) 調查，用主動語態即可。綜合以上，**A** 選項為正解。

36. The blood-type craze, considered simply harmless fun by some Japanese, may manifest itself as prejudice. There are reports of discrimination _____, ending of relationships, or loss of job opportunities due to blood type.

(A) led to kid bullies
(B) which lead kids to be bullied
(C) leading to kids bullied
(D) that it leads to kids being bullied

解 被有些日本人認為有趣且無害的血型風潮，可能變成偏見。曾有因為血型造成歧視，導致小孩被霸凌、關係劃下句點，或失去工作機會等的報導。

考點：對稱 / 分詞當形容詞。請見下方句構分析：

There are reports of discrimination _____, ending…, and loss…
　　主詞　動詞　　　　　名詞

再看下方細部分析：

…discrimination leading　to　kids　bullied, ending…, and loss…
　　名詞　　　形容詞　介係詞 名詞1　　名詞2　　　名詞3

從上方 1 個主詞和 1 個動詞可知句子結構已完整，故名詞 discrimination 後方應搭配 Ving 或 p.p. 形容詞，若用關係代名詞帶出來的關係子句當形容詞，則子句中需搭配完整的動詞，即非 Ving / p.p. / to V 原。discrimination 主動引發後續三個狀況，故應用表主動的 Ving 形容詞 leading to N。小孩「被霸凌」，名詞 kids 後方需搭配表被動的 p.p. 形容詞 bullied。若用關係子句當形容詞，則應寫成 discrimination which (或 that) leads to kids bullied。綜合以上，**C** 選項為正解。

37. The thriller, _____, mostly just follows a formula, adding nothing new to the "gather a group of friends and kill them off one by one" genre.

(A) which produces slickly
(B) though slickly produced
(C) if producing slickly
(D) to produce slickly

解 雖然製作手法嫻熟，這部恐怖片大多遵循一套公式，沒能為「召集一群朋友，再把他們一個個殺光」這體裁增添任何新意。

考點：分詞構句［變形1］

原句為：The thriller mostly just follows … / the thriller is slickly produced …。兩句主詞相同，都是 the thriller，可用分詞構句。is slickly produced 為現在被動式，應改成表被動的 p.p. 分詞構句 slickly produced。「製作手法嫻熟」(slickly produced) 和「了無新意」(adding nothing new) 文意上對沖，故可在分詞構句前，加上轉折文意的連接詞「雖然」though。綜合以上，**B** 選項為正解。

38. **Winning international recognition was _____ the main reason why Camake founded the Taiwu Elementary School Folk Singers in 2006. What really matters to him was to preserve and pass on their tribal culture.**

(A) not merely the original intention but  (B) either originally intent on or

(C) neither the original intention nor  (D) not originally intended but

解 贏得國際認可，既不是 Camake 創立 Taiwu 小學民俗歌手的最初意圖，也不是主要原因。對他而言，真正重要的是保存和傳遞他們的部落文化。

考點：對稱

從「真正重要的是傳遞部落文化」可知贏得認可「不是」camake 的意圖，「也不是」主要理由。「既不是 A 也不是 B」neither A nor B，A 和 B 兩者詞性和結構要對稱。句中，B (the main reason) 為名詞，劃線部份 A (the original intention) 也應為名詞。綜合以上，**C** 選項為正解。請見下方句構分析：

Winning … recognition was **neither** the … intention **nor** the … reason …
　主詞　　　　　　動詞　　　　　　名詞1　　　　　　名詞2

39. **The government is highly sensitive to its image and fully conscious of _____ the country from abroad. Thus, it comes as no surprise that it would turn to spyware to intimidate dissidents.**

(A) whom make such harsh criticisms  (B) who is criticizing

(C) who are the criticisms targeted at  (D) whose criticism is this

解 政府對它的形象高度敏感，且知道誰在海外批評國內。因此，政府利用間諜軟體來威脅異議份子，這一點都不令人感到意外。

考點：間接問句

介係詞 of 後方需搭配名詞。間接問句就是名詞子句，可放在介係詞後

方。間接問句的公式為：疑問詞 + 主詞 + 動詞...。套用公式可得：who（疑問詞 + 主詞）+ is criticizing（動詞）。who 當主詞時，應視為第三人稱單數，故搭配單數動詞 is。綜合以上，**B** 選項為正解。A 選項應改成：who makes such harsh criticisms。C 選項應改成：who the criticisms are targeted at。D 選項應改成：whose criticism this is。

40. The Writers Guild of America voted by a margin of 80 percent to authorize a strike. In all, 6,310 ballots _____, and 67.5 percent of eligible WGA membership voted.

(A) that are casting　(B) were cast　　　(C) to be cast　　　(D) had cast

解 美國作家協會投票以百分之 80 的差距授權罷工。整體而言，共投下 6310 票，百分之 67.5 的合格會員前來投票。

**考點：被動式**

ballots（票）「被投下」，需搭配被動式。連接詞 and 連接兩個動詞，兩個動詞時態應對稱。右邊 voted 為過去式，劃線處也應為過去式。綜合以上，**B** 選項為正解。

註 cast (v) 投；cast – cast – cast。

41. My parents don't want me to drop out of school in pursuit of some transient dreams, but if I _____ earnest about wanting a career in entertainment, they'll support me.

(A) am　　　　　(B) would be　　　(C) had been　　　(D) were

解 我爸媽不希望我輟學去追求一些瞬間即逝的夢想。但是假如我真心想當演藝人員，他們也會支持我。

**考點：假設語法**

if 針對「未來」they'll 做假設時，緊接在 if 後方的動詞需從未來往前跳一格，改用「現在式」，**A** 選項為正解。

42. The app itself is free, and _____ the first seven chapters of *November 9*. If you want more, you can subscribe for a monthly fee of $3.99.

(A) either has　　(B) as do　　　(C) neither is　　　(D) so are

解 這應用程式本身是免費的，November 9 這本小說的前 7 個章節也是免費的。若你想看更多內容，你可以註冊，繳月費美金 3.99 元。

**考點：附和用的倒裝句**

前 7 章「也是」免費。附和肯定句的「也」，共有 so / too 兩種寫法，但 too 只能放句尾。從句尾看到 too 可知本句是用副詞 so 寫成的。so 後方需搭配倒裝句，公式為：and so + be 動詞 / 助動詞 + 主詞。由於第一句使用現在式 be 動詞 is，那麼 so 附和句就會跟著使用現在式 be 動詞。複數主詞 the first seven chapters，需搭配複數 be 動詞 are。套公式，**D** 選項為正解。

43. **Historical interpreters, _____ in period garb, give tours to the Susan Constant, Godspeed, and Discovery. They often portray characters that would have lived and worked during the Columbus times.**

(A) dressed      (B) who dressed      (C) to be dressed      (D) dressing

解 穿著特定年代服飾的歷史劇演員，負責為 Susan Constant, Godspeed, and Discovery 三艘船導覽。他們常扮演在哥倫布時代生活和工作的人物角色。

**考點：分詞構句**

原句為：historical interpreters are dressed in (或 dress themselves in) period garb … / historical interpreters give tours …。兩句主詞相同，都是 historical interpreters，可用分詞構句。are dressed in N 為被動寫法，可改成表被動的 p.p. 分詞構句 dressed in period garb。dress themselves in N 為主動寫法，可改成表主動進行的 Ving 分詞構句 dressing themselves in period garb。綜合以上，**A** 選項為正解。B 選項，who 關係子句應搭配完整動詞，即非 Ving / p.p. / to V 原。B 選項需改成 who dress themselves 或 who are dressed。D 選項，應改成 dressing themselves。

44. **A study found that sampling while shopping convinces consumers to buy the featured product more often than does simply seeing the product _____ on the shelf.**

(A) to have displayed          (B) displaying

(C) displayed                (D) display

解 研究顯示，購物時，試吃比光讓消費者看架上展示的商品，更能說服他們購買。

考點：感官動詞

感官動詞 seeing，後方受詞 the product「被展示」，需搭配帶被動意味的「過去分詞」displayed，**C** 選項為正解。

45. **Hadn't I spent long hours on the beach without slathering on a generous amount of sunscreen the other day, I _____ severe sunburns.**

(A) didn't have to suffer

(B) might not have suffered

(C) wasn't going to suffer

(D) wouldn't be suffering

解 前幾天，假如我沒在沒厚塗防曬霜的情況下，長時間待在沙灘上的話，我就不會嚴重曬傷了。

考點：假設語法

從 the other day（前幾天）推知是針對「過去」做相反的假設，公式如下：

If 主詞 1 + 動詞 1（過去完成式 had (not) + p.p.），主詞 2 + 動詞 2 (would / should / could / might (not) + have p.p.)

套公式：If I hadn't spent…the other day, I might not have suffered…

也可去掉 if，並將 had 放句首，改成加強語氣版的假設語法，即：

Hadn't I spent…the other day, I might not have suffered…

由上可知，**B** 選項為正解。

46. **Cuba is renowned _____ foreign physicians and dispatching its homegrown ones to nations across the neighboring region.**

(A) as both the training of

(B) to either train

(C) in that it trains

(D) for both training

解 Cuba 以訓練外國籍內科醫師，和將本國籍內科醫師派遣至鄰近國家而聞名。

考點：對稱

片語「以 … 聞名」be renowned for + 特色 / be renowned as + 同位格。培養醫師是 Cuba 的特色，應搭配介係詞 for。片語「A 和 B 兩者都…」both A and B，A 和 B 要對稱，B 為動名詞 dispatching，A（即劃線處）也應為動名詞。綜合以上，**D** 選項為正解。A 選項，Cuba 和醫師的訓練，無法劃上等號，非同位格。B 選項，片語「不是 A 就是 B」either A or B，A 和 B 要對稱，to train 和 dispatching 不對稱。C 選項，連接詞 in that，即 because，應改成：in that it trains...and dispatches...。

**47. Though my objective seems _____, I will strive to achieve it with courage and perseverance.**

(A) rather intimidating　　　　(B) to intimidate

(C) very intimidatedly　　　　(D) like intimidation

解 雖然我的目標似乎讓人望而生畏，但是我會用勇氣和毅力努力達成它。

**考點：連綴動詞**

連綴動詞 seem，後方需搭配「形容詞」或「to 動詞原形」。objective 本身具有威脅挑戰性，有極高難度，應搭配表主動進行的 Ving 形容詞，**A** 選項為正解。rather (adv) 非常。B 選項應改成：to intimidate me。

**48. The North Carolina law requires transgender people to use public restrooms that correspond with their gender at birth. Only those who have their birth certificate _____ would not be affected.**

(A) changed　　(B) changing　　(C) to change　　(D) changes

解 North Carolina 州的法律要求變性人使用和他們出生性別相符的廁所。只有那些改過出生證明的人不受影響。

使役動詞 have，後方受詞 birth certificate「被改」，故搭配表被動的「過去分詞」changed，**A** 選項為正解。

**49. The minister refused to elaborate on his plans for dealing with Isis, saying "I wouldn't want them to know _____."**

(A) what are in my mind　　　　(B) what am I thinking about

(C) what my real thinking is　　　(D) what steps are taking

解 部長拒絕解釋他因應 Isis 恐怖份子的計畫。他說：我不想讓他們知道我真正的想法為何。

**考點：間接問句**

間接問句就是名詞子句，可放在動作後當受詞。間接問句的公式為：疑問詞 + 主詞 + 動詞 ...。套公式：what (疑問詞) + my real thinking (主詞) + is (動詞)，**C** 選項為正解。A 選項應改成：what (疑問詞 + 主詞)

+ is（動詞） in my mind。what 當主詞時，視為第三人稱單數，搭配單數動詞 is。B 選項應改成：what（疑問詞）+ I（主詞）+ am thinking about（動詞）。D 選項：what steps（疑問詞 + 主詞）+ are taken（動詞）。

**50.** She was one of the ten successful applicants out of a field of 800 from around the world _____ the three-year master's program in performing arts.

(A) who were admitted to

(B) that had admitted by

(C) admitting to

(D) where she was admitted by

解 從全球 800 個申請者中，錄取了 10 人參加三年表演藝術碩士課程。她就是那 10 個申請成功的人之一。

**考點：被動式。**請見下方句構分析：

She was one of the ten ... _____ the three-year master's ...
主詞 動詞　　　　名詞

從上方 1 個主詞和 1 個動詞可知句子結構已完整，故名詞 one of the ten successful applicants 後方應搭配 Ving 或 p.p. 形容詞。若用關係代名詞帶出來的關係子句當形容詞，則子句中需搭配完整的動詞，即非 Ving / p.p. / to V 原。十個成功「被學校碩士班錄取」的申請者之一，應搭配被動式，「被錄取」be admitted to 地點。二個動詞 was / be admitted to N 間，用不定詞（to V 原）處理一下。若用關係子句當形容詞，應寫成：who / that were admitted to。從 She was...可知本句需用過去式。綜合以上，**A** 選項為正解。

# Unit 11　特別收錄：五回試題
## 第四回試題

**01.** There is no convincing evidence that vitamin supplementation, as well as other supplements, _____ in important benefits such as the prevention of stillbirth or poor fetal health.

(A) are resulting　　　　(B) resulting
(C) have been resulted　(D) results

> **解** 沒有可信的證據顯示補充維他命，加上其他補充錠，可帶來重大好處，如：避免死產或胎兒不健康。
>
> **考點：主動詞一致**
>
> 關係代名詞 that 帶出一個句子。「A, as well as B」當主詞時，動詞單複數視 A 而定。單數主詞 vitamin supplementation，搭配單數動詞，**D** 選項為正解。

**02.** A recent Washington Post report finds that tourism to the US from countries _____ the travel bans or the electronics bans has dropped significantly.

(A) not targeting at　　　(B) isn't targeted by
(C) where they aren't targeted by　(D) which haven't been targeted by

> **解** 最近一則華盛頓郵報的報導發現，從未被旅遊或電子設備禁令鎖定的國家，前往美國旅遊的人次已顯著下滑。
>
> **考點：被動式 / 主動詞一致**。請見下方句構分析：
>
> …that tourism to the US from countries _____ the…bans has dropped…
> 　　　　主詞　　　介係詞　名詞　　　　　　　　　　動詞
>
> 從上方 1 個主詞和 1 個動詞可知句子結構已完整，故名詞 countries 後方應搭配 Ving 或 p.p. 形容詞。若用關係代名詞帶出來的關係子句當形容詞，則子句中需搭配完整的動詞，即非 Ving / p.p. / to V 原。這些國家「尚未被禁令鎖定」，應搭配表被動的 p.p. 形容詞 not targeted by。若用關係子句當形容詞，應寫成：countries which（或 that）haven't been targeted by ... 或 aren't targeted by ...，**D** 選項為正解。「物 / 主詞性質」的關係代名詞 which 代替 countries，複數主詞，搭配複數被動式。

**03.** There has been a global trend of airlines ramping up capacity, in part driven by lower fuel prices. Yet, this has in turn led to overcapacity, with airlines _____ fares to fill seats.

(A) by which slash    (B) slashing        (C) slashed        (D) slash

> 解 部份受到較低燃料價格的驅使，全球的航空公司興起增加容量的趨勢。然而，這反過來也造成超收，航空公司大砍價格求滿機。
>
> **考點：分詞當形容詞**
>
> 片語「伴隨 … 而來的狀況」with + N + adj。名詞 airlines 後方應搭配形容詞。航空公司可執行 slash fares（砍價）這動作，應搭配表主動進行的 Ving 形容詞，**B** 選項為正解。

**04.** A teeny-tiny mouse creeping around is scary enough to get diners _____ on chairs, not to mention the sight of rodents filing out for a lunch break, in orderly haste, into the filthy kitchen

(A) jumping        (B) jumped        (C) and jumps        (D) to jump

> 解 小老鼠四處爬的景象，就足以讓用餐者嚇得跳到椅子上了，更不用說看到大老鼠排隊吃午餐，倉促卻井然有序地衝進骯髒的廚房。
>
> **考點：使役動詞**
>
> 使役動詞 get，後方受詞 diners 可執行 jump 這動作，故搭配「to 動詞原形」，**D** 選項為正解。

**05.** Capoeira is a martial art that combines elements of fight, acrobatics, drumming, singing and rituals. _____ in movies and music videos, Capoeira is also believed to have influenced such dancing styles as breaking and hip-hop.

(A) Frequently performed          (B) To be performed frequently
(C) Having frequent performances  (D) Performing on a frequent basis

> 解 Capoeira 是種結合打鬥、雜技、擊鼓、歌唱和儀式等元素的武術。Capoeira 常在電影和音樂影片中被演出，相信也已影響了如：地板霹靂舞或嘻哈等舞蹈風格。
>
> **考點：分詞構句**
>
> 原句為：Capoeira is frequently performed in … / Capoeira is also

believed ...。兩句主詞相同，都是 Capoeira，可用分詞構句。is performed 為現在被動式，可改成表被動的 p.p. 分詞構句 frequently performed ... videos，**A** 選項為正解。

**06.** Until recently, the only option for hundreds of thousands of severe heart failure patients _____ heart transplants.

(A) to be      (B) having      (C) has been      (D) are

解 直到最近，成千上萬嚴重心臟衰竭的病患唯一的選擇就是心臟移植。

**考點：主動詞一致**

主詞「病患唯一的選擇」，重點為「唯一的選擇」。單數主詞 the only option，搭配單數動詞。又「直到最近」(until recently)，一段時間，得搭配完成式。綜合以上，**C** 選項為正解。

**07.** Even Republicans, _____ the base of O'Reilly's viewers, seemed to start turning against him: The previous week, 26 percent said his show should be canceled. In the latest poll, 31 percent did.

(A) comprising      (B) composed of      (C) making up      (D) included

解 即便民主黨黨員構成 O'Reilly 觀眾群的基礎，他們似乎也開始反他。上週，百分之 26 的人說他的節目應被取消。最近一次調查，百分之 31 的人持相同意見。

**考點：分詞構句**

原句為：Even Republicans (小團體) made up the base of O'Reilly's viewers (大團體) / Republicans seemed to ...。兩句主詞相同，都是 Republicans，可用分詞構句。made up 為過去式，可改成表主動進行的 Ving 分詞構句 making up ... viewers，**C** 選項為正解。The base of O'Reilly's viewers (大團體) comprises / is composed of / includes Republicans (小團體)，可改成分詞構句，分別為：comprising / composed of / including ... viewers。A、B、D 選項，主詞都是 the base of O'Reilly，和題目不合。

**08.** I initially approached the idea of corpse hotels with skepticism but _____ a recent research visit to one. I ended up wanting to open one in my hometown.

(A) was swayed by   (B) swaying to      (C) had swayed      (D) swayed

解 我一開始接觸到「屍體旅館」這點子時，滿心狐疑，但是卻被最近一趟研究訪查影響了。訪查後，我還考慮在我家鄉開一間屍體旅館。

**考點：主動詞一致 / 被動式。**請見下方句構分析：

I approached the idea ... skepticism but _____ a ... visit ...
主詞 動詞1　　　　　　　　　　　　　　　　　　　連接詞 動詞2

連接詞 but 連接兩個動詞，兩個動詞時態需對稱。從 approached 可知劃線處應為過去式。我「被這趟參訪」所影響左右，應搭配被動式。綜合以上，**A** 選項為正解。

---

**09.** Trump's order requires all federal contracts to use all-American steel products. Still, he'd review waivers that allow products to count as American-made if they're from countries _____ the US has trade agreements.

(A) except what　　(B) with which　　(C) whenever　　(D) that

解 Trump 的命令要求所有聯邦合約需使用美國生產的鋼鐵製品。然而，他也會審核免責書。免責書中，假如商品來自和美國有貿易協定的國家，就可視為美國製。

**考點：關係代名詞**

are / has 兩個動詞，代表兩個句子，故劃線部分應為具連接句子功能的關係代名詞。將先行詞 countries 放回後方句 the US ... agreements 排排看，得出：the US has trade agreements with the countries，由此可知需用「物 / 受詞性質」的關係代名詞 which，但因關係代名詞只能代替名詞 the countries，無法代替介係詞 with，故答案應為 with which，**B** 選項為正解。關係子句從關係代名詞開始，往後推，找不到第二個動詞，所以到句點為止。關係代名詞 with which 帶出來的關係子句 the US ... agreements 放在名詞 countries 後方，為「形容詞子句」。

---

**10.** The doctors explained that what pained them most _____ to choose who would live and who would die in their emergency rooms.

(A) to be forced　　　　　　　　　　　(B) and forcing them
(C) was being forced　　　　　　　　　(D) also forced it

解 醫生解釋，讓他們覺得最痛苦的，就是在急診室裏，被迫選擇誰生誰死。

**考點：主動詞一致。**請見下方句構分析：

... that what pained them most _____ to choose ...

<u>　　　　　　　　　　　</u>　　　<u>　　　　</u>
　　關係子句當主詞　　　　　動詞

從 explained / pained 可知本句為過去式。關係子句從複合關係代名詞 what 開始，往後推，到第二個動詞 (即劃線處) 前結束。1 句關係子句 what...most 放句首當主詞，單數主詞，搭配單數動詞。受詞 them (即 doctors)，讓醫生們覺得痛苦的 (what pained them most) 是在急診室裏「被迫選擇」誰生誰死，需搭配被動式。綜合以上，**C** 選項為正解。

11. **The doctors said that last month alone Syria saw 42 attacks on medical facilities _____ a medical facility in Syria is attacked every 17 hours.**

(A) and that　　　　(B) of them　　　　(C) among which　　(D) , which

解 醫生說，光上個月，Syria 就有 42 起對醫療機構的攻擊，且每 17 小時就有一個 Syria 醫療機構被攻擊。

**考點：關係代名詞**

動詞 said 後方有兩個受詞，都以關係代名詞 that 帶出來的名詞子句呈現，且用連接詞 and 連接這兩個受詞，形成結構對稱。綜合以上，**A** 選項為正解。請見下方句構分析：

... said that ... Syria saw... facilities <u>_____</u> ... a facility...is attacked ...
　　　that 關係子句當受詞 1　　　　連接詞　　　that 關係子句當受詞 2

12. **Not until Trump received a short history lesson from Chinese President Xi Jinping _____ how difficult it would be to disarm North Korea.**

(A) did he realize　　　　　　　　(B) realized he
(C) that he had realized　　　　　　(D) who led him to realize

解 直到中國領導人 Xi Jinping 替 Trump 上了一堂簡短的歷史課，Trump 才了解要北韓繳械有多麼難。

**考點：倒裝句。**請見下方句構分析：

Not until Trumps received ... Jinping <u>_____</u> ...
　　　　　　　時間　　　　　　　　　倒裝句

否定詞 not until 放句首，後方需搭配倒裝句。但得先將時間點說明清楚後，才開始造倒裝。時間點用句子寫成：Trumps (主詞) + received (動詞) ...。realize 不是 be 動詞，造倒裝句時，需搭配助動詞。從 received 可知本句為過去式。套公式：Not until 時間 + 助動詞 + 主詞 + 動詞原形...，**A** 選項為正解。

13. _____ at between 4 and 5 million years old, the fossil is the oldest remains ever found of a pantherine felid.

(A) Dated            (B) To be dated

(C) With dates falling      (D) Dating

> 解 這化石被鑑定有 4 百萬至 5 百萬年的歷史。這是至今被發現的貓科動物遺骸中最古老的。
>
> **考點：分詞構句**
>
> 原句為：the fossil is dated（被鑑定年代）at... / the fossil is the oldest...。兩句主詞相同，都是 the fossil，可用分詞構句。is dated 為現在被動式，可改成表被動的 p.p. 分詞構句 dated ... old，**A** 選項為正解。

14. The Spurs, _____ season came to an abrupt end, now have to turn their attention to their uncertain future earlier than they have hoped.

(A) when      (B) which      (C) whose      (D) where

> 解 馬刺隊的球季突然告終。馬刺隊現在必須比預期還早地將他們的注意力轉向未知的未來。
>
> **考點：關係代名詞**
>
> came / have 兩個動詞，代表兩個句子，故劃線部分應為具連接句子功能的關係代名詞。將先行詞 the Spurs（馬刺隊）放回後方句 season...end 排排看，得出：the Spurs' season came to ...，由此可知需用「人 / 所有格性質」的關係代名詞 whose，**C** 選項為正解。關係子句從關係代名詞開始，往後推，到第二個動詞 have 前（或斷句用的逗號）結束。關係代名詞 whose 帶出來的關係子句 season ... end 放在名詞 the Spurs 後方，補充說明 the Spurs 的表現，為「名詞子句」。

15. Aegean wall lizards are expert at picking out just the right background to minimize the chances that they _____ a hungry predator, like a crow or raptor.

(A) were spotting          (B) will be spotted by

(C) have been spotted by     (D) spot

> 解 Aegean 壁蜥蜴擅於挑選正確的環境背景，減少他們被饑餓的掠食者，如：烏鴉或猛禽，看見的機會。

考點：被動式

they（蜥蜴）「被掠食者看見」，應搭配被動式，**B** 選項為正解。C 選項，無法減少「已被看見」的機會。

16. The biologist praised the bees as one of the top ten most intelligent creatures. _____ in their hives but they engineer the very complex honeycomb structures for honey storage.

(A) Not only do they self-medicate     (B) They not only self-medicate

(C) Not only self-medicate they     (D) They don't self-medicate only

解 生物學家將蜜蜂譽為前十大聰明生物之一。他們不只能在蜂巢中自我療育，也打造出極度複雜的蜂窩結構來存放蜂蜜。

考點：倒裝句

否定詞 not only 放句首，後方需造倒裝句。從 engineer 可知本句為現在式。self-medicate 不是 be 動詞，造倒裝句時需搭配助動詞。套公式：

Not only + 助動詞 + 主詞 1 + 動詞原形 … + , but + 主詞 2 + 動詞 2

綜合以上，**A** 選項為正解。B 選項，「不只 A，連 B 都…」not only A but B，A 和 B 詞性、結構需對稱，而動詞 self-medicate 和句子 they engineer 不對稱。D 選項，「不是 A，而是 B」not A but B，文意不合，因為蜜蜂聰明之處在於它們既會自我療育，也會築蜂巢。engineer (v) 籌劃打造。

17. With its anti-bacterial properties, honey could be used to prevent wounds from becoming _____ in the first place.

(A) infecting     (B) infectious     (C) infectiously     (D) infected

解 憑藉著抗菌的特質，首先，蜂蜜可用來避免傷口變得受到感染。

考點：連綴動詞

連綴動詞 become，後方可搭配「形容詞」或「like + 名詞」。傷口「被感染」，應搭配表被動的 p.p. 形容詞，**D** 選項為正解。B 選項，傷口變得有傳染性（infectious），文意不合。

18. Liquefaction occurs when a quake shakes up water _____ in loosely packed sediment 20 meters below the ground and transforms the usually solid soil into liquid.

(A) sitting      (B) that are located   (C) which is lain     (D) situating

解 當地震搖晃位於地下 20 公尺深的鬆散沉積岩中的水，並將一般固態的土壤轉變成流質土壤時，土壤液化就發生了。

考點：分詞當形容詞。請見下方句構分析：

… when a quake shakes up water _____ in loosly …
           主詞      動詞      名詞   形容詞

從上方 1 個主詞和 1 個動詞可知句子結構已完整，故名詞 water 後方應搭配 Ving 或 p.p. 形容詞。若用關係代名詞帶出來的關係子句當形容詞，則子句中需搭配完整的動詞，即非 Ving / p.p. / to V 原。動詞「位於 …」分兩組。第一組：sit / stand / lie 得用主動寫法，應改成表主動進行的 Ving 形容詞，故 A 選項為正解。C 選項應改成：which lies。第二組：situate / locate / set / perch（棲息）得用被動寫法，應改成表被動的 p.p. 形容詞，故 D 選項應改成 situated。B 選項應改成 located，或 that is located。「物 / 主詞性質」的關係代名詞 that，代替前方的名詞 water，單數主詞，搭配單數動詞 is located。

19. Having multiple simultaneous diseases present _____ accurate diagnosis and proper treatment.

(A) to complicate             (B) complicating
(C) complicates             (D) have complicated

解 有多重疾病同時出現，將使正確診斷和妥善治療變得複雜。

考點：主動詞一致。請見下方句構分析：

Having … diseases present _____ accurate diagnosis …
主詞               形容詞   動詞

動名詞 having 放句首當主詞。1 個動名詞代表一件事，單數主詞，搭配單數動詞，故 C 選項為正解。present 放在名詞 diseases 後，為形容詞「出現的」。present (v) 提出呈現，放入句中，文意不合。

20. So _____ in New England that they could easily be captured at the shore and were consumed primarily by convicts and those stuck in poverty.

(A) abundantly lobsters found        (B) was the abundance of lobsters

(C) abundant were lobsters      (D) lived lobsters an abundant life

Unit 1
關係
代名詞

Unit 2
被動
語態

Unit 3
分詞
形容詞

Unit 4
分詞
構句

Unit 5
假設
語法

Unit 6
倒裝
句

Unit 7
間接
問句

Unit 8
特殊
動詞

Unit 9
主動詞
一致

Unit 10
對稱
結構

特別收錄
Unit 11
五回
試題

解 以前，新英格蘭可找到如此多地龍蝦，以致於岸邊就可輕易地捕到龍蝦，而且那時龍蝦主要是罪犯和窮人吃的食物。

**考點：倒裝句**

so 放句首的「如此地 ... 以致於 ...」倒裝句，公式如下：

So + 形容詞 + be 動詞 + 主詞 1 ... + that + 主詞 2 + 動詞 2

so 放句首時，緊接後方的句子需寫成倒裝句，但關代 that 後方句則不需倒裝。原句為：Lobsters were so abundant in New England that ...。套倒裝句公式：So abundant were lobsters in New England that ...，**C** 選項為正解。B 選項應改成：Such was the abundance of lobsters in New England that ...。so 為首的倒裝句，句中動詞只能用 be 動詞，所以 A 和 D 選項一看就是錯誤選項。

21. **The first red alert over air pollution in Beijing almost brought this city to a standstill, with schools shut, construction halted and _____.**

(A) restricted driving      (B) driving restricted

(C) restrictive to drivers      (D) drove restrictions

解 北京首次發佈紅色空污警戒，伴隨著學校關閉、建築工程暫停、開車受限，這些幾乎讓這都市停擺。

**考點：對稱。**請見下方句構分析：

..., with schools shut, construction halted and _____.
      名詞 1 形容詞 1     名詞 2    形容詞 2 名詞 3 + 形容詞 3

片語「伴隨而來的狀況」with + N + adj。為遵守對稱原則，連接詞 and 連接三組「名詞 + 形容詞」。開車這件事「被禁止」，名詞 driving 後方應搭配表被動的 p.p. 形容詞 restricted，**B** 選項為正解。句中，shut / halted 都是表被動的 p.p. 形容詞。

22. **Due to past food scares, consumers grow skeptical about goods produced domestically. To respond to their demands for safe, healthy foods, we have been enlarging our shelf space _____ to imported items.**

(A) which devotes      (B) and devoting

(C) as well as devotion      (D) devoted

解 由於之前的食安恐慌，消費者對國內製造的商品越來越不放心。為了回應他們對安全健康的食物的需求，我們已擴大專門放置進口商品的陳列空間。

**考點：分詞當形容詞。**請見下方句構分析：

..., we have been enlarging our shelf space ＿＿＿ to imported items...

主詞　　　　　動詞　　　　　　　名詞

從上方 1 個主詞和 1 個動詞可知句子結構已完整，故名詞 shelf space 後方應搭配 Ving 或 p.p. 形容詞。若用關係代名詞帶出來的關係子句當形容詞，則子句中需搭配完整的動詞，即非 Ving / p.p. / to V 原。上架空間「被奉獻給 ... / 被專門用於 ...」，需搭配表被動的 p.p. 形容詞 devoted，**D** 選項為正解。若用關係子句當形容詞，則應寫成：our shelf space which（或 that）is devoted（或 has been devoted）to N。關係代名詞 which 代替前方的單數名詞 space，故搭配單數動詞。

註 片語「專注奉獻於 ...」be devoted to N / Ving = devote oneself to N / Ving。A 選項應改成：which is devoted。B 選項應改成：and (we have been) devoting ourselves。物品「被進口」，名詞 items 前方搭配表被動的 p.p. 形容詞 imported。

23. Avoiding your allergens as much as possible makes sense. If you're not exposed to the substance ＿＿＿ you are allergic, you won't have an allergic reaction.

   (A) what　　　　　(B) when　　　　　(C) to which　　　　　(D) that

解 儘可能避免過敏原是很合理的。假如你不暴露在會讓你過敏的物質之下，你就不會有過敏反應。

**考點：關係代名詞**

are not exposed / are 兩個動詞，代表兩個句子，故劃線部分應為具連接句子功能的關係代名詞。將先行詞 the substance 放回後方句 you are allergic 排排看，得出：you are allergic to the substance，由此可知需用「物 / 受詞性質」的關係代名詞 which，但因關係代名詞只能代替名詞 the substance，無法代替介係詞 to，故答案應為 to which，**C** 選項為正解。關係子句從關係代名詞開始，往後推，到斷句用的逗號為止。關係代名詞 to which 帶出來的關係子句 you are allergic，放在名詞 the substance 後方，為「形容詞子句」。

24. Today, tea can be drunk at any time of the day, and it accounts for over two-fifths of all beverages ＿＿＿ in Britain, with the exception of water.

(A) consumed

(B) which are consuming

(C) that have consumed

(D) to consume

Unit 1
關係
代名詞

Unit 2
被動
語態

Unit 3
分詞
形容詞

Unit 4
分詞
構句

Unit 5
假設
語法

Unit 6
倒裝
句

Unit 7
間接
問句

Unit 8
特殊
動詞

Unit 9
主動詞
一致

Unit 10
對稱
結構

特別收錄
Unit 11
五回
試題

解 現在，一天當中任何時候都可喝茶。除了水以外，茶占了英國所有被喝的飲料的五分之二。，

**考點：分詞當形容詞。**請見下方句構分析：

... and it accounts for over two-fifths of all beverages _____ in Britain

主詞　　動詞　　　　　　　　名詞

從上方 1 個主詞和 1 個動詞可知句子結構已完整，故名詞 beverages 後方應搭配 Ving 或 p.p. 形容詞，若用關係代名詞帶出來的關係子句當形容詞，則子句中需搭配完整的動詞，即非 Ving / p.p. / to V 原。beverages「被喝」，應搭配表被動的 p.p. 形容詞 consumed，**A** 選項為正解。若用關係子句當形容詞，應寫成...all beverages which（或 that）are consumed（或 have been consumed）...。「物 / 主詞性質」的關係代名詞 which / that 代替前面的 beverages。從 accounts 可知本句為現在式。複數主詞 beverages，搭配複數現在被動式 are consumed。

25. **These programs were broadcast during the day and aimed at middle-class women _____ mindset leaned toward convenient foods for busy families.**

(A) that　　　　　(B) when　　　　　(C) of whom　　　　　(D) whose

解 這些白天放送的節目，瞄準了中產階級的女性。她們的心態傾向為忙碌的家人提供方便的食物。

**考點：關係代名詞**

aimed / leaned 兩個動詞，代表兩個句子，故劃線部分應為具連接句子功能的關係代名詞。將先行詞 women 放回後方句 mindset（心態）leaned ... families 排排看，得出：women's mindset leaned ... families，由此可知需用「人 / 所有格性質」的關係代名詞 whose，**D** 選項為正解。關係子句從關係代名詞開始，往後推，找不到第二個動詞，所以到句點為止。關係代名詞 whose 帶出來的關係子句 mindset leaned ... families 放在名詞 women 後方，為「形容詞子句」。

26. **On intense pollution days, there is a notable smell of smoke in the air and skyscrapers in the city _____ the haze.**

(A) has been obscured by

(B) are going to obscure

(C) are obscured by

(D) obscures

解 在空污嚴重的日子裏，空氣中有股明顯的煙味，且霧霾模糊了都市裏的摩天大樓。

**考點：被動式**

從 there is 可知本句為現在式。主詞「都市裏的摩天大樓」，重點為「摩天大樓」。複數主詞 skyscrapers，搭配複數動詞。且摩天大樓「被霧霾弄得模糊」，應搭配被動式。綜合以上，**C** 選項為正解。

27. I heard the girl _____ and threaten to expose Nathan's "prior misconduct" if he fails to pay her some hush money.

    (A) cursing      (B) to curse      (C) who cursed      (D) curse

解 我聽到那女孩邊咒罵、邊威脅。假如 Nathan 不付她一些封口費，她就要抖出他之前的不當行為。

**考點：感官動詞**

感官動詞 heard，後方受詞 the girl 可執行 curse（咒罵）這動作，應搭配「動詞原形」或「動詞 ing」，又為了和後方 threaten 對稱，**D** 選項為正解。

28. Two months after _____ their videos to 60 seconds, Instagram, a leading social network, grants the same privilege to regular users.

    (A) it lets advertisers to extend      (B) letting advertisers extend
    (C) let advertisers extending      (D) advertisers let it extended

解 Instagram 讓廣告商將影片延長至 60 秒，兩個月後，這首要的社群網絡也給一般使用者一樣的特權。

**考點：使役動詞**

使役動詞 let，後方受詞 advertisers（廣告商）可執行「延長影片」這動作，故搭配「動詞原形」。又介係詞 after，後方搭配（動）名詞。連接詞 after，後方搭配句子，即：主詞 + 動詞。綜合以上，**B** 選項為正解。A、C 選項應改成：it lets advertisers extend。D 選項，能授權延長影片的是 Instagram，而不是廣告商。

29. These big cats may have lived in a vast mountain refuge, formed by the uplifting Himalayas, _____ on equally remarkable species such as the Tibetan blue sheep.

    (A) are fed      (B) which feeds      (C) feeding      (D) fed

Unit 1
關係
代名詞

Unit 2
被動
語態

Unit 3
分詞
形容詞

Unit 4
分詞
構句

Unit 5
假設
語法

Unit 6
倒裝
句

Unit 7
間接
問句

Unit 8
特殊
動詞

Unit 9
主動詞
一致

Unit 10
對稱
結構

特別收錄
Unit 11
五回
試題

解 這些大貓可能住在由上升的喜馬拉雅山所形成的廣闊山區庇護所。它們以同樣引人注目的物種，如：西藏藍羊，為食。

**考點：分詞構句**

原句為：these big cats may have lived… / these big cats feed on ….。兩句主詞相同，都是 these big cats，可用分詞構句。big cats 自己會吃東西（feed），可改成表主動進行的 Ving 分詞構句 feeding…sheep，**C** 選項為正解。庇護所「被造山運動所形成」，名詞 mountain refuge 後方應搭配表被動的 p.p. 形容詞 formed。

30. That hound dog is a little bit weird. Its thin, tiny legs look _____ to the big chubby body.

(A) disproportionate

(B) disproportionately

(C) a huge disproportion

(D) that it is out of proportion

解 那隻獵犬有點古怪。它細瘦的小腳和肥胖龐大的身軀，看起來不成比例。

**考點：連綴動詞**

連綴動詞 look，後方可搭配「形容詞」或「介係詞 like（像）+ 名詞」，**A** 選項為正解。

31. The hunters have slaughtered thousands of rabbits in NZ as part of an annual 24-hour Easter shooting bonanza to curb the _____ species that cause devastation to the land.

(A) introduced

(B) immigrated

(C) invaded

(D) thrived

解 每年，在紐西蘭為時 24 小時的復活節射擊狂歡中，獵人殺死數千隻兔子，以抑制這對土地造成破壞的、被引進的外來物種。

**考點：分詞當形容詞**。請見下方句構分析：

The hunters have slaughtered thousands … to curb the _____ species…
　　　主詞　　　　　　動詞　　　　　　　　　　　　　為了…　　　　　名詞

從上方 1 個主詞和 1 個動詞可知句子結構已完整，故名詞 species 前方應搭配 Ving 或 p.p. 形容詞。物種「被引進」，應搭配表被動的 p.p. 形容詞 introduced，**A** 選項為正解。物種會執行 migrate（遷居）、invade（入侵）、thrive（蓬勃興旺）這三個動作，應搭配表主動進行的 Ving 形容詞 migrating、invading、thriving。

**32.** I receive brilliant advice from my parents often, yet I seldom follow it. This explains _____.

(A) if I often end up with failures

(B) what difficulty am I about to encounter

(C) what do I get myself into

(D) why I always get myself into trouble

> 解 我爸媽常給我很棒的建議，但是我很少聽從他們的建議。這也解釋了為何我常惹上麻煩。
>
> **考點：間接問句**
>
> explain 後方接「理由」、「為什麼」，需用間接問句。間接問句的公式為：why（疑問詞）+ I（主詞）+ get（動詞）...，**D** 選項為正解。A 選項應改成：why I often end up with failures。B 選項應改成：what difficulty I am about to encounter。C 選項應改成：what I get myself into。

**33.** Hair color helps determine _____. Blondes top the list with 146,000 follicles, while redheads have the least, averaging 86,000 follicles.

(A) that dense hair is on your head

(B) whether is the hair dense on your head

(C) why grows the hair denser on your head

(D) how dense the hair on your head is

> 解 髮色有助於決定你頭上的頭髮有多濃密。金髮髮量最多，有 14 萬 6 千個毛囊，而紅髮髮量最少，平均只有 8 萬 6 千個毛囊。
>
> **考點：間接問句**
>
> 從第二句可知，髮色決定頭髮是否濃密，多濃密。間接問句的公式為：how dense（疑問詞）+ the hair on you head（主詞）+ is（動詞），**D** 選項為正解。A 選項：濃密的頭髮是在你頭上，不合文意。B 選項應改成：whether the hair on your head is dense。C 選項應改成：why the hair grows denser on your head。

**34.** If Tim hadn't gobbled down his pizza, a chunk of crust he didn't chew so well _____ his airway.

(A) hadn't been obstructed      (B) would't have obstructed

(C) to obstruct      (D) was obstructing

解 假如 Tim 吃披薩時沒狼吞虎嚥，沒好好被咀嚼的那塊披薩皮就不會堵塞他的氣道。

**考點：假設語法**

從 hadn't gobbled 可知 if 針對「過去」做相反假設，公式如下：

If 主詞 1 + 動詞 1 (過去完成式 had (not) + p.p.)，主詞 2 + 動詞 2 (would / should / could / might (not) + have p.p.)

請見下方句構分析：

If Tim hadn't gobbled ..., a chunk of crust he didn't chew so well _____ ...
　　主詞 1　　動詞 1　　　　　　主詞 2　　　　　　形容詞子句　　　　動詞 2
套公式可知，**B** 選項為正解。披薩皮可阻擋氣道，應搭配主動語態。

**35.** The new \$1.2 billion concourse opened today _____ to boost the airport's capacity from 75m to 90m passengers annually.

(A) is expected        (B) which is expected

(C) to be expected      (D) expecting

解 今天開幕的這個 12 億的新大廳，預期能將機場每年的客容量從 7500 萬提升至 9000 萬。

**考點：被動式**

大廳「被預期」可容納 9 千萬名乘客，應搭配被動式。從 today 可知本句為現在式。綜合以上，**A** 選項為正解。大廳無法執行 open (開幕) 這動作，故名詞 concourse 後方應搭配表被動的 p.p. 形容詞 opened。請見下方句構分析：

The new \$1.2 billion concourse opened today _____ to boost ...
　　　　　　主詞　　　　　　　　　　形容詞　　　動詞

**36.** Acrylic paints are either applied using a knife or_____with a paintbrush.

(A) diluting and then spreading      (B) diluting to spread

(C) dilute and spread           (D) diluted and spread

解 壓克力漆可被用抹刀塗抹，或用筆刷稀釋，然後塗抹。

**考點：對稱 / 被動式。**請見下方句構分析：

Acrylic paints are **either** applied using a knife **or** ＿＿＿＿ with...

主詞　　　動詞　　　過去分詞 1　　　　　　　　過去分詞 2

壓克力漆「被塗抹」，需用被動式 are applied。「either A or B」不是 A 就是 B，A 和 B 兩者詞性和結構要對稱。A 為被動式中的過去分詞 applied，劃線處也應為過去分詞，**D** 選項為正解。

註 spread (v) 塗抹擴散；spread－spread－spread。

---

37. **When you are spraying pesticides out of an airplane from a couple hundred feet off the ground, it's much harder to direct ＿＿＿＿.**

　　(A) where they will land　　　　　(B) where it goes
　　(C) what direction is it　　　　　(D) which way do they go

解 當你利用飛機，從離地幾百英尺的高空噴灑殺蟲劑的話，很難引導這些殺蟲劑將落在哪兒。

**考點：間接問句**

空中噴殺蟲劑，引導殺蟲劑。當句中再次提及 pesticides 時，可換成代名詞 they。間接問句的公式為：where（疑問詞）+ they（主詞）+ will land（動詞），**A** 選項為正解。B 選項應改成：where they go。C 選項應改成：what direction they go。D 選項應改成：which way they go。

---

38. **The police said in a statement, "If these allegations against Mr. Wang ＿＿＿＿ true, we will not rest until he is held accountable for his wrongdoings."**

　　(A) is going to be　　　　　　　(B) were to be
　　(C) are　　　　　　　　　　　　(D) had been

解 警方在聲明中提到：假如這些關於王先生的指控結果是真的，我們將不眠不休地追查，直到他為他的罪刑負責。

**考點：假設語法**

if 針對「未來」we will 做假設，緊接在 if 後方的動詞需從未來往前跳一格，改用「現在式」。主詞「關於王先生的指控」，重點在「指控」。複數主詞 allegations，搭配複數動詞，**C** 選項為正解。

註 連接詞 until 遇到「未來」we will，until 後方動詞需改用「現在式」is held。

39. Roads in the U.S. had remained unsurfaced, crude or _____ gravel, until the beginning of the twentieth century.

(A) had covered　　　　　　　　(B) their covers were

(C) covered with　　　　　　　 (D) covering

> 解 直到 20 世紀初期，美國的道路仍然保持未鋪設的、粗糙簡陋的，或被碎石礫覆蓋的狀況。
>
> **考點：對稱 / 分詞當形容詞。**請見下方句構分析：
>
> Roads... had remained unsurfaced, crude or _____ gravel...
> 　主詞　　　　動詞　　　　形容詞1　形容詞2　形容詞3
> 動詞 remain（仍然）後方需搭配「形容詞」。為遵守對稱原則，連接詞 or 共連接了三個形容詞。道路「被碎石覆蓋」，需搭配表被動的 p.p. 形容詞 covered。cover (n) 封面 (v) 覆蓋。片語「被...覆蓋」be covered with N。綜合以上，**C** 選項為正解。

40. Attacks and chaos needed to come to an immediate end and humanitarian aid _____ through to desperate civilians who struggled to survive.

(A) should have allowed　　　　(B) had to be allowed

(C) hadn't been allowing　　　　(D) wasn't allowed

> 解 攻擊和混亂必須立即停止，而人道救援物資也必須被允許通過，送到掙扎求生的、心急如焚的老百姓手中。
>
> **考點：被動式**
>
> 從攻擊必須停止，可知救援物資還沒送到老百姓手上。所以 aid「必須被允許通過」，需搭配肯定的被動式。連接詞 and 連接兩個動詞，動詞時態需對稱。從 needed 可知，劃線處應為過去式。綜合以上，**B** 選項為正解。A 選項，should have p.p. 表示「過去該做卻沒有做」，文意不合，且也不是被動式，非正解。

41. The auto sales show signs of recession, _____ 6% to 1 million. The decline was exceptional for May, a month when people typically buy cars ahead of summer road trips.

(A) were to fall　　　　　　　 (B) falling

(C) have been fallen　　　　　 (D) fallen

解 汽車銷售出現衰退的徵兆，下降了百分之６，跌到一百萬輛。這跌幅在５月是很不尋常的，因為人們通常會在夏季旅遊前，就是五月，買車。

**考點：分詞構句**

原句為：the auto sales show … / the auto sales fall …。兩句主詞相同，都是 the auto sales，可用分詞構句。fall 沒有被動式，只能用主動語法，故改成表主動進行的 Ving 分詞構句 falling 6% to one million，**B** 選項為正解。

42. **If mobile phone roaming charges _____ across the EU from next year, cellphone users would be able to save up to 38 pence per minute on calls.**

(A) were to abolish                     (B) are abolished

(C) had been abolishing        (D) abolish

解 假如從明年開始，歐盟國家廢除了手機漫遊費，手機使用者打電話時，每分鐘將能節省多達 38 便士。

**考點：假設語法 / 被動式**

從 from next year 可知 if 針對「未來」做假設，緊接在 if 後方的動詞需從未來往前跳一格，改用「現在式」。複數主詞 charges，搭配複數動詞。漫遊費「被廢除」，需搭配被動式。綜合以上，**B** 選項為正解。

43. **Only through reproduction _____ the properties of a species.**

(A) that successive generations carry on

(B) do successive generations carry on

(C) can successive generations that carry on

(D) carry on successive generations and

解 只有透過繁殖，世代才能接連傳遞物種特質。

**考點：倒裝句**

only 加上介係詞片語放句首加強語氣，後方需搭配倒裝句。carry on 不是 be 動詞，倒裝時需搭配助動詞。

套公式：Only… + 助動詞 + 主詞 + 動詞原形…

綜合以上，**B** 選項為正解。C 選項，還原句子：Successive generations that carry on the properties of a species can only through production。can 為助動詞，後方缺動詞原形，非正解。

44. The organization promoted sculpture by standardizing procedures for competitions, _____ the professional status of sculptors, and encouraging commissions for sculpture works in public places.

(A) enhancement of

(B) which is enhancing

(C) enhancing

(D) enhanced

> 解 這機構藉由將比賽程序標準化、提升雕塑家的專業地位，和鼓勵公共區雕塑作品的委任等，來提倡雕塑。
>
> **考點：對稱。** 請見下方句構分析：
>
> The organization promoted...by standardizing... , _____..., and encouraging...
>
>     主詞         動詞        動名詞 1       動名詞 2       動名詞 3
>
> 介係詞「藉著」by，後方需搭配動名詞。為遵守對稱原則，連接詞 and 連接三個動名詞。劃線部份應為動名詞，**C** 選項為正解。

45. Water constitutes almost 96 perccent of the body weight of a jellyfish, so _____ a jellyfish dry out in the sun at this moment, it would virtually disappear.

(A) if          (B) were          (C) had          (D) should

> 解 水大約占水母體重的百分之 96，所以假如現在有隻水母晾在太陽下，它就會消失。
>
> **考點：假設語法**
>
> 從文意可知現在手邊並沒有任何水母。if 針對「現在」at this moment 做相反假設，緊接在 if 後方的動詞從現在往前跳一格，改用「過去式」。即：
>
> ..., so **if** a jellyfish **dried out** in the sun at this moment, it would disappear...
>
> 也可用助動詞 should（萬一）取代 if 造假設句。但需留意助動詞 should 後方要搭配動詞原形，即：
>
> ..., so **should** a jellyfish **dry out** in the sun at this moment, it would disappear...
>
> 由上可知，**D** 選項為正解。

46. One man interviewed calls the protests "embarrassing for the country" and wondered _____.

(A) why the disruptions are allowed to continue

(B) what have deterred the police from dispersing the protesters

(C) when is the chaos going to end

(D) who the chaos deals with

解 一名接受訪問的男子說，那些示威抗議讓國家難堪，並好奇為何這些騷動可以被允許持續下去。

**考點：間接問句**

從 wonder（好奇）可知有疑慮，後方應搭配間接問句，而非關係子句。間接問句的公式為：why（疑問詞）+ the disruptions（主詞）+ are allowed（動詞）…，A 選項為正解。B 選項應改成：what has deterred the police from dispersing the protesters。what 是疑問詞，也是主詞。what 當主詞時，應視為第三人稱單數，搭配單數動詞。C 選項應改成：when the chaos is going to end。chaos 為不可數名詞。D 選項應改成：who can deal with the chaos。

47. **The company courted considerable controversy with its tax avoidance strategies, _____ and its heavy reliance on lobbying to get its own way.**

(A) its shedding of domestic jobs  (B) shedding domestic jobs

(C) to shed domestic jobs  (D) which lead to shedding of jobs

解 這家公司因為它的避稅策略、它的國內大舉裁員，和它大量倚賴遊說，進而為所欲為等行徑，引發了相當大的爭議。

**考點：對稱。**請見下方句構分析：

The company courted … with … strategies, _____ and … reliance …
　　主詞　　　動詞　　介係詞　　名詞1　　　名詞2　　　　　名詞3

介係詞「因為」with，後方需搭配「名詞」。為遵守對稱原則，連接詞 and 連接三個名詞，都以「所有格 its + 名詞」呈現。「砍／減」shedding 為動名詞。綜合以上，A 選項為正解。B 選項，shedding 後方有受詞，所以 shedding 不是動名詞，而是分詞構句中表主動進行的 Ving 分詞構句。(the company) shedding domestic jobs and its heavy reliance 意指：(公司) 裁員，也砍了依賴性，文意不通。C 選項，「to 動詞原形」意指「為了…」。文意上變成：公司引發爭議是為了裁員，文意不通。D 選項，關係代名詞 which，代替前方的名詞 strategies，避稅策略不會引發裁員，文意不通。

48. **If we had a more intimate understanding of real, whole foods, we would be better equipped to evaluate what _____ in our grocery baskets.**

(A) should we put  (B) should be put  (C) are putting  (D) puts us

Unit 1
關係
代名詞

Unit 2
被動
語態

Unit 3
分詞
形容詞

Unit 4
分詞
構句

Unit 5
假設
語法

Unit 6
倒裝
句

Unit 7
間接
問句

Unit 8
特殊
動詞

Unit 9
主動詞
一致

Unit 10
對稱
結構

特別收錄
Unit 11
五回
試題

解 假如我們對真正的全食品有更深入的了解的話，我們就更有能力評估什麼東西該被放入我們的購物籃中。

**考點：間接問句**

從 evaluate（評估）可知尚未有結論，所以後方應接間接問句，而非關係子句。句中的 what 為疑問詞，而非複合關係代名詞。間接問句的公式為：what（疑問詞 + 主詞）+ should be put（動詞）...。what 既是疑問詞也是主詞。且 what 當主詞，應視為第三人稱單數，故搭配單數動詞。東西（what）「被放入」，需搭配被動式。綜合以上，**B** 選項為正解。A 選項應改成：what we should put。C 選項應改成：what is put。D 選項，東西不會「放我們」，文意不通。

49. **Nearly half of the 66 people killed in this tragic plane crash _____ Egyptians, many of them young men and women forced to look overseas for work.**

(A) were        (B) to be        (C) has been        (D) being

解 66 名在這次空難遇害的乘客中，約半數是埃及人。這些埃及人裏，許多都是被迫到海外求職的青年男女。

**考點：主動詞一致**

當主詞為「分數 of ...」時，動詞單複數必須視 of 後方名詞的單複數而定。 of 後方的名詞 the 66 people 為複數，故搭配複數動詞 were，**A** 選項為正解。killed 和 forced 放在名詞 people 和 women 後，為表被動的 p.p. 形容詞。

50. **If Earth _____, differences in air pressure would be the primary cause of air flow, with winds blowing from high-pressure to low-pressure areas.**

(A) hadn't rotated        (B) didn't rotate
(C) isn't rotating        (D) weren't rotated

解 假如地球不旋轉的話，空氣壓力的變化就成了空氣流動的主因，造成風從高壓地區吹向低壓地區。

**考點：假設語法**

從「地球不旋轉」可知 if 針對「現在」做相反假設，緊接在 if 後方的動詞從現在往前跳一格，改用「過去式」。地球自己會旋轉，得用主動語態。綜合以上，**B** 選項為正解。

# Unit 11

**01.** Information _____ on the fake banking website was stealthily captured by the criminals for their own fraudulent purposes.

(A) entering

(B) that was entering

(C) people was entered

(D) entered

解 為了詐欺，壞人偷偷地截取被輸入假銀行網站上的資訊。

**考點：分詞當形容詞。請見下方句構分析：**

Information _____ on the ... website was...captured...

<u>主詞 / 名詞</u>　　　　　　　　　　　　　<u>動詞</u>

從上方 1 個主詞和 1 個動詞可知句子結構已完整，故名詞 information 後方應搭配 Ving 或 p.p. 形容詞，若用關係代名詞帶出來的關係子句當形容詞，則子句中需搭配完整的動詞，即非 Ving / p.p. / to V 原。資訊「被輸入」，應搭配表被動的 p.p 形容詞 entered，**D** 選項為正解。若用關係子句當形容詞，則應寫成：information which（或 that）was entered...。「物 / 主詞性質」的關係代名詞 that 代替前方的不可數名詞 information，搭配單數動詞。C 選項改成：(that) people entered。

**02.** Andre Perache, head of programs at Doctors Without Borders, confirms to ABC News that a lack of vital hospital supplies such as antibiotics as well as fuel to run generators _____ doctors in Syria to make hard, horrible decisions.

(A) forcing　　　(B) are being forced　　　(C) and to force　　　(D) forces

解 無國界醫師的負責人 Andre Perache，向 ABC 新聞證實：缺乏重要醫療補給，如：抗生素和啟動發電機的燃料等，迫使 Syria 的醫生作出困難且可怕的決定。

**考點：主動詞一致**

關係代名詞 that 帶出一個句子。主詞「缺乏補給品」，重點在「缺乏」。單數主詞 a lack，需搭配單數動詞，**D** 選項為正解。請見下方句構分析：

...that a lack of ...supplies such as antibiotics ...generators _____ doctors...

<u>主詞</u>　　　　　　　　　　　　　　<u>舉例</u>　　　　　　<u>動詞</u>

03. _____ dogs were the first animal to be domesticated is generally agreed upon by researchers and scholars in the field.

(A) What      (B) Why      (C) That      (D) Whether

解 研究人員和學界學者大致都同意，狗是第一種被人類豢養的動物。

**考點：關係代名詞**

從 agreed 可知沒疑問，故句首應為關係字句。而非間接問句。were / is 兩動詞，代表兩個句子，故劃線部分應為具連接句子功能的關係代名詞。關係代名詞前無先行詞，故答案不是 that 就是 what。關係子句從關係代名詞開始，往後推，were / be domesticated 已用不定詞 (to V 原) 處理過，應視為一組動詞，所以到第二個動詞 is 前結束。關係子句 dogs were … domesticated「意思完整」，故 **C** 選項為正解。

04. Jackie Mclean's recordings have shown that he is one of the few musicians _____ style of playing has kept pace with the evolution of modern jazz.

(A) that      (B) for whom      (C) whose      (D) what

解 Jackie Mclean 的錄音顯示，他是少數演奏風格可與現代爵士樂同步演化的音樂家之一。

**考點：關係代名詞**

is / has kept 兩個動詞，代表兩個句子，故劃線部分應為具連接句子功能的關係代名詞。將先行詞 musicians 放回後方句 style of playing… jazz 排排看，得出：musicians' style of playing has kept pace….，由此可知需用「人 / 所有格性質」的關係代名詞 whose，**C** 選項為正解。關係子句從關係代名詞開始，往後推，找不到第二個動詞，所以到句點為止。關係代名詞 whose 帶出來的關係子句 style of playing…jazz 放在名詞 musicians 後方，為「形容詞子句」。

05. Companies need to have their employees_____ to implement the Six Sigma processes. During the rigorous training sessions, they would learn how to function well in a team and how to use the measurement and improvement tools.

(A) and to train      (B) to train      (C) trained      (D) training

> 解 公司需要讓他們的員工被訓練施行 Six Sigma 程序。在這嚴格的訓練期間，他們將學會如何在團隊中運作，及如何使用評估和改善的工具。
>
> **考點：使役動詞**
>
> 使役動詞 have，後方受詞 their employees「被訓練」，需搭配「過去分詞」，C 選項為正解。

06. A team of neuroscientists studied how the human brain responds to sharp noises using MRI brain scanners. As expected, after hearing a scream, activity increased in the brain's auditory centers where sound coming into the ears _____.

(A) is processed            (B) through the process

(C) to be processed        (D) have processed

> 解 一群神經科學家用 MRI 腦部掃描來研究人類大腦如何回應尖銳的聲音。正如預期地，聽到尖叫聲後，腦部聽覺中心的活躍度增加了。進入耳朵的聲音就是在聽覺中心被處理。
>
> **考點：被動式／主動詞一致**
>
> 關係副詞 where 帶出關係子句，請見下方句構分析：
>
> ... where sound coming into the ears _____ ...
> 　　　　主詞　　　　　形容詞　　　　　動詞
>
> 單數主詞 sound，搭配單數動詞。sound「被處理」，應搭配被動式。綜合以上，A 選項為正解。聲音直接進入耳朵，故名詞 sound 後方應搭配表主動進行的 Ving 形容詞 coming。

07. At the beginning of the 21st century, new cooking shows emerged to satisfy celeb-hungry, reality-crazed audiences. In these programs, chefs have become celebrities _____ fame rivals that of rock stars.

(A) who have     (B) with whom     (C) whose     (D) who's

> 解 21 世紀初期，新的烹飪節目出現，滿足那些瘋名人、瘋實境秀的觀眾。這些節目中，廚師已變身名人。廚師的名氣堪比搖滾明星。
>
> **考點：關係代名詞**
>
> have become / rivals 兩個動詞，代表兩個句子，故劃線部分應為具連接句子功能的關係代名詞。將先行詞 celebrities 放回後方句 fame rivals... stars 排排看，得出：celebrities' fame rivals（比得上）that（指 fame）

of rock stars，由此可知需用「人 / 所有格性質」的關係代名詞 whose，**C** 選項為**正解**。關係子句從關係代名詞開始，往後推，找不到第二個動詞，所以到句點為止。關係代名詞 whose 帶出來的關係子句 fame rivals … stars 放在名詞 celebrities 後方，為「形容詞子句」。

08. **The automakers say that lots of the weight saved _____ the increased use of aluminum in the engines.**

(A) is attributed to  (B) to attribute it to

(C) and attributed by  (D) are attributing

解 汽車製造商說，車體重量大減得歸因於引擎中鋁的使用量大增。

**考點：被動式**。請見下方句構分析：

that much of the weight  saved  _____ the increased use of…

　　　　主詞　　　　p.p. 當形容詞　動詞

省下來的重量「被歸因於」使用鋁製引擎，需搭配被動式。不可數名詞 weight，視為單數主詞，搭配單數動詞。片語「將 A 歸因於 B」attribute A to B，改成被動式也是搭配介係詞 to，be attributed to N。綜合以上，**A** 選項為**正解**。重量「被節省」，故名詞 weight 後方應搭配表被動的 p.p. 形容詞 saved。

09. **Our demand for a tuition freeze became _____ when our occupation of the college building made news.**

(A) apparently  (B) understanding  (C) like a sensation  (D) known

解 當我們占據學校大樓的消息上新聞後，我們學費凍漲的訴求也變得眾所皆知。

**考點：連綴動詞 / 分詞當形容詞**。請見下方句構分析：

Our demand for a tuition freeze became  _____ …

　　主詞 / 名詞　　　　　　　　　　動詞

連綴動詞 become，後方搭配「形容詞」。our demand「被人所知道」，應搭配表被動的 p.p. 形容詞 known，**D** 選項為**正解**。A 選項應改成 apparent。B 選項應改成 p.p. 形容詞 understood（被了解）。C 選項，become 可直接接名詞，不需介係詞 like，應改成 become a sensation（轟動的事）。

10. An influx of new immigrants to an area will appear _____ to local residents and therefore provoke their opposition and even racial tensions.

(A) threatened　　(B) threateningly　　(C) threatening　　(D) to threaten

> 解 新移民大量湧入一地，對當地居民似乎具威脅性，因而會激起他們的反對，甚至族群關係緊繃。
>
> **考點：連綴動詞 / 分詞當形容詞。**請見下方句構分析：
>
> An influx of new immigrants to an area will appear _____ to...
> ~~~~~~~~~~~~~~~~~~~~~~~~~~~~~~~~~~~~~~~~~~~　　　　　~~~~~~
> 　　　　　　　主詞 / 名詞　　　　　　　　　　　動詞
>
> 連綴動詞 appear，後方需搭配「形容詞」或「to 動詞原形」。大量湧入的移民會主動威脅到當地居民，應用表主動進行的 Ving 形容詞 threatening，**C 選項為正解。**D 選項，應改成：... appear to threaten local residents。

11. The military makes good use of the virtual reality simulations in training so that the first shot a soldier fires _____ against a real live enemy, but a virtual one

(A) isn't　　　　(B) and won't be　　(C) never being　　(D) not to be

> 解 軍方善用虛擬實境來訓練士兵，所以士兵開的第一槍不是對真的、活生生的敵軍，而是虛擬敵軍。
>
> **考點：主動詞一致**
>
> 從 makes / fires 可知本句為現在式。主詞「士兵所開的第一槍」，重點為「第一槍」。單數主詞 the first shot，搭配單數動詞，**A 選項為正解。**請見下方句構分析：
>
> ... so that the first shot (that) a soldier fires _____ against ... enemy...
> 　　　　　　~~~~~~~~~~~~~~~　~~~~~~~~~~~~~~~~　~~~~~~　~~~~~~~　~~~~~
> 　　　　　　　　主詞　　　　　　形容詞子句　　　動詞　　介係詞　　名詞

12. A merger is achieved when a company purchased the property of other firms, then _____ into one corporate structure.

(A) is absorbed　　　　　　　　　　(B) absorbed it
(C) absorbing them　　　　　　　　(D) they were absorbed

> 解 當某公司購買其他公司的資產，然後將這些公司合併成一家公司時，併

Unit 1
關係
代名詞

Unit 2
被動
語態

Unit 3
分詞
形容詞

Unit 4
分詞
構句

Unit 5
假設
語法

Unit 6
倒裝
句

Unit 7
間接
問句

Unit 8
特殊
動詞

Unit 9
主動詞
一致

Unit 10
對稱
結構

特別收錄
Unit 11
五回
試題

購案就已完成。

**考點：分詞構句**

原句為：... a company purchased ... other firms / a company absorbed other firms into one ...。兩句主詞相同，都是 a company，可用分詞構句。absorbed 為過去式，應改成表主動的 Ving 分詞構句。other firms 可換成 them。綜合以上，**C** 選項為正解。A、D 選項，副詞 then 無法連接兩個動詞 purchased / is absorbed，和 purchased / they were absorbed。

13. **To find out what makes human screams unique, neuroscientist Luc Arnal and his team examined a bank of sounds _____ sentences spoken or screamed by 19 adults.**

    (A) consisted of　　(B) containing　　(C) constituted　　(D) making up

    解 為了找出什麼因素讓人類的尖叫聲顯得很獨特，神經科學家 Luc Arnal，和他的團隊檢驗了一個聲音庫。這聲音庫是由 19 個成人尖叫或說出來的句子所組成。

    **考點：分詞當形容詞。**請見下方句構分析：

    and his team examined a bank of sounds _____ sentences...
    　　　　主詞　　　　動詞　　　　名詞

    從上方 1 個主詞和 1 個動詞可知句子結構已完整，故名詞 a back of sounds 後方應搭配 Ving 或 p.p. 形容詞。若用關係代名詞帶出來的關係子句當形容詞，則子句中需搭配完整的動詞，即非 Ving / p.p. / to V 原。原句為：...a bank of sounds（大團體）consists of / contain / comprise / is composed of / is made up of  sentences（小團體）...。前三個為主動語態，可改成表主動進行的 Ving 形容詞 consisting of / containing / comprising，**B** 選項為正解。後兩個為被動式，可改成表被動的 p.p. 形容詞 composed of / made up of 。

    註 補充說明另一個考點： ... sentences（小團體）constitute / compose / make up a bank of sounds（大團體）都是主動語態，可改成表主動進行的 Ving 形容詞 constituting / composing / making up。

14. **To work with the cutting-edge virtual reality device, _____ $800, users need a high-powered computer. This could easily mean $2000 out of the pocket, a huge expense for people who are eager to try it out.**

    (A) what price is　　　　　　　　　(B) where its price is around
    (C) and to be priced at　　　　　　(D) which is priced at

解 為了使用最先進的、售價約美金 800 元的虛擬科技裝置，使用者需要高效能的電腦。這意味著他們必須從口袋掏出美金 2000 元。這對渴望嘗試這裝置的人而言，是一筆很大的開銷。

考點：關係代名詞 / 主動詞一致 / 被動式。請見下方句構分析：

To work ... device, _____ $ 800, users need ...
　　　　　名詞　形容詞　　　　主詞　動詞

從上方 1 個主詞和 1 個動詞可知句子結構已完整，故名詞 device 後方應搭配 Ving 或 p.p. 形容詞。若用關係代名詞帶出來的關係子句當形容詞，則子句中需搭配完整的動詞，即非 Ving / p.p. / to V 原。裝置「被訂價」，應搭配表被動的 p.p. 形容詞 priced at。若用關係子句當形容詞，則應寫成：which is priced at $800。「物 / 主詞性質」的關係代名詞 which 代替前方的單數名詞 device。綜合以上，**D** 選項為正解。A、B 選項應改成：whose price is $800。C 選項，to be priced（為了被訂價）的主詞為 users，不合文意。

15. For centuries, pregnant women _____ attending funerals for fear that they might fall victim to souls searching for a host that will allow them to stay in the mortal world.

(A) are discouraging and      (B) have been discouraged from

(C) were discouraged in      (D) had discouraged when

解 幾世紀以來，懷孕女性被勸阻參加葬禮，怕她們可能淪為那些尋找宿主，好繼續待在人間的惡靈下手的目標。

考點：被動式

懷孕女性「被勸阻」參加葬禮，怕（for fear that...）有壞事發生，需搭配被動式。介係詞 for (centuries)，表示持續一段時間，需搭配完成式。片語「阻止某人做某事」discourage 人 from Ving。改成被動式：人 be discouraged from Ving。綜合以上，**B** 選項為正解。

16. In temples, some Indians simply have their hair _____ off for purification and as a gesture of gratitude to gods.

(A) that was shaved      (B) shaved

(C) to shave      (D) shaving

解 寺廟裏，有些印度人為淨身而剃髮，也藉此表示對神的感謝。

考點：使役動詞

使役動詞 have，後方受詞 hair「被剃除」，故搭配表被動的「過去分詞」，**B** 選項為正解。A 選項，that was shaved...放在名詞 hair 後，為形容詞子句，文意變成：讓他們被剃除的頭髮，文意不通。

Unit 1
關係
代名詞

Unit 2
被動
語態

Unit 3
分詞
形容詞

Unit 4
分詞
構句

Unit 5
假設
語法

Unit 6
倒裝
句

Unit 7
間接
問句

Unit 8
特殊
動詞

Unit 9
主動詞
一致

Unit 10
對稱
結構

特別收錄
Unit 11
五回
試題

**17.** **There are more than 2,000 species of fireflies known to exist around the world, _____ more than 60 species can be found in Taiwan.**

(A) which      (B) and where      (C) among which      (D) when

解 全世界現存的螢火蟲超過 2000 種，其中，台灣可找到超過 60 種。

**考點：關係代名詞**

are / can be found 兩個動詞，代表兩個句子，故劃線部分應為具連接句子功能的關係代名詞。後方 in Taiwan 已點出地點，故先行詞不是 world，而是 2000 species of fireflies。將先行詞 fireflies 放回後方句 more than...Taiwan 排排看，得出：among the 2000 species of fireflies, more than 60 species can be found in Taiwan，由此可知需用「物 / 受詞性質」的關係代名詞 which。關係代名詞只能代替名詞 the 2000 species of fireflies，無法代替介係詞 among，所以答案為 among which，**C** 選項為正解。關係子句從關係代名詞開始，往後推，找不到第二個動詞，所以到句點為止。關係代名詞 among which 帶出來的關係子句 more than...Taiwan 補充說明 2000 種螢火蟲分布的狀況，屬「名詞子句」。

**18.** **Only in the presence of dust particles _____.**

(A) can fog and mist be formed      (B) when fog and mist are formed

(C) form fog and mist      (D) have fog and mist formed

解 只有在粉塵分子出現時，才會形成霧。

**考點：倒裝句**

only 加上片語放句首時，後方需搭倒裝句。only 為首的倒裝句公式如下：

Only... + 助動詞 + 主詞 + 動詞原形 ...

Only... + be 動詞 + 主詞 ...

霧「被粉塵分子組成」，應搭配被動式。套公式，**A** 選項為正解。B 選項應改成：are fog and mist formed。

**19.** The glow behavior of fireflies serves multiple purposes, including intimidating predators as well as _____ illumination and camouflage.

(A) provision　　(B) providing　　(C) to provide　　(D) provides

解 螢火蟲發光有多重目的，包含威脅掠食者，還有提供照明和偽裝。

考點：**對稱**。請見下方句構分析：

…, including intimidating predators as well as _____ illumination …
　　　　 介係詞　　 動名詞 1　　　　　　　　　　　　 動名詞 2

介係詞 including，後方應搭配 (動) 名詞。為遵守對稱原則，連接詞 as well as 左方為動名詞 intimidating，右方劃線處也應為動名詞，**B** 選項為正解。A 選項，名詞 provision (準備) 和動名詞 intimidating 形式上不對稱。且名詞 provision 後方不會加受詞 illumination。

**20.** _____ only minimal power, the Myshake app detects shaking day or night and if the vibrations fit the profile of a quake, it relays the information, along with GPS coordinates, to seismologists.

(A) To consume　　　　　　　　(B) Having been consumed
(C) Consuming　　　　　　　　(D) Consumed

解 Myshake 應用程式只消耗極少的電力就可日夜持續監測震度。若震度符合地震條件，Myshake 就會傳送資料和 GPS 座標給地震學家。

考點：**分詞構句**

原句為：the Myshake app consumes … power / the Myshake app detects …。兩句主詞相同，都是 the Myshake app，可用分詞構句。consumes 為現在式，可改成表主動進行的 Ving 分詞構句 Consuming … power，**C** 選項為正解。

**21.** _____ that they spent most of their lives in swamps and shallow lakes where water could support them.

(A) So heavy were many dinosaurs

(B) Such heavy dinosaurs they were

(C) So heavy dinosaurs were many

(D) Such many dinosaurs were heavy

解 很多恐龍體重是如此地重，以致於它們大半輩子都在沼澤和水淺的湖泊

渡過。那兒的水浮力才足以支撐它們的身軀。

**考點：倒裝句**

so 放句首的「如此地 ... 以致於 ...」倒裝句，公式如下：

So + 形容詞 + be 動詞 + 主詞 1 + that + 主詞 2 + 動詞 2

such 放句首的「如此地...以致於...」倒裝句，公式如下：

such + be 動詞 + 主詞 1 + that + 主詞 2 + 動詞 2

從 spent 可知本句應為過去式。套公式，**A** 選項為正解。

Unit 1
關係
代名詞

Unit 2
被動
語態

Unit 3
分詞
形容詞

Unit 4
分詞
構句

Unit 5
假設
語法

Unit 6
倒裝
句

Unit 7
間接
問句

Unit 8
特殊
動詞

Unit 9
主動詞
一致

Unit 10
對稱
結構

22. **It's the Ikea curse: I spend four hours figuring out _____, only to be left with one component that doesn't seem to fit anywhere.**

(A) why does my furniture assembly fail

(B) what the assembly disaster results in

(C) how I can piece together my new furniture

(D) that something goes wrong with the assembled furniture

解 這就是 Ikea 的詛咒。我花了 4 小時弄清楚該如何組裝我的新家俱，結果居然剩下一個哪兒都塞不進去的零件。

**考點：間接問句**

從弄清楚 figure out 可知心有疑慮，後方應搭配間接問句，而非關係子句。間接問句的公式為：how（疑問詞）+ I（主詞）+ can piece together（動詞）...，**C** 選項為正解。A 選項應改成：why my furniture assembly fails。B 選項應改成：what results in the assembly disaster。其中，what 既是疑問詞也是主詞。what 當主詞時，應視為第三人稱單數，搭配單數動詞。D 選項應改成：what goes wrong with the assembled furniture。

23. **In his 1990 race for Congress, he frequently laid political bait for his opponent and relished watching him _____.**

(A) stumbling and fell       (B) stumble and fall

(C) to stumble and fall      (D) stumbled and falling

解 1990 年競選國會議員時，他常常為他的對手設下政治誘餌，然後享受看著對手失足跌倒。

**考點：感官動詞**

感官動詞 watching，後方受詞 him 可執行 stumble（跌倒）和 fall 這兩

個動作，故搭配「動詞原形」stumble and fall，或「動詞 ing」stumbling and falling。綜合以上，**B** 選項為正解。

24. After learning her son had been killed in a plane crash, she was stricken speechless and her face turned completely pale as if she _____ a ghost.

(A) was seen

(B) might see

(C) would have seen

(D) had seen

解 知道她兒子在空難中喪生後，她說不出話來，她的臉色變得慘白，彷彿看到鬼一般。

**考點：假設語法**

從 was / turned 可知 as if 針對「過去」做譬喻，as if 後方句中的動詞需從過去往前跳一格，改用「過去完成式」，**D** 選項為正解。實際上，她並沒見到鬼，所以 as if 後方不能用直說法。

25. When _____ heavy snow or melting snow, some rivers routinely overflow their banks.

(A) swollen by

(B) it swells

(C) they have swollen

(D) swelling

解 當大雪或融雪讓有些河流水位高漲時，這些河流常淹沒堤岸。

**考點：分詞構句［變形 1］**

河流水位「被融雪弄得高漲」，需搭配被動式。原句為：When some rivers are swollen by snow ... / some rivers routinely overflow ...。兩句主詞相同，都是 some rivers，可用分詞構句。are swollen by 為現在被動式，可改成表被動的 p.p. 分詞構句 When swollen ... snow。寫分詞構句時，也可保留連接詞 when。綜合以上，**A** 選項為正解。

26. Only if Tom _____ for his unfounded accusations will I make peace with him.

(A) apologizes

(B) will apologize

(C) were apologizing

(D) has apologized

**解** 只有當 Tom 為他的不實指控道歉，我才會跟他和解。

**考點：假設語法 / 倒裝句**

only 搭配 if 條件句放句首，需造倒裝句，但需先完成 if 條件句（if Tom...
accusations），才能開始造倒裝句。從 will I 可知 if 針對「未來」做假設，
緊接在 if 後方的動詞需從未來往前跳一格，改用「現在式」，**A** 選項為正
解。請見下方句構分析：

Only if Tom apologizes for his unfounded accusations will I make peace...

                    if 條件句                    倒裝句

27. **Whether you're a Kevin, Ashley, Mohammed or Felicia, _____ that distinguishes you from the crowd but it impacts your future success in surprising ways.**

(A) your name is not only an important part of your identity

(B) not only is your name an important part of your identity

(C) not only gives you the identity

(D) your name, an important part of your identity, gives not only

**解** 無論你是 Kevin、Ashley、Mohammed 還是 Felicia，你的名字不只是你身分
重要的一部份，讓你和別人不同，也以令人驚訝的方式影響你未來的成就。

**考點：倒裝句**

Whether ... Felicia 為第一句。逗號後就是第二句。從 it impacts 推知本
句為現在式。not only 為首的倒裝句，公式如下：

not only + be 動詞 + 主詞 2 + ... , but + 主詞 3 + 動詞 3。

套公式，**B** 選項為正解。若 not only 不放句首，則「不只 A，連 B 都...」
not only A but B，A 和 B 詞性需對稱。A 選項，名詞 an important part
of your identity 和句子 it impacts 不對稱，非正解。D 選項，not only 後
方為當「受詞」的名詞子句，而 but 後方加的是句子。不對稱，非正解。

28. **Have you ever wondered _____ after you pass away? Now you can nominate a "legacy contact," someone who helps manage your page, in advance.**

(A) what choices do you have as to your Facebook account

(B) if there had been ways to handle your Facebook account

(C) what might happen to your Facebook account

(D) that you could keep your Facebook account alive

解 你曾經好奇，你過世後，你的臉書帳號該怎麼辦嗎？現在你可事先指定一個代理人，來幫你管理你的臉書頁面。

**考點：間接問句**

從動詞 wonder（好奇）可知有疑問，後方應接間接問句，而非關係子句。間接問句的公式為：what（疑問詞 + 主詞）+ might happen（動詞）...，**C** 選項為正解。其中，what 既是疑問詞也是主詞。what 當主詞時，應視為第三人稱單數。A 選項應改成：what choices you have as to your Facebook account。B 選項應改成：if there are ways to handle your Facebook account。疑問詞「是否」if，後方動詞不需跳躍，對稱即可。D 選項應改成：whether you could keep your Facebook alive。

29. **I knocked Alice's new iPhone out of her hand and sent it flying onto the hot pavement. The case failed to protect her device and the screen shattered. Had I been more careful, the accident _____.**

(A) was then prevented

(B) could prevent it from happening

(C) could have been prevented

(D) would have prevented it.

解 Alice 手中的新 iPhone 被我弄掉了。我一揮，iPhone 飛到滾燙的人行道上。手機殼沒能保護手機，螢幕都碎了。假如我小心點，這意外就可被避免。

**考點：假設語法**

從文意可知 accident 已發生，無法被避免。if 針對「過去」做相反假設，公式如下：
If 主詞 1 + 動詞 1（過去完成式 had (not) + p.p.），主詞 2 + 動詞 2 (would / should / could / might (not) + have p.p.)

意外「可被避免」，需搭配被動式。套公式：
If I **had been** more careful, the accident could **have been prevented**.

也可去掉連接詞 if，將過去完成式中的助動詞 had 移至句首，即成加強語氣版的假設語法：
**Had I been** more careful, the accident **could have been prevented**.

由上可知，**C** 選項為正解。

30. **Music is a powerful medium for expression. It helps convey feelings which _____ into words and therefore is capable of touching people deeply.**

(A) can't be put　　(B) haven't put　　(C) aren't putting　　(D) don't put

Unit 1
關係
代名詞

Unit 2
被動
語態

Unit 3
分詞
形容詞

Unit 4
分詞
構句

Unit 5
假設
語法

Unit 6
倒裝
句

Unit 7
間接
問句

Unit 8
特殊
動詞

Unit 9
主動詞
一致

Unit 10
對稱
結構

特別收錄
Unit 11
五回
試題

解 音樂是強而有力的表達媒介。音樂幫忙傳遞難以訴諸文字的情感，因此也能深深地感動人心。

**考點：被動式**

「物／主詞性質」的關係代名詞 which，代替前方的名詞 feelings。主詞 feelings「被寫成文字」，需搭配被動式。從 is capable 可知，本句為現在式。綜合以上，**A** 選項為正解。

31. **On Easter morning of 1885, what appeared to be a simple enameled egg _____ to the palace. And to the astonishment of the Empress, the egg opened to a golden hen; inside the hen was a diamond miniature of the royal crown and a ruby egg.**

(A) to deliver　　　　　　　(B) had been delivering

(C) was delivered　　　　　(D) delivered

解 1885 年，復活節的早上，似乎像是琺瑯蛋的物品被送進了皇宮。令女皇大為驚喜的是，一打開蛋就看見一隻金母雞。金母雞裏面有個迷你版的鑽石皇冠和一顆紅寶石蛋。

**考點：主動詞一致／被動式。**請見下方句構分析：

..., what appeared to ...enameled egg _____ to the palace.
　　　　　關係子句當主詞　　　　　　　　動詞

關係子句從複合關係代名詞開始，往後推，到第二個動詞（即劃線處）前結束。1 句關係子句 what...egg 放句首當主詞，單數主詞，搭配單數動詞。「東西」（what）被送到皇宮，需搭配被動式。1885 年，需用過去式。綜合以上，**C** 選項為正解。

32. **If she _____ my daughter, I'd have no hesitation in phoning the police to report her drug abuse.**

(A) wouldn't　　(B) hadn't been　　(C) weren't　　(D) isn't

解 假如她不是我女兒，我就會毫不遲疑地打電話給警察，通報她濫用藥物。

33. Suffering massive losses, the party could neither afford to ignore minorities _____ continuing to alienate young voters or single women.

(A) and they couldn't either risk    (B) so couldn't they risk

(C) or they couldn't risk    (D) nor risk

解 選票大幅流失後，這個黨再也無法忽視少數族群，他們也無法冒險繼續離間年輕選民或單身女性。

考點：對稱

「既不是 A 也不是 B」neither A nor B，A 和 B 兩者時態、詞性和結構需對稱。neither 後方搭配動詞原形 afford，nor 後方也應搭配動詞原形 risk，D 選項為正解。

34. A poor roommate match is hard to undo. This is _____.

(A) why you should take your time singling out compatible roommates

(B) why to seek tips for filtering out the top matches

(C) why are these sites that promise to help find the ideal matches popular

(D) why some people hesitant to live with a roommate

解 選到糟糕的室友後，幾乎無法重選。這就是為什麼你該花時間慢慢來，選出和自己合得來的室友。

考點：間接問句

間接問句的公式為：why（疑問詞）+ you（主詞）+ should take your time（動詞）...，A 選項為正解。B 選項，疑問詞 why 無法寫成名詞片語，「why to V 原」為錯誤寫法，應改成：why people seek tips for ...。C 選項應改成：why these sites that promise to help find the ideal matches are popular。D 選項，缺動詞，應改成：why some people are hesitant to live with a roommate。

35. Hospitals are investing in new surgical devices and technologies. The moves are part of a growing shift away from conventional open procedures that involve big incisions, _____ and long hospitalizations.

(A) lose lots of blood      (B) lots of blood loss

(C) lots of blood is lost      (D) losing lots of blood

> 解 醫院正投資新的手術裝置和科技。這些舉動將改變傳統手術程序。傳統手術切口大、失血多，且住院時間長。
>
> **考點：對稱。**請見下方句構分析：
>
> …procedures that involve big incisions, _____ and long hospitalizations.
> <br>動詞　　　　　名詞1　　　　名詞2　　　　　　　名詞3
>
> involve 後方需加（動）名詞。為遵守對稱原則，連接詞 and 連接了三個名詞。劃線處也應為名詞，**B** 選項為正解。若用 D 選項，為求對稱，連接詞 and 應連接三個動名詞 Ving。

36. One of the easiest steps we can take to help mitigate the impacts of drought _____ water conservation. If we use water wisely at all times, we can reduce stress placed on our resources.

(A) has been      (B) and is      (C) being      (D) are

> 解 為協助舒緩乾旱的衝擊，我們能採取的最簡單的步驟之一，就是節約用水。假如我們總是能聰明用水，我們就能減少資源不足的壓力。
>
> **考點：主動詞一致**
>
> 主詞「最簡單的步驟之一」，重點在於「之一」。單數主詞 one，搭配單數動詞，**A** 選項為正解。請見下方句構分析：
>
> One of the easiest steps (that) we can take…drought _____ water…
> <br>　　主詞　　　　　　　　　形容詞子句　　　　　　動詞
>
> 關係子句從被省略掉的關係代名詞 that 開始，往後推，到第二個動詞（即劃線處）前面結束。關係代名詞 that 帶出來的關係子句 we…drought 放在名詞 steps 後方，為「形容詞子句」。

37. _____ our team trained harder, we would have been in better form and had a better chance of winning.

(A) Had      (B) However      (C) Even if      (D) Were

> **解** 假如我們隊之前訓練時更努力一點，我們可能狀況會更好，更有機會在比賽中獲勝。
>
> **考點：假設語法**
>
> 從 would have been，可知 if 針對「過去」做相反假設，公式如下：
> If 主詞 1 + 動詞 1（過去完成式 had (not) + p.p.），主詞 2 + 動詞 2（would / should / could / might (not) + have p.p.），套公式：
>
> **If** our team **had trained** harder, we would have been in better form ....
>
> 也可去掉連接詞 if，將 had 移至句首，即成加強語氣版的假設語法：
>
> **Had** our team **trained** harder, we would have been in better form ...
>
> 由上可知，**A** 選項為正解。C 選項，連接詞 even if（即使），文意不通。

**38.** A Los Angeles hospital succumbed to the anonymous hacker's demands, _____ a ransom of around $17,000 to restore normal operations of the computer systems.

    (A) paying him      (B) and was paid      (C) to pay him      (D) which paid

> **解** 某家洛杉磯的醫院，屈服於匿名駭客要求下，付給駭客一筆約美金 1 萬 7 千元的贖款，好讓醫院電腦系統恢復正常運作。
>
> **考點：分詞構句**
>
> 原句為：A Los Angeles hospital succumbed to... / a Los Angeles hospital paid him（即 the hacker）...。兩句主詞相同，都是 a Los Angeles hospital，可用分詞構句。paid him 為過去式，應改成表主動進行的 Ving 分詞構句 paying him... systems，**A** 選項為正解。

**39.** Altitude, climate, and the length of the growing season all determine _____.

    (A) where plants will grow

    (B) if the crops had high yields

    (C) what are the best crops for your farm

    (D) whether have farmers a good harvest

> **解** 海拔高度、氣候，和生長季的長度都決定了作物將在哪生長。
>
> **考點：間接問句**
>
> 間接問句的公式為：where（疑問詞）+ plants（主詞）+ will grow（動詞），**A** 選項為正解。B 選項應改成：if the crops will have high yields。

疑問詞「是否」if，後方動詞不需跳躍。海拔高度等因素可決定作物日後的生長狀況，故搭配未來式。C 選項應改成：what the best crops for your farm are。D 選項應改成：whether farmers will have a good harvest。

40. **Committed to cracking down on smuggling and _____ the flow of migrants to Europe, Turkey hopes to get financial and political concessions from the EU in return.**

(A) curbs      (B) curbed      (C) to curb      (D) curbing

解 土耳其全心投入取締偷渡，和遏止難民湧入歐洲，希望反過來可藉此取得歐盟在金融和政治上的讓步。

考點：對稱。請見下方句構分析：

Committed to cracking … and _____ the flow…
    介係詞  動名詞 1      動名詞 2

Committed ….Europe 為分詞構句。片語「全心投入」be committed to N / Ving。為遵守對稱原則，連接詞 and 連接兩個（動）名詞，從 cracking 可知，劃線部份也應為動名詞，**D** 選項為正解。

41. **The Gun-Free Schools Act demands that students who bring a weapon to school _____, a step beyond suspension.**

(A) to expel                (B) be expelled

(C) and are expelled      (D) expel

解 校園無槍法案，要求帶武器進入校園的學生應被退學。這是比留校查看更進一步的處分。

考點：被動式 / demand 特殊句型

特殊句型：建議、命令、要求 (demand)、堅持 that S +（should）V 原。當中，助動詞 should 常被省略，剩動詞原形。學生因帶武器到學校而「被逐出」，需搭配被動式。綜合以上，**B** 選項為正解。

42. **As the searing lava neared pockets of rotting vegetation, it ignited traces of the flammable gas _____ the decay.**

(A) given off by            (B) that had given off from

(C) by giving off            (D) and gave off

解 當熾熱岩漿接近腐爛的植被時，岩漿點燃了腐爛物所釋放出的可燃氣體。

**考點：分詞當形容詞。請見下方句構分析：**

..., it ignited traces of the flammable gas _____ the decay.

主詞　動詞　　　　　　　　名詞

從上方 1 個主詞和 1 個動詞可知句子結構已完整，故名詞 traces of...gas 後方應搭配 Ving 或 p.p. 形容詞。若用關係代名詞帶出來的關係子句當形容詞，則子句中需搭配完整的動詞，即非 Ving / p.p. / to V 原。可燃氣體「被腐爛物釋放出來」，需搭配表被動的 p.p. 形容詞 given off by，**A** 選項為正解。若用關係子句當形容詞，則應寫成：...which / that had been given off ( 或 was given off) by the decay.「物 / 主詞性質」的關係代名詞 which / that 代替前方的 gas，單數主詞 gas，搭配單數被動式。

**43.** **It is the number, kind and arrangement of teeth that _____, not the food that the animal actually eats.**

(A) explain what make a mammal carnivorous

(B) determine if a mammal is classified as a carnivore

(C) explain why is a mammal carivorous

(D) determine how do biologists differ carnivores from herbivores

解 牙齒的數量、種類、排列才是決定這隻哺乳類動物是否能被劃分為肉食動物的關鍵，而不是它吃的食物。

**考點：間接問句**

間接問句的公式為：if（疑問詞）+ a mammal（主詞）+ is classified（動詞）...，**B** 選項為正解。疑問詞「是否」if，後方動詞不需跳躍，只要和 is / eats 對稱，為現在式即可。A 選項，what 既是疑問詞也是主詞。what 當主詞時，應視為第三人稱單數，搭配單數動詞。A 選項應改成：explain what makes a mammal a carnivore。C 選項應改成：explain why a mammal is carnivorous。D 選項應改成：determine how biologists differ carnivores from herbivores。

**44.** **Astronomers believe that at the center of every galaxy _____.**

(A) is a huge black hole

(B) does a huge black hole have

(C) locates a huge black hole

(D) is a huge black hole situated

解 天文學家相信，在每個銀河的中央，都有一個巨大的黑洞。

**考點：倒裝**

關係代名詞 that，帶出一個以地點為首的倒裝句。公式如下：

at the center of every galaxy（地方副詞）+ is（動詞）+ a ...black hole（主詞）。還原句子：A huge black hole is at the center of every galaxy.，**A** 選項為正解。

地方副詞為首的倒裝句，句中動詞以 1 字寫成，不會有助動詞，也不會是被動式。B 選項，does...have，兩字動詞，非正解。且還原句子：A huge black hole **has** at the center of every galaxy，文法錯誤。C 選項，「位在 ...」locate / situate，需搭配被動式，不符合 1 字動詞的要求，需換成用主動寫法的「位於 ...」sit / stand / lie。C、D 選項改成：At the center of every galaxy sits / stands / lies a huge black hole。

45. Newspapers sensationalized the death of people _____ with the expedition to excavate Tutankhamen's tomb. They claimed that judging from the list of victims, only native Egyptians were not affected by the curse.

(A) who connected

(B) to be connected

(C) connected

(D) which connecting

解 報紙以聳動的手法報導和挖掘 Tutankhamen 墳墓相關人等的死訊。他們宣稱，從被害者名單看來，只有埃及本地人不受詛咒的影響。

**考點：分詞當形容詞。**請見下方句構分析：

Newspapers sensationalized the death of people _____ with the ...
~~~~主詞~~~~ ~~~~動詞~~~~ ~~~~名詞~~~~

從上方 1 個主詞和 1 個動詞可知句子結構已完整，故名詞 the death of people 後方應搭配 Ving 或 p.p. 形容詞。若用關係代名詞帶出來的關係子句當形容詞，則子句中需搭配完整的動詞，即非 Ving / p.p. / to V 原。people「被說和...有關」，應搭配表被動的 p.p. 形容詞，**C** 選項為正解。若用關係子句當形容詞，則應寫成...the death of people who were connected with...。「人 / 主詞性質」的關係代名詞 who 代替前方 people，複數主詞，搭配複數被動式。「和...有關」需用被動式寫。

46. Keep in mind that jeans with a price tag of less than $50 _____ for the masses; you'll have to try many pairs to find just the right fit.

(A) has made

(B) is to make

(C) have been making

(D) are made

解 記住：標價低於美金 50 元的牛仔褲是做給一般大眾穿的。你將必須試穿很多條，才能找到最適合你的牛仔褲。

Unit 1 關係代名詞

Unit 2 被動語態

Unit 3 分詞形容詞

Unit 4 分詞構句

Unit 5 假設語法

Unit 6 倒裝句

Unit 7 間接問句

Unit 8 特殊動詞

Unit 9 主動詞一致

Unit 10 對稱結構

特別收錄
Unit 11 五回試題

考點：主動詞一致 / 被動式。請見下方句構分析：

… that jeans　with　a price tag, … ＿＿＿ for the masses …
主詞　介係詞　名詞　　動詞

主詞「有…的牛仔褲」，重點在「牛仔褲」。複數主詞 jeans，搭配複數動詞。牛仔褲「被做」，需搭配被動式。綜合以上，**D** 選項為正解。

47. While normal speech sounds only have slight differences in loudness, between 4 and 5 Hz, screams can switch very fast, varying between 30 and 150 Hz and thus ＿＿＿ as being unpleasant.

(A) perceive
(B) perceiving
(C) is perceived
(D) perceived

解 雖然正常說話的聲音在響度上有些微差異，介於 4 和 5 赫茲間，但是尖叫聲可快速在 30 和 150 赫茲間轉換，因而被視為是不悅耳的聲音。

考點：分詞構句

原句為：…, screams can switch very fast, and screams vary between 30 and 150 HZ and screams are perceived as being unpleasant。主詞相同，都是 screams，可用分詞構句。vary 為現在式，應改成表主動進行的 Ving 分詞構句 varying …150 Hz。are perceived 為現在被動式，應改成表被動的 p.p. 分詞構句 perceived … unpleasant。且用 and 連接兩個分詞構句 varying … 和 perceived …。綜合以上，**D** 選項為正解。

48. The Executive Mansion, constructed in the 1790s, ＿＿＿ several renovations and now popularly called the White House, is the oldest public edifice in Washington, D.C..

(A) undergone
(B) undergoing
(C) had undergone
(D) is undergoing

解 行政大廈，建於 1790 年間，進行過幾次翻修，且現在被通稱為白宮。行政大廈是華盛頓特區最古老的公共建築。

考點：對稱。請見下方句構分析：

The … Mansion, contructed …, ＿＿＿ … and … called ... White House, is …
主詞　　　　　　分構1　　分構2　　　　分構3　　　　　動詞

原句為：the Executive Mansion was constructed in the 1790s, underwent several renovations, and now is called… / the Executive Mansion is the oldest … 。兩句主詞相同，都是 the Executive Mansion，可用分詞構句。

was constructed / is called 為被動式，應改成表被動的 p.p. 分詞構句 constructed in the 1790s / called the White House。underwent 為過去式，應改成表主動進行的 Ving 分詞構句 undergoing several renovations。接著用連接詞 and 來連接三個分詞構句。綜合以上，**B** 選項為正解。

49. _____ in December last year, the Paris Climate Agreement was widely seen as a big step forward in addressing climate change.

(A) Finalized　　　(B) To finalize　　　(C) That finalizing　　(D) Finalizing

解　巴黎氣候協定去年 12 月被定案。大家認為巴黎氣候協定讓各國在解決氣候變遷這議題上邁出了一大步。

**考點：分詞構句**

巴黎氣候協定「被定案」，需用被動式。原句為：the Paris Climate Agreement was finalized in December last year / the Paris Climate Agreement was widely seen as ...。兩句主詞相同，都是 the Paris Climate Agreement，可用分詞構句。又 was finalized 為過去被動式，應改成表被動的 p.p. 分詞構句 finalized...year，**A** 選項為正解。

50. The celebration of the end of the war with parades and parties _____ a complete disaster from the standpoint of public health, since it facilitated the spread of the flu in some major cities.

(A) which are　　　(B) have been　　　(C) being　　　　(D) was

解　從公眾健康的立場看來，用遊行和派對來慶祝戰爭的結束，完全是個大災難，因為慶祝活動加速了流感在一些主要城市的擴散。

**考點：主動詞一致 / 時態**

主詞「慶祝戰爭結束」，重點在「慶祝」。單數主詞 celebration，搭配單數動詞。從 facilitated 可知本句為過去式。綜合以上，**D** 選項為正解。連接詞 since（因為）必須連接兩個句子，但 A 選項，since 左方缺動詞，不成句，非正解。請見下方 A 選項的句構分析：

| The celebration of ... parties | which are ... disaster ..., | since | it facilitated ... |
|---|---|---|---|
| 名詞 | 形容詞子句 | 連接詞 | 句子 |

Unit 1
關係
代名詞

Unit 2
被動
語態

Unit 3
分詞
形容詞

Unit 4
分詞
構句

Unit 5
假設
語法

Unit 6
倒裝
句

Unit 7
間接
問句

Unit 8
特殊
動詞

Unit 9
主動詞
一致

Unit 10
對稱
結構

特別收錄
Unit 11
五回
試題

## MEMO

國家圖書館出版品預行編目 (CIP) 資料

必考！文法速解 / 大學堂英文編著. -- 初版. --
臺北市：創學堂文教，民 107.11　面；　公分

ISBN 978-986-97145-0-1（平裝）

1. 英語　2. 語法

805.16　　　　　　　107019033

# 必考！
# 文法速解

書　　　名：必考！文法速解

編 著 者：大學堂英文

發 行 人：創學堂文教事業股份有限公司

出 版 者：創學堂文教事業股份有限公司

版　　　次：初版

印　　　次：第一刷

地　　　址：台北市愛國東路 116 巷 23 弄 1 號 1 樓

電　　　話：0970-511-609

電子郵件：books@learnerhall.org

網　　　址：http://www.learnerhall.org

出版年月：民國 107 年 11 月初版

定　　　價：新台幣 320 元

代理經銷：白象文化事業有限公司

地　　　址：401 台中市東區和平街 228 巷 44 號

電　　　話：(04) 2220 - 8589

傳　　　真：(04) 2220 - 8505